HANGING DEVILS

Professor He Jiahong is one of China's top experts in criminal evidence, evidential investigation and criminal procedure. He obtained his doctorate in judicial science from Northwestern University in Illinois and is currently a professor at the school of law, Renmin University of China. As well as publishing extensively on legal matters, he has written several bestselling crime novels, including *Black Holes* the second in a series of four books featuring the character of Hong Jun. He has also published widely on the subject of criminal law and wrongful conviction, including the Penguin Special *Back from the Dead* about a landmark case of wrongful conviction.

He Jiahong

HANGING DEVILS

Hong Jun Investigates

Translated from the Chinese by Duncan Hewitt

CHINA LIBRARY

PENGUIN BOOKS

UK | USA | Canada | Ireland | Australia
India | New Zealand | South Africa | China

Penguin Books is part of the Penguin Random House group of companies
whose addresses can be found at global.penguinrandomhouse.com.

Penguin
Random House
PENGUIN BOOKS CHINA

This paperback edition published by Penguin Group (Australia)
in association with Penguin (Beijing) Ltd, 2015

1 3 5 7 9 10 8 6 4 2

Text copyright © He Jiahong, 2010
Translation copyright © Duncan Hewitt, 2012

Originally published in Chinese as *Xue Zhi Zui* by Renmin University Press, Beijing.

The moral right of the author has been asserted.

Cover design by Di Suo © Penguin Group (Australia)
Text design by Steffan Leyshon-Jones © Penguin Group (Australia)
Printed and bound in China by South China Printing Company

National Library of Australia
Cataloguing-in-Publication data:

He, Jiahong, 1953-
Hanging devils: Hong Jun investigates/He Jiahong.
9780734399571 (paperback)
Legal stories, Chinese.

895.136

penguin.com.cn

A NOTE ON CHINESE USAGE AND NAMES

In Chinese, a person's given name always follows their surname. Therefore, the protagonist of *Hanging Devils*, Hong Jun, has the surname Hong and the given name Jun. Pinyin, the standard Romanisation method for Chinese characters, has been used throughout this novel.

HANGING DEVILS

CHAPTER ONE

HONG JUN SAT at his large desk and looked around the office. He felt a glow of satisfaction. It was perfect for the times. Very 1990s, he thought, but with a nod to Chinese tradition. The room was large, the ceilings high and there was a good light from the window on the right-hand wall which, when the dust died down, gave him a view of the busy cranes changing the skyline around him. Along the left-hand wall stood two handsome, wide bookcases heavy with China's laws, as handed down by the National People's Congress, and a television tuned to China Central Television. Against the far wall stood a long sofa in a coarse red fabric, two matching chairs and a little tea table. Above the sofa was an oil painting of the Tianshan Mountains and the Tianchi, the Heavenly Lake, and near the door, to the right, was a pot of ornamental turtle bamboo. A dark, finely knotted and patterned rug from Central Asia covered a large expanse of the industrial grey carpet tiles, under which ran the cables for the telephone and computer on his otherwise clear, semi-matt black desk. Hong Jun leaned back in his chair and thought the office far nicer than the one he'd had in America. Better still, here he was the boss, responsible only to himself and his business, his only master the rule of law, which sounded noble but was, in the new China he had come home to, almost impossible to define.

He was considered tall at 5 feet 11 inches, liked to be active and appeared slim in the black suit he had bought that morning from one of the new foreign boutiques opening up all around Beijing. It fitted him well and, with its classic lines, spoke professionalism. His large, bright eyes glinted through silver-framed spectacles, which gave his face a kindly if somewhat austere expression. His wide forehead and black hair, neatly combed to the right, gave him an academic air. His watch was a classic but relatively common timepiece he had worn for years, slim and accurate. What more did a watch need to do but tell the time? Though Hong Jun was only just past the age when the ancients say you should stand on your own two feet – thirty to be precise – he appeared and acted older. His manner was solid, unflappable; his words pithy and to the point; his humour so dry that others often missed it.

The office was in the commercial building of the old Friendship Hotel, in the northwestern corner of Beijing. It was close to the People's University of China, where he had begun his studies, and his law degrees hung on the wall in the reception room. Hong Jun had learned to love the law at the People's University.

He swivelled his high-backed chair to face the window, edged by the red leaves of an old maple that grew in the sunlight starved garden below. The tree was a reason for his taking this office. He liked to think that, from the third floor, he could see China's modernisation while not losing touch with the earth.

'Coffee, boss?'

He slowly turned his chair back to the desk. The fashionably dressed young woman walked across the room and put a steaming cup before him.

'And I didn't put any sugar in it this time, boss,' she said.

'Thank you, Miss Song . . . But, for the third time, please knock on the door before you come into my office.' His years in America had led him to see knocking as a matter of basic courtesy, even if the door was already open.

'Oh, dammit, I forgot again,' said Song Jia, who could keep track of a dozen complicated tasks at a time and needed only to look at a telephone number once to remember it, but needed a calendar to tell her what day of the week it was. 'But if you correct an error immediately, you can still be a good comrade,' she added cheerfully, and retreated to the door, where she stood at attention and knocked theatrically. 'Excuse me, boss. May I enter, please?'

Hong Jun could not maintain his stern look and laughed, 'You may, Miss Song,' and with a sweep of his arm waved her in. He adored her ability to use humour to prick at anything she thought pompous. During her interview for the job, she was quick to pick up that Hong Jun's name sounded like 'red army' in Chinese.

'Wow, your parents must be pretty important. I bet you come from a revolutionary family and your father's some old cadre whose father was probably on the Long March . . . I should be quiet now, shouldn't I?'

If he was brutally honest, what most intrigued him about her was how much she looked like his former classmate, Xiao Xue – fair skinned, with a delicately shaped face, a sharply defined nose, big eyes and fine, dark eyelashes. When she smiled, the world seemed to be bathed in sunlight, her lips parting to reveal neat white teeth, shallow dimples appearing in the rosy flush of her pale cheeks.

At university, it was Xiao Xue's alluring smile that led all the boys to vote her 'the most beautiful girl on campus'. And their voices were very similar too, though Song Jia's words contained more than a hint of the sarcasm and teasing mock seriousness so typical of young people in Beijing.

Song Jia was perceptive. She quickly sensed that this handsome man with the doctorate from abroad felt some special emotional connection to her, and she wanted the job, so if she had an advantage over the others why should she question her good fortune? She had studied administration at the police college and had worked in the Public Security Bureau for two years after graduating, before resigning to work in public relations for a private company. It was all about making money back then, and no one was sure how long it would last. Everyone wanted to get rich. She changed jobs several times in the space of a few years, working in a hotel, a bar and a nightclub, but though the money was better than good, she found no satisfaction in what she did. What she wanted was, as she so forthrightly put it to Hong Jun, something 'not too tacky, but not too much like hard work'.

For the past few years, she'd been studying psychology in her spare time and would have had a master's degree if she had formally enrolled at a university. She preferred to sit in on classes and read the suggested books, and other books besides. She was never caught, and she never had to sit examinations. Miss Song, Hong Jun had soon worked out, would forever be a student, which was not such a bad thing. She had analysed Hong Jun's personality and decided she should take the initiative to reduce the psychological distance between them. And so, even before her one month probation was over, she stopped addressing him as Lawyer Hong and began calling him 'boss', talking to him in a casual manner. As she put it, if you are in a senior position you should treat your subordinates with respect; if you're in a junior position you should treat yourself with respect.

Hong Jun took a sip of his freshly brewed coffee. He learned to like coffee in the United States, where proper Chinese tea meant having to go all the way to Chinatown in Chicago. Otherwise, it was dust in a teabag. So he drank coffee.

'How are you finding the job?' Hong asked as Miss Song was almost out his door.

'Pretty good, boss, I'm certainly having a relaxing time.' Her facial expressions constantly changed whenever she spoke, as though keeping time with some beautiful rhythm. 'I've been here almost a month and we haven't had a single proper case. Just a few enquiries on the phone and that's all. You didn't just come back to China to have a rest, did you?'

'One should strike a balance between pressure and relaxation,' said Hong Jun, his eyes narrowing as he sipped his coffee. 'As a lesser man would say, "One should not sweat unnecessarily."'

'If things carry on like this we'll have to change our name from "law office" to "rest home".' Song Jia held her head to one side and frowned. 'Are things that serious?'

'If we just go on doing what we said in the newspaper, I don't think we'll be able to survive much longer.' Song Jia, who knew the company's balance sheet down to the last *fen*, pointed a manicured finger at a copy of the *Beijing Evening News* lying on the table.

Hong Jun knew the article, which he had circled in red.

Hong Jun Law Office, recently opened in Beijing, is the latest privately owned law practice to open in the city.

The firm's principal, Hong Jun, formerly taught at People's University and also worked as a lawyer before going to the United States to study in 1988.

During his five years in America, he received his doctorate in law, and worked for two years at a famous legal practice in Chicago.

Unusually for a returned foreign-educated lawyer, Dr Hong specialises in criminal cases of all kinds.

'I want to help ordinary people defend their rights,' said Dr Hong, adding that he wanted to help China build the 'rule of law'.

In a slightly exaggerated tone, Song Jia said, 'Most lawyers these days would give anything to get themselves a commercial case or work on foreign investment deals. That's where the money is. And there's lots of it to go around and more on the way. How come we insist on only taking criminal cases?'

'It's what I'm interested in, it's what I'm best at,' said Hong Jun.

'But you're not going to earn much from criminal cases. I know they say money is just a transient possession, but if you ask me, that only applies to the person whose pocket it's in.'

'In the US, criminal lawyers are rich, too.'

'Yes, but that's in the US . . .' she said.

'Just relax,' he told her. Rather than be annoyed, he enjoyed arguing with Song Jia, who was clever enough to know not to push too far.

'As the philosopher Mencius once said, "Before heaven grants me an important mission, it will first send me mental and physical privations to endure," and so, we must endure.'

'But no one's going to grant me an important mission,' said Song Jia. 'Why do I have to endure all that stuff too?'

Hong Jun abandoned his attempts to look older than he was and burst out laughing, and Song Jia was giggling too when the door buzzer sounded and their faces became masks of seriousness.

'Perhaps it's someone bringing us some transient possessions . . .' she said and headed down the short hallway, which was flanked by two empty offices, and past the reception area facing the door to admit the visitor.

✳

He was a red-faced man in his forties, with big eyes and thick eyebrows, a scraggly moustache and sideburns, of medium height, with a pronounced beer belly. His suit was new, his loosely knotted tie slightly askew and his briefcase was scuffed but still smelt of new leather. Miss Song escorted him as far as the door and sent him across the rug to Hong Jun, now standing in front of his desk, whose hand he shook heartily. 'So you're the famous Dr Hong, the lawyer,' the man said.

'Hong Jun,' he replied, proffering a business card.

'No need to be so polite,' the man replied, and handed Hong Jun his own card, which was printed on good quality card with a hard, though not inelegant, typeface.

'Zheng's the name, Zheng Jianzhong.'

Hong Jun invited him to sit on the sofa, and took a chair opposite. He looked at the name card.

BINBEI CONSTRUCTION PROJECTS COMPANY
ZHENG JIANZHONG
MANAGING DIRECTOR

Zheng took out a packet of Marlboro. 'Dr Hong, would you like a cigarette?'

'Thank you, no, I don't smoke.' Hong Jun crossed his legs and gently nudged, with the toe of his passing shoe, a little sign on the coffee table.

PLEASE DON'T SMOKE UNTIL FORMAL DISCUSSIONS CONCLUDE.

Zheng Jianzhong had just lit a match and, slightly embarrassed, quickly shook it out, removed the cigarette from his mouth, put the evidence of his transgression in his left jacket pocket and waved his right hand to dispel the sulphur in the air between them. 'Please don't take offence, Dr Hong . . .'

'That's okay. It's just that cigarette smoke makes me dizzy. You're from the northeast, judging by your accent.'

'Yes, Heilongjiang,' Zheng said.

'I thought so. I have friends in Harbin. Been in Beijing a while?'

'Yes, quite a few years. I'm in construction, and there's not so much going on back home. Beijing's a big place, so it's easier to make money here than most other places. Like they say, "Don't hang yourself on the first tree you come to – if you must hang yourself, try a few different trees first". Ha ha, ain't that right, Dr Hong?'

Zheng's laugh gave in quickly to a rasping cough, which he covered with a folded handkerchief from his left jacket pocket. 'Beijing is so dusty these days,' he said by way of apology.

'Sounds like you must be talking about "money trees", the kind we always say produces money when you shake it, but you have to cultivate it first to yield a good crop,' said Hong Jun, ignoring his comment about the dust, which was everywhere now but not worth talking about. 'I don't get the impression that you've come here today because of money.'

'You're sharp, you are,' Zheng said. 'No, I didn't come to see you about money. I came about my brother's case. A very strange case, it is. I swear you'll be fascinated when you hear about it.'

'Really? Why is that?'

'Where should I start?' said Zheng Jianzhong.

'With some tea, I think,' Hong Jun said, and crossed to his desk and pressed the button for Song Jia's extension, asking for tea. A minute or so later, she brought in a tray with a lidded tea cup for the visitor and a coffee mug for Hong Jun. Miss Song closed the door behind her as she left.

Hong Jun, now with a yellow legal pad on his knee and pencil at the ready, said, 'Please, start at the beginning.'

'It was a case of rape and murder that took place ten years ago at the state farm where I lived. It was an isolated little place, just a few hundred people in all, everyone knew everyone. Sure, you got quarrels and fights, plenty of 'em. Stealing, sleeping with the neighbour's wife, it all happened. But rape and murder? Never! People always said nothing big could ever happen in a small place like ours. But, well, this time it sure did.'

Zheng paused, sipping at his tea.

'Strange thing was, though, that no one was really sure how she died. If there's a rape, there ought to be screams, right? But her dad was in the next room, and my house was next door, and we didn't hear anything at all. A fully grown adult attacked and killed and not a sound, and no clue how she died. Weird, isn't it?

'And, there's something even stranger. I can tell you, for sure, my kid brother definitely didn't do it. But he confessed to the crime and now he's in prison. I just can't understand it. It didn't look like the police had got rough with him and forced him to confess, and he never said they did. It was as if he was under a spell. Nothing I said could get through to him. They gave him a suspended death sentence. But I know he didn't do it. Even after all these years, I can't figure it out.'

'Why have you waited until now to do anything about it?' Hong Jun was watching Zheng Jianzhong closely, trying to read in his face and body language the truth of what this case was about. Experience and study had taught him that people rarely tell the truth, even when it's in their own best interests to do so. There are always secrets, and in criminal cases those secrets are always closely guarded.

Zheng held his cup in both hands, looking into it, as if trying to find answers in the large unfurled leaves.

'It's not really that I waited . . .' he said. 'At the time I thought, well, maybe it's just my little brother's fate. If he's not going to appeal, why should I waste my time trying to help? And what would it achieve? Sometimes you just have to accept things.'

'That is, unfortunately, sometimes true,' Hong Jun said.

'All these years I was so busy trying to make money, but the more I earned, the more uncomfortable I got.' He sighed. 'I felt I'd let my brother down, let down my dead mum and dad too. I got to thinking that if I'd been a big boss back then, there's no way my kid brother would have gone to the slammer. Over the last couple of years, I've talked to a lot of lawyers back home, but none of them dare take the case. They all say there's no way I'll get it overturned. All it'll do is attract attention and cause trouble, and no one wants to be labelled a troublemaker, even these days when it's all about "righting past wrongs", y'know? But I still haven't given up.

'I saw your advertisement in the evening paper . . .'

'It was a news article.'

'I understand. These days getting a journalist to write an article is even better than an advertisement. No bullshit! Anyone who read that article would come to you if they had to go to court. Just like me . . .

it made me feel there was new hope for my brother, that's why I came to see you. You're an American lawyer.'

'I am a Chinese lawyer, Mr Zheng, be clear about that.'

'But you worked as a lawyer in America? That bit's not made up, is it?'

'No, it isn't. I passed the Illinois state bar examination, but I am also qualified to practise law anywhere in China. That's all that matters here. A lawyer is a lawyer, Mr Zheng. What does it matter if he is Chinese or American so long as he does his job well?'

'I've seen the films, Dr Hong, and those American lawyers are fearless. Doesn't matter what the case is, if they take it on they win, because the law is the law and no one can trample over it. Not even the American president is immune. Remember Nixon? When he came to China, it was such a big show, but then he got in trouble with the law and had to quit. Quite something, ain't it? If our officials had to face the law, think what fun we'd have.'

'China is different, Mr Zheng. The rule of law is still young and we have to tread carefully. This is not America.'

'I know that. Anyway, I'll stop rambling,' said Zheng Jianzhong. 'There's another reason why I came to see you. I read in the paper about a group of lawyers in Chicago who specialise in getting defendants in rape cases released. They've even got some fancy name for it? "The Innocence Project", is that right? Took a lot of effort for me to remember that name, I can tell you. Those lawyers use some kind of new technology . . . What's it called? Damn it, this one I really can't remember!'

'Forensics? DNA?' suggested Hong Jun.

'Yeah, that's it, DNA. I reckoned you'd know all about it. It's like a fingerprint in your blood, innit? Amazing . . . '

'It doesn't actually mean there are fingerprints in people's blood,' Hong Jun smiled. 'It means you can use DNA testing to identify a specific person from a sample of blood, hair or semen, because we each have unique DNA, some of which comes from our mother and some from our father. It's like a computer code of everything we are.

And it is just as accurate as a fingerprint, probably better, but it's very expensive and not yet in wide use in China.'

'Well, however it works, it's real scientific, ain't it?' said Zheng. 'And I know you worked as a lawyer in Chicago before you came back to China, so I reckoned you might be able to use this kind of technology to get my brother's verdict overturned.'

'To use DNA, you've first got to have an uncontaminated sample from the crime scene to test, such as blood or semen.'

'That's no problem. In this case, we've got the lot.'

'Even so, getting the verdict overturned in a ten-year-old case like this is going to be very difficult and by no means certain.'

'This is why I've come to a great lawyer like you, Dr Hong. Do you think I'd waste your time if I didn't think you could win? To tell you the truth, I think you're the only person who can get my brother's verdict reversed.'

'Hmm . . .'

With his right hand, Hong Jun squeezed the joints of the fingers of his left until they cracked, a habit of his when he was trying to come to a decision, though not one he'd been aware of until Miss Song pointed it out to him when he was interviewing her for the position.

'Taking on a case in Heilongjiang would be pretty inconvenient,' Hong said.

'Money won't be a problem,' Zheng said. 'As they say these days, I'm so poor all I have left is money.'

Zheng Jianzhong reached inside his jacket and pulled out two tight stacks of crisp banknotes, which he placed on the table. 'Take this first twenty thousand, as . . . what do you call it, a retainer? That's right, isn't it? If it's not enough let me know and I'll send you some more. And when you win the case, I'll give you another hundred thousand. Does that sound okay?'

'As regards our fees, we have our own set rates, as laid down by the relevant authorities. Miss Song will explain it to you, give you a receipt, and have you sign a letter so I may act on your behalf in this case,' Hong Jun said. With handling money, he felt it was better to keep things formal and official, lest clients assume they are buying more than his services as a lawyer, buying more than he could legally provide.

'Then we'll stick to your rates,' said Zheng, sounding satisfied with the arrangement. 'I'll do whatever you say.'

'Do you have documentation regarding the case? A copy of the court judgment, for example?' Hong Jun asked.

'Yes, and not only the judgment. I've had someone put together a whole set of material. Believe me, I came well prepared.' Zheng reached down to the briefcase at his feet, took out a battered manila folder bulging with papers and put it neatly on the table.

Hong Jun swiftly scanned the court's brief judgment, flicked through the background material, scribbled a few notes on his pad and sat back in his armchair.

'I'll take the job,' he said, 'but I need to make my own investigations to assess whether there's a chance of getting a retrial for your brother, and whether there's any hope of overturning the original verdict. We can decide what the next step should be once I have done that. In other words, I can't give you any guarantees. Is that understood?'

'I understand. Lawyer Hong, so long as you agree to take the case on, that's fine by me. I know you will do your best and I will accept whatever the outcome.'

Still seated, they shook hands.

Hong Jun rose and went to his desk, picked up the phone and summoned Miss Song. She arrived with a stenographer's pad and they talked quietly for a few minutes and she left, taking with her the documents and the cash. 'Miss Song will just prepare our contract, in which you have engaged me in this case. She will be able to explain anything in it you don't understand.

'Now, please tell me more about the details of the case, and particularly about the relationship between your brother and the victim.'

CHAPTER TWO

ZHENG JIANZHONG LIVED on the Binbei State Farm, about fifty kilometres from Binbei County Town, northeast of Harbin. During the Cultural Revolution, the farm had been renamed a Production and Construction Corps, and a lot of 'educated youth' from schools in the big cities were sent down there to carry out manual labour and 'learn from the peasants'. After the Cultural Revolution, in the late 1970s, most of them returned to the cities and it reverted to being a state farm – a relatively prosperous one, given the rich black soil that had been tilled and harvested for centuries.

He was sixteen years old when both his parents died of Keshan disease, a heart condition caused by a lack of selenium, common in the 1960s in northeast and southwest China. By 1970, thousands had died in Heilongjiang before doctors worked out what was happening. Dietary supplements curbed the problem, but a lot of children were left with weak hearts. Before he died, Zheng's father told him, 'Your brother is much weaker than you, both physically and in temperament, so you must be sure to look after him.' Zheng Jianzhong gave up his studies, and went to work on the farm. His little brother, Zheng Jianguo, was just ten, small and scrawny, sometimes the target of bullies, and often led into trouble. Once, he and some friends sneaked into the communal canteen's melon patch to steal some musk melons, but were caught by the young watchman, who let all the other children go, but gave Jianguo a good hiding. That evening, Jianzhong heard his sobbing brother's story. The next morning, he took a pickaxe handle and went looking for the watchman, found him on a farm road, and with a single blow broke his leg. For this, he spent three days in the farm's punishment cells and the old people declared he was bad, a troublemaker, the type who, before the Revolution, would have ended up a bandit in the hills. From then, Zheng Jianzhong was known as 'Big Axe'.

When Zheng Jianguo was eighteen, he started work on the farm too, in the mechanical section, where he learned to drive a combine harvester. Big Axe was pleased. He himself had done almost every job on the farm: in the fields and farmyard, feeding pigs, herding sheep, driving the horse cart, breaking rocks, building houses. But he'd never been promoted to the mechanical section. There was a rumour Big Axe had bribed the section chief with a bottle of the local Two Dragon Mountain liquor to get his little brother the job.

Zheng Jianguo wasn't tall, but he was well proportioned. He wasn't handsome, but he had regular features. He wasn't outgoing, but he was clever. He liked reading, and sometimes wrote poetry in a rustic style that earned him the nickname 'Peasant Poet'. One of his love poems became quite famous around the farm, and was considered a classic of the genre:

> Brother on this side of the field,
> Sister on the other;
> They can't keep hold of their hoe handles,
> A furrow filled with love.

*

The Zheng's neighbour was a man named Li Qingshan. His wife died young, of Keshan disease, and he brought up his three daughters on his own, which everyone said had made him old before his time, his face etched with wrinkles from an early age. When the educated youths from the cities first arrived in the village, he was only in his early thirties, but the city kids all called him 'grandpa'. The skin on his hands was dark and his palms calloused like old leather, and his finger joints were swollen, reminding many who saw them of chicken's feet. Li Qingshan didn't talk a lot and wasn't brave and, while he tried not to offend anyone, he rarely helped anyone either. There were some who said he treated his pigs better than his daughters. In those days, it was very hard to get antibiotics, and though it was known Li had a supply, he kept it from his daughters, even when one of them caught pneumonia. Only his piglets got special treatment. It wasn't that he didn't care about his children. He simply believed they would get better, but his pigs could die quite quickly if left untreated, and pigs were valuable and worth even more money when the pigs of other farmers were all dead.

Had that been the extent of the treatment of his daughters, it might be argued that Li Qingshan was putting the needs of the farm before the needs of his family. But he was also mean. The family kept a dozen or more chickens, but never ate the eggs, which were sold for cash. When the girls were little, they noticed that other children had eggs to eat, and demanded eggs too because their chickens made lots of them. Li Qingshan let some of the eggs go bad and cooked and served the stinking mess to his children to eat. Li told them that eggs came out of a hen's backside, and the daughters had only to see an egg to feel sick. That was too much for the villagers and from then on he was known as 'Rotten Egg'.

The three girls were all very pretty, particularly the youngest, Hongmei. The characters of her name meant 'Red Plum', and she had big eyes, delicate eyebrows, finely proportioned features, and her skin was unusually smooth. When she was about seventeen or eighteen, the boys and young men on the farm began to call her the 'Beauty Queen'.

She was more beautiful than any of the other girls on the farm, even the educated girls sent down from the city. The Beauty Queen was a warm-hearted, generous girl who talked a lot, laughed a lot and liked to look her best. She didn't wear the standard farm overalls or the sexless garb unlike most of the other women, and she got sharp looks from them for drawing attention to herself, but to her it was just fun. She was fond of tight clothes to show off her figure, notably her bust. The other girls looked at her with a mixture of jealousy and admiration. They would slouch, hunch their shoulders and pull in their chests, but Li Hongmei always walked with a straight back, head held high, even in summertime when she was only wearing a thin T-shirt. She was appreciated by the farm youths, and married men, who often got slapped by their spouses for looking too long. When chatting and laughing, her breasts would quiver a little, drawing the gaze of everyone, even the married ones prepared to risk hisses from their wives. When she began working, she was assigned to the canteen. At every mealtime, all the young men would line up in front of her window, even if there were shorter queues at other windows. They couldn't see her face through the little serving window, but they hoped to catch a glimpse of her breasts, well covered by a long apron though they might have been.

Zheng Jianguo and Li Hongmei were schoolmates as well as neighbours and had played together since they were little. 'Childhood sweethearts', clucked many of the grandmas. As they grew older, and she became a beauty, feelings for her began to stir in the Peasant Poet's heart. He never told anyone, though it was fairly clear from his poems. The two of them met almost every day, but they spoke less and less. If they met in the street, the Beauty Queen was always warm and friendly to the tongue-tied and flushed Zheng Jianguo. He sometimes thought of asking her to meet him after dinner, under the big tree at the back of the farmyard, but he never dared. He knew he wasn't rugged or handsome, and he sensed her attitude towards him was simply the friendship of a neighbour and a classmate. But in his heart he could hope and dream.

*

The grain harvest of 1980 was good across the country and at Binbei State Farm, as far as the eye could see across its vast fields, ranks of harvesters marched like ants, reaping the wheat, disgorging the grain into trucks and wagons, filling the silos. The farm had many mechanised harvesters, but mostly they were pulled by tractors. That year, the star was the new East Wind combine harvester, a huge machine with a comfortable, spacious enclosed cab and so many levers and switches and gauges that the farm children thought it was like a spaceship. And Zheng Jianguo was its driver. He was smart and studied hard and his technical expertise made him one of the best drivers and mechanics on the farm.

At lunchtime, Li Hongmei brought food for everyone working one of the fields, which included Zheng Jianguo, and after lunch she walked over to the East Wind and looked at it with great interest. Zheng Jianguo rushed to show her the machine, suddenly loquacious as he explained how it worked and how much grain its sharp blades could gather in a single turn.

He showed her the driver's cabin and let her touch its many levers, but feeling hot and flustered so close to her, he suggested they look at its cutting machinery. As Zheng Jianguo explained in some detail how it worked, Hongmei noticed an oil leak and pointed this out to him. Zheng Jianguo took a look. 'That's no big problem,' he said. 'It's just a little leak in the joint of the oil pipe on the hydraulic lift mechanism. I'll just tighten it up a little.' He climbed into the cab, raised the cutting machinery, and jumped down with a spanner in his hand, clambering under the array of blades.

Hongmei squatted, peering in. 'Can I help?' she asked.

'No need.' As he lay underneath the cutting platform, Zheng Jianguo's heart was bursting with happiness and pride. He found the leaking joint and tightened it with the spanner, but the blue-black oil kept dripping. He figured the rubber washer was damaged. He had one in his pocket and began to loosen the nut, as he had done many times before in the workshop. But as the nut came off, fluid began spurting from the high-pressure line and, as the massive cutting platform lost its hydraulic support, he heard a sharp creak and it came crashing down. He had forgotten to use a jack to secure the cutting gear. Zheng Jianguo cried out in pain, and then there was silence.

Li Hongmei was on her feet, mouth open, but couldn't make a sound. She could only stare at the blood-red blades embedded in his mangled flesh. She caught her breath and finally managed to scream. The workers on the far side of the field came running. Some of the women held Li Hongmei and led her away from the harvester. The senior men began barking orders. By the time they raised the cutting gear and pulled him out, Zheng Jianguo was unconscious and bleeding profusely. They loaded him carefully onto the trailer of an Iron Bull 555 tractor, blood-covered men surrounding him, trying to keep pressure on his many wounds, and drove as fast as the lumbering machine would allow to the farm hospital.

It was dusk by the time Zheng Jianguo regained consciousness. When he opened his eyes, he saw Li Hongmei. He thought he was dreaming and tried to rub his eyes with his right hand, but could not move his arm. Then he remembered. He saw his now broken right arm suspended in a rigid plaster cast, and felt sharp pain across his heavily bandaged torso. The doctor explained that his wounds were serious: he had suffered severe muscle damage to his arm, which was broken in two places. But fortunately he had escaped internal injury, and if he hadn't instinctively raised his right arm when he did, he'd have probably been killed. Seeing that he was awake, people clustered around him, asking how he was and trying to comfort him. But he didn't notice them. All he could hear was Hongmei, murmuring softly, 'It's all my fault.'

During the time he was in hospital, she came to see him almost every day, her visits often ending with tears. His right arm healed with time, but he was told he could no longer do heavy work. His stomach was scored by the scars of the blade. Yet he thought his injuries worth it, since it had won him Hongmei's love, or at least that's what it felt like.

Big Axe joked that there were other, less life-threatening ways to attract the attention of a beautiful woman, and although he was happy for his brother, that happiness turned to concern as he noticed things cool between Jianguo and Hongmei, and that several other young men were making plays for her affection. He urged his brother to seize the moment, but Jianguo merely shrugged, smiled sadly and said, 'Forget it.' He asked him why, but never got a straight answer. His brother drew more and more inside himself and Zheng Jianzhong felt angry, but there was nothing he could do.

Then came the spring morning in 1984, when, still in bed despite the busy day ahead, Zheng Jianzhong heard a pitiful wailing from Li Qingshan's house. He quickly dressed and rushed out, almost colliding with Jianguo who was coming out the opposite door, and together they ran to the Li's house. They stopped at the front door, letting their eyes adjust to the dark interior. The house was just like their own, dingy, a centre room with a stove and square table, all manner of things piled up about the floor, Li Qingshan's room on the east side, Hongmei's on the west. They found Li Qingshan sitting on the floor of the west room, weeping, and on the raised earthen bed was Hongmei, motionless, naked from the waist down. Zheng Jianguo crossed wordlessly to the bed and pulled the quilt over her. More neighbours arrived, and soon the doorway was crowded with faces looking in at the weeping Li Qingshan and the dead Hongmei and Zheng Jianguo standing, numb, beside the bed.

Two Public Security Bureau officers from county headquarters, at the farm on another investigation, were called to the scene and Section Chief Gu Chunshan took charge, snapping orders to his junior officer, a big pockmarked fellow named Wu Hongfei, to clear the scene and get everyone away from the house.

Rumour was that the PSB were on a political case involving Xiao Xiong, an 'educated youth' who had decided to stay on the farm. He was a bit of a loner. His father had been labelled a 'rightist' in the late 1950s and he had a sister whom he seldom saw since coming to the farm. Xiao Xiong was a likeable guy, strong, but not too bright and easily tricked. His nickname was 'Dumb Deer', the name hunters gave to a local deer species. They were easy marks. It was common knowledge that Dumb Deer was one of Li Hongmei's admirers, and wagers had been taken that he had the best prospects. Some hinted they were already engaged.

Section Chief Gu ordered the house sealed as a crime scene and told everyone to go home, but most people stayed and watched from a distance. A police van arrived. Throughout the afternoon, a number of people were summoned to the farm office for questioning, the Zheng brothers among them. Most of the questions were about Li Hongmei's relations with various young men, and whether each of the subjects had an alibi, which was checked. Once confirmed, they were free to go back to work, but no one was to leave the farm.

On the previous evening, the Zheng brothers had eaten dinner together at home. After dinner, Jianguo went to his room to read, while Jianzhong and his wife sat up playing cards. In the middle of a game, Jianzhong had gone out to the toilet and saw the light on in his brother's room. At about ten o'clock, he went to bed and called out to his brother not to stay up too late. Jianguo replied, 'I'm just going to bed now.'

Rumours swept the farm like wildfire. One line was that the police pathologist had inspected Hongmei's body and confirmed that she'd had sex with someone the night she died, that she had lost her virginity long before, and there were no signs of injury on her body. That the Beauty Queen wasn't a virgin was an explosive piece of news on Binbei Farm, and the gossips would have it that every man on the farm had slept with her. Others were more circumspect; some thought Zheng Jianguo, some thought Xiao Xiong. Consensus was that more than a dozen men might have 'done it' with the Beauty Queen, and there was a plausible case to make for each one, but it was all conjecture.

Then another rumour began, that the coroner couldn't verify the cause of death. Suffocation was a possibility, but she might also have had a weak heart – Keshan disease, they whispered. Some said she'd been raped, and the man who did it had been so aggressive that she died. Others thought she had gotten carried away in illicit passion with her lover and this had brought on a heart attack. Opinion was divided. Some people felt sadness for Hongmei, others took secret delight.

On the third morning after her death, Zheng Jianguo was called in again by the PSB. A blood test was administered. In the afternoon, Zheng Jianzhong was summoned to the farm office. He was questioned by Section Chief Gu, who asked him repeatedly about the evening of Hongmei's death, and many of the questions focused on what his younger brother had been doing. Big Axe realised that the police suspected his brother, and he swore, over and over, that Jianguo had spent the evening with him and his wife, and hadn't gone out at all.

That night, Zheng Jianguo was taken from the farm by the PSB. Big Axe ran about trying to find out what was happening and learned that his brother was suspected of rape and murder. He could get no more details from the PSB and wasn't allowed to see him.

A few months later, Zheng Jianzhong told Hong Jun, when the case was about to go to trial, he learned some of the details. A half-peeled apple had been found at the scene, along with a fruit knife with traces of blood on its blade. It seemed the person who had peeled the apple had accidentally cut themselves. There were no wounds on Li Hongmei's hands, but Zheng Jianguo had a cut on his right index finger. Tests showed that his blood was of the same type as the traces on the knife, and the blood type of the semen in the victim's vagina. Li Qingshan made a statement saying he'd had a bit to drink that evening and had fallen asleep straight after dinner. In the middle of the night he'd got up to go to the toilet and had seen a figure darting into the yard of the Zheng's house. The PSB pushed him on the question of whether the figure looked like Zheng Jianguo and he finally said it did. On the basis of this evidence, and the fact that Zheng Jianguo and Hongmei had previously had a romantic relationship, the Public Security Bureau determined that Zheng was the rapist and murderer. After several interrogations, he confessed.

In court, Zheng Jianzhong watched as his brother was led in wearing handcuffs. He waved at him, but the expression was blank. Throughout most of the trial, Jianguo stood with his head bowed as the prosecutor presented the PSB evidence against him, and its conclusions that he had committed the crimes for which he was charged. He only raised his head to give brief replies to questions from the judge and the prosecutor. The court sentenced him to death, suspended, because he had confessed to his crimes. After the verdict, Zheng Jianzhong went to see his brother in the detention centre and urged him to lodge an appeal. He was entitled to do so but he never did.

With his brother in prison, Big Axe felt it would be too much of a loss of face to carry on working at the farm, and so he set off to make his own way in the world. He went to Harbin and worked for a while laying tiles for a building firm. He took to the chaotic atmosphere of the early years of China's market economy like a duck to water. He was quick-witted and not scared to speak out if he could see cheaper and quicker ways to do a job, and backed up his words by proving it. He was much sought after as a site foreman. Within a few years he'd become the head of his own team of building workers, and before long started his own construction company. And once he'd succeeded in Harbin with a fairly decent amount of capital, he made forays into the bigger Beijing market and was soon well established there, too. He could keep expanding, but he was satisfied with his life. All that he really wanted was to get his little brother out of prison and the verdict overturned, so their departed parents might be at rest.

Hong Jun had filled many pages of his yellow pad with notes of Zheng Jianzhong's recollections. He had written questions circled many times, and drawn boxes of names with interconnecting lines that jumped back and forth across the pages. He would need time to sort through his thoughts, but he saw some patterns and was sure there was more to the case than met the eye. He needed more information. First, he wanted to talk to Zheng Jianguo so they could lodge an appeal.

CHAPTER THREE

IN SUMMERTIME, THE Songhua River runs crystal clear through Harbin, as beautiful as a fairy, singing softly and dancing gracefully. But in winter, it has another kind of charm, that of a beautiful woman, asleep on her side, now and again snoring gently. Its waters rest quietly under the ice, which reflects the gentle embrace of the sun's rays. No little boats bobbing on the waves around Sun Island, no crowds of people along its green banks talking and laughing.

A few children were making the most of the pleasures of winter. They'd cleared an ice run on the steeply sloping riverbank, and were taking it in turns to slide down on sledges. Some of them even skidded right out to the middle of the frozen river. They laughed and shouted cheerfully, even when they were bumping into each other and falling over on the ice, or crashing into the snowdrifts on either side of the ice run.

A few people walked the path beside the river, mostly young lovers with their arms round each other, and grey-haired old couples, mittened hand in mittened hand. Visitors took photographs of each other in front of the grand Flood-Fighting Monument. In the distance, Central Avenue was overwhelmed by cars and people.

*

It took Hong Jun several days of rushing back and forth, from one office to another with one form after another, to get permission to see Zheng Jianguo in Harbin Prison. He was taken to a bare meeting room, and twenty minutes later a warder brought in a man dressed in a blue cotton prison uniform.

Hong Jun had tried to imagine what Zheng Jianguo might look like after ten years' incarceration. But he was quite unprepared for the man he saw in front of him. Zheng Jianguo was at least 160 centimetres tall and weighed less than fifty kilograms. His face was sallow, his cheeks gaunt and he looked old. Wrinkles rolled across his forehead like waves, breaking into crow's feet around his eyes, which were cloudy, slow and blank. A thin growth of new white hair covered the top of his round head. Hong Jun could hardly believe he was looking at the Peasant Poet, a man of little more than thirty.

Zheng Jianguo was led to the table. He was dragging his right leg and favouring his right arm, the one injured in the harvester accident. He cast a slow, suspicious look at Hong Jun before sitting at the table. The warder withdrew, but stayed near the door. Hong Jun introduced himself and handed him a letter from Zheng Jianzhong.

Zheng Jianguo took the letter, opened it and read it slowly, still standing. When he finished, he looked up, his face expressionless, and asked, 'What the hell should I appeal for?' The voice was quiet, almost hushed.

Hong Jun gestured to him to sit, and took a seat diagonally across from him. 'First of all,' he said calmly, 'we're not talking about an appeal, because your case was concluded ten years ago. The only thing we can do now is petition the court for a retrial under the judicial supervision procedure. As for why, well, your brother says you're the victim of a miscarriage of justice . . . that you're innocent.'

The corners of Zheng Jianguo's mouth twitched. After a moment he said slowly, 'What's the point? They reached their verdict ten years ago.' He stopped and wrinkled his brow, thinking, and then asked,

'My brother says in his letter that you're a lawyer but you don't work for the state. What does he mean by that?'

'I'm a lawyer in private practice. I'm not paid by the state.'

'Who pays you then?'

'My clients, in this case your brother.'

'How much is he paying you?'

'You can ask him that. Of course, it's entirely up to you whether you want to apply for a retrial or not.'

'Can you guarantee I'll get out?'

'No, I can't. I can only try and I will do my best. I understand how you feel.'

'No!' He slammed his left fist on the table. The outburst was sudden, unexpected. 'You don't understand! How could you possibly understand? Can you imagine what I've been through the past ten years? I'm innocent. I didn't kill anyone. I didn't hurt anyone. Why do I have to suffer in here?' Zheng Jianguo's words were lost in tormented sobbing, as his fist slammed the table again.

The warder rushed forward, but Hong Jun gestured to him to stay back.

If Zheng Jianguo was innocent, Hong Jun thought to himself, life in jail must be a nightmare without an end. How had he kept going? How long can a person endure injustice, isolated from the world, before life loses all meaning?

Hong Jun reached out and patted Zheng Jianguo lightly on the shoulder. His sobbing gradually grew quieter, and subsided. But he remained slumped at the table, like an exhausted child. After a while, he raised his head, looked Hong Jun in the eye and said, 'Lawyer Hong, tell me what I should do. I'll do whatever you say. Just get me out of here.'

'Good, then I have a few questions. If you don't want to answer them you don't have to say anything.'

'As long as I know the answers, I want to talk.'

'Did you always love Li Hongmei?

'Yes, I did.'

'So why did the two of you split up?'

'That was because I wasn't the right person for her. She just felt sorry for me, after the accident. She didn't really love me.'

'Do you know who she was in love with?'

'It was the Dumb Deer, I mean, Xiao Xiong.'

'Can you tell me about it?'

Zheng Jianguo paused, as though putting his memories in order, then began.

'The thing about Hongmei is that she wasn't just nice-looking, she was really kind-hearted too. She treated everyone well. If she heard that someone was sick, you could be sure she'd cook him a bowl of hot noodles and take it to him. If he didn't know better, the guy would think she had feelings for him, and he'd be so bowled over that he could hardly remember his own name. Only after a while would he realise that she was this nice to everyone,' Zheng Jianguo said, speaking softly and carefully. He'd had ten years to remember how things really were, and his memories had been stripped of any romantic exaggeration.

'Hongmei was also very good-tempered. All the guys loved to tease her, and she liked a bit of banter too. Didn't matter whether what they said was true or not, she never got angry. Sometimes, if you said a couple of dirty words, she'd just curse you back, but she wouldn't really be annoyed. You could only tease her with words, though. You couldn't touch her.

'Once, one of the guys from our mechanical unit tried to kiss her hand as a dare, and I was sent to watch what happened, because I was the newest boy in the section. Before his lips could touch the back of her left hand, which he had taken in his, she lifted her right hand and gave him a good smack across the chops and cursed him something rotten. She looked quite scary when she got angry, and the guy ran away in terror. I did, too.

'After I got crushed by the harvester, Hongmei was pretty good to me. She often came to see me, even helped me wash my clothes. For a while, I really thought the two of us had become an item. I wrote her a love poem, and she took it. Once, at my house, when no one else was around, I plucked up courage and stroked her hand. She didn't say anything, but she gave me a look, and I knew she wasn't happy. I knew I wasn't good enough for her, but she treated me so well, and I just couldn't quite give up. I was pretty confused, really.

'One evening after supper, Hongmei came to see me, said there was something she wanted to tell me. I was very excited. I even put on clean clothes before I went to meet her. We walked to the west side of the house. There was no one around. We were standing very close, and she kept looking at me. I was so nervous I couldn't speak. Finally she told me that she knew I liked her, and she knew I was a good person, very clever and very capable, but the two of us couldn't be a couple. She said she'd thought about it for a long time, and she felt it was best to make things clear.

'I guess I'd been expecting this for a long time. I asked her why, and she said her dad and her sisters were against it. So I asked what she thought. She said that since that time when I got hurt, she'd always felt it was her fault, that she owed me something, so she wanted to be nice to me, but she knew it wasn't love, and it couldn't carry on long-term. She said she'd thought it over carefully, and she felt the two of us just weren't right for each other.

'I told her that I understood and that I'd be okay, just so long as she was happy. She wanted to let me kiss her once, as a souvenir, but only on her cheek, like friends do when they say goodbye in those foreign films. So I kissed her on the cheek. It seemed a satisfactory way to bring things to a close. It was the first time I'd kissed a woman's face in my life, and it'll probably be the last.'

Hong Jun said nothing. The thought of being incarcerated like this forever and that a kiss on the cheek was the closest Zheng Jianguo would ever get to finding love was too overpowering. He made a show of turning the pages of his pad. They sat in silence for a few moments.

'Now, I guess you want to know about Dumb Deer? Well, he was a clever guy, but a real loner. His father lived in their hometown and his sister was studying in Beijing. We worked together, but we hardly ever spoke. He looked down on me, but I didn't care. I've got plenty of self-respect, and if he didn't want anything to do with me, well, the feeling was mutual. I knew he liked Hongmei too. He never said so, but I could tell, so he must have been pretty annoyed when he saw how good she was to me.

'Then something happened to make us friends . . .

'It was autumn and we were ploughing the fields for the next plant-ing. Me and Dumb Deer had to do extra shifts driving the tractors and we were sent to field number nine to relieve a couple of drivers. Field nine was a few kilometres from the workshop and we had to cross a fallow pasture of wild grass to get there. There was no moon, but the stars were very bright. We were going along a little path. Neither of us was much for talking, so we just walked in silence, though the grass rustling in the wind was a bit spooky. We were far enough north that we sometimes saw wolves in that field.

'We just kept going, him in front. We were each carrying a long wooden stick – little more than kindling for a fire, to be honest, and if we really met a wolf we wouldn't stand much of a chance.

'About midway through the field, I felt a sudden chill and kept thinking someone was behind me, but whenever I looked round there was nothing there. It was pitch black, but I thought I saw two green dots of light move behind me. When I moved, the dots moved; when I stopped, they stopped. My hair stood on end. "Dumb Deer?" I called out. "Is there something behind us, or am I just seeing things?" He turned around and looked where I was pointing. Two green dots were suspended in the air again, completely still. Xiao Xiong crouched beside me, grabbed my arm and pulled me down. "Wolf," he whispered. As I squinted in the starlight, I finally made out a shadowy shape around what resolved into the eyes of a wolf. The beast was about twenty metres behind us.

'Xiao Xiong got up and said, "Ignore it, but let's get a move on." He was tall and he took big strides. I was almost running to keep up with him. Was he trying to teach me a lesson? We were love rivals. But the minute I stopped concentrating on where I was going, I tripped on a clump of grass, fell flat on my face, and heard the swish of grass as the wolf made a dash for me. In an instant, Xiao Xiong was between me and the wolf, lashing out with his stick, which he held two-handed like a fighting staff. I scrambled back to my feet, but I'd lost my stick when I fell, and my right arm was pretty useless in a fight, so I pulled up some grass clods and flung them at the beast, bellowing for all I was worth.

'Maybe Dumb Deer had landed some effective strikes, or maybe we were just too much trouble, because the wolf simply gave up and lumbered off. I wanted to ask if he was okay, and thank him for rescuing me, but Dumb Deer got in first. "Get a move on. We're late." He had me walk in front and he followed, carrying his stick in both hands. We were out of the meadow soon enough and, cresting a hill, saw the lights of the tractors and as we got closer to the well lit work camp, I saw that the wolf had ripped the sleeves and trouser legs of Dumb Deer's uniform, and the backs of his hands and his calves were covered in bloody claw marks.

'From that night on, we became good friends and, though we didn't talk much, I discovered that Dumb Deer was very smart, read a lot and knew a lot of things that had nothing to do with the farm. When he spoke about what was happening in China, he knew what he was talking about. I felt sure he'd go on to do great things.

'We never talked about Hongmei, but I knew that if he was serious I didn't stand a chance. This I confirmed one evening after dinner when there was a power cut and I went to the garage to get kerosene for the lamps. I was just heading back when I saw two people walking towards me, from the farmyard. I hid behind one of the tractors. I couldn't make out their faces, but from their silhouettes and the way they walked I knew it was Hongmei and Dumb Deer. They went hand in hand to the corner of the wall between the garage and the drying room, a spot that's hidden from the path.

'I knew I should leave, but I couldn't move, and by then I'd been there too long so I had to stay, to avoid embarrassing them. They weren't doing anything I could see, except standing close to each other. This lasted about an hour. A lot of things went through my mind. I'd be lying if I said I wasn't upset. But I realised then that the right person for Hongmei was Xiao Xiong, and I'd just have to live with it.'

*

Hong Jun had said nothing while Zheng Jianguo spoke, scribbling notes at various points but otherwise remaining silent and attentive.

'Lawyer Hong, did I talk too much?'

'No . . . No, I'm sorry. I'm just a little tired and my concentration slipped for a moment.' Hong Jun stood, stretched his arms above his head while he worked his neck, then picked up his yellow pad and, still standing, flipped through the recent pages. 'Did you see Dumb Deer . . . I mean . . . Xiao Xiong around the time of Li Hongmei's death?'

'The last time I saw him was a couple of weeks before it happened. He was often away from the farm, but when he came back that time, the PSB were there looking for him, so he didn't stay long.'

'Why were the police looking for him?' Hong Jun watched Zheng Jianguo's reaction to the question.

'I dunno. He never breathed a word to me about what he did when he was away from the farm.'

'Do you think Xiao Xiong could have killed Li Hongmei?'

'No. That's impossible.' Zheng Jianguo looked shocked. 'Lawyer Hong,' he said, 'you won't get me putting the blame on someone else just to save my skin. And that doesn't make sense. Why would Dumb Deer have raped Hongmei? She was already his, and besides, Xiao Xiong wasn't like that.'

'What if it wasn't rape and murder, as the police say, but an accident?'

'An accident? What do you mean? What sort of accident? I don't understand.'

Hong Jun made a note on his pad, which he set back on the table again, and sat down. He asked Zheng Jianguo to tell him what he was doing on the night Li Hongmei died. What he told him fitted exactly with what his brother, Zheng Jianzhong, had already said. There was just one more thing he wanted to ask. Doing his best not to stare too pointedly, and choosing his words carefully, he said, 'If you weren't responsible for her death, why did you make a confession?'

'Oh . . . that.' Zheng Jianguo stared at the floor.

'Did the police beat you?'

'No, they didn't. I can't really explain what I was thinking at the time. It just seemed like if Hongmei was dead, there wasn't much point in me being alive. I guess I was feeling pretty confused, and the police were pretty convincing, and I guess I figured if they thought I'd done it, then I must have. They took it in turns to interrogate me, non-stop, for days, and if I started to fall asleep, they sprayed cold water in my face. They kept asking the same questions, over and over, and I kept answering them until I wasn't sure what I was saying. It was hard to take. I couldn't tell the difference between what was real and what was a dream.'

'A dream, what do you mean by that?' Hong Jun's eyes sharpened on Zheng Jianguo's face.

'Well I did dream about . . . you know, that I did it with Hongmei. It was long before she died. I dreamt that I got up in the night and met her in the yard. She'd been to the toilet. I went back to her room with her, and wanted to do it with her. She didn't agree at first, but then she did. I did it lots of times, and I shot my bolt every time. Sometimes at night when I couldn't sleep I'd think about that dream, and I'd come again. And on the morning after she died, when I saw her in the bedroom, naked from the waist down, it was pretty much like what I'd seen in my dreams. Later, the police kept asking me whether I'd had relations with Hongmei. They must have asked me that question more than a hundred times. After a while, I started feeling pretty mixed up. What if I'd really had relations with her, but just didn't remember? And by then I couldn't take it any longer. I wanted everything to be over, quickly. So I made a confession. It didn't seem like there was much point denying it. They said they'd found my semen on Hongmei's body and, even without my confession, they had enough evidence to convict me. I could keep my life if I confessed.'

'But you only dreamt about it? You didn't have sexual relations with her?'

'Of course not.' Zheng Jianguo shook his head and glared at Hong Jun, then, with a deep sigh, dropped his chin to his chest. 'If I'd really had relations with Hongmei, then even if I'd been sentenced to death I wouldn't have felt I'd died in vain!'

Hong Jun leant back in his chair, ran his right hand through his hair several times, and asked, 'Have . . . have you ever sleepwalked?'

'What's that mean?'

'It means that when you're asleep in the night you get up and do things without realising it. It's really like being in a dream. Do you talk in your sleep, for example?'

'My brother says I did when I was little, but after that I don't know. I definitely never went . . . "sleepwalking"? I'm a sound sleeper. Do you believe me?'

'I do.' Hong Jun believed Zheng Jianguo, and logic, based on his physical infirmities and common sense, dictated that he wasn't a killer or a rapist. But could he have done something subconsciously, something which he was unable to control, while sleepwalking? He remembered a case in the US involving a young man who stabbed his father to death without ever waking up. Thanks to the combined efforts of his lawyer and psychiatric experts, he was found not guilty of murder. In Illinois, Hong Jun had spent most of his free time in the Cook County Courthouse, sitting in on trials and studying the techniques of some of Chicago's best lawyers. There was often a political undertone to high-profile cases. Prosecutors were under a lot of pressure to win because the district attorney, their boss, was an elected official judged on his record of convictions and not his sense of justice. Defence lawyers might be either court-appointed or paid for by the defendant. It was all very adversarial, and Hong Jun loved it. But this wasn't Chicago; it was China and the rules were different. Everything rested on the evidence gathered by the Public Security Bureau, and the court's job was to check whether the PSB had done its job properly, deliver a verdict based on the evidence before it and mete out punishment.

Hong Jun glanced at his watch. He pulled out the letter authorising him to seek a retrial, and asked Zheng Jianguo to sign. He noticed that Zheng wrote his name with his left hand. 'Are you left-handed?' he asked.

'No, not originally. I learned to write with it after my right arm was crushed.'

'Can you still write with your right hand?'

'No. It's pretty useless now. I can carry a bowl or a basin for cleaning my teeth, that kind of thing, but nothing more. I can't grip a pen. They told me the muscles and tendons were pretty badly damaged, and the bone breaks were pretty bad and would probably never heal.'

'It looks like there's something wrong with your right leg, too. Was that also from the accident?'

'No. That I got here.'

'Who did it?'

'One of my cellmates, but don't bother telling anyone. In this place if you don't beat people up, they'll beat you. If you're scrawny like me, you're bound to suffer. When I first got here I didn't know that, and I talked back, tried to stand my ground. I got plenty of beatings before I learned to shut up and take whatever they dished out, and do what they tell you. So I played along, and I got beaten up a lot less.

'There was just one time I got really angry.' Zheng had fixed his eyes on the wall, as if he was digging down deep to recall a painful memory. 'You'll probably laugh, but I'm writing a novel about my own story, really. The warders were quite supportive, and even brought me writing paper. I'd written a thick sheaf of pages, and really thought I was on to something good.

'I don't know why, but the boss of our cell ripped it up, every page. That book was my whole life. I was furious and went for him. I bit a chunk out of his arm before his boys pinned me down and gave me a good beating. After they'd staunched the bleeding, the boss stood over me and, with one kick, broke my leg. I was in the infirmary for a fortnight. Anyway, that was a long time ago.'

Hong Jun shook his head in sympathy and asked, 'Did you finish writing the book?'

'I started again and I've finished the first draft now. But I'm still working on it.'

'What's it called?'

'It's called *Broken Bones, Unbroken Spirit*.'

The warder signalled to Hong Jun that their time was up and began to lead Zheng Jianguo back to his cell somewhere deep inside the prison. In the doorway, the Peasant Poet stopped for a moment and turned to look at Hong Jun, who saw something that had not been there when they began their meeting . . . hope.

*

On the train from Harbin to Binbei, Hong Jun reflected on what Zheng Jianguo had told him. He couldn't help feeling that the Peasant Poet's love for Li Hongmei had a certain tragic beauty – a reminder of the power of that most indefinable of human emotions. He found himself thinking of Xiao Xue, his own first love. It was hardly surprising – she'd barely been out of his thoughts since he'd arrived in Harbin – this was her part of the world after all.

He closed his eyes as the train lurched along and remembered that night when he and Xiao Xue had gone cycling through the darkened streets outside the university and two thugs tried to steal their bikes, how he chased them away, and how, when they got back to the campus, in the silence of the playing field, Xiao Xue turned towards him expectantly, and, for the first time, they kissed. They had a magnificent summer, but the more they learned about each other and their dreams, the more they understood how divergent their paths were. He wanted to do things with his life, as did she, and neither was worth sacrificing. To ask that one give up their dreams for the other was, to him, unfair. They were just not meant to be together. But he'd never been able to erase her image from his memory, in which she was very much alive. And nagging questions returned: how was Xiao Xue now? Was she happy? These thoughts had become ever more pronounced over the past few months, since he'd returned to China.

She was the most beautiful female student in the People's University Law Department, and very talented; lots of people on the campus were in love with her. Hong Jun had faced tough competition to win her favour, not least from Zheng Xiaolong, the quick-witted head of the student union. When she finally chose Hong Jun, he became the envy of his classmates.

In the spring of 1985, both he and Xiao Xue were accepted for postgraduate study in the law department. It was a blissful time for them. Most of their classmates were busy worrying about what jobs the government would assign them after graduation, or trying to make plans, but they had no such cares. Every evening they went for a walk together, or went dancing, or watched films, or just strolled in the park. They were determined to make the most of this carefree period so they could return to the pressure cooker world of academia in a cheerful frame of mind. The greatest source of joy was that they were, then, deeply in love. But before they could even begin their postgraduate studies, it all came to an end. One day, Xiao Xue suddenly told him her father was dying, and she had to go back to Harbin to care for him. She had always refused to talk about her family before. Hong Jun sensed there were other problems back home too, and, on the pretext that they were parting, perhaps forever, he learned that her father had been labelled a 'rightist' and she had a brother who had been sent away as an educated youth. Apparently he had become involved with some radical political group and got into trouble with the authorities, but she was unwilling to discuss it any further. It was a sad, tearful parting at Beijing Railway Station. Hong Jun wished he could get on the train and go back to Harbin with her, but he knew he could not abandon his studies. They promised to stay in contact, but in those days it was hard even to make a telephone call to another city. They wrote often at first, but time and pressure intervened, and their career paths diverged, and gradually they lost touch with each other.

Just before he left for America, he had seen some of her academic papers on criminology, which had impressed him. He knew she was in Harbin, but he wasn't sure where to start looking. He imagined them meeting again after so many years, catching up on events in each other's lives, a pleasant evening together comparing what happened to each other, and afterwards personally reflecting on what might have been.

CHAPTER FOUR

BINBEI WAS A county town with aspirations of greatness. Headquarters of the regional administration and Chinese Communist Party Committee, with a bustling and lively downtown area, it already behaved like a regional city. Binbei Avenue, the main street, had an urban grandeur about it, running wide and arrow straight for several kilometres from the station in the south to the county hospital in the north. It boasted a strong mix of shops and restaurants, and the stretch of video parlours and nightclubs, now such a part of modern life, had a look of permanence and prosperity.

It was past three o'clock in the afternoon when Hong Jun left Binbei Station. Heavy snow had only recently fallen, and the houses, trees and ground were a pristine white, though the roadway was already a black river of slippery slurry from the tyres of cars and trucks, the drivers of which leaned on their horns and cursed. Cyclists and pedestrians paid little heed to the traffic, focused instead on making their way through the soft snow banks as quickly as they could.

Hong Jun headed north into town, following the icy narrow footpath established by countless pairs of trampling feet. A bitterly cold northerly wind blew up clouds of powder. He put down his suitcase, turned up his collar and zipped his leather jacket up to the neck, and pulled his woolly hat further down over his burning ears. Inwardly, he thanked Song Jia for running out to the shop to get it for him before he left.

Picking up his case, he set off again. The little trail through the snow was very slippery, and his leg and calf muscles soon ached as he took one precarious step after another. A passer-by confirmed he was going the right way, and assured him that the Songjiang Hotel, the biggest in town, was close by. It was a big five-storey building and boasted the latest facilities for the modern businessman, including in-room TV, fax machines and a computer-equipped business centre. The description sounded good, but what really impressed Hong Jun was not the phone or TV but the gleaming white bathroom and endless hot running water. He stripped fast and flung himself under a hot shower, not only to wash away the dust and dirt of travel but to drive the cold from his bones. He'd forgotten just how bitterly cold the northeast could be.

Hong Jun felt much better after the shower, and the room was cosy and warm from the central heating, but now his stomach was starting to grumble. He dressed in layers and was determined to find somewhere to eat that let him take a look at the town.

His watch showed it had just gone five o'clock. It was already dark outside and the streetlights burned like beacons. There were fewer people about than before, but the atmosphere was still lively. Roadside traders were undeterred by the cold, as were the shoppers, who sifted through goods of all kinds, many made in Russia, looking for bargains.

On the corner, not far along the street, Hong Jun noticed a row of big neon characters declaring Binbei Restaurant, and he headed towards it.

The restaurant was on two floors, with brightly lit plate-glass windows along its street-front. On either side of the entrance's colourful sign lanterns swayed in the wind. Hong Jun pushed the door open and found himself inside a little porch with a steel grate floor, where he could stamp his boots clear of snow and shake his coat. As he lifted the thick curtain separating the porch from the main room, a wave of warm air surged over him. The dining room was big, with large round tables in the middle and small square tables around the edges, all white tablecloths and vases. There were only a few diners. It was early.

A waitress with painted eyebrows and bright lipstick came over, smiled, and asked, 'Would you like to try the deluxe dining room upstairs, sir?'

'This will do fine,' he said, and took one of the small square tables beside the window while the waitress fetched the menu.

'Not from round here, sir?' she asked.

'No, I'm not,' said Hong Jun, flipping through the menu.

'From Beijing, then?'

'You're very smart,' he said, and gave her smiling face more than a glance.

'It's nothing to do with being smart. In this job you talk to different people all day long. After a while, you only have to hear them say a couple of words to guess where they're from, and nine times out of ten you're right. You're from Beijing all right, and born there. It's all about inflection and the pitch of your tones. But never mind,' she said and talked him through the menu, compiling for him a meal of local mountain vegetables, stewed meat and a bottle of beer.

When the food and drink arrived, Hong Jun did not rush, chewing each mouthful slowly as he looked out of the window. In fact, his mind wasn't on the street or on what he was eating, but focused on the Zheng Jianguo case. He turned the particulars over in his mind, weighing up possibilities and sifting details he needed to confirm. It was simply a matter of lining up what was logical concerning motive, means and opportunity, laying out the evidence and arguments for and against its inclusion, and deducing from all that the most likely solution, which was usually the simplest. He sipped his beer and was planning what he needed to get done the next day when a sad, monotone song broke his train of thought. He turned his head towards the sound.

The restaurant had become crowded while he was thinking, and he had to look for gaps between the other diners to catch sight of the singer, a woman with long, unkempt flowing hair, sitting in an ill-lit corner, face unclear, hands waving in front of her chest. She had a low, gravelly voice like some of the blues singers he had come to appreciate while in Chicago. He concentrated on the words, which were the same, over and over again.

> My brother's a big official, hah
> My home is in Harbin, ah
> Who wants to suck up to me, eh?
> Take me home to be your mother, hey!

Frowning, Hong Jun got to his feet and walked towards the toilet, slowing as he passed the woman. To say she looked like a scarecrow would have been no exaggeration. Her grey-black hair was like wild grass flattened by a fall of frost and strewn randomly about her head and face. She was dressed in ragged clothes of indeterminate but mismatched colours. In places all over her coat, the black cotton padding showed through. She wore disintegrating cotton shoes, useless in such weather, particularly as he could see filthy, raw toes poking through the holes. Her face was a dirty yellow, but the whites of her eyes were clear, and appeared especially bright. However, they weren't animated, and he wondered what they might have looked like when life burned behind them.

Back at his table, he pondered what life was like for those who weren't on the fast train towards modernisation. He could no longer enjoy the food in front of him and gestured for the waitress to bring him the bill. When she brought him his change, he asked, 'Who's that woman?'

'Just some crazy person.'

'Is she a local?'

'No. I think she's from Harbin. She's only been here a couple of months.'

'She doesn't have anyone to take care of her?'

The waitress made no attempt to hide her astonishment. 'Who takes care of other people these days? People don't even take care of their own mothers, let alone those of others. Is she your mother?' She realised how harsh she sounded, and added, 'Don't judge by her looks. She's quite young, only about thirty. Most likely just someone who has lost her way is all. If she makes it through this winter, she'll be fine.'

His attention was drawn back to the crazy woman by a surge of laughter around her and he got up to see what was happening. Four fashionably dressed young men eating at a table near the mad woman were trying to persuade her to sing them a song, and one was waving a half-chewed bone in front of her face, as if to get an animal to perform a trick. Hong Jun was not alone in his anger and revulsion at the scene, but no one made a move. A disturbing number of diners tried to pretend nothing was happening at all.

Hong Jun began to move towards the four drunken louts when the waitress gripped his shoulder. 'You don't want to get out of your depth here,' she said quietly. 'They're a pretty nasty bunch. The one with the great big nose is called "Old Maozi", the one with eyes like a toad is "Commander Tang". Do you want to provoke them?'

Well aware of his own limitations, Hong Jun had no desire to stir up trouble, but he couldn't let this helpless woman be tormented. The initiative was taken from him when a fist slammed loudly on a table in the middle of the restaurant and a big, deep, male voice bellowed, 'Goddammit!'

It wasn't hard to locate the source. Every head turned towards a huge man, in his forties or fifties, with big eyes and thick eyebrows and whiskers covering most of his face. He had a prominent scar on the right of his forehead, and his face told the story of a man used to hardship. Deerskin coat over deerskin waistcoat, and a bandolier of shotgun cartridges hung low around his waist. His worn canvas breeches were tucked into a pair of high felt inner boots, and over them were leather boots lined with grass – wula sedge, Hong Jun recognised, which had excellent thermal qualities. A double-barrelled hunting gun leaned against the table, gleaming in a dull metal grey.

Eyes ablaze, the man closed on the four louts and slapped the guy with the bone with an open hand, behind which was enough power to send him sprawling to the floor. The other three came at him with broken beer bottles, but he had them marked and in swift blows left them sprawling, spread-eagled. The guy he had slapped wasn't ready to surrender and was about to jump him from behind with a bottle when Hong Jun saw his opening, stretched out a long leg and tripped him so he fell flat on his face. The big man shouted, 'Get the hell out of here,' and they scrambled for the door. Commander Tang stuck his head back through the curtain and shouted, 'Just you fucking wait!'

The big fellow began to laugh, and many of the other diners started laughing too, but Hong Jun didn't join them. The now forgotten mad woman cowered in her corner, but from whom he couldn't tell, the big man or the louts?

The man looked at Hong Jun. 'Thanks, brother,' he said, went back to his table, drained the liquor in his drinking bowl, cradled his gun, left a crumpled handful of banknotes on the table and strode out. Hong Jun glanced at the mad woman and, through her dishevelled hair, caught an extraordinary expression of adoration, delight and a look that declared her far from insane.

She began singing again.

My brother's a big official, hah . . .

CHAPTER FIVE

BINBEI DISTRICT INTERMEDIATE People's Court was a three-storey building, as unimaginative a piece of utilitarian architecture as could be found across China. Not even the snow could soften the Party's past grim preference for concrete, and more concrete, in all its buildings. Hong Jun pushed open a grimy aluminium-framed door, no different from the type found on all government buildings, and approached the clerk at the front desk. 'Take a seat,' she said before he even reached her, and went to refill her flask of hot water before fussing about with sheets of paper on her desk. Hong Jun was the only other person there, and he watched her watch him from the corner of her eye for half an hour. The wall clock made an audible 'click' as the minute hand moved every sixty seconds. Hong Jun knew she would talk to him when she was ready, and there was nothing he could do about it. So, he sat.

'What do you want?' she asked him, and he rose and approached the long desk. He explained the reason for his visit. She looked at his lawyer's licence, scrutinising the Ministry of Justice stamp and comparing, again and again, his face with that in the headshot on the card, and then turned to Zheng Jianzhong's letter appointing Hong Jun as his lawyer. 'You're a lawyer from Beijing,' she said. 'Why have you come here? It's a long way and a lot colder.'

'As the letter explains, I have been engaged to investigate a case handled by this court. My licence gives me permission to go anywhere in China.'

'But this case is . . .' she squinted at the letter again, '. . . ten years old? I doubt we have the documents you want to see.'

'Perhaps you could check for me? Would that be possible?'

'That's not my job.'

'Could you tell me who I should talk to?'

'She's not here. Come back later, maybe three or four o'clock.'

'Would it be possible to have a word with the Chief Judge of the Court?' he asked. It was a long shot, but he felt he would not be playing his part properly if he didn't ask, and the clerk, who had expected the question for the same reason, had a ready reply.

'He's not here either . . . up at the District Party Committee on a training course.'

Hong Jun stood his ground. He looked at her, she looked at him.

'Look, just come again this afternoon. When our section chief gets back, I'll tell her you want to see her.'

'And her name is?'

'Wang. Section Chief Wang.'

Hong Jun jotted the name in his pocket notebook. 'All right. I'll come back then.'

'Your first time in Binbei, is it?' the clerk asked, dropping her formal tone and lapsing into a more relaxed, northeast manner. 'Go for a walk. It is really lovely here. Cold, but lovely. Turn north when you leave. In no time you'll be at Binbei Park. I heard there are people doing ice sculpting there. Have a look, get some lunch. We should be ready for you mid-afternoon, okay?'

The clerk had a friendly smile that suited her round face, and she meant well, in a just-doing-my-job way. He wasn't getting anywhere, so he smiled too, and turned back toward the street.

The day was very cold, but the sky was clean and clear. He headed north.

✳

Binbei Park was an old stretch of wood with a large lake on the edge of the town, and he hoped it would be left alone as the population grew, but at the same time Hong Jun knew he was being too optimistic to think that the city would not cash in on such valuable real estate. Everything had value in China, and dirt was more valuable now than gold. A bulldozer and a load of concrete was all it really took to turn a centuries-old forest into a building that would be torn down and replaced with another in a decade.

At this time of day, there weren't many people around and it was very peaceful. Hong Jun walked into the wood, scuffing his boots through the soft, powdery snow, until he came to the shore of the lake. Its surface was a layer of pure white, though a makeshift ice rink had been cleared and a handful of skaters were moving around, some lithely, some unsteadily. Now and again one of the littler skaters skidded over and fell, hard, but laughter and giggles and a helping hand forestalled tears, reminding everyone that it was all part of the fun. Nearby, a big sign announced that an exhibition by famous ice sculptors would be held there, but not any time soon.

Hong Jun kept walking and followed the path all the way around the lake, which really was quite large. Depending on the stream that fed it, this would be a nice fishing spot in summer. He felt relaxed, and happy. Like so many other towns in China that were growing into cities, he felt affection for Binbei, a link with its collective past, and hoped it wouldn't make too much of a mess of its coming prosperity. He looked at his watch. It was nearly eleven o'clock and he was hungry. He turned and headed back towards the entrance, through the little wood, listening to the snow crumble under his feet. In the distance, he caught sight of a figure and, shielding his eyes from the glare, recognised him as the hunter from the Binbei Restaurant.

As Hong Jun got closer he saw that his beard was frosted white from his frozen breath, and he shouted out, 'Hello brother.'

The big man turned around, alert. 'Eh . . . ? You are . . . ?'

'Last night at the Binbei Restaurant.'

'Yes . . . hello, brother,' said the man, and their gloved hands met in an awkward shake. 'From your accent, I'd say you're not from these parts.'

'No, Beijing.'

'Beijing, eh? A right big place, that is. What you doin' here then?'

'Work.' Hong Jun noticed a big grey rabbit hanging from the rifle on the hunter's back. 'Did you just *shoot* that?' he asked.

'Trapped it,' he said.

'Trapped? How?'

'With this . . . ' and the hunter raised his left hand. Hong Jun saw a fine wire with rings, not unlike a garrotte.

'You can catch a rabbit with that?'

'Sure.' The big man continued walking, stopping now and again to crouch down and inspect the snow for the faintest disturbance by a fleet-footed rabbit, or a fox. 'You just put this trap on the path the rabbit uses, securing it at one end to a rock or something, and when they come out at night, they can't see it and get caught in the trap, which tightens around them as they struggle. They always struggle. Pretty soon, they strangle themselves.'

'But how do you know where the rabbits will be?'

'They always take the same path, going out of the burrows and coming back. Find their prints, and you simply lay the trap and wait. Of course, there's a knack to setting the traps. Moonlight, for instance. A rabbit moves faster when it's in moonlight, so you set the trap high. If it's dark, they creep more slowly, so you set the trap low.'

Hong Jun was fascinated. Maybe it was the mystique, or personal rebellion against his bookish nature, but he admired real hunters who tracked and killed their prey, not for sport but to eat, to survive. It was all about careful observation, working out the rhythm and distinguishing disturbances in the natural order of things. He remembered Magic Ma, the footprint expert who was a legend in the PSB. He could track anyone, under any conditions; even when logic insisted that heavy rain had washed away all trace of a person's presence, Magic Ma would find something, some clue, some irrefutable evidence.

The hunter halted. 'Hah,' he exclaimed. 'I've been so busy blabbing, and I don't even know where you're heading, and we're getting further and further from town.'

Hong Jun looked up and saw they were almost at the edge of the wood. Ahead of them, snowy fields stretched into the distance, an occasional house dotted among the network of pathways that crisscrossed the cleared landscape. 'Yes,' he said with a smile. 'I ought to go back. My name is Hong Jun. Might I ask yours?'

'Bao's the name, but everyone calls me "Old Bao".'

'Thank you, Old Bao,' said Hong Jun. 'See you again, I'm sure. Good hunting.'

Hong Jun had a steaming bowl of noodles at a shack in the park, tromped aimlessly around in the snow for a while and got back to the courthouse at three o'clock. The clerk at the front desk smiled at his ruddy face, but did not leave her seat. 'Lawyer Hong. I do hope you enjoyed your walk.' She swivelled on her chair and bellowed towards a side corridor. 'Section Chief Wang? He's here.' Her voice loud enough to frighten a wolf, he thought. And she directed him, more quietly, 'Third office on the left.'

Section Chief Wang turned out to be a friendly woman in her mid-thirties with a well-proportioned figure and a pleasant face, a neat, understated business suit which seemed a little beyond her pay grade, and fine, pale skin quite unsuited to the dryness and glare of a winter sun. As Hong Jun approached, she got up from her desk and shook his hand gently. 'Hello,' she said, 'I'm Wang Xiuling.'

'Section Chief Wang, delighted to meet you. My name is Hong Jun. Please, my card.'

Wang Xiuling apologised for having used up her name cards and asked him to take a seat. Looking at his card, and running a judgemental thumbnail over the engraved printing, she said, 'So, you're Dr Hong, and you're a returned PhD from abroad, I believe, with impressive credentials. What brings you *here*?'

Hong Jun got the message – she had checked up on him and would cooperate, within reason. He explained the purpose of his visit, handing over his lawyer's card and letter of authority. Wang Xiuling glanced at the letter. 'Ah, Zheng Jianguo. That was the case at the Binbei State Farm. I vaguely remember it. I was a clerk then.'

'Did you work on the case?'

'No, but it was a big case. We all talked about it. The trial judge was our own Deputy Chief Judge Han? I'm not absolutely sure, but I'll check.'

She made a note on a discreet pad to the right of the desk, returning her hand to rest in front of her, the pen held loosely between her fingers.

'I wonder when you think I might be able to read the case documents.' Hong Jun was keen to get past the preliminary banter. He wanted to read the papers, which was his right, but what did he have to do to get them?

'Read the papers? In a ten-year-old case like this? I think I really have to ask the Chief Judge of the Court.'

'I understand. When do you think you'll be able to do that?'

'Well, all the top officials are on a study course at the District Party Committee until tomorrow afternoon. So why don't you come back the day after tomorrow, in the afternoon.'

Hong Jun knew she knew that holding him in Binbei for so long might be very inconvenient for a lawyer like him, and no evening train stopped at the station.

'As you know, I've come from Beijing, and I really need to get back as soon as possible. Could you just phone the Chief and ask him?'

'Oh no, I couldn't do that.' She shook her head gravely. 'The bosses have gone to the district to study the documents from the Party Central's last plenary session. Before they set off, they specifically told us not to phone unless it was an emergency. I don't really think your request for court papers from a ten-year-old trial is an emergency. And that being so, would a few days more make much difference?'

'But . . . ' Hong Jun surrendered. He lacked the skills to outtalk a northeasterner.

'Dr Hong, I know you must be in a hurry to get things done. All lawyers are. In America, where they charge by the hour, this would be a big bonus.' Their eyes met and he conceded the amusement of such a comment. She had done her homework. 'So, how about this . . . ?

'As soon as I get in, day after tomorrow, I'll tell the Chief about your case and he'll make a decision. You can come at, say, ten o'clock that morning, for our answer. Is that okay? I know the courts should help lawyers, but you also have to understand the way we work. "Long live understanding", eh?' Wang Xiuling stood, indicating the end of their meeting.

Hong Jun said, 'Thank you,' and left Wang Xiuling's office. The clerk at the front desk smiled a farewell, and he was sure her eyes said, 'Sorry, better luck next time'.

Outside the courthouse, zipping up his jacket and pushing his gloved hands deep into his pockets, he pondered his next move. He looked around, thinking a bar might be a warmer place for such thoughts, when he saw a young man standing by the side of the road, staring at him. Hong Jun turned and headed back to his hotel. The young man ran after him. 'Are you Dr Hong?'

'Sorry, you are . . . ?'

'Chu Weihua, People's University, I enrolled in the law department in eighty-five. You used to lecture us. We played basketball together, too.'

Hong relaxed and looked him up and down, trying to remember. 'Ah yes, Chu Weihua . . . you were pretty good, despite not being so tall . . . good at free throws. But, I think you were probably a little slimmer back then?'

'I was, Dr Hong, much slimmer. Now, I have no time for exercise. I have grown busier, and lazier, and fatter.' He laughed and patted his round belly. 'They say I look like a man of standing, but if you ask me I'd say I look more like a woman ready to drop her baby soon.'

Hong Jun joined him in laughing.

'But, Dr Hong,' he said, 'I thought you were abroad? Why are you here?'

'I came back from the US in the spring and opened my own legal practice, in Beijing. I'm here on a case.'

'Well, there's certainly good money in being a lawyer now. Since Deng Xiaoping set the ball rolling, a lot has changed. Dr Hong, you must be feeling the cold. I certainly am. Please, come to my office. It's not every day we have such a special guest.'

Hong Jun loved teaching, and there were days he missed the energy of his students and how hard the best of them made him think, but to teach he had to learn, and to learn he had to do. And he did like practising law, as much as he did teaching.

Chu Weihua's office was on the second floor. It wasn't very big, and it contained three narrowly parted desks. 'Everyone else is out. We cover a huge area and there are only three junior judges. They'll be gone for quite a few days. Please take a seat, Dr Hong.' He made tea for Hong Jun and himself from a hot water flask and a small tin of leaves. Chu Weihua was from Binbei County, he said, and had chosen to come back after graduating. He was now working as a trial judge in the criminal sentencing department of the intermediate court. Impressive title, he said, but not a lot happened in Binbei County.

'I read a lot, especially your books and articles. What are you doing here?' he asked. Hong Jun explained Zheng Jianguo's case, and the problems he'd encountered in the last two days.

Chu Weihua said, 'As long as the court documents are still on file, I don't think there'll be any problem for you to read them. But since Wang Xiuling said she'd have to ask the Chief Judge of the Court, I'm afraid it's not really appropriate for me to intervene. She's a nice person, but quite stubborn; a stickler for protocol. Her husband's the Deputy Party Secretary of Binbei County, so she goes by the book. Nothing gets done in a rush around here, so perhaps you could just find something else to do tomorrow, and then come back again the next day? I'll try to talk to Deputy Chief Judge Han about it so there are no further delays. He's in charge of criminal trials now.'

'Thanks,' said Hong Jun. 'I'll go to the Binbei State Farm tomorrow, see what I can learn there.' The joints of his fingers made their cracking sound again.

'Do you want me to arrange a car for you?' asked Chu Weihua.

'There's no need, thanks. I've already checked and I can take the public bus. It's quite convenient and will give me time to think.'

They chatted about the pace of progress in China, and its strain on the legal system amongst other things. They could have talked all night, but it was time to say goodbye, and as they did, Hong Jun thought of something else he wanted to ask. 'Weihua,' he said, 'are you still in touch with other graduates from our department who are now living in Heilongjiang?'

'Sometimes, but not very often.'

'Do you know a woman named Xiao Xue?'

'Xiao Xue? Doesn't ring any bells.'

'She graduated in eighty-five.'

'Ah, well that's quite a few years before me. But I'll ask around. Last year there was a party in Harbin for People's University law graduates. I couldn't go, but they sent me a contact list. She may be on it. I'll look for it when I get home tonight.'

'No hurry,' said Hong Jun. 'We were both in the same year, and it would be good to catch up while I'm here.'

CHAPTER SIX

AS WAS SO often the case on clear days after a snowfall, the sun was exceptionally brilliant. His eyes hurt and he had a headache, which the too-crowded bus did nothing to make easier to bear. He was thankful he had a window seat and tried to take comfort in that. Hong Jun squinted at the distant mountains and thick forests beyond through the foggy window. The road was unkind and the bus jolted over the rutted surface, its tyres fighting for purchase through the filthy morass of mud. He caught sight of a patch of mostly dark grey buildings nestled among the white grasslands.

The Second Branch of the Binbei State Farm was built on and around a lonely hill; the settlement was dominated by a big hall used for political meetings and as a communal canteen. To the south were stables for horses and sties for pigs, in the east stood a clinic and machine shop, while the farm office, single men's dormitory and family quarters lay to the north, and to the west was a large yard for drying crops and sifting grain, enclosed by an earthen wall half as tall as a person. Spread out around the hill was an intricate and undulating quilt of fields. In the far distance was the peak of Mount Erke.

The bus stopped on the forecourt in front of the meeting hall. Hong Jun was the last to get off. On a remote farm like this, he thought, the arrival of the morning bus was probably the liveliest event of the day. The bus filled up again with bags big and small, the doors closed and it drove around the yard towards the county town an hour away.

Hong Jun watched the arriving passengers disperse towards the residential quarters, and the forecourt sank back into quiet lethargy. Winter was the slack season on the farm. There were repairs and refurbishments to be made, but without the sense of urgency that accompanied the harvest. Hong Jun looked around him and saw only a few pigs snuffling past the drying yard. Wisps of white cooking smoke rose above the family area. He heard a door open and saw a ruddy-faced girl come out carrying a basin of water, which she poured, steaming, onto the ground. She turned back towards the door and he followed her to the far end of the canteen.

He was instantly engulfed in a cloud of warm, damp steam, and had to wipe his glasses. Two young women were lifting a large, heavy basket of steamed buns from an enormous iron wok. They placed it on a plank and lowered another batch into the scalding vapour, sealing the wooden lid with two strips of yellowing cloth. As the younger of the two girls swept her face with the back of her forearm, she noticed Hong Jun standing in the doorway. 'Looking for someone?'

'Yes. May I ask for your assistance?' he said, putting his glasses back on.

The younger woman looked him over for a moment. 'Hey, are you from the city? Come in, come in.'

Hong Jun thanked her, and asked whether she knew where Li Qingshan lived.

'Li Qingshan?' She looked stumped. 'I don't think there's anyone of that name round here.' She called out to her friend. 'Hey, Fatso, we got anyone here called Li Qingshan?'

The plump girl came over. 'Li Qingshan? Never heard of him! What's he do?'

'He's an old worker from this farm,' said Hong Jun. 'One of his daughters was murdered here ten years ago.'

'Oh, that,' said the young one. 'I think the family moved away a long time ago. They were gone by the time I got here, and that's a good few years ago. But everyone knows the story, don't they Fatso?'

'What story?' She was already at work preparing the ingredients for the next batch of steamed buns, and sounded irritated at being left to work on her own.

'You know, that incredibly beautiful girl. The one who was raped and murdered? They called her the Beauty Queen. Her dad was called Rotten Egg.'

'Of course I know.'

'Hah, you never remember anything, pea brain.'

'I remember there are supposed to be two people doing this job, not one.'

The younger girl snorted and turned back to Hong Jun. 'Go to the building at the south end of the row opposite, and ask for Mr Gao. He's the Deputy Farm Director. He knows everything that goes on here. And,' she called out as he left, 'don't forget to come back at lunchtime to try our buns!'

'Just come in, what you knocking for?' The voice was gruff and impatient. Hong Jun opened the door and saw a middle-aged man at a desk, writing carefully in a ledger. He had a red face, with thick lips and a little beard. The top button of his grey tunic was undone, and the collar of his not very clean white shirt underneath stuck out at a comical angle. A not-quite-new black padded jacket was draped over his shoulders. 'What is it?' he asked. He didn't look up.

'I'm looking for Director Gao?'

The man put down his pen, flexed his fingers, revealing the hard, calloused hands of a working man, and glared at Hong Jun. 'I am Gao. What do you want?'

'My name is Hong Jun. I am a lawyer from Beijing. I was hoping you might be able to help me with some information.' Hong Jun approached the desk and placed his business card in front of Director Gao, who looked at it closely, shrugged off his padded jacket and adopted a friendlier posture.

'A man of education is most welcome here. It is an honour, Dr Hong. Please, take a seat. How can I help you?'

Hong Jun tried to copy the friendly, direct manner of speaking favoured by northeasterners and said, 'Director Gao, I hear you know everything about this farm, past and present.'

'That is so. I've been 'ere thirty years, man and boy.' Hong Jun thought he detected a hint of Shandong in his accent.

Gao took a pouch of tobacco from his tunic pocket and offered it to Hong Jun. 'We roll our own here. And we grow it ourselves. Good for all that ails ya. Better than the machine stuff. It makes me look like a yokel, but . . .'

'That's very kind of you, but I don't —'

'Guess you Beijingers only like foreign smokes.' Gao took a strip of white paper from a packet inside the pouch, folded it down the middle, spread a pinch of tobacco leaves torn between his fingers down the centre and, as quick as magic, turned it into a perfect cigarette, which he placed between his moistened thick lips and lit with a match. Exhaling a sweet-smelling bluish stream of smoke that began to play in the sunlight from the window, he asked, 'So, Lawyer Hong, what would you like to know?'

Hong Jun had been fascinated by the cigarette ritual and it took a moment for the question to register. 'I'm trying to contact someone called Li Qingshan,' he said quickly. He didn't feel ill at all from the smoke made by Gao's cigarette.

'Li Qingshan?' Director Gao shifted slightly, more alert. 'What do you want to find him for?'

'We're reinvestigating a case, and we want to check some information with him.'

'What case?'

'The murder of his daughter, Li Hongmei.'

'But that was ten years ago. And the PSB closed the case. Why are you investigating it now? And who is "we"?'

'The defendant is seeking a retrial. I am investigating on behalf of his brother, now a prosperous Beijing builder, who wants the verdict overturned.'

'I see,' said Gao. He seemed to be weighing Hong Jun's forces against those he would need to contend with locally. 'It really was tragic, poor Hongmei. Zheng Jianguo always seemed like such a good kid. No one thought he could do something like that. You think you know someone, but you never really know what's going on inside their head. You think he's innocent?'

Hong Jun didn't want to debate the case and tried to steer the dialogue back to his question, to give him some leads. 'Does Li Qingshan still live here?'

'Oh no, he's been gone a long time. He moved away soon after it happened.'

'Where did he go?'

'I think he maybe went to Harbin with his older daughter. She married one of those urban youths working on the farm, and then later they moved back to the city. Yes, that's it – he went with them.'

'Do you know where they live in Harbin?'

'No, I don't. And it's not the farm's business to keep track of where people go after they leave here. If I had to do that . . . ' Gao waved both hands over the papers piling up on his desk, his left eye squinting at the smoke trickling up from the cigarette in the corner of his mouth. 'Nothing to do with us.'

'Where do you think I might find out Li Qingshan's address?'

Director Gao thought for a moment. 'Well,' he said, 'I suppose you could ask Chen Fenglu. He lives in Li Qingshan's old house now. The two families got on quite well, so he might know.

'The problem is,' he added, leaning forward and lowering his voice, 'he's a great talker, but you never know how much of it to believe. Everyone on the farm calls him "Big Mouth" and he's loud. You can hear him across two fields.'

'Thanks, I can keep my hat down over my ears if he doesn't invite me inside.' Hong Jun got to his feet. 'How do I get to his house?'

'Head a little ways north from here, then . . . oh, too complicated. It'll be a lot easier if I just take you. I need to go that way to see some-one anyway.'

Hong Jun thanked him for his kindness.

'What you bein' so polite for?' said Gao. 'C'mon, let's go.'

Passing through the residential area, Hong Jun saw row upon row of brick houses, neatly arranged, all identical, though he noticed a few decrepit mud houses scattered among them. It was already almost lunchtime and the tantalising smells stirred his belly, so Hong Jun concentrated on steamed buns at the canteen as he followed Director Gao west along a neatly cut path a metre or so wide. A makeshift fence had been thrown up to make a small compound in which stood closely stacked bales of hay. They passed more rows of houses built around courtyards and at the westernmost edge they halted outside a courtyard gate, beyond which, Hong Jun realised, was the scene of the crime.

'Hey Big Mouth, you home?' Director Gao shouted.

A small, wizened head peered out from behind a half-open door. 'Director Gao, what do you want?' The voice was croaky, and with raspingly loud, laboured breaths, a little old man shuffled out in cloth slippers.

'It's not me who wants to see you. This is Dr Hong, a lawyer from Beijing. There's something he wants to ask you about.' He turned to

Hong Jun. 'Dr Hong, you two have a chat. I've got things to do so I'll leave you to it. Find me if you need more.'

'Thank you, Director Gao,' he said.

'No need for thanks. As I said, I was coming this way. Hey, Big Mouth, this is a special guest from Beijing, and he has impeccable manners, so watch what you say.'

Chen Fenglu snorted and spat into the snow as Director Gao waddled off through the snow, and invited Hong Jun into the house. There were no windows. Hong Jun blinked a little in the darkness after the bright white outside, and slowly his eyes adjusted and he could make out a stove, a water barrel, kitchen cupboards and Chen Fenglu standing at a door. He followed him into the room with two *kang*, one at the south end, one at the north. One of the earthen beds was piled with clutter and on the other a few quilts were folded. A glow of embers was still visible, remnants from a small pile of ash that had spilled out from the fireplace underneath. Between the *kang* stood a pair of wooden trunks with pictures of grain harvests painted on them. On the wall was a mirror, with a couplet pasted vertically on either side. *Remember that our rice and our porridge are hard-earned*, said one line, and the other, *Never forget that the merest thread is hard to come by*. Across the top of the mirror, another line was pasted. *Make your cloak before the rain comes.*

Hong Jun sat on the edge of the *kang* beside a little table. 'Interesting couplet you've got there, Grandpa Chen,' he said. 'You write it yourself?'

'How could I write something like that?' he laughed. 'No, someone in town did them for me. At the time, the lines really chimed with my innermost feelings, you know, so I paid someone to write them. Nice brush strokes. Life is much better now, but to keep a family and make a living still requires great frugality. As the old saying goes, "You can eat well and dress well, but if you don't get your sums right you'll end up poor." There's a lot in it, wouldn't you say?'

'Absolutely right,' Hong Jun nodded.

'You smoke . . . ?' asked Chen Fenglu, fondling his pipe. 'Or how about an apple? We got a good orchard here. I've got a knife here somewhere. I know you city folk like things to be clean, and peel apples before you eat them. We just bite right into them.'

'I'm okay. Thank you. There's really no need.'

'Anyway, I know you're a busy man. I won't keep blathering away. What do you want to ask me about?'

'Director Gao said you were quite friendly with Li Qingshan. I was wondering if you know where he lives now.'

'Li Qingshan? Oh, you mean Rotten Egg,' Chen laughed. 'Yes, we got on pretty well. He's a couple of years older than me, so he was like my older brother. But all I know is that he went to Harbin, don't know exactly where.'

'Did he go there with his daughter?' asked Hong Jun.

'Yep, he did. His older daughter was going anyway and took him along with her. He's had a tough life. He really loved his youngest daughter. Who could have imagined it would end like that. I suppose you must have heard all about it, right?'

'Yes. I'm here because of Li Hongmei's death.'

Chen Fenglu seemed to ignore Hong Jun. 'After Hongmei died, Li Qingshan was quite ill. He used to be pretty tough, that guy. He could carry a hundred kilo sack of wheat on his own, but after, he could hardly fetch a bucket of water. His temperament changed too. Never quarrelled or fought with anyone and just laughed when people called him Rotten Egg, but then he was always swearing and cursing at people and if anyone called him Rotten Egg, he'd want a fight. At first, everyone felt sorry for him and made allowances, expecting him to get better. He didn't, so they just ignored him. I think I was the only one who still talked to him. When his older daughter wanted to move away, she couldn't leave him here alone, so she packed him up and took him with her. Wow, did he curse her. I swear I could hear him all the way to Harbin. He wanted me to get the house, I think to apologise for having become such a mean old bastard. Well, that's life. And destiny is destiny, no point fighting it.'

He stopped talking and began rummaging again, presumably still looking for his knife. Hong Jun changed the subject. 'Is this the room Li Hongmei used to live in?'

'Sure is,' said Chen, giving up his search and sitting back down. 'After Li Qingshan moved away, the farm assigned this house to me. But my two daughters refused to live in this room, even though it had the two *kang*. They said it was unlucky. Me and the wife took it. It is a lot nicer than the other room. My eldest got married and moved away and so the youngster, still at home, stays in the other room. She's scared of meeting strangers, silly girl, and when we have visitors she shuts herself up in her room. Sometimes I forget she's there. Can't even hear her radio because the doors are solid and the walls are pretty thick. It's a good house.'

Hong Jun noticed the doors, and that the builders hadn't scrimped on the brick walls: the room was warm.

'I've heard that Zheng Jianguo used to live in this row of houses too.'

'He was just over there, on the east side. Both the brothers lived there. When Jianguo was put in prison, Jianzhong left. I heard he's pretty rich now. To tell you the truth, of the two of them, Jianguo was the honest, hard-working one and I still find it hard to believe he did what he did. His brother, Big Axe, could be vicious when he got worked up. A real temper he had. If it wasn't for the proof, the blood on that knife . . . '

'Do you think they got the wrong man?'

'I dunno. For a start, Jianguo was such a little guy and he had a bad arm. And, even if he did, I can't see how he could have been able to overpower Hongmei. She may have been called the Beauty Queen, but she was tough as old boots, that girl, strong as any field man. So this rape business . . . even if Jianguo had the urge and the will, and I just don't think it was in his nature, certainly he didn't have the strength.

If those two had got into a fight, Hongmei could have decked him. But Big Axe? Now *he* could have done it. Not only was he strong, but he could be pretty violent and he had an evil streak too. If that guy saw an old sow in the farmyard, he'd give it a couple of pokes.' Chen suddenly stopped. 'Oh, sorry, Dr Hong, you'll have to forgive me, I'm just a vulgar old man, and I talk so much I forget who I'm talking to.'

'No problem, Grandpa Chen. You should hear how they talk sometimes in Beijing. I like the way northeasterners talk.' Hong Jun tried to steer the conversation. 'Tell me more about Big Axe.'

'Y'know, he really was a nasty character. The year all the city kids, the educated youth, arrived? The two of us were working in the livestock section. He was herding sheep and I was driving the feed truck. One day, the farm vet brought in a stallion he'd borrowed to breed with our mares. So Big Axe rounds up all the girl students in the section to come and watch. He told them it was an important part of being "re-educated by the poor and lower-middle peasants". The girls didn't know what was going on, and watched very carefully. When the stallion mounted the first mare, one of the youths asked, "What's it doing?" Big Axe says, "It's fucking." The girls were so shocked they all ran off, covering their faces in embarrassment.' He paused for a moment to catch his breath. Chen liked to talk, but age was catching up with him.

'What a nasty guy. I tell you, if his wife hadn't kept him on a tight leash, there's no telling what bad things he'd have done. But every dog has its master . . . if he didn't obey her she'd soon sort him out. Don't know how she did it and don't know what she saw in him, y'know? But, anyway, it's not just me that says this about him. Ask any of the old people on the farm, they'll all tell you the same. Like I say, if you'd said it was Big Axe who committed the crime, most people would have believed you. But no one believed it was Jianguo. Even the girl's dad, Rotten Egg, he said to me later that he always felt bad about Jianguo going to prison.'

'Why?'

'Because he didn't think Jianguo did it, that it wasn't Jianguo he saw that night.'

'Did he say who he thought it was?'

'Nope. And once Jianguo was found guilty, well, he must have done it. The PSB had the evidence, and evidence doesn't lie. If he suspected someone else, he never said so and I don't make things up, though I'm sure you've been told otherwise.'

Chen went quiet, brooding, and Hong Jun looked around the room, searching for clues he knew he wouldn't find into what happened here on that night ten years ago.

'Tell me, Grandpa Chen, have you changed the room much since you moved in? These *kang* look like they have been here a long time.'

'Yes. I've added a few more coats of varnish to the tops, and I redid the walls, changed the newspaper . . .'

'So the wall at the head of the *kang*, that's changed?'

'I couldn't just leave a dead girl's things on my bedroom wall, now, could I?'

'Do you remember what was there before?'

'There was some personal stuff of hers, secret stuff.'

'What do you mean?'

'Well,' Chen Fenglu was clearly thinking he'd said too much. 'Oh, I suppose she's been dead for so long now, it can't do any harm to talk about it.'

'Go on,' said Hong Jun. 'Tell me about what was there. It might help me.'

'Over there, I . . .' He lowered his voice, and pointed to the corner by the head of the *kang*. 'Behind the newspapers on the wall there I found a letter from Dumb Deer to Hongmei. You've heard of Dumb Deer? His real name was Xiao Xiong.'

Hong Jun nodded. 'Yes, I know who he is. And I know he was Li Hongmei's boyfriend.'

'Okay. Well, there was a letter from him. It was personal. So I burnt it.'

'But it could have been important evidence. You should have given it to the PSB.'

'I never thought of that,' Chen said. 'After I found the letter . . . well, the case had been closed a long time, the PSB had all gone home and it was no use to anyone. Hongmei was dead and if I showed the letter around I'd just be raking up all the things those kids had said to each other and it wouldn't have been fair on Li Qingshan, my friend. Don't you agree?'

'That depends. Do you remember what was in the letter?'

'Oh, it was that kind of lover's talk young people like to use. I felt embarrassed just reading it.'

'So there was nothing in the letter except lover's talk?' Hong Jun pressed him for more. 'Try to remember, please.'

'Hmm, let me think. There was love stuff, and Xiao Xiong was asking Hongmei to hide something . . . no, to keep something hidden and he said he was planning to come back to the farm, but asked her not to let anyone else know. Yes, that's it. At the time I thought that if he'd really come back, maybe Hongmei wouldn't have died.'

'Was there anything else?'

'I honestly can't remember.'

'Did you tell anyone else about this letter?' Hong Jun asked.

'No. Li Qingshan had already left. Who else could I talk to about it? You're a special guest from Beijing, see, that's the only reason I'm telling you. I've been keeping this secret for ten years now. Just talking about it now is a real weight off my mind, I tell you. But now you've got me thinking, there was a photo in the letter.'

'A photo? Did you burn that too?' Hong Jun tried to remain calm.

'No, I don't think I did. It was a nice picture of the Flood-Fighting Monument. I have it here, somewhere . . . ' He began rummaging again, and Hong Jun left him to it. Minutes went by. 'Here it is,' said Chen at last.

'Is this Xiao Xiong?'

'It is,' said Chen. 'A very good likeness.'

Hong Jun examined the photograph carefully. The focus was sharp and he could see Xiao Xiong clearly, even his eyes. He had an odd feeling, but he didn't have time to work out why. 'May I keep the photo?' he asked Chen Fenglu.

'Take it. If it has any link with what happened to her, I don't want it here. I just thought it was a nice picture of the fountain.'

Hong Jun was silent for a moment. Another question occurred to him. 'Where is Li Qingshan's second daughter? There were three, weren't there?'

'Yes, three. Y'know, I'm really not sure. I think she might be in Binbei County Town. Let me think . . . When she got married, she moved to a village not far away but I went there once and heard that she and her husband had left the village to go into business. I saw her in Binbei one time, but didn't ask where she was living, though I got the feeling she lived in the town, but don't ask me why.'

Hong Jun had nothing more to ask and he got up, thanked Chen Fenglu and said he would see himself out. Back on the path, he took a quick look in at the house where the Zheng brothers had lived, making a note in his pocket pad of its location in relation to Li Qingshan's home, and headed for the canteen. He felt he had earned some steamed buns.

*

After lunch, Hong Jun found Director Gao out among the farm's livestock, talking with the vet, but it was apparently just a routine visit because he excused himself and led Hong Jun back towards his office to answer some questions about Xiao Xiong.

The Harbin Public Security Bureau had asked the Binbei County PSB to investigate Dumb Deer because he had taken part in the democracy movement back then. But by the time the police were at the farm, Xiao Xiong was spending all his time in Harbin, and had never come back. And after what had happened to Li Hongmei, he had vanished without a trace. Director Gao said he had heard a rumour that Xiao Xiong had gone to America, but stressed it was only rumour.

On the bus back to Binbei, Hong Jun thought it far from being a wasted day, and the steamed buns were delicious.

Hong Jun was looking forward to soaking in a hot bath as he entered the lobby of the Songjiang Hotel, but his day wasn't over yet. Chu Weihua was waiting for him. 'Dr Hong!'

'Weihua? Hello. Something urgent?'

'I saw Deputy Chief Judge Han this afternoon and he'd already heard you were in town and asked where you were. I said you'd gone to the farm and would be returning later. Just as I was leaving my office he came to find me and said that Party Secretary Gu had also heard you were here. He's the Deputy Secretary of the Binbei County Party Committee, and his wife is our own Section Chief, Wang Xiuling. Secretary Gu felt it was a matter for celebration for such a learned man as yourself to visit our humble little county town. And Chief Han agreed with him. They have sent me to take you as their guest to a welcome dinner at the Binbei Restaurant . . . ' Chu Weihua looked at his watch, ' . . . right now.'

'I am just a lawyer. Strictly speaking, they ought to be my guests.'

'Chief Han is really impressed. He started out as a soldier and didn't go to university. He got a diploma from the television university. He has a lot of respect for educated people. And Secretary Gu —'

'All right, all right,' said Hong Jun. 'Let me go and have a quick wash in my room and I'll be right back down.'

As he reached the door of his room, Hong Jun had the feeling he was being followed and, when he looked behind him, glimpsed a shadow in the stairwell, but then it was gone. He shook his head, opened his door and went inside, making straight for the bathroom.

CHAPTER SEVEN

CHU WEIHUA DROVE Hong Jun the short distance to the Binbei Restaurant in a car belonging to the court. This time, Hong Jun would be eating upstairs, in a quiet and elegant private room. There were four people in the room and they all stood when he arrived. Chu Weihua did the introductions.

Han Wenqing, Deputy Chief Judge of the Binbei District Intermediate People's Court greeted him first. He was in his forties, tall and big, with the air of a senior official and a 'general's belly' to match.

Gu Chunshan, Deputy Secretary of the Binbei County Party Committee and Secretary of its Political and Legal Affairs Committee, was next. He was around forty, of medium build, with a rectangular face, a slightly protruding chin and thin lips. He had a pale complexion, lively eyes and the smart, confident air of someone who is used to getting things done.

Beside him was Hao Zhicheng, the Binbei County PSB Chief. He was around fifty, tall and still slim, with pale, sallow cheeks and gleaming black hair, neatly brushed. His eyes were small and there was an enigmatic quality to his gaze, hard to pin down.

Finally, there was Wu Hongfei, head of the Binbei PSB Criminal Investigation Unit, in his late thirties, powerfully built, with a pockmarked, ruddy face. He had big eyes and a pointed mouth which, if he wasn't talking, looked tightly shut.

Hong Jun shook hands and exchanged formal greetings and presented each of them with his name card. After they sat, with Hong Jun in the honoured position, Han Wenqing began. 'We feel deeply honoured that Dr Hong should not only have come such a long way to return to the motherland, but also travelled another not inconsiderable distance to visit our humble little town. I have read Dr Hong's important book on criminal investigation, a work of the highest quality. And today Secretary Gu has invited us to extend to you our warmest welcome, Dr Hong.'

'Hear, hear,' said Gu Chunshan. 'As Confucius once said, "There is no greater pleasure than a friend coming from afar." Dr Hong is a big lawyer from Beijing. We're delighted that he has come to visit our county, and we'll certainly do everything we can to make him feel welcome.'

'Hmm . . . It seems that Secretary Gu has only to meet a doctor from the capital to acquire the sophistication of a doctor in his own speech,' said Han, to the laughter of the others. 'You really know how to say the right thing to each person, most impressive.' Hong Jun got the distinct impression that Han's polite words concealed another meaning.

'Chief Han, how could I possibly hope to compete with your eloquence,' said Gu. 'A man of such high education and knowledge, acquired the hard way through a vocational college, was it, or the television university? A dedication not to be sniffed at, either way.' There was clearly a tension between the two men that intrigued Hong Jun, but the banter wasn't finished yet. Gu Chunshan raised his glass and said, 'Chief Han? Will you make the toast?'

'Oh I couldn't do that, Secretary Gu. You are the host, so it's for you to make the first toast.'

'Forgive me,' said Gu, and turned to Hong Jun. 'Dr Hong, we welcome you to Binbei, and we will be grateful for any guidance you can give us in our lowly work. Today, however, our main duty is to drink together. When it comes to drinking, we northeastern people have a rule. If you feel close to someone, you should drain your cup; if your feelings aren't deep, just take a sip. Everyone, let's empty a glass to Dr Hong.'

Hong Jun looked at the full glass of *baijiu* grain spirit in front of him, and knew the sort of evening that lay ahead. 'My dear sirs,' he said, 'I am deeply grateful for your kindness, but I really can't drink spirits. If you give me a little beer, I could just about manage it. But could I possibly be excused this toast?'

It was too late. Even as he spoke, he saw Gu Chunshan raise his glass to his lips, as did the other four officials, and each drained the liquor in a single gulp. Chu Weihua, at his elbow, whispered to Hong Jun, 'No matter what you say, you must drink at least the first glass.'

Hong Jun, still holding his glass, gave the flushed faces around the table a broad smile. He had never drunk *baijiu* and disliked such games. At university, his stubbornness was widely known, how he refused frequent attempts by other students to engage him in beer drinking contests despite their curses and taunts. But he wasn't among undergraduates now. He was in a world of grown-up games, and they were played for other purposes. If he wanted to win their trust and make any headway in his investigation, he would have to sacrifice himself. Watched by five pairs of unwavering eyes, he poured the contents of the glass into his mouth and swallowed in a single gulp, turning his glass upside down on the table to show it was empty. Fire surged down his throat, blazing the length of his oesophagus, before spreading into his stomach, where the heat only intensified and threatened to retrace its path. He grabbed a teacup and swallowed its tepid contents, but it made no impact on the fire in his belly. Some of it went down his windpipe and he started to cough. The others gave him a big round of applause, and Chu Weihua was behind him, slapping his back. It took a few minutes for him to recover, but he managed to think of a way to save face.

'Wow, you northeasterners really are a tough lot.'

They all laughed and cheered and declared Hong Jun to be a brave man, and a convivial mood was established.

'Now,' said Gu Chunshan, 'for Dr Hong, let's switch to hops. Bring beer . . . '

'Bring both,' called PSB Chief Hao.

Han Wenqing, who was already chewing on a piece of venison, called, 'Bring us food,' and said to Hong Jun, 'The main thing is to eat. I'm sure you know the expression, "You don't get fat from a single mouthful, but you can still get fat one mouthful at a time." I make no apologies. I just love meat, especially this venison. From our own mountains. It is a real local specialty, Dr Hong, eat. Authentic cuisine of the northeast.

'As you Beijingers would say, it's "really hot". I was just at a conference in the capital and a friend took me to a northeastern restaurant just behind the Beijing Hotel. They not only served game, but wild mountain vegetables too. Beijing people love them. Times have certainly changed. I remember when we gathered and ate wild vegetables because we had no money for food and that was all there was. Now you eat them in restaurants and pay a month's salary.'

'Chief Han, what was Beijing like when you were there?' asked Hao

'How do I put this? When you go to Shenzhen and see all those "newly rich" you realise how little money you have, when you go to Hainan Island and meet all those beautiful women you realise how feeble your body is, and when you go to Beijing and see all those big officials you realise how little power you have.'

'And when you come to Binbei and taste our food, you realise how dull your food at home is,' added Chief Hao, to much laughter.

Hong Jun was starting to get caught up in the atmosphere, and said excitedly, 'You certainly do have a lot of wild animals here. Yesterday morning I went to Binbei Park and saw a hunter who had caught a big rabbit in the woods.'

'Nothing special about that,' said Han Wenqing. 'You often see wolves on the edge of town, even leopards.'

Deputy Secretary Gu turned to Hong Jun. 'Do you like hunting, Dr Hong?'

'When I was younger, it fascinated me, but I've never had the chance.'

'Would you like to go hunting?' asked Han Wenqing.

'Yes, I'd love to.'

'That's easy to arrange,' Han said. 'Secretary Gu is an expert hunter, and quite the tracker. The last Sunday of every month is officially designated a hunting day around here, and nothing interferes with the hunt. Isn't that so, Secretary Gu?'

Gu Chunshan smiled but said nothing.

'How about it, Dr Hong?' asked Han. 'Stay a few more days and, though it's not the last Sunday, Secretary Gu will lead an "unofficial" hunt. You'll learn a lot.'

Something was nagging at the back of his mind. 'Only if that's okay with Secretary Gu,' Hong Jun said.

'No problem, no problem at all. If Dr Hong is really interested I'd be delighted to arrange it. However,' Gu Chunshan pulled out a diary and consulted its pages, 'I don't think this weekend is possible.'

'No hurry,' said Hong Jun. 'Whenever it fits in with your schedule. Please, don't make any special arrangements for my sake. I'll probably be around for a while longer working on the case.'

Han Wenqing, his face bright red from alcohol, seemed not to hear him. 'Secretary Gu is one of Binbei's most outstanding officials. He's upright in his work, and he keeps his word. He is a model Party member and, Dr Hong, a model husband. You've met his wife, Wang Xiuling. She is an important member of our court. Sometimes when she's working late, he comes to pick her up on his bike. Tell me the name of another husband, such an important official, who treats his wife so well.'

Gu Chunshan nodded behind an awkward smile, his face red too, but from embarrassment. Hong Jun though he detected a hint of anger in his eyes at Han's eulogising.

Han Wenqing didn't catch the look, or if he did, ignored it and kept going. 'There was another time, when we all went to Harbin for a meeting, and our hosts invited us to go to a sauna. And after the sauna, there were women to give you a massage. It was pretty obvious what kind of massage they were offering. Secretary Gu said he wasn't interested. Now, that really is a model husband.' Hong Jun was watching Gu for a reaction, but he was very good at masking his feelings. Han continued, 'I don't know if you realise it, Old Gu, but all the female staff in our court are always going to see Xiuling for advice, asking her how she trained her husband to be so ideal! And can you guess what Xiuling tells them, Old Gu?'

Gu Chunshan carried on looking at Han Wenqing, a thinning smile on his face.

'Xiuling says a woman gets a model husband because she's earned one. No training required. Ha ha!' No one else laughed and Han finally picked up that the enthusiasm of the table for this particular topic had waned. He drank off the beer in his glass and changed the subject. 'Dr Hong, you are very young to have done so much. You must be no more than thirty?'

'Yes, I am just thirty,' replied Hong Jun.

'Married?'

'Not yet,' he said, adding, 'To be honest I just haven't really had time for such things.'

'Another model,' declared Han. 'A model of late marriage, as the government always advocates.'

PSB Chief Hao, who hadn't been able to get a word in, took up the interrogation of their guest. 'Do you have a girlfriend, Dr Hong?'

'Well . . .' Hong Jun hesitated a moment, wondering how to respond in a manner that would prevent things getting bawdy.

Han wagged a finger, 'Old Hao, you're so out of date. Dr Hong is young, energetic and talented. Lots of women must like him and I bet he has a lot of telephone numbers. But I understand how he feels. These days, young people want love affairs and don't want to get tied down too soon. Isn't that right, Dr Hong? What is it they say now? "Marriage is the graveyard of love"?'

'To be honest, Chief Han, I've been hoping to find someone to take me to this "graveyard", but they all seem to think it would be too much like hard work, so no one wants to do it.' The officials all laughed at that, even Secretary Gu. 'And I must say I'm getting impatient, but there's nothing I can do about it.'

'Well said, Dr Hong.' Han raised his refilled beer glass. 'I like you, Dr Hong. Educated but with no airs and graces. Come on, let's drink a toast.' And he clinked glasses with Hong Jun, gulped down the beer and wiped his mouth with the back of his hand. And belched.

'Weihua told me a little about what you're working on, Dr Hong. You may not know yet, but I was the presiding judge in the Zheng Jianguo case and I think, if memory serves . . . yes . . . Old Gu, you were still with the Public Security Bureau back then. Didn't you work on that case?'

Gu Chunshan looked at Han Wenqing. 'Zheng Jianguo?'

'Oh come on! The case at the Second Branch of the Binbei State Farm, ten years ago, it was rape and murder. The woman was called Li Hongmei, and we sent Zheng Jianguo to prison, suspended death sentence.'

'Oh yes, I remember now,' said Deputy Secretary Gu. 'It was the district PSB who handled the case. I just happened to be at the farm on another matter, so I was first on the scene. I've worked on so many cases over the years.' He looked across the table. 'Old Wu, weren't you involved in that case, too?'

Hong Jun had almost forgotten Wu Hongfei, the head of the Criminal Investigation Unit, was also at the table, so quiet had he been, too busy eating and drinking to bother making conversation. Wu nodded, wiped his mouth with the back of his hand, and managed, 'Yup.'

'There was a lot of evidence in that case, and the accused signed a confession.'

'Let's just keep to the facts,' Wu Hongfei cut in. 'He confessed to his guilt, but he never said how he did it, or why.'

'He didn't deny the charges in court,' said Han. 'And he didn't appeal the verdict.' Han looked at Dr Hong, and remembered why he was here, and he was suddenly sober. 'But now that the defendant has applied for a retrial, I think we should carefully reinvestigate the case. If we made any mistakes, we must admit them and take all necessary steps to correct them.

'Dr Hong,' he continued, 'let me assure you our invitation this evening has nothing to do with this case. You are a man of great learning, and we simply want to show our respect. So far as your work here is concerned, you must do whatever you need to do. And we will give you all the help we can. Young Chu, when you get to work tomorrow morning your first assignment is to find the case documents and give copies to Dr Hong. We welcome his scrutiny of our work and should think ourselves lucky to have such valuable supervision.'

PSB Chief Hao picked up the point. 'You're absolutely right. Any error must be acknowledged and rectified. If all our comrades in the courts were as upright as Deputy Chief Judge Han, correcting miscarriages of justice would be a lot easier.'

'When I was at the conference in Beijing this last time,' said Han Wenqing, who retained his newfound sense of sobriety and sipped his beer at a more leisurely pace, 'I heard a very interesting speech by an expert. The expert said that, at the moment, China's criminal procedures are like a production line. The law requires the police, the prosecutors and the courts to scrutinise each other, and provide checks and balances, but in practice it's the first part of the process that is the most important. The gathering of evidence and interviews by the police that, when examined together, make the case. If something goes wrong at the beginning, the error is more likely than not compounded at other stages in the process.'

Gu Chunshan nodded. 'Chief Han is absolutely right. Anyone can make mistakes. If we didn't make mistakes, the "correct political road" would have been gridlocked years ago. I confess to past mistakes and fine myself a glass of *baijiu* as punishment.' And he raised his glass and drained it in a single gulp.

'Now, when it comes to miscarriages of justice,' Gu continued, 'the police, prosecutors and courts all bear a responsibility. Regardless of whose fault it is in a specific case, it's always the result of errors in our political and legal work, and we must be determined to put these right. Dr Hong, I also want to make a pledge that whatever you need for your work, all of us – the Party, the police, the prosecutor's office and the courts – will give you our full backing.'

Gu Chunshan raised his glass and said they should seal the pledge with a toast, and drank it down. Everyone followed, including Hong Jun. More toasts were proposed, and more rounds drunk. Hong Jun was falling behind as the alcohol got the better of him. Gu Chunshan noticed his predicament, and proposed they should all finish their glasses and bring the dinner to a close. After protracted goodbyes, Chu Weihua drove Hong Jun back to the Songjiang Hotel.

In the car, Hong Jun said to Chu Weihua, 'That Wu from the . . . Criminal Investigation Unit . . . is a funny one . . . All he did was eat beer . . . I mean drink food . . . Anyway, he hardly said a word all evening.'

'Dr Hong, I think you drank quite a lot tonight.'

'I'm not so bad at drinking, am I?'

'You're pretty good. And a smart move, staying away from the *baijiu*.' Chu Weihua was driving very carefully, and very slowly. 'Chief Wu doesn't talk much, but that's just how he is. Everyone calls him "Dopey Wu". He knows what he's doing, and he's especially good in the interrogation room. He's lazy, but he usually gets it right first time so he doesn't have to do it again.'

'Something going on between Chief Han and Secre . . . Secretary Gu?'

'It's a long story,' said Chu, who looked both ways at an intersection so many times Hong Jun's head began to spin. 'Recently there've been all these rumours that Binbei District might be upgraded to a city and they need to promote a bunch of officials. Both men are front-runners for the post of Secretary of the Municipal Political and Legal Commission, so there's a lot of calling in favours and twisting of arms.'

Chu finally made his turn and narrowly missed a lorry. 'I think it will work in your favour. They both want to be seen to be helping you and come out of it looking good. So they'll exploit each other's weaknesses. It might give you some leverage.'

The car pulled up in front of the Songjiang Hotel and Hong Jun, with some difficulty, opened the door and fell into the snow. His legs didn't work. Chu Weihua got out and helped him to his feet, but it took a few moments before he could find his equilibrium, and a few moments more before he could get his eyes to focus. All he wanted to do was go to sleep, but the icy wind was clearing his head.

A huddled figure lurched around the corner and staggered behind the car. Hong Jun looked more closely and saw it was the crazy woman from the restaurant. He watched her disappear into the darkness.

'Dr Hong? Dr Hong? Can you hear me?'

'Yes, sorry, she looks like someone . . . I used to know . . . too much to drink.' He shook his head and turned unaided towards the hotel door, then stopped. 'Weihua? Have you had time to dig up anything on what I asked you about yesterday?'

'What thing?'

'An address for Xiao Xue.'

'Oh. Sorry. No, not yet. I'll check tonight and let you know in the morning.'

Hong Jun was starting to feel the cold, and began to sober up. He thanked Chu Weihua, quickly pushed open the door and walked into the warmth of the hotel lobby.

CHAPTER EIGHT

AT HALF PAST eight the next morning, Hong Jun arrived at Binbei Courthouse. The clerk at the front desk greeted him by name, asked him to wait a moment and picked up the telephone. Chu Weihua was at his side a minute or so later and said he had all the papers on the Zheng Jianguo case in his office. He invited him to read them there. The photocopier was broken and the file couldn't leave the building. Once Dr Hong was done, Chu would have to put it back into the archives.

The file was well organised, Hong Jun saw. He declined Chu Weihua's offer of tea and asked instead if his former student could find him some coffee, black, no sugar. The young judge said he'd be right back. Hong Jun laid out the papers on one of the empty desks. He had the indictment from the public prosecutor's office, notes of the interrogation of the accused, affidavits of witnesses, records from the investigation of the crime scene complete with photos, a report of the post-mortem, the results of blood tests, trial notes, the court's judgment and the official announcement of the criminal verdict. 'No autopsy,' Hong Jun wrote on his pad and drew several swirling circles around the words. There were procedural documents, such as the receipt for the transfer of the defendant, certification that the indictment had been delivered, the defence lawyer's letter of authorisation and notes from the sentencing meeting.

The file wasn't very thick. The investigation didn't seem to have gone very deep. Once Zheng Jianguo was identified as the primary suspect, all other avenues were closed. The facts seemed to have been quite clear, and the prosecution was straightforward. Zheng Jianguo hadn't mounted a defence, which made for a short trial. Hong Jun made notes as he examined each of the documents. He sifted the pages for the parts he wanted to more closely study, starting with the crime scene notes and photos, which were thorough: wide shots and close-ups and detailed shots of the corpse, as well as the knife and the apple. Having been to the scene, the pictures seemed familiar, and the written descriptions were reasonably clear. He laid the photographs out on the other vacant desk. Li Hongmei's body lay on a padded mattress at the top of the *kang* on which he'd sat, her head facing south. She was dressed in a sweater, her trousers pulled down below her knees. A pillow and quilt lay beside her on the *kang*. A little table stood near the end of the *kang*. On it was a half-peeled apple and a fruit knife.

Hong Jun read the post-mortem report and the results of the blood tests. External examination revealed the victim's hymen had been broken at some time in the past, with no signs of fresh tearing or trauma to the genital area, seminal fluid was present in her vagina, there were no obvious injuries to her hands or other parts of her body to indicate a struggle. There was a purpling of the face and the eyes were bloodshot, leading the coroner to conclude the cause of death was suffocation. Time of death was estimated to be between eight in the evening and midnight on April 17, 1984. Blood analysis stated the deceased was blood type O. The semen in the vagina was blood type A, as was blood found on the fruit knife. Hong Jun flipped a page. The accused, Zheng Jianguo, was blood type A.

Nothing in this evidence struck Hong Jun as doubtful, or suspicious.

The interrogation notes comprised three reports on Zheng Jianguo's questioning by the PSB. He had initialled each page and signed a declaration, 'I have read the above materials and they are an accurate record.' A print of his right index finger was also inked on each page.

Hong Jun read each of the interrogations and made notes of the key parts:

Record of the first interrogation:

Question: What is your name?

Answer: Zheng Jianguo.

Q: Why have you been brought to this police station?

A: Because I raped and killed someone.

Q: Where did you rape and kill this person?

A: In the home of Li Hongmei, in the residential area of the Binbei Farm.

Q: How did you rape and kill her?

A: I don't remember clearly.

Q: Did you go to Li Hongmei's home on the evening of April 17?

A: I did.

Q: Did you have sexual relations with her?

A: Yes.

Q: Did she resist?

A: At first she didn't consent.

Q: Did you cover her mouth with a pillow?

A: I don't remember clearly.

. . .

Record of the second interrogation:

Q: How do you feel about your problem?

A: I've said everything there is to say about it.

Q: Did you rape and kill someone?

A: No.

Q: How did you get the wound on your finger?

A: I was chopping vegetables at home the previous day, and I accidentally cut it.

Q: For your information, our policy is leniency to those who confess, severe punishments for those who resist. Do you understand this?

A: I understand.

Q: Did you love Li Hongmei?

A: Yes, I loved her.

Q: Were you very upset when the two of you split up?

A: I was very upset.

Q: Did you ever have sexual relations with Li Hongmei?

A: No.

Q: Think it over again carefully.

A: I wanted to have sexual relations with her, but I never did.

Q: For your information, our policy is that you should stick to the facts, and seek to demonstrate a good attitude. Did you ever have sexual relations with Li Hongmei?

A: I did not.

. . .

Record of the third interrogation:

Q: What is your name?

A: Zheng Jianguo.

Q: Why have you been brought to this police station?

A: Because I raped and killed someone.

Q: Where did you rape and kill this person?

A: In the home of Li Hongmei, in the residential

area of the Binbei Farm.

   Q: How did you rape and kill her?

A: I don't remember clearly.

   Q: Did you go to Li Hongmei's home on the evening of April 17?

A: I did.

   Q: Did you have sexual relations with her?

A: Yes.

   Q: Did she resist?

A: At first she didn't consent.

   Q: Did you cover her mouth with a pillow?

A: I don't remember clearly.

Hong Jun was at first confused, and then excited at such an obvious error. The suspect admitted to rape and murder in the first interrogation. In the second interrogation, the suspect had not yet confessed and the third interrogation was exactly the same as the first, word for word. He checked the timing of the interrogations, as recorded on the three sets of notes. The second interrogation was conducted the day before the first and the third, which were identical in all respects, including time. There were three interrogations. That much was officially noted and certified. And there should be the notes of each. The first interrogation had been removed and, needing a properly certified substitute to take its place, whoever had done so simply replaced it with a copy of the third. But the time stamp was the same.

Hong Jun flipped some more pages and found that the interrogators in all three sessions were PSB Section Chief Gu Chunshan, Wu Hongfei and two other detectives.

Hong Jun turned to the pages on the court hearing. According to these records, the presiding judge had begun routinely, confirming the name and identity of the accused, introducing the members of the judging panel and explaining the rights of the accused as laid down by the law, including the right to silence, before commencing the hearing. He first asked the public prosecutor to read the indictment and then asked the accused if he wished to make a statement regarding the charges contained in the indictment. The record showed Zheng Jianguo said he had nothing to say.

Then the judge began his questioning.

> Q: Do you admit to the criminal acts of which you are accused in this indictment?
> A: I am guilty.
> Q: How did you rape and murder Li Hongmei?
> A: I don't recall clearly.
> Q: Is the confession you made to the public security officials a true statement of the facts?
> A: Some of it is, not all.
> Q: Which parts of it are true?
> A: I can't really say for sure.
> Q: Are these the crimes which you confessed to the public security officials.
> A: Yes.
> Q: Did the investigators beat you?
> A: No.

After reading out the notes from the interrogations and of the questioning of witnesses, along with the report on findings from the scene of the crime and the conclusions of experts, and after presenting items of evidence, the judge allowed the public prosecutor and the defence lawyer to question the defendant. It was a brief process, because Zheng Jianguo's answers were simple. Then the judge announced that the court had concluded its investigations, and called for statements from the prosecutor and the defence. The public prosecutor repeated the key elements of the charges. The defence entered a guilty plea, and asked the court to take into account the defendant's previous exemplary behaviour and his relatively positive attitude towards confessing his crimes, pleading for leniency in the sentencing. The judge asked the defendant if he had any last comments. Zheng Jianguo said, 'I have faith in the government.'

The date of the trial hearing was recorded in the court documents as September 18, 1984. The presiding judge was Han Wenqing.

Three days later, the court found Zheng Jianguo guilty of rape and murder, and sentenced him to death, suspended for two years. He was ordered to participate in re-education through labour, where his behaviour would be assessed. He would also be deprived of his political rights for life. In the court notes from the sentencing hearing, Zheng Jianguo initially wrote the words 'don't accept; wish to appeal' in a box marked Defendant's Opinion of the Sentence. But the word 'accept' was later crossed out, so the notation read, 'Don't wish to appeal.' There were no initials beside either the comment or the change.

Hong Jun put down the papers and closed his eyes. He saw problems with the original investigation of this case, but those were not sufficient to get the verdict overturned. Identification of the defendant as the perpetrator based on the evidence of matching blood types alone was not forensically acceptable, but he could only use that to demonstrate that the verdict *might* have been wrong. It didn't prove wrongful conviction. He thought about asking the court to order a DNA test of the traces of blood on the fruit knife, and on the semen, which would almost certainly have to be done in Beijing, but Hong Jun didn't know what state the material evidence was in after ten years, or whether a usable sample could be successfully taken. It was a thin thread on which to hang a case, particularly a sensitive one involving a miscarriage of justice that might point who knows where.

The interrogation notes were incomplete, and a blunder, but was there deliberate tampering with the evidence? He didn't have enough. He looked again at the photographs of the crime scene, and scrutinised the close-ups of the half-peeled apple and the blood-speckled fruit knife. A smile began to play at the corners of his mouth. Hong Jun ran from the room, startling several court officers as he skidded around corners in the highly polished linoleum hallway.

'Are you hungry, Dr Hong?' asked Chu Weihua when he returned to his office and saw Hong Jun peeling a bag of apples. Several already stood lined up, half white with their skin dangling. 'The canteen opens in half an hour. We can go have lunch then.'

'No rush. I'm fine. More than fine. These apples are really sweet and tasty. Want one?' Hong Jun handed him an apple and the fruit knife.

'Great, thanks. Fuji apples? From Japan? Did you buy them from the stall on the corner? He always has the best produce.' Chu Weihua began to work the knife. 'When I was a kid I remember the only things we could get in winter were frozen pears, but sometimes you could buy a few "National Glory" apples, which were a real treat. Now, if you've got money you can buy anything.'

Hong Jun watched as Chu Weihua peeled his apple. When the task was finished, and his former student took a large slice of the flesh and put it in his smiling mouth, Hong Jun said, 'Weihua, I've finished reading the file on the case, and I have a few ideas I'd love to discuss with Deputy Chief Judge Han. Is he around?'

'I'll go and have a look,' Chu said, munching on his apple. 'If he's here, we can go up to his office.'

'See if you can get him to come here.'

Chu Weihua found Han Wenqing in the corridor on the third floor. 'Chief Han, Dr Hong asks if you have time to see him now.'

'Goodness, he doesn't waste any time!' Han replied. 'Where is he?'

'In the Criminal Case Office on the second floor,' said Chu. 'He asks if you would come down, please.'

'Lead the way.'

There was a lift in the building, but it seldom worked, so they took the freezing concrete fire stairs.

'So, Dr Hong,' said Han Wenqing as he entered the office, 'have you already uncovered what we got wrong? What should we write in our self-criticisms?'

'Not wrong,' Hong said lightly, playing to Han's good humour, 'just some things that raise a few questions in my mind, which I'd very much like to discuss with you, Chief Han.'

Han Wenqing took a chair, glancing at the files laid out on one desk, the photos on the other and the row of half-peeled apples, the aroma of which was filling the room and making him salivate.

'I've been through the documents in this file,' Hong Jun began, 'and it seems there were four main pieces of evidence used to identify Zheng Jianguo as the rapist and murderer. There was the semen in the deceased's vagina, the traces of blood on the fruit knife, the testimony of her father, Li Qingshan, and the defendant's own confession.' Han Wenqing gave no indication he was in dispute. Hong Jun continued.

'The results of the blood tests show that the semen and traces of blood on the fruit knife were both type A, the same blood type as Zheng Jianguo. However, we know that being of a certain blood type can only provide a partial verification and is not a definitive identification. Many people share the same blood type. Zheng Jianzhong, his brother, might logically be type A too, as might Xiao Xiong, or any number of people on the farm. Is my logic correct, Chief Han?'

'Of course,' said Han slowly. 'Blood type is, at best, circumstantial. But it can be used to support other evidence. In this case, Zheng Jianguo had motive. He admitted being after Li Hongmei for a long time, but she wasn't interested in him, so he raped her and then killed her.'

'If you will indulge me, I have some doubts about the way this case was resolved. An old man at the farm told me that Li Hongmei was a strong woman. Zheng Jianguo was small and scrawny, and one arm was virtually useless. Would he really have been capable of raping and killing her? The investigators concluded that he suffocated her with a pillow *while* he raped her, though I would have thought it pretty hard for a one-armed man to rape *and* suffocate a woman at the same time.'

'Hmm . . . When men get that urge, they can do anything.'

'But if she was raped and suffocated, surely there ought to have been some injuries on her body from when she tried to resist? She was a strong woman. Yet the post-mortem found no injuries, anywhere. How could anyone be raped and asphyxiated without fighting back?'

'Dr Hong, investigating a case is different from theoretical supposition. Only those who were there know precisely what happened, as you know. It is the investigator's job to reconstruct as clear a picture as can be got from evidence at hand, establish the basic facts and from there identify the perpetrator. In this case, the key was not *just* that Zheng Jianguo had the same blood type, but also that he had a knife wound on his finger. You're not going to tell me you believe in coincidence? I can assure you, Dr Hong, that when we examined the evidence, we were very thorough in corroborating it all.'

'Excuse me, Deputy Chief Judge, let us look at the knife wound on Zheng Jianguo's finger, shall we?' Hong Jun was worried the discussion was becoming adversarial, and such a turn would not be useful to him.

'Weihua, would you please peel an apple for me. Fuji apples, from Japan, they're really sweet. Won't you try one, Chief Han?'

'I don't want an apple,' said Han Wenqing, his uncertainty about Hong Jun's direction having robbed him of his earlier anticipation.

'Please explain the cut on Zheng Jianguo's hand.'

Hong Jun proceeded, slowly, deliberately. 'Please note the location of the cut, as shown in this photograph, the index finger of his right hand. What does that tell us? It says Zheng Jianguo was left-handed. Whether he was peeling an apple or chopping vegetables, if the cut was on his right index finger then he must have held the knife with his left hand. Correct?'

'Zheng Jianguo was born right-handed, but he injured his right arm, a farming accident I think it was, and learned to do things with his left. So, yes, he would most probably hold a knife with his left hand. We know all this. Please, get on with it.'

Hong Jun stood beside Chu Weihua, who was still peeling the apple. 'Chu also peels apples with his left hand. Thank you, Weihua, you can stop now.'

The apple was about half done, and a long strip of peel hung loose. Hong Jun placed the apple with its attached peel on the desk beside Han Wenqing. He picked up a crime scene photo of the apple and placed it next to Chu's apple.

'If you look at this apple, you'll see that it's very similar to the one in the photograph. They're both half peeled and both have a long piece of skin still attached. But I'm sure you've spotted the difference between the two. In the photo, the peel hangs to the right, but the peel of Weihua's apple hangs to the left. When Weihua peeled the apple, his knife moved from left to right, but whoever peeled the apple at the scene of the crime was cutting from right to left, holding the knife in the right hand. In other words, the person was right-handed.

'And you will have observed that as Weihua peeled the apple, the index finger of his right hand, which was holding the apple, trailed the blade as it turned and could not have been cut by accident. All of which makes it more likely that the cut on Zheng Jianguo's hand was made when he was chopping vegetables, as he claimed.

'My final point, judging from this photograph, whoever peeled this apple did so quite skilfully. Now, Weihua peeled this one quite well too – the skin is still attached, and it is of an even thickness. Have you had a lot of practice, Weihua?'

'Well, my wife loves apples, and she often asks me to peel one for her.'

'Whoever peeled the apple in the photograph was equally proficient. Now, I've been told that when the people on the Binbei Farm eat apples they usually don't bother peeling them first. So, from that we can conclude this person probably wasn't brought up on a farm, which Zheng Jianguo most certainly was. I think you have to agree, Chief Han, the logical conclusion is Zheng Jianguo did not peel the apple.'

Han Wenqing made no reply. He carefully examined the apple in the photograph and the apple on the table. He picked up the fruit knife and the apple and moved them back and forth in his hands.

'Dr Hong, I acknowledge that your observations are highly detailed,' he said, 'and your reasoning is very convincing. We missed this in our own investigations. But the question of the peeling of the apple is of only secondary importance in this case. Based on the evidence at the crime scene, the Public Security Bureau investigators inferred that the person who peeled the apple was the killer, but that doesn't rule out the possibility that someone else had been in Li Hongmei's room before the killer arrived, and had peeled half an apple. On its own, I don't think that you have sufficient reason to overturn the verdict in this case.'

Han watched Hong Jun closely, but he said nothing and his face gave nothing away.

'Tell me, Dr Hong, if Zheng Jianguo wasn't the killer, why did he confess? In court, I specifically asked him whether the investigators had beaten him, and he clearly said they had not. His conduct in court was that of someone who has committed a crime in a moment of madness, regrets what he did and presents himself for punishment. His death sentence was suspended because he admitted his guilt in court and had no prior criminal record. We could have sentenced him to immediate execution – don't forget this was the middle of a "strike hard against crime" campaign.'

'Chief Han, I absolutely agree with you that my deduction about the apple is not enough to overturn the original verdict on its own, but it does tell us that, according to the evidence we possess now, the identification of Zheng Jianguo as the guilty party was not completely satisfactory. If I may . . . Li Qingshan's testimony doesn't really have much value as evidence, either, since all he said was that the silhouette of the figure he saw *looked* like Zheng Jianguo. As for Zheng's confession, I was quite baffled at first. After all, if a suspect pleads guilty, voluntarily, and there is no coercion or torture to extract the confession, then that ought to be pretty reliable. However, after looking at the documents, it seems clear to me that there were problems with the interrogation.'

'What problems?' Han Wenqing sat forward. He wasn't enjoying this meeting and he didn't like surprises.

'Court documents are held in a secure archive and can't be tampered with after a trial. Is that correct?

'Yes.'

Hong Jun flipped through the file until he came to the interrogation records, and pointed out the times and dates of the three sessions. 'Please look at the first and third records of interrogation.'

Han Wenqing frowned. 'Hmm . . . well . . . during the "strike hard" campaign, the emphasis was on cracking down on crime as hard and quickly as possible, and the documents relating to the cases weren't always prepared as carefully as they should have been. But, I concede, Dr Hong, this really is a mess.'

'Before I came to Binbei, I went to Harbin Prison to see Zheng Jianguo, and he said that while the investigators didn't beat him during the interrogations, he wasn't allowed to sleep. He said there were two shifts and they took it in turns to question him for more than fifty hours, without rest. This kind of questioning, of sleep deprivation, is covert torture, psychological rather than physical, and any confession obtained in such circumstances is most unreliable. None of us can survive without sleep. He may well have been hallucinating when he signed the confession.'

'Covert torture?' said Han Wenqing. 'That's a new one on me. Can you prove it?'

'I think what Zheng Jianguo told me is enough to prove his confession was not freely given, though I would probably have to argue it before a judge, and the falsification of the records by the interrogators provides additional circumstantial evidence. There are also problems with the way they questioned the suspect. The investigators described all the details of the crime in their questions and Zheng Jianguo had only to agree with what they said. With a line of questioning like this, there must be suspicion that the suspect was induced to confess.'

Han Wenqing leafed through the interrogation records. Hong Jun saw the flicker of a pause at the page identifying the interrogators, which he had marked with a turned down corner. 'Hmm . . . so the interrogators obtained a false confession through the use of covert torture and inducements, and falsified the case notes, resulting in a miscarriage of justice. This line of your investigation is most interesting, Dr Hong.'

'I have one more thought about Zheng Jianguo's confession,' said Hong Jun. 'There was a time when I was very interested in criminal psychology, and I studied the psychological patterns of victims of crime. We know that there can be both direct and indirect victims of crime. In this case, I think Zheng Jianguo might actually be an indirect victim. From meeting him, and what I've heard from others, I believe he loved Li Hongmei very deeply, almost to the point of worship.

'What's more, an introverted character with a sense of low esteem like his is highly susceptible to self-loathing and self-condemnation. In certain circumstances this can turn into a desire for punishment. This phenomenon is sometimes known as compulsive guilt syndrome. If something unfortunate happens to affect such a person, even if it's not their fault, it may give rise to an uncontrollable sense of guilt and they will be overwhelmed by a psychological need to blame themselves and seek punishment. I think Zheng Jianguo has compulsive guilt syndrome and because of this he felt he deserved to be sent to prison because Li Hongmei died, not because he killed her.'

Han said nothing.

'Zheng Jianguo's love for Li Hongmei also seems to be quite special. Some people say love is selfish, that it excludes others, and that's quite normal. But if love develops to the point of worship, then it may go beyond the bounds of selfishness and exclusivity, particularly if the admirer believes they have no chance of having that person for themselves. In *this* case, Zheng Jianguo accepted that Li Hongmei didn't love him, but so long as she remained near to him, and was happy and enjoying good fortune, he could derive a measure of contentment.

'But for his "idol" to be violated and killed in such a brutal fashion was an attack on the core of his being, and left him with extreme pain buried deep in his heart. His nature was such that he couldn't scream or shout or kick up a fuss, or go and commit murder and arson, and so his pain turned inward, and led him to blame himself, even to punish himself. Being sent to prison would enable him to take on some of Li Hongmei's burden of suffering. It's a rather complicated logic, but I'd argue that this was the state of mind Zheng was in when he went on trial. He had failed to protect the object of his worship. So, in his mind, he was as guilty as the person who committed this crime. Am I making myself clear, Chief Han?'

Han Wenqing was thinking over questions of his own and was a little taken aback at the question. But he replied quickly, covering his inattention.

'Dr Hong, your analysis makes a lot of sense. Why don't you write an application for a retrial, and we'll give it to the judicial committee to consider whether there are sufficient grounds to reopen the case in accordance with the regulations on scrutinising verdicts. Personally, I think it should be reinvestigated. Of course, I have to keep my distance from such matters, but I'll help you if I can. I've tried more than a thousand cases, and of course we sometimes make mistakes, and if a judge discovers that he may have made an error, he shouldn't attempt to cover it up, but should do all he can to correct it. That's the true spirit and ethics of our profession.'

Hong Jun thought he detected a hint of Han's own machinations at play in his eagerness to support the reopening of the investigation, and it was worth exploiting.

'There's something else I would like to try. Forensic science now has at its disposal a powerful tool, DNA identification, with which we can match a person to a drop of blood found at a crime scene, or even just a strand of hair.'

'I've heard of it, but we can't do it here, or in Harbin. We simply don't have the facilities or the training.'

'I understand. But it can be done in Beijing. Would it be possible to have the material evidence, in particular the fruit knife, sent there for testing?'

'The fruit knife?' said Han. 'Material evidence is returned after trial to the PSB for safekeeping. It should be easy to find.' Han turned to Chu Weihua and said, 'Contact the PSB and have that knife sent to my office. You can pick it up there.'

'Yes, sir.'

Han Wenqing got to his feet. 'Dr Hong, will you join me for lunch in the canteen?'

'Thank you, Deputy Chief Judge Han, but I'm afraid I won't be able to join you. I'm going back to the hotel to draft a letter of appeal.' He put the file back in order and handed it to Chu Weihua, then followed Han Wenqing out of the office.

They parted at the fire stairs. Hong Jun headed for the ground floor, skipping two steps at a time, humming an old blues number, *Sweet Home Chicago*.

CHAPTER NINE

SONG JIA ANSWERED the telephone with a clear, measured, professional voice, 'Hong Jun Law Office, how may I help you?' As soon as she heard Hong Jun's voice at the other end, she shed her ladylike manner and vented her fury at his failure to check in with *his* office on at least a daily basis to keep *her* informed about his movements. Hong Jun was struck dumb. After a long audible breath that hissed down the phone line, she said, 'Hi, boss, how's it going? What do you need?'

Hong Jun was stunned, but understood perfectly Song Jia's annoyance, and decided the best approach was to deal with it later. He gave Song Jia a quick outline of what he'd been up to, and asked her to do three things for him. He needed a reputable, accredited lab in Beijing that could run a DNA test on a ten-year-old blood sample as quickly as possible. He also needed fast, discreet enquiries about Zheng Jianzhong and what he'd been up to in Beijing. And could she call Zheng Jianzhong and ask him to come to the office tomorrow. He would be back from Harbin early.

'Got it, boss. On it now. Just, how do the Americans say? Keep me in the loop. Okay?'

Hong Jun felt like a child, chastised by his mother for some wrongdoing, and smiled at Song Jia's boldness.

'Yes, Miss Song. Message received and understood. See you in the morning.'

'Bye, boss.'

He was still smiling as he hung up the phone. Of course, Song Jia was right. He was running a business, not some one-man crusade. He settled down to concentrate on drafting his letter of appeal in the case of Zheng Jianguo, but it was slow going and involved lots of crossings out and revisions as he tried to set out the reasons and cite from memory the pertinent laws as simply and clearly as possible. It took a while, but he got there. Someone at the business centre would type it up for him.

Hong Jun was pleased with how smoothly his investigations had gone so far and ventured the hope that his first case would come to a perfect conclusion. DNA evidence clearing Zheng Jianguo would be perfect, and might be good publicity, but even if there was no DNA to work with, or even if it identified his client, everything could still be wrapped up in a satisfactory way. He was sure Jianguo was not guilty, but someone wanted him convicted and he needed to anticipate the as yet unidentified forces working against him. He would have to work hard to get the verdict overturned.

Calling down to the business centre, he explained what he wanted, and a girl arrived at his hotel room door, all brisk efficiency, and took away his handwritten pages, promising to return in an hour or so.

At this stage, Hong Jun thought, there was nothing more he could do. He liked the idea of a hot bath as a reward for his hard work, but as he put his hand on the hot water tap, potential issues of the case drew him back to his yellow pad. If the DNA test was inconclusive, or confirmed a match with Zheng Jianguo, what would his next move be? In the American court system, where it was normal to challenge verdicts, and where procedural justice and the protection of individual rights were so revered, a judge might accept 'murder while sleepwalking' as a defence and hear his argument. But a Chinese judge was unlikely to embrace such a novel idea, particularly in a retrial. Hong Jun knew that, under the prevailing Chinese legal system, it was far easier for the courts to allow a wrongful verdict to stand than to get it overturned. Righting past wrongs was a propaganda slogan, pretence being cheaper than practice.

The sleepwalking defence was, at best, a final option and he would have to exhaust a long list of what ifs before he'd need to try it. He had faith in his own instincts and in his analysis of the case documents, particularly his deduction regarding the fruit knife. He was now absolutely sure Zheng Jianguo wasn't the killer. If not him, then who did it? As a lawyer, Hong Jun didn't have to answer that question, just prove his client was innocent, or show that the evidence on which the original conviction was based was unreliable or incomplete. Still, he also knew that the best way to get an innocent person's conviction overturned was to expose the real perpetrator of the crime. And he began to accept that tracking down the rapist and murderer of the Beauty Queen was going to be his job. Hong Jun would not only have to prove that Zheng Jianguo did not rape and murder Li Hongmei, he would also have to prove to the court the identity of the real killer. A crime had been committed, and someone had to be punished. It was all about balance and harmony.

When he was little, Hong Jun loved puzzles and mathematics problems, the harder the better. He even won quite a bit of money at school betting he could solve any puzzle put in front of him. One boy had a Rubik's Cube brought home for him by his father, a high Party official in the Foreign Ministry. He asked for a few minutes to look at it – none of them had seen one before – and turned it over and over in his hands before they started the clock. Five minutes. Everyone was impressed by his cleverness, even the boys whose money he took.

Hong Jun smoothed his hand over the blank page of his yellow legal pad and wrote Xiao Xiong's name at the top. He couldn't account for Dumb Deer's movements and he had been missing for a long time.

He was allegedly connected with the democracy movement back then, but it was pretty unlikely that he'd have gone so far as to kill his own lover, even if she was a witness to, or an unwitting collaborator in, his activities.

Hong Jun recalled conflicting theories concerning the cause of Li Hongmei's death, that she had been deliberately suffocated, that she had died accidentally while having sex because of a heart condition, which couldn't be ruled out given the area's connection with the outbreak of Keshan disease. Why wasn't an autopsy performed? And what other deaths looked like asphyxiation?

He drew circles around the name Xiao Xiong. He had means, motive and opportunity. But how could he prove it? He would need to put Dumb Deer at the scene, and if the blood and semen were his, he'd need a sample. If Dumb Deer had gone to America, he may be able to find him through contacts, but that relied on *if* he'd left the country.

What about Big Axe, Zheng Jianzhong, his own client? He was an obvious suspect, and Hong Jun would need to rule him out. Hong Jun knew enough to know that Zheng Jianzhong had not only the motive and the ability to have committed the crime, but also the time and the opportunity. But if he were the killer, why would he try to get his brother's sentence overturned, and risk exposing himself?

He lay back on the bed, closed his eyes, ran his fingers several times through his hair and let his thoughts wander. A shadowy figure, or was it two, took shape in his mind, and he was trying to make out their faces when his eyelids snapped open at the sound of the room's loud doorbell. Groggy from his unplanned nap, he was sure he'd hung the DO NOT DISTURB sign on the doorknob. Maybe it was the business centre, bringing him the typed pages. He rolled off the bed, stretched and rubbed his face vigorously. An envelope with a clip fastener was on the floor, slipped under the door. He picked it up and pulled open the door.

'Oh, Weihua . . . Come in, I must have dozed off.'

The envelope did contain the typed pages he was waiting for, and he scanned them for errors while Weihua launched into his report.

After lunch he had gone to the County PSB headquarters, but Pathologist Yu Jinghui, the only one who could sign over the evidence, was away, and would be 'back soon', which might mean an hour or a week, so, no knife. Chu Weihua had reported this to Chief Han, who suggested that, under the circumstances, Hong Jun should return to Beijing and the court would send someone with the knife. He would have to sign for it personally. Chu Weihua had agreed on Hong Jun's behalf, because he thought it best that the court remain responsible for requesting the DNA test. Hong Jun congratulated him on his initiative, and, after signing the letter of application, sealed it in a hotel envelope addressed to Deputy Chief Judge Han Wenqing and asked Weihua to deliver it. 'I must leave for Beijing tonight.'

'I understand,' said Weihua, and handed Hong Jun a page torn from a small notebook. 'Here are the details of the person you asked me to look up.'

'Thanks,' said Hong Jun, and unfolded and read it. *Xiao Xue, Deputy Division Chief, Municipal PSB, Harbin.* Underneath, Chu had written her correspondence address and two telephone numbers, one her direct line, the other her home.

He had a quick dinner in the hotel restaurant, packed his bags, checked out and headed for the station.

∗

It was a misty night, with an icy winter wind, and there weren't many people on the main street. Maybe the town could make it as a summer city, Hong Jun thought, because its winters left a lot to be desired, ice sculpting notwithstanding. He'd only walked a little way before he had that familiar feeling of being followed; the crunching boots behind him were too measured for a random walker and tried to match his own. When he sped up, so did the footfalls, when he slowed, they did too.

He stopped, bent down to adjust the lace of his boot and, between his legs, saw a man in a medical facemask, not out of place given it was winter and flu season, apparently engrossed by his map and the street around him. Hong Jun turned into a nearby department store, and ducked behind a counter. The man with the mask also walked in and stood in the doorway for a moment, looking around, before heading deeper into the store. Hong Jun thought there was something familiar about his pursuer, but he could reflect on it later. He quickly left the store and made for the station. He waited until the last moment to board the train, much to the annoyance of the guard, and was sure the man had not followed him.

CHAPTER TEN

HONG JUN WATCHED the cabin passengers on the crowded flight to Beijing jostle and push each other, forcing their way into the pack trying to get off the plane. He trailed after the crowd towards arrivals. Song Jia was waiting for him, grabbed the handle of his bag and shouldered his carry-on. 'Just remember, you're the boss, and I carry your bags. Okay?' she said.

'I really *should* fire you, y'know?' He smiled at Song Jia.

'Hey boss, don't scare me,' she said, feigning melodrama. 'I'm really a coward and I totally hate it when people scare me.'

Hong Jun burst out laughing, and Song Jia smiled. 'Welcome back,' she said, and changed the bag handle to her other hand.

The company VW Santana, bought when Hong Jun got back to China using a generous government subsidy for returning overseas students, was parked very close to the terminal. How did she do it? He always ended up so far from the terminal he had to take a shuttle bus to get there. Song Jia put his case in the boot, dangled the car keys from a slender finger, and said, 'Boss, I'll drive, you rest.'

'No, thank you,' he said. 'My company. My car. My responsibility. Keys, please.'

'I have passed the police driving test, which I believe you commended, and can handle this baby against all comers.'

'I have no doubt, but watching you drive stresses me more than driving myself.'

'Yes, boss.'

He lifted the keys from Song Jia's outstretched manicured finger, opened the door and got into the driver's seat. She walked around to the passenger side and got in. Seat belts buckled, he drove to the exit, paid the parking fee and headed onto the access road to the airport expressway.

'So, Miss Song,' Hong Jun said once they were on the highway, 'what have you found out for me? I'm all ears.'

'Okay. First, the DNA tests. There are several places that meet your criteria: the Second Research Institute of the Ministry of Public Security, the Municipal Police Forensic Science Laboratory and the Technical Evidence Identification Centre at People's University – all three come highly recommended, and have provided evidence for the highest courts. Second. Zheng Jianzhong has a contract to build a shopping centre in Beijing, the company is in the thick of the current construction boom and he's doing pretty well. His company is privately owned. He lives in a flat by the Asian Games Village with his wife and son, who is fifteen and goes to a nearby fee-paying school, which is not cheap. She is a housewife buying her way onto the social ladder, while the son came top of his class and will probably have the choice of any university he wants in any country he wants. Our client has done well for himself, but there's a shady side, nothing too deep that'll get him into any real trouble, though, to be fair, name me one person in construction who doesn't know what it takes to get things done.'

'Very good, Miss Song, but may I ask how you know all this?'

'I have friends.'

'Do you think your "friends" can get a sample of Zheng Jianzhong's blood without him knowing about it?'

'You suspect our client?'

'I'm not sure, but I do want to know his blood type.'

'Hmm, tricky. Let me think about it while I finish my report, boss. Your third request. I've been in touch with Zheng Jianzhong and he apologises but he asked if you would meet him tomorrow evening at the East Beijing Leisure Garden. He says he'll send a car to pick you up at five o'clock.'

'The Leisure Garden . . . ?'

'His idea, boss. He said it's ideal for talking business. You can have a sauna, a massage, sing a little karaoke, enjoy yourself. His version of "classy", I suppose. And there are girls to, well, keep you company.' Song Jia gave him a sidelong glance. 'I said I would confirm with you and call him in the morning. It's a highly regarded establishment, which means he wants to throw some cash around to impress you. Yes? No? Up to you, boss. Work is work.'

The car had reached the expressway toll booth. He slowed, rolled down the car window, handed over a ten-yuan note, and smoothly shifted through the gears to get back to the one hundred and ten kilometre an hour traffic flow. He arched his back and settled into his seat, holding the wheel with two fingers of his left hand.

'Did you do a lot of driving in America?' Song Jia asked him. 'The roads there must be fantastic.'

'In America, cars are like legs. Everyone has them. Everyone needs them. People drive everywhere. Even the dishwashers in Chinese restaurants have cars. America's road network is amazing. I drove across most of the country, from the Pacific Ocean to Niagara Falls and the Atlantic. Try driving across China. Ha!' They both laughed.

'Seriously, *the* best thing about American highways is the bends, so beautifully cambered. The degree of slope and curve are perfect for speed. In Beijing, you ride the brakes on a bend, even if there are no other cars nearby, otherwise you skid out.'

The car had reached the Sanyuan Bridge, where Hong Jun turned off the airport expressway and headed onto the north section of the Third Ring Road. Traffic was heavier and slower. They had caught the beginning of the afternoon rush hour and cars were already slowing to a crawl. They were lucky. In fifteen minutes, traffic would be at a standstill.

'Of course,' Hong Jun continued, unfazed by the road conditions around him, 'driving on those roads can be tiring too. Once, I drove from San Francisco to LA, and part of the way was on Highway One, which is cut into the cliffs along the Pacific coast and is said to be the most scenic highway in the country. On one side there are lovely wooded hills, on the other side, the Pacific Ocean. It really is beautiful. What I got to see of it. Cliff face on your left, long drop into the ocean on your right, and it's steep and winding. It gets so dangerous the speed limit is only twenty kilometres an hour in parts. On that road, my palms were sweating. *Fantastic.*'

They passed the Big Bell Temple, and Hong Jun steered the car into the right-hand lane and took the exit down from the Third Ring Road for the final run to the office.

'I would like to hear more about America sometime,' said Song Jia. Her boss had turned out to be a more interesting person than he let on, not all shop-talk and keep your private self to yourself. 'Sounds like you had a really fascinating time there.'

'It wasn't all wonderful. But America has its moments.' He steered the car into the Friendship Hotel parking lot and slid it into the space marked HONG JUN LAW OFFICE.

He hadn't been away that long, but there were stacks of letters waiting on his desk, sorted by Song Jia according to priority. One pile, already opened, was routine legal correspondence. A smaller, unopened pile was for his immediate attention. He emptied his satchel on the desk and sorted out the pads and papers and pens.

Song Jia knocked on the open office door. 'Boss?' she asked.

Hong Jun looked up and smiled.

'Coffee or anything?'

'Nothing for now, thanks,' he said, but as Song Jia turned to leave, Hong Jun called her back.

'Miss Song, when you were checking about DNA testing, did you ask them about testing old blood samples?'

'Yes, I did, and they all said that so long as the sample wasn't too degraded, as in ruined, or contaminated, it should be possible to get a DNA identification on samples of any age.'

'Would you choose the forensics lab you think we can deal with, while I phone Binbei and tell them to send someone over with the knife as soon as they can, so we can get the test done.'

He checked his watch and called Han Wenqing's office.

'Chief Han,' he said, 'I'm back in Beijing and we've checked with the experts here about the DNA testing, and they can do it, even for ten-year-old blood samples. When do you think you can send someone with the knife?'

'Dr Hong, I'm afraid we're not going to be able to do the test after all.'

'Why not?'

'It's not ideal to go into the details on the phone. I'll . . . I'll tell you all about it when you get back to Binbei.'

Hong Jun replaced the receiver, and a feeling of frustration washed over him.

CHAPTER ELEVEN

THROUGH THE GATEWAY of the East Beijing Leisure Garden, Hong Jun tailed Zheng Jianzhong's grey VW Jetta. A blue-uniformed guard directed him to a parking space. By the time he got out of the car, Zheng Jianzhong and his two companions were already standing behind his car, waiting for him. Hong Jun had been introduced to them earlier. He knew the man with the yellow teeth was Zheng's deputy managing director. The younger guy, his hair prematurely grey, was his driver and probably bodyguard, too.

Zheng Jianzhong came over. And they shook hands. 'Have you been here before, Dr Hong?'

'No, it's the first time I've ever been, but I hear it has a very good reputation.'

'Don't they have saunas in America?' asked Yellow Teeth.

'There are clubs, but nothing like this, and on such a grand scale.'

'All the rage in Beijing now, Dr Hong,' said Zheng Jianzhong. Hong Jun followed him through the entrance, where a young woman stood ready to greet them. 'Boss Zheng, how many guests are with you tonight?'

'Three guests,' he said. 'But today, our honoured guest is my friend here, the famous lawyer Dr Hong.'

Hong Jun figured that Zheng thought it was important to show off how well-connected he was, and he had already decided that he would go along with whatever Zheng wanted. It was a chance to get a good, up-close look at his client's motivations.

Zheng Jianzhong clasped his 'honoured guest' about the shoulder and said, 'Dr Hong, I've invited you here today to have a bit of fun. You've had a tough trip to the northeast and you need to relax. In a minute we'll go and have a sauna, and then we can go upstairs for a massage. They've also got billiards, mah-jong, game machines, karaoke, a disco . . . whatever takes your fancy. Please, you are my guest tonight.'

'Thank you, Zheng Jianzhong. No problem. It's always a pleasure to spend someone else's money.'

Hong Jun was given a locker key at the reception desk, changed his shoes for a pair of slippers, and followed Zheng Jianzhong and the others into the bath house. He found his locker, inside of which lay crisp and neatly folded pyjama trousers and a bath towel. He undressed and went into the bath house, which consisted of three round plunge pools, two cold and one hot with massage jets, and two little timber-clad rooms, which he took to be the saunas, and another with an aluminium door, the steam room. Hong Jun first washed himself with soap under a nearby shower, and they went into one of the saunas. It was about three by four metres square. He lay on a pine bench, wiped his face with a wet towel, and let the hot, dry air bake his body. It was a very pleasant experience, completely unlike lying in a hot bathtub at home, alone with his thoughts. This was more stimulating than relaxing.

After a quick shower, and dressed in his light blue pyjama trousers, he found Zheng Jianzhong waiting for him. 'How was it, Dr Hong?'

'I feel pretty good. Thank you, Mr Zheng.' He ran his fingers through his thick, dark hair, trying to make it presentable.

'Let's go upstairs and get a girl to give us a massage. You'll feel even better after that,' said Zheng, and laughed.

The massage parlour was a long narrow room, divided into little cubicles by shoulder-high partition walls. Each cubicle held either one or two massage couches with a curtain that could be drawn for privacy. Someone was already having a massage in one of the cubicles. The rhythmic clapping sound and grunting left Hong Jun wondering what sort of massage was on offer.

Two young women came over and greeted them. 'Massage, gentlemen?'

'Sure!' said Zheng Jianzhong. 'Give us a good massage. Us old guys need to relax.'

They were led to separate cubicles, and the woman with Hong Jun asked him to lie on the couch. 'Shall I draw the curtain?' Her accent was southern, Guangzhou. Hong Jun said there was no need and she guided him with her hands to lie on his back and began to massage his head and face with her strong fingers. He had never had a massage like this, and was alert to the experience, trying not to think that it was a woman doing it, which made him feel awkward. He closed his eyes.

When she had finished massaging his front, the woman asked him to turn over, and began massaging his back. She clasped her two palms together, and began drumming on his back, shoulders, buttocks and thighs. Now his body too was making the clapping sound, and he was grunting too.

She worked hard and triggered sharp pains in his neck and shoulders, which eased the more she worked the knots out of the muscles. 'Shall I stand on you, sir?'

'What?' Hong Jun was taken aback.

'Stand on you, sir?' she repeated, louder this time.

Before he could reply, Zheng Jianzhong called out from next door, 'You should let her stand on you, Dr Hong. It's really good.'

The woman asked him to lie flat, took off her slippers, climbed up onto the bed, and stood on Hong Jun's back. He held his breath, expecting even her slight weight to break his back or do him some serious injury. She grasped a pair of handles above the bed and began treading, ever so lightly, on his back, one foot after the other, but she managed to reach every muscle, and not all of them welcomed the pressure.

He lost track of time, but eventually the pain ended, and he covered himself and thanked the woman. She called him back, 'Please sign this, sir.' He wrote his key number on the piece of paper, noticing that it had just cost one hundred yuan to be beaten and walked on, and went for a walk around the club's large premises. Grey Hair and Yellow Teeth were playing billiards. He went downstairs and saw Zheng Jianzhong in the corridor.

'Don't you want to play some games, Dr Hong?' he asked.

'I'm not really interested in things like that,' he replied. 'We need to talk about the case. Is there somewhere quiet we can go?'

'I've reserved a private room,' he said. 'Let's go there to talk.' He had words with Yellow Teeth and Grey Hair, and he led Hong Jun up the stairs.

The private room was fourteen or fifteen metres square, with leather sofas around three sides, a coffee table in the middle and a big TV on the wall by the door. Zheng Jianzhong and Hong Jun sat down on one of the sofas. A young woman opened the door and asked with a smile, 'Boss Zheng, do you want the girls now?'

'Later, we'll have a rest first,' he replied.

'What are you drinking today?'

'A bottle of Remy Martin, I think.'

Hong Jun looked at the drinks list. It was priced at eight hundred yuan. 'Director Zheng, by all means open it if you feel like it, but I can't drink those foreign spirits.'

'It's nothing to do with whether I want to or not,' Zheng replied. 'If we use the room we have to have one, a kind of cover charge. Anyway, it's nothing.'

The young woman quickly brought in a tray with a bottle and two wine glasses, knelt at the table and opened the bottle, half filled each glass, and, taking the tray with her, left them with a good view of her well-shaped bottom.

Zheng Jianzhong picked up his glass and said, 'Dr Hong, let's drink a toast.' He took a big swig, and continued, 'To tell you the truth, this stuff is nowhere near as good as a nice bottle of *Erguotou* spirit, but if you ordered that here they'd laugh you out of the bleedin' house. In this day and age, what men fear most is being poor, or appearing poor, and what women fear most is being ugly. If a man has no money he can't get anything done, if a woman is ugly she can't get anything done. Guys who can't get things done shouldn't blame women for being too pragmatic, and women who can't get things done shouldn't blame men for being too superficial.'

Hong Jun had barely let the alcohol moisten his lips, its fumes alone making him light-headed, before putting his glass back on the table. He said nothing. Zheng Jianzhong's comments were as alien to him as the taste of the foreign spirits, he thought, and he didn't like either.

Zheng Jianzhong sensed Hong Jun's feelings and quickly changed the subject. 'Tell me more about your trip to Binbei. I want to hear all the details.'

Hong Jun began with his meeting with Zheng Jianguo, making a point of emphasising how tough his life was in Harbin Prison and relating the story about his broken leg. He watched Zheng Jianzhong's reaction.

'My poor brother, he suffers so much.' Zheng Jianzhong hung his head and stared at the glass on the table. After a long while, he gave a deep sigh. 'Ah, let's not discuss him any more. There's nothing we can do to change the past. Let's talk about the chances of overturning the verdict. What's your opinion?'

'I think we can apply for a retrial, and I'm very confident of overturning the original verdict,' Hong Jun said. He described his conversations with Han Wenqing, and explained his theory about the apple at the crime scene. Zheng Jianzhong listened intently. 'Of course! Why didn't I think of that at the time?'

Hong Jun looked him in the eye. 'The traces of blood on that fruit knife are important evidence for proving who the killer was,' he said. 'I'm planning to get the experts to carry out a DNA test, the test you mentioned last time, like the American lawyers use, remember?'

'I certainly do,' said Zheng.

'It will tell us whose blood is on the knife.'

'You mean it could also show who the real killer was?'

'You're absolutely right!'

'But what use is that?' he asked.

'Why wouldn't it be useful?'

'Well, I reckon the real killer is Xiao Xiong,' said Zheng. 'And he went to America long ago, so even if you can show it's him, what good does that do us?'

'But how can you be sure that Xiao Xiong was the killer?'

'Well, who else could it have been, Dr Hong? You don't expect me to believe that Li Qingshan raped his own daughter, do you?'

His words reminded Hong Jun of something. 'Ah yes, now you mention it, I wanted to ask you about Li Qingshan. Do you know where he is now?'

'He's in Harbin.'

'Do you have his address?'

'No, I don't. All I know is that he went to Harbin with his oldest daughter. Seems his son-in-law was also in the building trade there for a while. But I don't know anything else about it.'

'And do you know where his middle daughter is?'

'She's in Binbei. She works in a restaurant in the county town, a big place, the Binbei Restaurant. Last year I went back to Binbei and invited some friends for dinner there, and I bumped into her. Of course!' he exclaimed. 'You could go and look for her. Her name's Li Hongxing.'

Hong Jun looked at Zheng Jianzhong. 'And there's something else. Did your brother ever sleepwalk?'

'What are you asking that for?'

'People heard him talking in his sleep,' Hong Jun lied.

'Really? I know he talked in his sleep when he was little, but then it stopped. What'd he say in his sleep?'

'He talked about his relationship with Li Hongmei. I think there was even something about having sex. Actually I wanted to ask you, how far did his relationship with Li Hongmei go?'

'You want to know about that kind of thing too, Dr Hong?' Zheng Jianzhong took a big swig of cognac.

'It may have a bearing on the case.' Hong Jun raised his glass too.

'I don't think the two of them went that far. You're not telling me he really did it with her? No, it can't be true. What did he tell you?'

'He told me he hadn't,' said Hong Jun.

'I don't think he did. If he had, how could Hongmei have split up with him?'

The door opened again, and the young woman stood in the doorway. 'Hey Boss Zheng, have you two had enough rest?'

Zheng Jianzhong asked Hong Jun whether there was anything else he wanted to discuss. Hong Jun shook his head. 'Okay,' said Zheng to the young woman. 'Bring us two girls. You know what I like.'

'All our girls here are like honey, Boss Zheng. If you don't believe me you can taste them for yourself,' she said, and, fluttering her eyelashes, she closed the door.

Hong Jun was now pretty sure he was out of his depth, and he sank further when two young women entered, dressed in tight blouses tied at the waist, short-short skirts and stiletto heels. 'Hello big brother,' they said together. One sat next to Zheng, the other next to him, encouraging them to finish their drinks, and now and again touching them with more than sisterly intimacy.

'Let's go and have some fun,' said Zheng Jianzhong, draining his glass. 'Do whatever you like' he told Hong Jun. 'This place is completely safe.' To the girl, he said, 'Look after this boss well. If he is happy, I'll be happy and it'll be worth your while.'

'Yes, Boss Zheng, everyone will be happy,' she replied and moved closer to him.

Before Hong Jun had time to speak, Zheng and his companion were gone. 'Shall I lock the door, boss?' the girl asked him softly.

'There's no need,' said Hong Jun.

'But if we don't lock the door, how can we enjoy ourselves?' she asked, giving him a teasing glance. 'Aren't you worried someone might see?' When he didn't reply, she giggled and asked, 'Hey boss, which bit of me do you like best?'

'Actually I'd like it if you were a bit further away,' he replied sternly, and went and sat down on the other side of the table.

The girl looked at him a little uncertainly.

Reverting to his normal tone of voice, he asked here where she was from.

'I'm from Hubei Province,' she said.

'Did you go to university?'

'I was never very good at school.'

'What are your plans for the future?'

'My future . . . ?' She looked as though she'd never been asked the question before.

Hong Jun was feeling more and more uncomfortable. He made a show of looking at his watch and stood. 'I'm sorry, I've got to go; there's something I have to do, okay?'

The girl's lips remained firmly shut in contemplation.

Yellow Teeth was standing in the corridor outside. 'Where's Director Zheng?' Hong Jun asked him. 'I'm afraid I have something to do, I need to leave now.'

Yellow Teeth blocked his way. 'Calm down, Dr Hong, why the hurry?' he said, but quickly added, 'Wait a moment.' He went over to the door of the private room next door, and knocked loudly. 'Director Zheng,' he called. 'Dr Hong wants to leave.'

After a little while, Zheng Jianzhong opened the door and came out. 'Dr Hong? Why the rush? Wasn't that girl to your taste? I can get you another one?'

Hong Jun wanted to get out of there, fast. 'Director Zheng, I'm afraid I have something else to do. I need to leave now.' He nervously turned his back on them and marched down the corridor to the changing room, put on his clothes and went to the lobby to return his key.

Zheng Jianzhong, Yellow Teeth and Grey Hair appeared in the lobby.

'My dear Dr Hong,' said Zheng, 'I'm very sorry you didn't enjoy yourself. Next time we'll go somewhere else.'

'I've really learned a lot today,' Hong Jun said. 'Thank you very much, Director Zheng for your generous hospitality. My office will call when I have more information for you. I really have to go. Goodbye!'

Hong Jun walked out to his car and drove out of the gate of the East Beijing Leisure Garden. 'Two brothers, one locked up in jail for crimes he didn't commit, the other, probably guilty of stepping outside the law a few times, living a life of wine and women,' he muttered to himself. 'Sometimes destiny . . . ' he searched for the correct word, and came up with a few in English that would work, but not given to profanity, settled on one that seemed appropriate, ' . . . *sucks* . . . Sometimes destiny *sucks*.' He tore through the gears of his car as he sped through the dark streets back towards the city.

CHAPTER TWELVE

ON HIS RETURN to Binbei County, Hong Jun was welcomed by all the staff at the front desk of the Songjiang Hotel. He didn't want to be here, but made a show of courtesy because he feared he might become a regular customer. It was mid-morning and he could get in a good day's work before travel fatigue caught up with him. He unpacked. The room looked exactly the same as his last one, though he had a good view of the main street below and he could see the wooded park and the countryside beyond. His first stop was the court, where the desk clerk greeted him and quickly arranged for an officer to show him up to Deputy Chief Judge Han's office.

Han Wenqing was ready for him. After brief pleasantries, Hong Jun's impatience got the better of him, and he asked Han to tell him about the fruit knife. Han explained that after having the knife sent over from PSB headquarters, Chu Weihua had shown it to the coroner. The coroner had told him that the traces of blood on the blade had already been completely corrupted by rust, and there was no way they could be used for identification.

Hong Jun asked if he could look at the knife. Han Wenqing readily agreed, and went to a bank of filing cabinets, unlocked a drawer and took out a very old manila envelope, which he placed on the table. On it was written, among other things, the words CASE OF 17

APRIL 1984 and LI HONGMEI. Han opened the envelope and took out a plastic evidence bag, and from this, he carefully removed the knife. It was a very ordinary folding fruit knife, its handle inlaid with red glass that had faded and lost its lustre. He opened the knife. Most of the shiny metal plating had long since come off the blade. In the middle, on the edge of the blade, there was one small dark red speck, merging into the rust marks that covered areas where the plating was missing.

After inspecting the knife closely, Hong Jun sat for a moment, lost in thought. Then he looked up. 'Chief Judge Han, could I have another look at the case files?'

'Of course you may.' Han Wenqing took the file from the same filing cabinet drawer and placed it in front of him.

Hong Jun quickly turned to the photos of the fruit knife, looked at them, and then turned to the reports of the investigation of the crime scene and read through them. 'Chief Han,' he said, 'this is not the original fruit knife.'

'What? It's not the same one? That can't be possible.' Han stared at him, wide-eyed, yet Hong Jun didn't think he was particularly surprised by the revelation. Han had half risen from his chair, but resumed his seat and asked, 'Please, Dr Hong, explain.'

'Well, my memory's usually pretty good,' he said, 'and from what I remembered from the files, the fruit knife wasn't red. You see, in the report from the crime scene it says it had a black handle. And look at this photo,' he placed the picture in front of Han, 'even though it's black and white, you can see that the colour of the handle is quite different from the colour of the specks of blood.'

'Can this really be true?' Han Wenqing's face was a picture of anger, though at whom Hong Jun was curious. 'What the hell do they think they're playing at? That gang of cops have got a nerve. This is fabricating evidence, obstructing an investigation.' Han slapped the top of his desk with the open palm of his right hand.

The joints of Hong Jun's fingers cracked. 'I think this is to our advantage,' he said calmly, drawing in Han as an ally. 'If we can find out who swapped the fruit knives, it will be a major step forward for us in reinvestigating Zheng Jianguo's case.'

'We've definitely got to get to the bottom of this!' Han Wenqing's anger quickly subsided as he calculated the personal political advantage of Hong Jun succeeding. 'Here's where we are, Dr Hong,' he said, and reported that the court's sentencing committee had discussed the case and decided to investigate Zheng Jianguo's conviction. Chu Weihua was in charge of the day-to-day work. He left for Harbin the day before, and had gone to visit Zheng in the provincial jail to check some of the details. Han finished by telling Hong Jun, 'Don't worry, we'll definitely give you all the support we can. I'll call the County PSB right away.'

*

Public Security Bureau Chief Hao Zhicheng was loudly dressing down Wu Hongfei, head of the Criminal Investigation Unit for all to hear beyond the thin partitions of his office. 'Well done, Dopey Wu, you really lived up to your name this time, didn't you,' he yelled. 'You sure know how to get things done! What the hell were you thinking, substituting the fruit knife? Whose stupid idea was that?'

'It was my idea,' replied Wu expressionlessly. 'We couldn't find the original knife, so we had to find another one to replace it. It's not like we've never done this kind of thing before.'

'Don't give me that. What was done back then . . . This is a completely different era. Secretary Gu himself is taking a serious interest in this case. A lot of people are looking for errors in our work. So, well done, you've just dumped one steaming blunder right on our doorstep.'

'That's why I tried to find another knife. If we admitted we'd lost the knife, they'd put all the blame on us,' Wu said.

'Wu Hongfei, you've normally got a pretty good head on you. Why suddenly turn into such a dumb ass now?'

Those outside the office had long since stopped working and the lengthening silence from within only fuelled the suspense of listeners.

Chief Hao spoke first. 'So, you looked for a new knife, but you've got to find one that looks the same. The real one had a black handle, and you get one with a red handle? Who the hell's going to fall for that?'

'It's not easy to find an old knife like that,' said Wu Hongfei. 'I had to look all over the place just to find this one. Who'd have thought they'd work it out? If you ask me, it must have been that big shot Beijing lawyer.'

'Don't you underestimate that lawyer,' the chief said. 'I've heard he's got friends in Beijing, and in the provincial HQ too. Who else knows about this?'

'Just me and Old Yu. But it's got nothing to do with him,' Wu added. 'If anyone has to take responsibility, it'll be me alone.'

'I don't want to hear that kind of nonsense,' Chief Hao said. 'Listen, don't tell anyone else about this – I'll go to the court and explain things to them. But I'm telling you, Wu Hongfei, don't ever try to pull a stunt like this again, okay? If anything else goes wrong, that'll be the last of you as head of the Criminal Investigation Unit.

'And one more thing,' he said, 'If that lawyer comes here to investigate, be sure to help him. At the very least we've got to make him think we're cooperating. I don't mind him knowing that some stupid cop tried to cover his arse, but I don't want him thinking we tampered with the evidence. Have you got that?'

After Wu Hongfei left, and the rest of the office had reluctantly got back to their business, Hao Zhicheng lit a cigarette and stood looking out of the window. He'd decided a while ago that he would have to stand by Deputy Secretary Gu Chunshan. And it wasn't just because Gu was a former PSB man and they'd been comrades in arms for many years. He'd hitched himself to Gu's political career and if Gu

was promoted to Secretary of the Political and Legal Committee of
the new Binbei City, he was sure to get Executive Deputy Head of the
Municipal Police Bureau at the very least. Hao's aspirations were not
excessive. He wanted to retire on at least a deputy provincial police
chief's pension, which was more than enough for him. He stubbed
his cigarette out in the ashtray and strode out of the office, full of
optimism. A cloud of gossip descended over the office as soon as he
left the building.

That afternoon, Hong Jun arrived at the County PSB. He told the
officer at the gatehouse he had come to see Chief Hao and was shown
inside, but Hao Zhicheng wasn't in his office, and someone said he
had gone out a while ago. Was there someone else who could help
him? He asked for the Criminal Investigation Unit, Wu Hongfei. The
door was ajar, and he could see people inside. He knocked and a voice
immediately called out, 'Come in.'

It was a big room, but so full of desks, cupboards and field cots,
haphazardly arranged, it felt like a closet. Two young men were im-
mersed in a game of chess, while another was lying on a cot with a
newspaper over his face. One of the young men looked up and shot a
quick glance at Hong Jun, then returned to the chess board. He moved
a piece, then asked without raising his head, 'Who are you looking for?'

'Wu Hongfei, the head of the unit,' he replied.

Now both the young men lifted their heads and looked Hong Jun
up and down, then smirked at each other. One of them pursed his lips
and nodded towards the figure on the bed, and the other said loudly,
'You're looking for Chief Wu? Better come back a bit later.'

'Who's looking for me?' The newspaper rose from the breath underneath and he pulled it free of his face, and struggled to a sitting
position. The two young officers hunched over the chess board, but

their concentration was not on the pieces but another, more interesting game.

'Hello, Chief Wu,' said Hong Jun.

'Ah, Dr Hong!' Wu Hongfei stretched lazily, and strolled over to a chair in front of one of the desks. 'Please sit down. What can I do for you?'

'I've just got back from Beijing today, and . . . ' He stopped, and glanced at the two men playing chess.

'Don't worry, Dr Hong,' said Wu Hongfei, 'there are no secrets in our office.' As he spoke, he lit a cigarette.

'I'd like to know more about that fruit knife,' Hong Jun went on. 'I hear you couldn't find it at first, is that right?'

'Uh huh! It's awful that something like that could happen!' said Wu. Then he called out to one of the chess players. 'Hey, Dongsheng!'

'Yes, Chief.'

'Go and get Old Yu.'

'Yes, Chief.' But before the young man could get to the door, Wu Hongfei called him back. 'Forget it,' he said. 'It'll be easier if we just go see him ourselves.'

The next office was smaller, but more orderly, with only two desks and a lot of cupboards. In one glass-fronted cabinet there were bottles of various sizes. Several of the larger ones contained human body parts preserved in fluid. On the bottom shelf was part of a human skull.

At the sound of the opening door, a short, greying middle-aged man got up from behind the desk. He had a pale face and glasses. 'Chief Wu, what can I do for you?'

Wu Hongfei gave him a sidelong glance. 'This is Lawyer Hong from Beijing, he wants to know about that fruit knife, tell him all about it.' He turned to Hong Jun. 'This is Comrade Yu Jinghui, he's been a police pathologist for about twenty years. Last year he was made a master pathologist.'

Wu Hongfei sat down on a chair in the corner of the room. Hong Jun came straight to the point. 'Dr Yu, could I ask you whether the fruit knife has always been kept here in your office?'

'Yes, that's right,' Dr Yu replied. 'It was always my responsibility, I can't deny it. As soon as the court had finished with the knife, after the trial all those years ago, I put it straight into this cupboard, where I keep all the major case evidence, and never took it out again.'

'And when did you discover it was missing?'

'When Chief Wu told me the court wanted it sent over so they could check the traces of blood, I went to fetch it, but the evidence envelope was empty. The knife had gone. I immediately reported it.'

'So the knife might have gone . . . ?'

'When it went missing I really couldn't say,' Dr Yu said. 'In a grass-roots level unit like ours we're quite short-staffed, and our management's not great either. We moved offices a couple of years ago, and everything was in a big mess. We didn't really pay too much attention to anything that wasn't an open case. If the evidence envelope was gone too, I'd have presumed it got lost in the move.' Dr Yu shrugged his shoulders, as if to say, Let's be reasonable.

Hong Jun nodded. 'Dr Yu, when you tested the blood traces on the knife back then, did you test for anything except blood type?'

'I know there are lots of different kinds of blood tests, and the more you do, the more chance you have of making an absolutely accurate identification. But as I say, we're the grassroots here and our facilities are pretty primitive. We can only do blood type ABO. You'll probably laugh at me when I say we even had trouble doing that test.'

'What kind of trouble?' asked Hong Jun.

With a glance at Wu Hongfei, Dr Yu went on, 'Well, at the time, the first test I did on that knife actually seemed to suggest that there were two different types of blood on the blade.'

'Really?' Hong Jun said.

'Yes. We got type A and type O. That's what I wrote in my first report. I still have it in my own files. Right, Chief Wu?'

Wu Hongfei had been sitting listening in silence. Now he frowned and said, 'Yes, that's what happened.'

'In the traces of semen on the victim's body we also identified traces of both A and O,' Dr Yu continued. 'But that was only to be expected, because the victim was type O. But how could there have been two people's blood on the knife in the exact same places? How could the victim's blood have got onto it? There were no wounds. It was quite bizarre. I figured the sample must have got corrupted so I ran a new test and, because I couldn't explain it, issued a lab report saying it was blood type A.'

'Do you still believe the original test results were right?' Hong Jun asked.

'Yes, I do.' Dr Yu seemed rather emotional. 'I always take my work very seriously, and this was an important case. I'm sure I didn't spoil the samples, and I'm also certain there were two types of blood on that knife.'

'Could someone else have contaminated the samples?'

'I really couldn't say,' he replied. 'I just carry out tests on what I'm given. What happens before evidence gets to me is not my business. But we do have a strict chain of evidence, and I know what I saw.' Yu glanced at Wu Hongfei, who was sitting alongside him, looking apparently disinterestedly at the skull bone in the cupboard.

'Dr Yu, I've heard that at the time there were differing views on the cause of Li Hongmei's death?'

'That's right,' he said. 'The corpse did show some signs of mechanical asphyxiation, her face had turned purple, and there was blood from the ruptured capillaries in her cornea, but it wasn't a textbook case, especially since there were no injuries on her body. At the time, my analysis was that, if asphyxiation was the cause of death, and there was no bruising around her neck, which ruled out being throttled or strangled with a rope, all that's left is that she would've been smothered. But, when people are smothered there would normally be marks on their body from where they tried to resist, at the very least there would be superficial abrasions on the mouth or nose as they fought to get free of the obstruction. But there was nothing like that on Li Hongmei's body.

'It did make me wonder whether she had suffered from heart problems. That's not uncommon around here. If she had coronary disease, then being raped could have brought on a heart attack, and that could also have been interpreted as asphyxiation. At the time, I did suggest a full autopsy, but our leaders wanted the case cleared up as quickly as possible, and the deceased's family didn't want me cutting up her body. So, we just settled on asphyxiation as the cause of death.'

'And from your examination of the body, could you at least be certain that she was raped?' Hong Jun asked.

'To tell the truth, no I couldn't,' said Dr Yu. 'There was no bruising or evidence of forced entry, and no signs of a struggle elsewhere on her body. I could only establish that sexual intercourse had taken place shortly before she died, but as to whether it was consensual or rape . . . '

Wu Hongfei glared at Dr Yu.

'Lawyer Hong asked me and I'm just telling him what I know,' said Dr Yu. Hong Jun noticed he was annoyed by Wu's attempted intimidation.

'Thanks. You've both been a great help. I'm very grateful to you both,' said Hong Jun. He wasn't getting any more from Dr Yu than he had already and he wasn't going to get any straight answers from the PSB. Besides, he was hungry.

✳

Hong Jun walked deep into the restaurant, to where the cash register stood next to a steel spike holding paid bills and a long rod with pegs holding open bills. He saw his waitress working some tables to the right and she gave him a wave. Another waitress was working the till and he asked her whether Li Hongxing was there.

'She just waved at you,' she said. 'Over there.'

'Oh,' he said, 'I've never met her before. Would you mind asking her to come over here? There's something I need to talk to her about.'

'Sure. But don't keep her long, please. We're really quite busy to-night.' The waitress giggled at the mystery of it all and returned quickly with Hong Jun's waitress. 'Li Hongxing? Hello, again.'

'Oh, my friend from Beijing, isn't it? How do you know my name?'

'I'm a lawyer. Hong Jun. I'm working on a case and I'd like to ask you a couple of questions.'

'What case?'

'An old case, the murder of your sister, Li Hongmei.'

'Ah . . . ' Li Hongxing appeared to relax a little. 'You scared me there. I thought something else had happened. Come on, let's go and sit down. I think I've earned a short break.' Hong Jun followed her to a quiet corner and took a seat. 'I'll try to be quick. When the case took place, were you at Binbei Farm?'

'No,' she replied. 'I was living in a village about four or five kilo-metres from the farm. Someone else told me what happened. I didn't get there until the next day.'

'Do *you* think that Zheng Jianguo was the killer?'

'Well, what can I say? We'd known each other since we were kids, and I always thought he was a good, honest sort. But you can never see into someone's head, can you, so who knows what he was really thinking? Besides, the blood type matched up, and the court sentenced him. Anyway,' she sighed, 'it's ten years since it happened. Why are you asking about all this again?'

'We're reinvestigating the case. I don't think Zheng Jianguo did it.'

'He didn't?' said Li Hongxing. 'Then who did?'

'That's precisely what we need to find out,' he said. 'Who do you think it might have been?'

'I really couldn't say. I wasn't living at the farm at the time, so I didn't really know too much about what my sister was up to. I only know there were a lot of guys who wanted to be her boyfriend.'

'Did your father ever talk about that kind of thing?'

'My dad? Well, he did say there was one guy who Hongmei really seemed to like. I think he was called Xiao something.'

'Xiao Xiong?'

'Yes, that's the name,' she replied. 'I just remember they called him Dumb Deer. I met him. He was much better looking than Peasant Poet.'

'After Hongmei died, did your father ever talk about who might have killed her?'

'At that time my dad spent all his time sighing and saying how unlucky he was. Whenever we asked him about what happened that night, he always just mumbled and muttered. But at first I don't think he particularly suspected Zheng Jianguo and even when they arrested him he didn't really believe that Zheng Jianguo could have done something so terrible. Oh yes, and one time he did mumble something about how he suspected someone else. But when I asked who it was, he refused to tell me. After they found the match with Zheng Jianguo's blood, he never said any more about it. He would only say, "You can know someone from the outside, but you'll never know what's in their head."'

'And where is your father living now?' asked Hong Jun.

'With my older sister in Harbin.'

'Would you mind giving me your sister's address?' he said. 'I'd really like to go to see your father and hear what he has to say.'

'Sure!' she replied. 'In fact, I just got a letter from my sister yesterday. I think it's still in my coat pocket. Wait a minute, I'll go and check.'

Hongxing got up and went to the rear of the restaurant, returning a moment later carrying a letter, which she handed to Hong Jun. 'My sister's name is Li Honghua,' she said. 'When are you planning to go? I'd like to send something to my dad with you.'

'I can take it for you, sure,' said Hong Jun, as he copied the address into his pocket notebook, 'as long as you're not scared I'll run away with it!'

'As if you would,' she chuckled. 'We've met already, the last time, and I could tell you were a respectable person. Anyway, I only want to send him things like wild mushrooms from the mountains and fungus, nothing valuable. But only if you're sure it won't be too much trouble for you, brother.'

'It's no problem at all,' said Hong Jun. 'I'm leaving tomorrow morning, so I could come and collect them before I set off. Would eight o'clock be too early?'

'Fine, that's settled then.' Li Hongxing glanced at her watch. 'Hey, it's five o'clock, why don't you stay for dinner? I'll get the kitchen to make you some of our local specialities.'

Hong Jun didn't take much persuading.

＊

After he finished dinner, he went back to the hotel, where the receptionist gave him a message chit: *Please call Miss Song in Beijing.* He went to his room and phoned the office. To his surprise, Song Jia was still in the office, waiting for his call.

'Hello, Song Jia?' he said. 'How come you haven't gone home yet?'

'I need to report back to you on the things you asked me to do,' she said. 'I can't leave until the job is done. At least you didn't stay out boozing.'

'What do you have for me?'

'How about Zheng Jianzhong's blood type?' she asked.

'Have you been able to find it out?'

'I have. He's type O.'

'Aha, very good,' he said. 'But how did you find out?'

'I used a trick or two,' she said. 'But I'm not going to tell you about it now.'

'I'll find out. You forget I'm a clever lawyer. Anything else?'

'That's it for now.'

'Very good. Now go home, or go out. I hope you're not late for something.'

'Night, boss.'

*

No sooner had he hung up when the phone rang again. He thought it might be Song Jia calling back, but it was a man's voice.

'Hello, Dr Hong?'

'Yes it is,' he replied. 'Who is this, please?'

'This is Gu Chunshan.'

'Oh, Party Secretary Gu, good evening. Is there something I can do for you?'

'Old Han from the court told me you were back in town, and this coming Sunday is my hunting day. Would you like to join me?'

'Of course, I'd love to. Let me see . . . today is Wednesday . . . Yes, I should still be here. That would be fine.'

'Then it's a deal,' said Gu. 'We'll pick you up from your hotel at five o'clock on Sunday morning. No lazing around in bed for hunters, eh?'

'No problem.'

'By the way, how are you getting on with the case? Is everything going okay? I hear from Chief Han that the court's decided to reinvestigate. You must forgive me, I'm afraid I've been very busy recently so I haven't been paying close attention to how you're getting on.'

'Thank you, Secretary Gu, but really, there's no need,' Hong Jun said.

'Well, if there's anything we can do to help, please say. We'll do all we can.'

After he hung up, Hong Jun felt pleased. This was good news, both professionally and personally. He had a hunch that this hunting trip would prove very useful, a chance to kill two birds with one stone, since he was not only fulfilling a long-held wish, but, he hoped, he would also have a chance to learn more about Zheng Jianguo's case from Gu Chunshan himself. He swung his right arm round and round a couple of times, and in his enthusiasm began humming:

My sweet home, Chicago . . .

CHAPTER THIRTEEN

ON THE EVENING he arrived in Harbin, Hong Jun followed the directions given him by Li Hongxing and went straight to her older sister's house, but Li Qingshan was no longer staying there, having found a job as a janitor at a primary school where he lived on the premises. It was in the Daowai District, too far to go at that hour, and it was first thing the next morning when he found the red brick Russian-style building with a sloping roof. Entering the main door, he found himself in a large entrance hall, trying to work out where the janitor's room might be and thinking he might need to descend to the basement.

Classes were underway and the hall was silent. Hong Jun stood in the entranceway, expecting the janitor to be about his duties, when a small peephole in the wall clacked open and revealed a face full of wrinkles.

'Comrade, who are you looking for?' a croaking voice asked.

'Are you Li Qingshan?' said Hong Jun, speaking into the hole. 'I've come from Binbei. I have something for you from your daughter Li Hongxing.'

'Really? Then please come in and sit. Take the first corridor on the left.'

Hong Jun went round the corner and saw the door of the janitor's office standing open, and occupying the doorway was a thin old man with a slightly hunched back. 'Please, come in, come in,' he said. 'What was she thinking of, Hongxing, asking you to carry things such a long way? I'm really sorry for putting you to so much trouble.'

The janitor's office consisted of two rooms. In the outer room were two chairs, a table with a telephone and a quartz clock radio, and a small chalkboard hanging on the wall, divided into rectangles for days of the week and hours of the day. It looked like his duties, some daily, some weekly, with an empty column for teachers to write up things that needed to be fixed. The door to the inner room was only partly open, but Hong Jun assumed it was his bedroom.

He gave Li the bag he had brought for him. After one look inside, Li Qingshan couldn't stop thanking him as he took the bag into the inner room, returning to sit opposite Hong Jun. 'What can I do for you?'

'My name is Hong Jun. I'm a lawyer in Beijing. I am on a case in Binbei, and I met Hongxing. I told her I was planning to come to see you, so she asked me to bring you something. She is a good daughter.'

'Hah,' said Li. 'However good she is, a daughter is not the same as a son. You were looking for me?'

'Yes.'

'Why?'

'It's about the murder of your daughter, Li Hongmei.'

'Hongmei?' Li was startled and drew back from the table. 'What do you want?'

'I am trying to find out what really happened that night she died. I believe Zheng Jianguo to be innocent and the court is examining its guilty verdict to see if there may have been a mistake in his conviction.' Hong Jun let the information sink in, and spoke quietly to the old man. 'I've heard she was a very good daughter, and very kind to everyone.'

'Hah, good people don't necessarily have good fortune, do they?' said Li with a shrug. 'Fate's been pretty cruel to me, to lose a daughter so full of life so young. She should have had a long, happy life.'

'If Zheng Jianguo is innocent, he's spent ten years in jail for a crime I don't think he committed. Is that fair?'

'Huh, what's the point of reinvestigating after all these years? It ain't going to bring my daughter back to life, is it?' said Li.

'But if Zheng Jianguo wasn't the murderer, then we need to find the real killer. Otherwise, Hongmei's soul will never rest in peace, her death unavenged.' Hong Jun didn't like playing on the superstitions of old, which the Party tried to eradicate, but they run deep in Chinese culture.

'The dead are dead, and the living have to go on living,' Li muttered, almost as though talking to himself. 'Innocent people get punished all the time, and the guilty will never be punished. You are too young to know how these things work.' He snorted. 'If they couldn't get to the bottom of it at the time, what's the point talking about it now?'

'You don't think Zheng Jianguo killed your daughter, do you?' Hong Jun asked, but saw Li Qingshan wasn't going to answer his question.

'I wonder if you could tell me about Hongmei's health, Mr Li. Did she ever have heart problems? Keshan disease had quite a hold on Heilongjiang for a while,' he said.

'Heart problems?' Li looked surprised. 'No, strong as a horse, she was a tough girl, never got sick, not even in winter. Mind you, her mum's heart wasn't so good. We lost her so young.'

'What do you remember about the day of the crime?'

Li Qingshan thought for a moment, then said slowly, 'Well, that evening, I had a few drinks, and fell asleep soon after it got dark. Hongmei said she'd tidy up before she went to bed. I always sleep like a log, but during the night, I thought I heard some noises, and got up to take a leak. When I opened the door, I thought I saw a dark shape slip out of our gate, heading east, but the moon was bright and it took my eyes a while to adjust. I just figured it was a tree moving or something, and didn't think anything of it. I went inside and went straight back to sleep. The next morning when I got up, nothing had been done about breakfast and the fire was cold. Hongmei is always up early to do those things, so I went to her door and called her a few times. Maybe she was using the toilet. I waited, but she didn't come back, so I knocked loudly on her door and called her name and when she didn't answer, I went in. What I saw there was so shocking I could hardly move. I almost fainted . . . I know I must have screamed because the Zheng brothers arrived, and I'm sure you know what happened after that.'

'The dark shape you saw. Did it go into the Zheng's courtyard?' asked Hong Jun.

'Maybe. I can't remember for sure. As I said, the moon was bright. Maybe it was just another tree. It was a long time ago.'

'Did the shape look like anyone?'

'Look like . . . ? Well, I've said it looked like Zheng Jianguo but I spent a lot of time thinking about it over the years and, y'know, I can't say for sure.'

'I met Chen Fenglu on the farm, Old Big Mouth? He said you were pretty good friends.'

'That's right, we got on very well.'

'He told me that after Hongmei died, you once said to him that you always felt bad for Zheng Jianguo. Is that right?'

'Oh? Did I? Hmm . . . yes . . . I think I did say that.'

'Why would you feel bad for him?'

'Well,' Li paused for a moment. 'I suppose I thought I shouldn't have said that the shape looked like him when I didn't know for sure. We'd been neighbours for a long time. I just figured they'd always get better evidence and my statement would never come up.'

'Do you think Zheng Jianguo was the killer?' Hong Jun asked.

'What can I say? They matched the blood types, didn't they?'

'The same blood type doesn't necessarily prove it was the same person. Lots of people have the same blood type. For example, maybe both you and Hongmei were type O.'

'Yes, I've heard that children have the same blood type as the father.'

'Not necessarily.' It was too complicated to explain, so Hong Jun moved the conversation on. 'Your daughter Hongxing told me that after it happened, you mentioned that you suspected someone else.

Could you tell me who it was?'

Li sat upright. 'I never said that!' He sounded adamant.

'Then why would Hongxing have said that you did?'

'She's talking rubbish, such a silly girl.' He was angry, but why?

The bell rang for the end of classes, and the corridor was filled with the sound of children shouting in the hallways, which reminded Hong Jun of the 'frog chorus' beside a village pond on a summer evening. Several teachers came to the janitor's room to collect newspapers or letters. One of them wrote a note on the chalkboard for Li Qingshan to deal with, commenting as she got a look at the stranger, 'No particular rush.' After a few minutes, the bell for the next class rang, and peace was restored.

'Dr Hong,' said Li. 'I'm sorry if I sounded angry just then. It wasn't with you, it was with Hongxing. She must have remembered wrong. But she shouldn't say things if she's not sure they're true. I didn't raise her to be a gossip.'

'Well,' said Hong Jun, 'it's really no big deal. After all, you only said you suspected someone. You didn't name anyone for sure. So no harm done.'

'But we can't just suspect anyone, can we?' Li seemed perturbed. 'This is a legal matter. It was up to the government to determine, and they did. Case closed.'

Hong Jun made several attempts to get Li Qingshan to voice his suspicions, but none worked and he wasn't going to give him the name. Hong Jun decided it was time to go. He got up, made his excuses, and, looking at his watch, figured he would catch the evening train to Binbei.

Li Qingshan hadn't given him the information he'd hoped for, but he had at least confirmed that he could not identify the shadow he saw that night and that he wasn't certain it was Zheng Jianguo. No positive witness identification was better than nothing. Hong Jun decided to talk to Chu Weihua when he got back to Binbei, and ask him to come with him to see Li Qingshan another time. Li might be more willing to talk to someone from the court. And he also had a nagging sense that Li knew something, and that knowledge frightened him. He thought back over what he had said, but he couldn't quite pin it down.

CHAPTER FOURTEEN

A HAZY CURTAIN of mist parted to release the orange morning sun. As its brilliant rays shot across the azure sky, a dazzling white glow rose from the vast snow-covered plain. A bright green jeep cut across this great snowy expanse, racing down hills, shooting through woods, sliding on ice, bouncing around as if it were being tossed on a choppy sea.

At the wheel was Liu Yongsheng, driver for the Binbei Party Committee. He was known as 'Big Liu', and with good reason, since he was tall, with a broad face, big eyes, a big nose and a loud voice. He was an excellent driver, a keen hunter and knew the best tracks through the snow. Gu Chunshan always used him for his hunting trips.

Hong Jun and Gu Chunshan were hunched next to each other in the back of the closed jeep, surrounded by the hunting gear, their heads up against the canvas roof. Talk was difficult above the revving and roaring of the engine, but for Hong Jun, it was too good an opportunity to miss and he figured Gu wouldn't allow talk once the hunting began.

'This place really is beautiful in the snow,' he said. 'I noticed it on the bus when I first went to the Binbei State Farm . . . Secretary Gu, you were on a case at the farm when Li Hongmei died. Do you remember what you were investigating?'

Gu Chunshan took a while to answer. 'Yes, I think it was something to do with the democracy movement. Harbin asked us to help investigate, and we were following a lead on someone of interest, but it was a dead end.'

'I've heard you were looking for Xiao Xiong, and he was Li Hongmei's boyfriend,' he said. 'Is that right?'

'That's right. At one point we suspected he might have killed her to stop her talking. We even sent for an arrest warrant. But we never found him and the evidence in her case took us in a different direction. We reported that Xiao Xiong had left the area and passed that case back to Harbin.'

'Tell me more about Xiao Xiong.'

'What's to tell? I never met him. All the time we were at the farm, I heard he was in Harbin. Later I heard he'd run off to America with some of those other troublemakers.' The jeep jolted over a hump of snow, and Gu cursed as his head struck one of the canopy struts.

'At the time, we took cases like that so seriously,' he continued after shouting at Big Liu to try not to kill them. 'When I think about it now, it was pretty pointless. But so was most of the work we did back then, chasing ghosts or mediating rows between neighbours, sometimes sorting out husbands who loved the drink more than their wives, or their work. If you ask me, we ought to spend more time looking at nature. Nothing better.'

Hong Jun unclipped the plastic window beside him and let a blast of icy wind hit him full in the face, breathing in the clean air until his lungs hurt. 'It is quite magnificent,' he said, clipping the window closed, and went back to thinking about the hunt.

Big Liu slowed the jeep at a mountain pass and turned into a gully. There was no apparent road, but faint depressions indicated a rutted track carved by the logging trucks that came to take trees from the forest. Big Liu steered the jeep along one of the deeper tracks, clutching the steering wheel tightly with both hands. The engine gave out a high-pitched whine as the wheels struggled to find purchase. Hong

Jun and Gu Chunshan clung tightly to the straps, trying to stop their heads banging on the roof struts.

They passed a couple of hillocks and came out onto what would be broad lush pasture in the summertime. From a clump of trees up ahead, they saw a hunter emerge. He was big and tough looking, bushy beard, a double-barrelled hunting gun on his back, a scar on his forehead. Hong Jun recognised him immediately. Big Liu stopped the jeep and cut the engine. Gu Chunshan jumped out and walked towards him, all smiles. 'Hello Old Bao,' he said, 'I hope we're not too late?'

'Mr Gu, I was starting to worry whether the icy conditions had got the better of you.'

Gu Chunshan laughed and indicated Hong Jun, who was extricating himself from the jeep. 'Old Bao, I'd like to introduce you to a friend. This is Dr Hong Jun, a lawyer from Beijing. Dr Hong, this is . . . '

'Old Bao, hello again,' said Hong. 'We have already met.'

The grizzled hunter was startled to see him. 'What are *you* doing here?'

'Eh, how come you know each other?' asked Gu Chunshan.

'You remember I told you last time that I met a hunter who was trapping rabbits in Binbei Park?' Hong Jun replied. 'Well, it was him. So, you're old friends, are you?'

'Fellow hunters,' said Gu. 'We met a while ago. He's a true hunter, y'know . . . he can track any animal, big or small, he's a crack shot and he knows the lay of the land like no other guide. I arranged for him to come with us because I want to be sure you get a true hunting experience, Dr Hong.'

'Well, brother,' said Old Bao, nodding uncertainly at Hong Jun. 'You were right interested in hunting last time, but I didn't know you actually wanted to do it.'

'This is my first time,' said Hong Jun quickly.

'Your first time?' Old Bao paused. 'Can you shoot? Have you ever handled a gun? We're not here for fun and games, y'know. And this can be dangerous.'

'I can shoot, and I'm not such a bad shot. No marksman, but I hit more than I miss.' In America, Hong Jun's friends often took him to shooting ranges. He could handle a shotgun quite well, and a rifle too, but he preferred the pistol range and the calmness required to sight the target and gently squeeze the trigger, three times in quick succession, without his aim going astray.

'Ah, that's okay, then. No need to remind you that the gun is always loaded and the horse always kicks, so careful where you point your gun,' said Old Bao. 'This is a great place to come for your first time.' He pointed towards the mountain on the other side of the pasture. 'That there is Black Bear Mountain. If you come here with sincere intentions, I can guarantee you won't go home empty-handed.'

Hong Jun gazed across at the mountain and, squinting a little, he began to see the huge black bear crouching on the ground, dense black forest of its slopes like thick fur on its flanks. Two little ridges stretched out from its northern side the bear's hind legs. To the south, its peak rose steeply, as though the bear was raising its head. Below it was a big cave, as though it was opening its mouth wide, which Hong Jun found rather intimidating.

'Is that cave as big as it looks?' he asked.

'Quite big,' said Old Bao. 'Black Bear Cave, it's called. I have my den in there. I'll take you to have a look if you like. We can get pretty close in the jeep and start from there.'

Old Bao pushed the gear from the front passenger seat and sat next to Big Liu to show him the path. They drove across the pasture and through the thickening forest at the foot of Black Bear Mountain. Old Bao tapped Big Liu's shoulder and pointed to an almost invisible break in the trees and he turned, engaging the four-wheel drive. The heavily laden jeep jerked and lurched but held and they climbed a winding track to the bottom of a hillside. Old Bao signalled for Big Liu to stop. 'We walk from here,' he said. They left the jeep in a sunny and sheltered spot and the four of them got out, shouldered packs and weapons, and climbed, scrambling in places on hands and knees, up the path to Black Bear Cave.

The mouth of the cave was more than a dozen metres wide and as much as ten metres high. Inside, it stretched for twenty or thirty metres before the light gave out. On the craggy cliff face to the right of the entrance were carved eight lines of poetry, in giant characters, which Big Liu read with grace and eloquence, the pleasing bass timbre of his strong voice amplified by the cave.

Black Bear Mountain rises to the blue sky,
In Black Bear Cave there resides a spirit;
Its sharp eyes can perceive good or evil,
Its wise heart can distinguish between the loyal and the treacherous.
It laments that greed and lust have destroyed man's noble nature,
Pities that one day they will be just white bones on the mountain;
Don't despair that karma does not punish the evil,
In the world of men justice will one day prevail.

They stood silently at the mouth of the cave until the last deep notes, like an incantation from some ancient opera, finished playing off the rock walls.

Even Old Bao was impressed. 'Inside, you can just see a couple of smaller caves leading off the main chamber. The one on the right is about fifteen metres deep, and that's where I've got my den. The one on the left is much deeper, but the further you go the narrower it gets. I once squeezed my way in more than a hundred metres until I reached a drop-off. One time I dropped a piece of burning wood into it and I didn't see it hit the bottom. I explore a little bit now and then, using string and chalk, but you don't want to get lost in there. You'll be the big black bear's dinner for sure.'

Hong Jun turned to Gu Chunshan. 'I'd hate to spoil Old Bao's sanctuary, but you could develop this place for tourism. I'm sure it would do very well.'

'We thought about it,' said Gu. 'But it's just so difficult to get here and hunters don't like to share their secrets, eh Old Bao?'

Big Liu, who had gone into the cave with a flashlight, re-emerged and asked Old Bao, 'Don't you get scared sleeping here alone at night?'

Old Bao roared with laughter, a rich sound that bounced deep into the cave. 'What would I be afraid of? I've never done anything shameful so I don't need to worry about the ghosts coming to carry me off.'

'Have you heard the black bear growling?' Big Liu teased, putting on a timorous voice.

'Of course I have. And if you don't believe me then try staying a night here, I can promise you'll hear it!'

Big Liu became more serious. 'What does it sound like?'

'I can't copy it. You need to hear it for yourself. But it can be quite frightening. I think it comes from the cave on the left.'

At this point Gu Chunshan interrupted them. 'Gentlemen, we are burning daylight. I think it's time to go up the mountain, Old Bao.'

Old Bao checked each of them over. He didn't want to lose a hunter to the snow, or risk any injuries. Hong Jun was handed a shotgun and water canteen by Gu Chunshan and was ready to go, filled with excitement. 'Hey brother,' Old Bao said, pointing at his feet. 'You're not going up the mountain like that. Your feet will freeze and your toes will fall off.'

Hong Jun looked down at his black combat boots, and looked at the others. Old Bao was wearing high leather boots lined with white felt; Gu Chunshan and Big Liu both had army boots with steel toe-caps, and puttees were wrapped about their boots to below the knees. Gu said, apologetically, 'He's right, Dr Hong. You can't just leave your trousers loose like that. The snow up on the mountain is very deep and your boots will be full of snow before you know it. Then,' Gu snapped his fingers, 'frostbite.'

Old Bao went into the cave and came back with a couple of lengths of cord, which he wrapped tightly around Hong Jun's jeans, from below his knees to about halfway down his combat boots. 'It'll have to do,' he said, 'but if your feet go numb, tell me immediately. Okay?'

The four of them set off from the cave, Old Bao leading the way, then Hong Jun, Gu Chunshan, and Big Liu taking up the rear, and they climbed along the path up the hillside. Gu told Hong, 'We'll split up into two groups soon.'

'Yup,' said Old Bao, adding for Hong Jun's benefit, 'When you're tracking animals you can't all huddle together. They're damn cunning you know. If they hear us moving, they'll vanish. We have to work them so if they bolt from one group, they'll be heading straight for the other.'

Taking charge, Gu Chunshan said, 'Dr Hong, you and Old Bao take the left side, Big Liu and I will head to the right. Keep a distance of a hundred and eighty metres, and keep your aim forward, Dr Hong, if you please, no shooting to the side.'

'Okay,' said Old Bao. 'Let's all meet up again at that outcrop over there. We'll see who gets lucky, eh?' He tapped Hong Jun's shoulder and pointed forward. Off we go, thought Hong, taking a deep breath to calm his nerves. Gu Chunshan and Big Liu set off in a perpendicular direction.

Hong Jun unslung his shotgun, cracked it open and slid a shell into each barrel. He closed the gun, checked the safety catches, placed his thumb over them and nestled the gun barrel downwards in the crook of his arm, angled away from Old Bao ahead of him. They walked a little way towards the left and after a while headed off the path into the woods. The snow was deeper, up to his knees in places, so he felt like he was wading. Old Bao examined the snow for any deep drifts as he led the way uphill, crouching as he went, carrying the gun in two hands, eyes scanning the ground in front of him. Old Bao signalled to him to stop. Hong Jun straightened up, and looked round to see where the others were, how the others were carrying their guns. But he saw no one.

It was a poplar wood, and the straight, black trunks towered above him, like poles. Occasionally he caught sight of a silver birch, bent to one side by the wind. There were lots of low bushes and shrubs among the trees. Reaching the crest, he crossed a short stretch of open ground and entered a grove of small oak trees, stopping every now and again to check his direction. He thought he heard a far-off gunshot, but couldn't be sure. There must be wildlife here somewhere, though he had yet to glimpse, let alone see, a single animal. Remembering Old Bao's advice, he squatted and began to examine the snow around him for signs of animal tracks. As he concentrated, what was a blank shroud revealed crossings in all directions cut through the grove; some were obviously made by birds, while others were unclear. Crouching low, he moved forward, still keeping his eyes to the ground.

A flapping sound startled him and, looking up, he saw a pheasant with variegated markings and long tail feathers flying up from the bushes in front of him. He raised his gun and took aim, but the bird was gone. A shot rang out to his right. At least he'd flushed something out for someone else. He felt despondent. He needed to stay alert. He scrutinised the bushes up ahead. Now and again a gunshot echoed across the mountainside. He wanted to shoot something, even a sparrow, but even if he hit a feathered quarry there'd be nothing left. Big Liu had said the shells were loaded with buck shot for roe deer, not bird shot.

Two hours had passed and he was approaching the meeting point, when he saw Old Bao again, gun angled down in his right hand, a pheasant hanging from his belt. Hong Jun walked over and stroked its long feathers, admiringly. He was sure it was his pheasant, but said nothing.

'Eh? Empty handed?' said Old Bao, chiding him and patting the pheasant. 'Nice bird. Lucky for me it was flushed out and flew straight in front of my gun. Pop.'

'I didn't even fire a shot.'

'A lot of hunting is teamwork, brother.' Old Bao's eyes told Hong Jun the pheasant was indeed his. 'And there's a knack to tracking animals. Not something you can just learn in a few hours. Come with me.'

Hong Jun followed, noticing that while Old Bao walked very fast, his footsteps were light and he stopped every few paces to inspect the snow, glance around him and gauge the wind direction. He waved Hong Jun forward as they worked their way quietly downhill and against the wind.

Hong Jun tried to step quietly, glancing all around as he went, dropping about a dozen or so metres behind him. Old Bao stopped and raised his gun. Hong Jun followed the direction of its barrel and caught sight of what looked like a deer behind a clump of bushes at about twenty-five metres away. It must have sensed they were there, because it turned, but it had only got in a couple of graceful paces, readying to leap, when Old Bao's gun boomed and the animal crumpled headlong into the snow. It happened so fast, Hong Jun hadn't even raised his gun. The deer twitched a little in the snow, which was turning red around its head, and then lay still. Old Bao straightened up slowly, called up Hong Jun and they set off down the slope.

Hong Jun gave a little cheer of excitement and began bounding down the hill. When he was about ten metres from the deer, he couldn't resist raising his gun and loosing off a shot at the motionless beast. He missed; the shot peppering a nearby tree. 'What the hell are you doing?' Old Bao yelled, but realising how excited Hong Jun was on his first hunt, smiled and let it rest. The deer lay peacefully on the ground, its head resting on a maroon pillow. The scorched tear in its skull revealed a perfect headshot. As he looked at the lifeless creature, Hong Jun's joy and excitement suddenly evaporated. How cruel people can be, he thought.

Old Bao killed for food and, taking a rope from his pack, skilfully tied the feet together, strapped the carcass onto a makeshift sled. Handing Hong Jun a piece of rope, they began dragging it up the hill. They hadn't gone very far when Old Bao stopped and turned. 'Look, a monkey's head.'

Hong Jun half expected to see some sort of snow primate, but looking to where Old Bao was pointing, at the fork of a big tree, he saw something the size of an apple with yellowish-black wrinkled skin.

'A monkey's head mushroom – they're quite special, real nourishing.' As he said this, Old Bao started clambering up into the tree. He plucked the mushroom and handed it to Hong Jun, adding, 'A real local delicacy. There should be another one over there, too.' Old Bao walked across to the trees opposite, inspecting each one carefully, and on a tree about fifteen metres away found another monkey's head and picked it.

Big Liu's voice boomed. And they continued up the hill, dragging the deer behind them.

CHAPTER FIFTEEN

AS CHANGEABLE AS the face of a child, the weather in the Xing'an Mountains was unpredictable. By the afternoon, the boundless clear blue sky of the morning had been replaced by a sea of dark clouds, and the north wind howled madly.

A goshawk circled a couple of times, dived sharply, skimmed over the woods on the mountainside and plunged into a clearing, trying for one last kill. It reappeared, clutching something in its talons, wheeling steeply, and vanished into a cleft in the rock face.

Gu Chunshan and the others made their way down from the mountain top, taking it in turns to drag the deer. Old Bao had a brace of pheasants over his shoulder, plus the one at his belt. Hong Jun was excited, even if he hadn't shot anything. His feet were aching and his legs were a bit shaky.

Black Bear Cave faced south and was sheltered from the wind. The forest near the cave mouth afforded an effective windbreak. Once inside, Hong Jun and Gu Chunshan were sent to fetch Old Bao's straw mattress and leather sleeping bag from his den. Old Bao and Big Liu built a good-sized fire, surrounded by heavy rocks, inside the entrance to the cave, and once they got up a good mound of hot glowing embers, Old Bao produced an iron wok that fit snugly into a hot corner and soon a delicious cooking smell filled the cave. Stewed pheasant with monkey's head mushrooms bubbled in the wok while a haunch of venison roasted on a spit, dripping hissing fat. To the four tired and hungry men, it was a lavish feast. Big Liu pulled out a bottle of *baijiu* and they all sat around the fire and ate. Hong Jun felt a sense of camaraderie he had not experienced before. He was a hunter among hunters.

*

With food and drink in their bellies, they became a lot livelier and more talkative. Holding up a piece of monkey's head mushroom, Hong Jun, who was getting used to the fiery *baijiu*, asked Old Bao, 'When you found the first mushroom, how did you know there'd be another one nearby?'

Old Bao wiped the venison grease from his beard with the back of his hand. 'Monkey's head mushrooms are like couples. Find one, and its mate won't be too far away. I dunno if it just makes it easier for them to procreate, but the Mountain God looks after life. And it's hard to live on this mountain, so it helps where it can.'

Big Liu asked, seriously, 'You believe in the Mountain God?'

'How could I not? The Mountain God's damn powerful.' He turned to Hong Jun, 'There's a grand old tree stump in the middle of the forest. There's a saying round here that that tree stump is the Mountain God's seat, and no one else can sit on it.' Old Bao paused for a moment. Three shining faces around the fire were watching him intently. 'I once knew a man who didn't believe in curses. He came up here to chop trees and insisted on sitting on that stump, Mountain God be damned. The same day he was crushed to death by a Hanging Devil.'

'What's a "Hanging Devil"?' asked Hong Jun.

'A big branch that's caught up in higher trees,' said Old Bao. 'When you bring down a tree, a lot of the forked branches high up get caught by the trees around it and they just hang there, swaying. Or a rotten branch falls off and gets snagged by others around it. You never know when they're going to fall, but they do, even on a completely still day. Standing there thinking what a lovely day it is to be on the mountain and then a tree branch skewers you through the head and out here that sort of traumatic head injury and brain damage means it's lights out. We mountain people call them "Hanging Devils". I've heard others call them "Widow Makers".'

'You see, Dr Hong?' Gu Chunshan said. 'Up here in the mountains there are lots of local customs. If you come here hunting often, you'll learn a lot.'

'This isn't a custom,' said Old Bao. Gu's oversimplification clearly annoyed him, and he wasn't afraid of his position. 'It's about the spirit of things. The mountains are living and lots of things up here have spirits and I'm not talking about ghosts,' he said for Big Liu's benefit. 'That is what nature is, a living collective of spirits. You should take it seriously. Mr Gu? Have you heard the story they tell about this cave?'

'Yes, I have, Old Bao,' Gu Chunshan said, rather curtly, before changing the subject. 'Now listen, Old Bao, it's the Spring Festival soon. How about you come and stay with us in town for a few days?'

'No thanks!' he replied. 'Mountain folk can't be away from the mountains.'

'As you say, mountain man,' said Gu Chunshan, his words meant affectionately, and looking at his watch, said to the others, 'It's getting late, we really ought to be on our way or our dear friend Old Bao will frighten us to death with his stories.'

Everyone got to their feet. Old Bao turned to Gu Chunshan. 'You take the deer and the pheasants with you,' he said.

'Of course we couldn't!' he replied. 'You shot the deer, and one of the pheasants is yours too!'

'If you respect me, please take them. I have more than enough,' said Old Bao.

Seeing that he was serious, Gu Chunshan had no choice but to agree. Carrying the pheasants with them and pulling the deer along behind, they left the cave and went down to the jeep. They lashed the deer across the bonnet, which fortunately, Big Liu could see over.

The sky was starting to darken, and the wind was very strong. After saying goodbye to Old Bao, the others climbed into the jeep. Big Liu turned the key, and pumped the accelerator. The starter motor turned and turned for several nervous moments before the engine caught. Big Liu let it warm up while they rearranged the gear in the jeep to make more room in the back. With the jeep idling smoothly, they slowly set off along the track.

Hong Jun couldn't remember when he had last felt so invigorated and turned to Gu Chunshan with some questions about the case. Gu's eyes were shut and, soon enough, his own eyelids started to get heavy, so he closed them too.

He was drifting into sleep when he suddenly heard a series of explosions coming from the exhaust pipe and the jeep slowed to a standstill. Big Liu cursed, pumped the accelerator and was rewarded with a succession of loud oily bangs, and the engine died. Big Liu turned on the ignition but the engine wouldn't turn over. The petrol gauge read empty. 'This can't be right,' Big Liu said, and got out of the jeep. Hong Jun joined him on the snow, staring at the jeep. They were in the middle of the open pasture and the wind was biting. Big Liu went to the rear of the jeep, opened the petrol tank and tried to see inside with a flashlight. He jounced the jeep on its suspension, ear to the side, but heard nothing. 'The petrol tank's empty,' Big Liu told Hong Jun. 'I filled it myself before we left and it should still be more than half full.' He crawled under the jeep with the flashlight. Hong Jun heard a muffled curse. 'Of all the bloody . . . ' he muttered as he slid himself out from under the vehicle. 'We've lost the drainage cap from under the petrol tank.' Hong Jun had no idea what he was talking about.

'You sometimes need to drain the fuel tank to clean it, mostly because they water down the petrol too much. Cheap bastards sell what they save on the "grey market". Water sinks to the bottom of the tank and you have to drain it off. But if the cap isn't screwed back on tightly, it falls off after a few bumps. This model of jeep is notorious for that happening. I didn't bring any spare fuel since we were only going out for the day. C'mon, let's see if we can find that useless cap.' They walked back a few kilometres, following discoloured patches of snow before Hong Jun's flashlight picked up a glint of metal. The missing cap.

They trudged back to the jeep. Gu Chunshan had slept through it all, but when Big Liu woke him to explain the situation, his temper exploded and he cursed Big Liu for all he was worth. 'I checked the jeep before we left. How could I know the drainage cap was going to fall off?' he grumbled. 'Where we've been today, we're lucky the whole jeep didn't fall to pieces.'

Hong Jun was surprised at Gu Chunshan's volatile temper. 'Let's try to think of a solution.'

'It's cold and dark and we're in the middle of the mountains with a jeep that won't go because it's run out of petrol,' screamed Gu Chunshan. 'What solution would you suggest, Doctor!?'

Big Liu said, quietly, 'Let's go back to Black Bear Cave.'

Gu Chunshan's anger had subsided a little. 'Does anyone remember seeing a place that might have some petrol? A farm house?'

'There ought to be some farms nearby,' said Big Liu, 'but I don't remember seeing any and I wouldn't go wandering off in the dark.'

'Why don't we go back and ask Old Bao?' asked Hong Jun. 'He knows his way around. If he can't think of anywhere, at least he's got a cave and a fire and we won't freeze to death in the middle of nowhere.'

Logic won out and they headed back to the cave, following, losing and finding the jeep tracks all the way. Big Liu remembered the turn-off and they found Old Bao sitting beside the fire, drinking the *baijiu* they'd left him. 'Hello, again. Didn't you just leave?'

'Dammit,' said Gu Chunshan, irritably. 'The jeep's run out of petrol.'

'Hmm . . . not good. I've got plenty of wild boar oil here. It burns. Would that be any use to you?' said Old Bao, lurching to his feet to fetch it.

Gu Chunshan burst into peals of near-hysterical laughter. Big Liu closed a huge hand over Old Bao's equally huge shoulder. 'Petrol. We need petrol. Not cooking oil.'

'Ah, I see,' said Old Bao. 'Sorry, I'm not an expert on all those machines. Come on, take a seat and get warm. So what are we going to do about that then?'

'Are there any farms or villages nearby where we could borrow petrol?' asked Gu Chunshan, who was already in front of the fire.

Old Bao thought for a moment. 'There are villages, of course,' he said. 'There's one about a dozen kilometres to the west, but I don't think they even have a tractor, and there's a farm to the south, that's pretty well off. It has lots of machinery and trucks, but I reckon it's got to be a good fifteen kilometres by road.'

After talking it over for a while, they decided it would be safer to try for the farm to the south. But who should go? Old Bao was content by the fire and nominated Hong Jun and Big Liu. But Big Liu insisted Old Bao go with him, because Hong Jun would just get lost in the dark and freeze to death. Old Bao agreed and said he'd go instead. He told Big Liu to bring his gun and they left Hong Jun and Gu Chunshan alone in Black Bear Cave.

The fire was comforting and Hong Jun stared into the flames, feeding in firewood he had begun setting out to dry around the rock circle and choosing each piece with care. It kept him from looking into the blackness beyond the cave mouth. The mountain forests seemed alive to him, a great black bear, watching malevolently. The north wind swept through the trees with a strange high-pitched whistling sound that made the hair on the back of his neck stand on end. Hong Jun was a rational man, a man of logic. He knew there was nothing to fear, but, in the absence of daylight, Black Bear Cave took on an even more forbidding, frightening atmosphere.

Gu Chunshan drafted Hong Jun to help build another fire deeper in the cave so they were less exposed. They laid out the straw mattress and the sleeping bag beside it, and both sat down. Neither had anything to say, so they just sat and listened to the sounds of the mountain.

'We're both tired,' said Gu Chunshan, 'and should get some sleep. But we need to keep the fire going. How about you have a sleep first, and I'll wake you up in an hour's time. We take turns and we should get through the night.'

Hong Jun argued that, being younger with more stamina, he ought to be the one to take responsibility. 'I'm not tired, you sleep first, and I'll call you in a little while if I get sleepy. How about that?'

'All right,' said Gu Chunshan. 'I think the alcohol's starting to get to me. I'll just doze for a bit, and you can wake me up in an hour.' He looked at his watch. 'It's six-forty now.' As he spoke, he climbed into the leather sleeping bag, and was soon snoring loudly. If there were ghosts in the caves, thought Hong Jun, they'd be awake soon enough.

The bonfire at the entrance to the cave gradually died. Hong Jun had no desire to leave his warm, bright little world, so he just watched until it was swallowed up by the dark shadows of the mountainside opposite. A gust of wind rolled down from the mountain top and swept across the ashes, sending little red sparks leaping into the air like so many sprites, flitting in and out of the trees. Hong Jun felt his head growing heavy as a wave of weariness took hold of his body. He tried to stay awake, but he knew he was drifting off, his right hand mechanically continuing to throw stick after stick of wood onto the fire.

*

A noise woke Hong Jun with a start. He wasn't sure how much time had passed, but the fire in front of him was now down to glowing embers. He must have been out for a while. His ears took priority and all he registered was the cave's silence, then Gu Chunshan's snoring, and beyond that the steady wind outside. He threw more wood on the fire, but not all of it was dry, and the fire hissed at him until the wood took. The flames leapt up with a crackling sound and the light flickered around the cavern. Hong Jun looked at his watch. Ten past eight. He would be fine now, for a while, so he let Gu Chunshan sleep.

His ears caught it again, a faint snatch at first, and then it grew in volume. A strange howling from inside the cave, he was sure from behind him. He turned, but all he could see was his own vast shadow cast by the fire multiplied on the rocky roof and walls of the cave. He felt for the briefest moment surrounded by spectres, which he knew was irrational. Hong Jun, doctor of law, widely published and respected, was frightened by his own shadow. Still, he shifted to one side so the light of the fire could reach deeper into the cave. The sound came at him again. The wind, he decided, blowing through a fissure that opened out somewhere deeper in the cave. Except, it wasn't a wind sound, more like sobbing, a woman's sobbing. The imagination has a whole deck of tricks to play, Hong Jun considered, and turned back to the fire to feed it more fuel, arranging the damp wood around the pit so it would dry when he needed it.

It was the sound of sobbing. There was no mistaking it. 'Wake up Mr Gu, quick, wake up,' he shouted. 'Wake up!'

Gu Chunshan opened his eyes, reluctantly. 'What? What is it?'

'Listen,' he said. 'That sound?'

They both looked back into the cave, listening carefully, but the sound had disappeared. 'There's nothing there,' said Gu Chunshan with a laugh, though not happy about being woken with such a fright. 'Dr Hong, surely you're not afraid on your first night in the mountains, are you?'

Hong Jun didn't answer. He felt embarrassed, but he was still listening. Gu Chunshan crawled out of the sleeping bag, stretched his stiff limbs and sat beside Hong Jun on the straw mat. He added some dry wood to the fire and listened to the crackle, and heard the same low, long-drawn-out howling echoing from somewhere deep inside the cave. 'You hear that?' said Hong Jun. Gu Chunshan had heard. The sound continued, in fits and bursts, getting closer. They heard a rustling noise and looked at each other. It sounded like something crawling towards them. Gu Chunshan grabbed his shotgun and cranked a shell into the chamber. Hong Jun picked his gun up too, but his hands were shaking and he kept dropping the shells as he tried to load it.

'Get a hold of yourself, Dr Hong,' hissed Gu as he swept his gun aimlessly at the darkness. The howling stopped. So did the rustling. The silence frightened Hong Jun more, as if the danger was now close by, waiting. He caught a glimpse of movement and his head snapped to the entrance of the left cave. He held his breath.

A female figure with long, wildly flowing hair, in a long black gown appeared before them. She moved softly, almost as if she were floating. In the glow of the fire, Hong Jun caught sight of a pale face and two blood-red eyes. She let out an anguished scream and rushed towards them. She raised her hand up in a wide arc and an intense light filled Hong Jun's vision. He screamed . . .

Wood crackling in the fire, the wind blowing outside and the faint sound of wolves howling up in the hills could be heard. He must have passed out, he thought. Gu Chunshan was lying on the mat, not in the sleeping bag, and he wasn't snoring. Hong Jun called his name a few times. He found the bottle of *baijiu*, and poured the last few drops into Gu's mouth which seemed to revive him. His eyes opened. They were filled with terror and he appeared to be in shock. Hong Jun heard the tread of feet outside the cave and pointed his gun at the opening. 'Who's there?' he shouted, trying to sound braver than he was.

'It's me, Big Liu.'

Hong Jun's knees gave out at the sight of the driver and he crumpled beside the fire. 'Hong Jun, what's the matter?' Big Liu rushed to his side. Hong Jun tried to explain what had just happened. 'Go slowly, Dr Hong.' When he had finished, Big Liu looked at Gu Chunshan, not sure whether this was some camp prank, and though Gu Chunshan appeared more or less normal again, he couldn't speak, simply nodding that what Hong Jun had said was true. Now there was a look of fear in Big Liu's eyes.

Hong Jun slowly collected his wits and tried to think clearly. He scanned the area around the fire and picked up what looked like a small birch wood branch from the straw mat on the ground. It was a rolled up strip of birch bark. Gu Chunshan and Big Liu were watching him. In the light of the fire, he saw that there were some drawings scrawled on the surface of the bark, the outlines of which were not clear. Big Liu looked too, but shook his head.

It was a thin piece of bark, and had been so neatly cut that it looked like a piece of writing paper. The drawings on it were unusual, and looked rather like a prehistoric cave painting. Turning it this way and that, they managed to work out that it was divided into two parts. At the bottom left was what appeared to be a male reproductive organ, while the top right seemed to show a wicker basket hanging on a tree, and in the middle there was a red circle. Everything else was drawn in black.

Gu's voice returned, but it was a hoarse, uncertain whisper. He said he'd take the drawings and have them studied. Hong Jun handed him the roll of bark. Gu Chunshan picked up the now empty *baijiu* bottle, held it hopefully to the light of the fire, and cast it aside in frustration. 'Big Liu, how come you're back? Did you find some petrol? Where's Old Bao?'

Big Liu hung his head. 'The wind's so strong out there, the snow's blowing everywhere. I couldn't see my hand in front of my eyes. Before I knew it, I'd got separated from Old Bao. I didn't dare just wander around in that weather. I always have my compass with me, my dad gave it to me, I could keep going south, but didn't know exactly where the farm was and could easily walk straight past it, so I thought I should come back. Once I reached the treeline, it was easy. Old Bao must be still out there somewhere. He's probably gone to the farm alone.'

They huddled around the fire, guns beside them, silent, listening.

*

At two o'clock in the morning, the cranking of engine gears and the roar of a truck motor broke the mountain silence. Hong Jun and Big Liu ran to the entrance of the cave and saw Old Bao below, climbing down from the cab of a Liberation truck.

Old Bao went straight to the fire and pulled off his gloves. It was a moment before he sensed the fear around him and saw Gu Chunshan's face. 'Hey Mr Gu, what's the matter?' he said. 'You look terrible. Are you ill?'

Big Liu declared, 'Old Bao, you live at the mouth of the underworld. Party Secretary Gu and Dr Hong are lucky to be alive.'

'Don't be so dramatic,' Hong Jun said and explained they had heard the black bear howling, a woman with straggly hair came out of the cave and attacked them . . . or did something. He wasn't sure what happened.

'What? You really saw a woman?'

'Yes,' Hong Jun said, 'dressed all in black.'

'Well, I've heard that bear growling plenty of times, and it was a bit frightening the first couple of times. But it's just the wind. I've never seen a woman up here. Are you sure?' Old Bao thought for a moment. 'Maybe it was the Black Bear God.' He appeared to be addressing Big

Liu, and Hong Jun wondered if he was just trying to scare him. He was about to say as much when Gu Chunshan made it clear that he wanted to leave immediately.

They gathered up their gear and, at the entrance to the cave, Hong Jun asked Old Bao, 'Don't you want to come back to town with us?'

Old Bao thanked him, but declined.

'I know what I saw, Old Bao. Are you sure you will be safe here, alone?'

At this, Old Bao laughed loudly. 'What do mountain people have to be afraid of? As they say, "If you've never done anything to be ashamed of, you don't need to be scared of ghosts knocking on your door." Ain't that right, Dr Hong?'

They all said goodbye to Old Bao and set off down the hill. When they got to the truck, the driver told them to get in and they drove out to where they'd left the jeep. The wind had dropped off and Gu Chunshan immediately got into the back of the jeep and covered himself with coats and blankets. Hong Jun stood with Big Liu and the truck driver beside the jeep. The driver looked at the deer slung across the bonnet. 'Nice kill,' he said.

'Sorry for giving you so much trouble in the middle of the night like this,' Hong Jun said.

'No trouble at all,' replied the driver. 'I was on the night shift anyway. I'd just finished my late-night snack when Old Bao appeared and told us that County Party Secretary Gu's jeep had broken down on Black Bear Mountain. I asked what the problem was, and he said the jeep had run out of petrol. The petrol cap had fallen off, or something. Made no sense to me, so I said he must be talking about the oil in the sump,' he went on. 'He said he needed petrol, not oil, and once he said it was a jeep, I knew right off what happened. So I just grabbed this can of petrol and we set off. But I keep some oil in the truck, just in case, so we're covered either way. Let me see what the problem is.'

The driver had Big Liu lift the petrol out of the truck and Hong Jun showed him the dislodged cap. 'Yup, just as I thought.' He crawled around under the jeep, then stuck his head out the side and called out to Big Liu to start refilling the tank.

'How far is it from here to your farm?' Hong Jun asked.

'About ten to twelve kilometres by road, if you can call it a road . . . maybe twenty minutes' drive?'

'And how long on foot?'

'Well,' said the driver, 'it depends which way you go. If you take the road, it's a long way round. But if you take the path through the mountains, that's much shorter, so probably not much more than an hour at a brisk pace. On a night like this, I'd say two hours.'

He shouted to Big Liu to try the engine. After sputtering a few times, it began to roar. Hong Jun thanked the truck driver for his help. Gu Chunshan was already snoring away in the back. Hong Jun decided to ride up front with Big Liu.

Hong Jun admired how Big Liu expertly handled the driving conditions. On the way back to Binbei, Hong Jun closed his eyes and thought about what had happened. The black-clad woman, dishevelled hair flying. The image of another dishevelled woman flashed into his mind, and that monotone snatch of song, sung in a hoarse voice, seemed to fill his ears:

> . . . *My brother's a big official, hah.*

CHAPTER SIXTEEN

HONG JUN, ACHING all over, wanted to take a bath but he knew he'd fall asleep. He had a shower in his Songjiang Hotel room and went to bed. It was past lunchtime when he woke, cursing at having lost so much of the day. He phoned Chu Weihua and told him about his trip to Harbin to visit Li Qingshan the previous week. He explained that he wanted to go back to the city, and expressed the hope that Chu would join him.

If Li Qingshan would agree to give an affidavit to the court declaring that he had not seen the shadowy figure enter the Zheng family's courtyard, and that he couldn't positively identify it was Zheng Jianguo, it would be a big boost to their case to overturn the verdict. Chu Weihua agreed, but said it would have to wait until the next day, as he was busy with another case.

There was no point staying another day in Binbei, so Hong Jun decided to head back to Harbin and arranged to meet Chu at the exit of Harbin Station the morning after next, telling him he wanted to have a chance to talk more to Li Qingshan first.

Of course there was another reason, too, for spending some time in Harbin – the hope of catching up with his classmate, Xiao Xue. He had such fond memories of their university days together and maybe it would have gone further, if he hadn't been so fixated on his dreams for a better China and she hadn't had to return to Harbin to look after her father in her brother's absence. They had talked many times about what they wanted to do with their lives but circumstances beyond their control meant that they couldn't be together.

He always considered her his first love, and his true love, and she probably would always be so. It was comforting to know what love felt like, but Hong Jun was getting maudlin, which he disliked in other people, a reason why he didn't drink a lot.

He got to the station an hour before the scheduled train, bought his ticket and went into the overly warm waiting room to think. The air reeked of cigarette smoke and sweat, but it was still preferable to the icy fresh air outside. All the benches were full. Some people were sleeping, some chatting, some reading books or newspapers. On the right-hand side of the room, a few young people were sitting on the floor playing poker, their laughter and curses adding to the general hubbub. Near them, beside the radiator in the corner, a woman with dishevelled hair lay curled up, her head resting on a bundle wrapped up in a ragged piece of patterned cloth. She appeared to be asleep. The way she was dressed reminded Hong Jun of the crazy woman in the Binbei Restaurant, and he found his attention divided between the card players and the woman.

Perhaps because of the shouting, perhaps because of a dream, the woman sat bolt upright, glaring angrily around her, but being uncertain of the offender, lowered her head back down, eyes open, staring blankly.

It was the same crazy woman, Hong Jun realised, the third time he'd encountered her, and she was looking at him. He looked away, pretending to watch the card players, but she kept her eyes fixed on him. Her eyes appeared dull, empty. Drug addicts got that look after a while, so did soldiers too long in the field. She looked straight at him, as though her attention were drawn to something beyond this world. He shook his head to clear his mind of such uneasy thoughts.

The barriers opened to let passengers for the Harbin train onto the platform, and Hong Jun followed the crowds in his leisurely manner through the gate, letting most of the waiting passengers rush to wait again on the platform for the train that had yet to show its southbound lights at the final distant curve before the station.

Hong Jun watched the locomotive draw level with the platform and listened to the screech of its final braking sequence as the carriages jolted to a standstill. Attendants flung open the doors, around which knots of people immediately formed, those trying to get off pushing against those trying to get on. He found his carriage and waited. He was the last to board, by which time the seats were all occupied and the corridor crowded with standing people and baggage rolls. A few had slipped under the seats and made a makeshift bed. The air in the carriage was barely breathable. Several signs in the carriage said PLEASE DON'T SMOKE, but dozens of cigarettes were already going like chimney stacks.

Hong Jun wedged himself in a corner next to the car door. It was colder, but quiet and he could breathe. He put down his case, leaned back against the door and gazed out of the window.

The train slowly set off and gradually picked up speed, its wheels making a rhythmic bumping sound as they passed over the rails. The lights of Binbei disappeared behind the hills. Outside the window it was pitch dark, with only the occasional patch of brightness flashing by. In the distance, somewhere between the earth and the sky, a few tiny pricks of light soared and sparkled, but whether they were stars or electric lights was hard to say.

Hong Jun felt the train was moving too slowly, much like his case, twisting and turning, negotiating obstacles, but it would reach its destination, of that he was sure. But when? And would it be what he expected? He needed more evidence. He stopped thinking about what was missing, and focused on what he knew. Li Qingshan was an important key, if only because he, maybe mistakenly, put Zheng Jianguo near the scene. What had he said when they met?

'The dead are dead, and the living have to go on living. Innocent people get punished all the time, and the guilty will never be punished. You are too young to know how these things work. If they couldn't get to the bottom of it at the time, what's the point talking about it now?'

Hong Jun broke it down, phrase by phrase. 'The dead are dead' was Li Hongmei. Those who 'have to go on living' might be Li Qingshan himself, but it could also apply to someone else. 'Innocent people get punished all the time' was Zheng Jianguo. But the phrase 'the guilty will never be punished' seemed to mean someone, or indeed others, would get away with their crime. Perhaps they weren't punished because they had run away and couldn't be found? Or they were too powerful and above prosecution, or there wasn't the evidence to prove their guilt?

Li Qingshan had said, 'If they couldn't get to the bottom of it at the time, what's the point talking about it now?' Could it be that he had other important information that he had yet to divulge, which might go a long way to explaining his comment to his daughter Hongxing that he 'still suspected someone else'?

Hong Jun was anxious to get to Harbin, but there were still many hours to go. He sat on his suitcase and shut his eyes. His mind wandered to Black Bear Cave, another puzzle. Was it related to his case, and if so, how? What did the bark drawings mean? Were the petty political machinations of Binbei somehow linked to his ten-year-old case? These questions circled in and out of his mind, in time with the click-clack of the rails as the train clattered over the tracks.

Hong Jun's neck was stiff and his shoulders hurt from the little sleep he got in his corner of the train carriage. He tried to stretch out the soreness as the carriage emptied onto the platform. At five o'clock in the morning, in the winter dark, he was cold, tired and hungry. He cleaned himself up in a rank-smelling station men's room, scrubbing his face with ice-cold water and running wet fingers through his hair. A line of taxis idled outside the station. He told the driver to take him to the primary school in Daowai District. The driver looked at him briefly in the rear view mirror, grunted, and turned up the radio, which screeched traditional opera. He liked Chinese opera, but there was a time and place for everything, and five in the morning sliding back and forth on the back seat of a speeding taxi was not one of them.

The roads were relatively empty and the driver paid little heed to speed limits or stop signs. The sun was just rising as the taxi pulled up at the school. Hong Jun saw Li Qingshan was already up, standing on the small patch of grass in front of the main school building, doing stretching exercises. Hong Jun hailed him politely, 'Good morning, Mr Li.'

Li continued stretching. 'Morning. And you are . . . ?' He squinted and stopped his exercise. 'Oh, Lawyer Hong. What brings you back here again, and at such an early hour?' He sounded nervous.

'I came to see you, sir.' Hong Jun put his suitcase down. 'Is that some special type of exercise discipline you're practising there?' he asked, casually.

Li Qingshan was puzzled by the suitcase. 'Oh, nothing in particular. I always get up early, and start off the day with a bit of stretching. Don't want to get too old too soon, eh?' He glanced at the suitcase again. 'You on your way back to Beijing, Lawyer Hong?'

'Not yet, still looking for answers. That's why I've come to see you again. Shall we chat out here so you can continue your regimen?'

Li Qingshan, noticing people were now out the street, said reluctantly, 'Let's go inside and talk.'

Hong Jun followed him to the janitor's office. They sat and he came straight to the point. 'Mr Li, after we talked last time, I thought very carefully about what you said, and I think you don't really believe it was Zheng Jianguo who killed your daughter.'

'Ah,' Li sighed, 'it happened ten years ago. Why do you keep going on about it? None of this can bring Hongmei back to life!'

'No, Hongmei can't come back to life,' said Hong Jun. 'What about Zheng Jianguo? You were neighbours for all those years, you watched him grow up . . . and I think you know he's not the killer. He's been locked up in prison for ten years. Can you imagine how hard that must be for him? He gets beaten, you know, and one of the prisoners broke his leg. Think about what that's like.'

'I never said he was the killer,' Li said quietly.

'Didn't you suspect someone else before?' Hong Jun asked.

'But that was only a suspicion.'

'Well, who did you suspect?' he said, gently but quickly.

Li Qingshan was silent. He sat at the table, looking out of the window, frowning, deep in thought. 'Lawyer Hong? Last time you told me the court had reopened the case, right?'

'That's right.'

'Well could you get the court to send someone for me to talk to? It's not that I don't trust you, but you're working on behalf of Zheng Jianguo.'

'A judge, Chu Weihua, has been assigned to this case and will be in Harbin tomorrow morning. If we come back together, will that be all right?'

'Yes, okay. If the government's retrying the case, I'll talk . . . if they want me to. After all, I'm only telling them my suspicions, right? Even if I'm wrong, they can't say I'm trying to frame anyone, can they?'

'You will be perfectly safe,' said Hong Jun. 'You are only doing your duty as a citizen to provide the court with all the information you know.' He got up. 'Thank you, Mr Li. I'll see you again tomorrow morning.'

'Try to come early, before the classes start. We don't want other people seeing you and starting to gossip.'

As he walked out of the school gate, Hong Jun felt he'd made significant progress. With Chu Weihua's assistance, Li Qingshan would tell them everything he knew. He waited a few minutes for an empty taxi, waved it down and headed to the hotel.

CHAPTER SEVENTEEN

HONG JUN MET Chu Weihua in front of the railway station. 'We're in a bit of a hurry, my friend. I'll explain on the way,' he said, bundling his former student into a taxi. Chu Weihua was excited and eager to find out who this new suspect might be. But when they got to the school gate, Li Qingshan wasn't outside doing his exercises. Hong Jun went to the main door. It wasn't locked, so they went inside. In the entrance hall, he saw that the light was on in the window of the janitor's office and rounded the corner to the office door and knocked. There was no sound from inside. Hong Jun knocked again and called loudly, 'Mr Li? Mr Li?'

His voice echoed in the silent corridor. 'Mr Li? It's Lawyer Hong and Judge Chu.' No response.

'Maybe he's doing his rounds?' Chu suggested.

'No,' said Hong Jun. 'He knows we're coming.'

They walked around to the outside of the building, until they reached the window of the inner room of the janitor's office. The curtains were closed, but there was a narrow gap between them. 'Give me a boost,' Hong Jun asked Chu Weihua, who linked his hands to make a step for Hong to look through the gap. A pair of legs . . . but sitting or lying down, he couldn't tell. He banged on the window. The legs didn't move. 'This doesn't look good,' he said to Chu Weihua.

He was sure that something was wrong. It was too early for staff to be on the premises and breaking in wasn't an option. 'Stay here while I call the police. There's a phone out on the street, near the entrance.'

'What about calling your friend at Harbin PSB?' Chu suggested.

'Good thinking.' Hong Jun had Xiao Xue's numbers in his pocket. What use is *guanxi* if you don't use it, he rationalised. He figured she would not have left for work yet. He called her home number. She answered, and skipping over the abruptness of his phone call, there being no time for pleasantries, he explained what had happened and that he needed her help.

'Is he dead?' she asked.

'I'm pretty sure he is.'

'Okay. Stay put. I'll be there as soon as I can, but the detectives should get there first, and a forensics team. See what you can do to secure the area.'

He trotted back to Chu Weihua. 'On their way,' he said. They waited in the entrance hall, until sirens echoed down the street and soon a patrol car screeched to a halt outside the schoolhouse. Three officers jumped out. They were followed by another unmarked car. A tall woman in a uniform glinting with silver insignia got out, and briskly marshalled the three detectives as they approached the school entrance. As elegant as ever, Hong Jun thought, his heart suddenly beating a little faster.

Seeing him, she walked straight over and shook his hand warmly, a faintly amused smile playing on her lips. Hong Jun smiled and, with a slightly embarrassed shrug, thanked her for coming. It felt bizarre to see her for the first time after all these years in such circumstances. After introducing her to Chu Weihua as Deputy Division Chief Xiao Xue of Harbin Municipal PSB, he explained to the police officers what had happened, though he held back his own suspicions.

The three detectives checked the doors and windows, and confirmed they were all locked from the inside. One of them fetched a crowbar to pop the lock on the office door when school staff began to arrive for work and one of the administration staff called out to them not to break it. She would fetch a spare key. They waited, but though the key turned, the door didn't open. 'He must have a latch on the inside. If he's tripped that, you won't get the door open, and if you try to break it down you'll just hurt your shoulder. These doors are good and solid,' the staff member said, matter-of-factly.

'There's a window on the outside,' suggested Hong Jun. 'But you need a boost to reach it.' Two detectives trotted outside and, a minute or so later, one of them had jemmied the lock and opened the door from the inside. Hong Jun noted the detectives were now wearing latex gloves and tried not to touch anything in the room.

By now, a group of students was gathering outside the door, no doubt excited by seeing police cars outside. Chief Xiao identified herself to the head teacher and said the corridor was being closed. Was there another way the students could get to their classrooms? The head teacher said she understood and opened the side door of the building, instructing staff to take the pupils up to their classrooms by a side staircase. Calm returned to the investigation scene. The gloved forensics team had arrived and went into the room first.

Xiao Xue asked Hong Jun to come into the room to act as a witness to the discovery of any pertinent evidence. One of the detectives was busy taking photographs of the outer room. They waited in the doorway. Hong Jun glanced around him. The room looked just as it had the day before.

The forensic pathologist emerged from the inner room. 'Liver temperature suggests at least four to five hours dead. I can only guess at time of death . . . any time between eight last night and four this morning? Sorry, Chief, I can't do better than that right now. I'll know more later. You want to take a look before we move him?'

Hong Jun followed Xiao Xue into the inner room, but he was in no rush to see. He let his eyes wander, starting with a large wardrobe, a single bed beside the wall, covers and a quilt piled up on it, and next to it a square table and two chairs. On the table was an empty beer bottle and another half full, two unfinished plates of food, a bowl and a pair of chopsticks. In the corner of the room was a radiator. It was not on. One end of a rope, thick as a finger, was tied to the water pipe on the wall feeding the radiator, leading to a noose around Li Qingshan's neck. His body was more or less in a sitting position, his back resting against the radiator pipe, buttocks a dozen or so centimetres off the floor, legs stretched straight out in front of him, heels on the ground. To his right, on the floor in the middle of the room, was an upturned four-legged stool. The smashed remains of a beer glass lay on the ground between the stool and the table.

Hong Jun's instincts said murder, staged to look like suicide. If Li Qingshan had wanted to hang himself, the school had plenty of better places that would give him a good drop. But he had only a superficial knowledge of forensic medicine, and asked the pathologist, 'Would you say that given the position of the body, this isn't very likely to be suicide?'

The pathologist seemed rather unimpressed. 'Why shouldn't it be?' he said. 'It's perfectly plausible. This is what's known as atypical asphyxiation. People can hang themselves from a doorknob, you know. In this room, it'd be the best way to do it, and asphyxiation would fit, but, let me do the autopsy first. I don't like to speculate.'

Hong Jun didn't say any more, partly because he wasn't going to get any facts, and partly, too, because he was feeling guilty. If Li Qingshan had killed himself, had Hong Jun driven him to it by insisting he relive Hongmei's death? Had his attempts to rescue an innocent man from prison driven another innocent man to his death? But Li Qingshan was not distressed by their conversation and seemed to welcome the chance to unburden himself of whatever secret he had carried for ten years. Had someone overheard them talking, or become aware of what Li Qingshan was about to say? Who had he spoken to about Li?

Xiao Xue was standing next to him, directing the photographer and the fingerprint team. As the flash went off again and again from different angles, Hong Jun noticed something glinting on the corpse's trouser leg. He waited until the photographer paused to reload his camera and squatted next to the leg. 'Chief?' he called over his shoulder. It was a piece of broken glass. She had one of the forensics guys pick it out with tweezers and mark it for closer examination, but first got the photographer to take a picture of it where it lay.

'All done?' asked the pathologist. The Chief looked around. Everyone nodded. She gave him the all clear. The body was released from the noose and carried to the bed for a cursory external examination. Everything was done in a very orderly fashion, choreographed almost. Each officer moved in a precise fashion, making sure not to disturb anything until its precise location had been photographed and documented. All were on their best behaviour. Hong Jun wasn't sure whether to be impressed by the PSB's investigative discipline or irritated that they only seemed to be taking this apparent suicide seriously because a prominent Beijing lawyer and a judge, albeit of relatively junior rank, were involved, and a deputy division chief was supervising.

Hong Jun gazed at the broken glass on the floor, its shards and fragments now circled in chalk. He left the room and looked at the main door, scrutinising the spring deadlock. Donning a pair of latex gloves, he pulled the little button down to drop the latch, so that the lock would no longer turn. Then he lifted it up again. The lock turned normally. He opened and shut the door a couple of times. Although the button seemed fairly loose, it couldn't have dropped into place by accident. It was a keyhole lock. He got close to the door and crouched down, put his eye to the keyhole under the door handle, and looked through. He scanned the floor inside the door, working slowly, focusing on small sections at a time.

Xiao Xue watched Hong Jun's slightly curious behaviour for a minute or so. She knew Hong Jun, had followed his rise to prominence and had read all his books and articles, finding in them invaluable tips for her own study of criminology. 'Have you found something?'

'Oh, Xiao . . . Chief, I didn't realise you were there. Forgive me if I'm interfering, but I think I may have found proof that Li was murdered.'

'Show me,' she said.

He walked them away from the door, ran his hands through his hair, which felt strange until he realised he had gloves on, and put them in his pocket. 'Just now, when I heard what the pathologist said, I felt that, given the position of the body, we had to accept the possibility that it was suicide. But, not wanting to second-guess the autopsy, I thought it all a little suspicious. The explanation was plausible, certainly, and maybe that's the conclusion we should draw. But . . .'

The three detectives had stopped what they were doing, and were now also listening to his assessment. '. . . for one thing, if Li Qingshan was going to commit suicide, would he bother latching the door? Was he scared that someone would break in and stop him killing himself? Why make it so hard to get in? For someone who's about to kill himself, this seems a little excessive. On its own, it doesn't prove anything, but there's the smashed glass on the floor in the other room. If we assume Li Qingshan did commit suicide, it seems to me that his final sequence of actions ought to be that he stands by the table, drains the alcohol in his glass, throws the glass on the floor, goes to the corner, sits on the stool and puts his head in the noose. He knocks over the stool, hangs himself on the rope and dies. Right?' He looked around at the others. There was no sign of disagreement.

'The crucial thing is the broken glass. From the position of the fragments, the glass broke close to the side of the table. Did Li Qingshan drop the glass, or someone else? A fragment of the beer glass was found on the trouser leg of the deceased. And . . .' indicating the turned over stool, '. . . another two small pieces of broken glass are inside the base of this stool.' He looked up. 'So the glass wasn't dropped until after the stool tipped over and Li Qingshan was suspended by the noose above the floor.' The detectives were muttering to each other, but he had the Chief's full attention.

'Someone else was in the room after Li Qingshan died. Someone who dropped the glass on the floor. Why would this person have been there, at that time? To make sure Li Qingshan was really dead? Or arrange the scene so that murder looked like suicide? The autopsy will give us the precise cause of death, and we simply work back from that.'

Xiao Xue was impressed and made appropriate remarks for her subordinates. 'No matter how perfect the crime, a killer always makes a mistake.'

'The killer probably felt extremely pleased with the way he'd arranged the suicide scene, and couldn't restrain himself from adding a *pièce de résistance*. He thought he was "finishing the eyes on a painting of a dragon" when in fact he was "painting legs on a snake".' The detectives smiled at his apposite use of these old sayings. 'Either way, though,' Hong Jun added, 'I'd say the murderer has studied or knows police work, making sure all the clues were arranged in such a way that they would lead to a simple conclusion.'

One of the detectives spoke. 'But if the killer was in the room when Li Qingshan was hanged, how did he leave the scene? All the doors and windows were locked from the inside.'

Hong Jun led them to the main door of the outer room. Chu Weihua, who'd been leaning against the window, came forward to join them. Hong Jun pointed at the lock. 'Do you see . . . there's a thin, irregular, dark line running down from this latch button on the top lock, past the handle, to the keyhole below . . . ?

'Now here's what I think the killer did. Before he left the room, he tied a thin piece of string or cotton to the button on this upper lock, and threaded it through the keyhole to the outside. Then he went out and closed the door behind him, so the lock sprang shut. He tugged on the string, which pulled the button down and dropped the latch. A neat trick was setting light to the end of the string from the outside, probably already dipped in oil so it burned quickly, leaving only these faint traces and no string. I expect that if you take off the lower lock and open it up, you'll find traces of ash.'

One of the detectives whistled at the cleverness of it and Xiao Xue shook her head in admiration. She, too, had sensed something was wrong with the scene when Hong Jun first pointed out the shard of glass on the dead man's trousers, and the glass in the upturned stool, and though she would probably have worked it out back in the crime room, she was amazed at how quickly he had deduced murder. 'Thank you, Lawyer Hong. Thank you very much for your help.'

Hong Jun smiled. 'It may well turn out that we're all helping each other.'

Hong Jun accompanied Xiao Xue in her car to the PSB headquarters to await the preliminary lab results. Chu Weihua excused himself, saying he hadn't got any sleep on the train the night before, and needed a couple of hours rest. Hong Jun told him to use his hotel room, handed him the key and said they'd meet up for lunch.

The car journey was a little awkward after their rushed reunion; they mostly discussed Hong Jun's case and how it had reached out to embrace Harbin. He even told her about his eventful hunting expedition and Old Bao before broaching the subject of the time that had passed since their last contact. After deferring her studies and returning home, Xiao Xue had managed to get into the PSB, despite the emotional strain of her family's circumstances. Hong Jun was impressed: she hadn't had it easy.

Xiao Xue used her clout to rush the coroner's report, which confirmed that Li Qingshan had died of asphyxiation. There were no injuries on his body. He had a large quantity of alcohol in his stomach, and his blood showed an alcohol level equivalent to the consumption of a moderate amount of beer. Toxicology showed no traces of drugs or anaesthetics. From the contents of his stomach, mostly beer but also partly digested meat, time of death was fixed at between nine and eleven the previous evening. Forensic tests of the keyhole revealed a small amount of ash, from a cotton fibre, common sewing thread of undetermined colour. The detective reported that a canvass of all the staff revealed that two teachers working late had passed the janitor's office at ten past nine as they were leaving, and recalled seeing Li Qingshan sitting alone in his room drinking.

Hong Jun felt sure Li Qingshan's death had something to do with his investigation into Li Hongmei's murder. He voiced his thoughts to Chief Xiao and said he wanted to pursue other lines of inquiry, but would keep her informed and they'd talk later in the day. 'I think Chu Weihua has had more than enough beauty sleep,' he said. She offered him a driver to take him to the hotel, but he said he'd be fine.

He woke Chu when he let himself into his room. The junior judge had undressed and put on a bathrobe from the bathroom, found the room's extra blankets and had curled up on the bed cover. His jacket and trousers were neatly arranged over the back of a chair. He gazed blankly at Hong Jun.

'Hey Weihua, what's up?' he asked, laughing. 'Brain not awake yet? C'mon, get up.'

Chu Weihua shook his head a few times, took a gulp from a bottle of water by the bed, and said, 'I just really needed to close my eyes. If I don't get enough sleep I go into a kind of trance.'

'Well my friend, here's a question to test how alert you are. Do you think Li Qingshan's death is linked to the case of Li Hongmei?'

'Not necessarily,' said Weihua. 'I know you dislike coincidences, but maybe that's all it was. Robbery or something unrelated to our case. The old guy might have had a stash of cash. There was no money, or valuables, in his rooms, except a few yuan in his pocket, but maybe that's all he had. I don't know. There've been a lot of cases of robberies of old people leading to murder over the past few years,' he added.

'But if you kill someone during a robbery, why go to so much trouble to make it look like suicide?'

'True . . . But if you think there's a link, then what would be the point? Killing him to stop him talking? Why didn't they do it before now? They've had ten years to silence him if indeed he had something that incriminated another person. And how did they know we would be coming that morning? I didn't know until you got me at the station.'

'Maybe they didn't think it was necessary to silence him before,' said Hong Jun. He thought for a moment. 'Who did you tell that we were coming to see Li Qingshan?'

'I told Chief Judge Han that I'd be interviewing him,' he replied. 'I have to brief the court chief on all my trips.'

'Anyone else?'

'No, no one else . . . mind you, in Binbei, news gets around pretty damn fast,' said Chu Weihua as he took his clothes into the bathroom to dress. His voice echoed as he continued speaking. 'You know, everyone's talking about your hunting trip and what you saw in Black Bear Cave. Some people say there is a creature, half-bear, half-woman, that drinks men's semen. All kinds of rubbish. Curiously, it's all aimed at Gu Chunshan. He's become a laughing stock: the Party Secretary who's terrified of ghosts. I'd say he's got no chance of making Secretary of the Municipal Political and Legal Commission now.'

'Why would what happened at the cave make a difference?'

'At an important time like this, a small incident can easily get blown up into something big.'

'You're talking about political power struggles in the bureaucracy?' Hong Jun thought for a moment. 'That's something I really don't understand much about. I'll let you keep thinking about it. By the way, do you know the old legend of Black Bear Cave?'

'I've heard the stories, yes,' said Weihua, knotting his tie in front of the big mirror in the room.

'Can you tell it to me?' he asked.

'Well, I heard it when I was kid,' replied Weihua. 'It's some kind of ghost story they tell to stop us being too adventurous in exploring dangerous areas. But, to be honest, I don't believe in that sort of thing and don't remember too many of the details . . .'

'A ghost story?' said Hong Jun. He fell deep into thought.

Hong Jun checked in with Deputy Division Chief Xiao, but there was nothing new to report in the PSB's investigation, which she had classified as a homicide. A crime team, under her supervision, had been formed. He told her they were going back to Binbei that evening, and they promised to keep each other posted on any new developments.

The train ride was uncomfortable and they were glad to be headed towards the platform exit when Hong Jun saw a familiar looking figure descend from the carriage ahead of them. He nudged Chu Weihua. 'Isn't that Chief Wu?' What was Wu Hongfei, head of the Binbei PSB detective squad, doing on the train from Harbin? Chu Weihua ran forward a couple of paces. 'Chief Wu . . .'

Wu Hongfei stopped in his tracks, trying to locate the source of the voice, and saw Chu Weihua and Hong Jun.

'Hey Chief Wu, where are you coming back from?' asked Chu Weihua.

Wu Hongfei greeted Hong Jun. 'From Harbin,' he said.

'Really?' said Chu as they walked out of the station together. 'We've just come back from Harbin too. How come we didn't see you last night when we boarded the train?'

'Where did you get on?' Wu asked.

'At Harbin Station.'

'Ah, no wonder . . . I got on at Three Trees Station, on the other side of town. That's where the train starts and not many people board there, so it's easy to get a seat.'

'Did you go to Harbin for a case, Chief Wu?' asked Hong Jun.

Wu Hongfei looked at him for a moment. 'Yes. There's a case we're working on and we needed the help of Harbin PSB. Secretary Gu knows Section Chief Li . . . '

'Did Secretary Gu go to Harbin too?' Hong Jun asked.

'Yup,' Wu nodded.

'But he didn't come back with you,' Chu Weihua said.

'He came back yesterday. I had something else to do, so I stayed an extra day.'

'I took the train to Harbin on Monday evening. When did you set off?' asked Hong Jun, fishing for information but content with nibbles at the bait.

'Tuesday morning,' Wu said.

Still chatting, they passed through the ticket barrier. Wu had a marked car waiting for him. He didn't offer them a lift.

CHAPTER EIGHTEEN

HONG JUN LAY on the bed in his hotel room, staring at the ceiling. He didn't smoke and wasn't one for pacing back and forth. When he needed to think, he liked to lie down, try to remain as still as possible and empty his mind so it was a blank canvas on which he could put together the pieces of the puzzle, shuffling them around until they started to fall into place. Sometimes he found he started working from the centre, sometimes he started at the edges and worked inward. Slowly, sections became clearer, though pieces might still be missing.

The room grew darker, but he was too busy thinking to bother with the lights. For some reason, Black Bear Cave kept turning up next to Binbei Farm. Did he have two puzzles, or were they all part of the same?

He could have remained lost in thought for hours when a loud banging on the door broke his concentration. He fumbled for the light switch on the bedside console and went to the door. Zheng Jianzhong stood grinning at him from the hallway.

'Surprised, Dr Hong?' said Zheng with a laugh, chest thrust forward, and began pushing himself into the room.

'Director Zheng . . . oh, please come in. What a surprise,' said Hong Jun, as he yielded to the man's imposing presence. 'Sit, please.'

'So what d'ya think? Binbei sure has come a long way.'

'It's a nice town. I like it,' he replied, and sat on the chair by the desk.

'How's the food?'

'Very good. I like northeastern food.'

'And how's the case going? Making any progress?'

Zheng Jianzhong was the client, he was paying Hong Jun to do a job and he was not a man for extended pleasantries and courtesies. Time was money. Hong Jun was never one to take offence, so long as none was intended.

'Not so good,' he said.

'Why? What's the matter?' Zheng took a packet of cigarettes from his coat pocket, hesitated and put the pack down on the table.

'They can't find the fruit knife, so no DNA. And Li Qingshan's dead.'

'What? Li Qingshan's dead?' Zheng Jianzhong took a cigarette from the pack. 'Sorry, Lawyer Hong, but that is really bad news.' Hong waved off his concern and threw him a box of matches from the ashtray on the desk. 'He wasn't so old, was he? He could only have been about sixty, maybe a little bit more.'

'He was murdered.'

'Murdered? Someone killed him? He was in Harbin, wasn't he?' Zheng took a long drag on his cigarette and held the smoke in for a while before exhaling. Hong Jun stifled the urge to cough.

'Yes,' said Hong Jun. 'He was killed the night before he was going to tell me and a judge from the court a key piece of information concerning the case. Someone didn't want him to talk.'

'I wonder what he was going to say? That sounds pretty stupid, but I thought Li Qingshan had to have been mistaken to say it was my brother he saw. And I know he had his own suspicions. And just as he's about to say who he thought the real criminal was . . . he's killed. Dr Hong, do you think you have enough to keep moving forward? You mentioned last time the killer ought to be right-handed, and my brother can only use his left hand. Isn't that proof enough he wasn't the killer?'

'No . . . it's only circumstantial, not hard evidence. We can prove he didn't peel the apple, but we need to find who killed Hongmei to get your brother released.'

'Hang on, Dr Hong. That wasn't our deal.' Zheng Jianguo was staring hard at him and angrily stubbed out his cigarette before immediately lighting another. 'I hired you to get my brother's verdict overturned, not to help them crack the case. You clear about that? My brother didn't do it. That's all you have to prove. I'm not paying you to do the PSB's job for them. Okay?'

'Of course, Mr Zheng, of course.' The cigarette smoke was becoming annoying, but he wanted Zheng to stay calm, and if the smoking helped, he could live with it. 'But please understand that the only path left to us to prove your brother's innocence is to find out the identity of the killer. I'm not the one with the power to revoke his sentence. It's up to the court to decide. The case is open again, but the court needs answers, not my deductions, if it's going to reverse its own verdict. We need to prove they got the wrong man, and produce the right one. That's just the way it is.'

'Ah, I see now, so it's the court . . . ' Zheng Jianzhong smiled awkwardly. 'I suppose I got a bit carried away just now, please don't hold it against me, Dr Hong. I'm just worried about my brother. And this case must be very difficult for you, what with them losing the knife and Li getting murdered. It's like every door you manage to open, there's nothing but a brick wall. Something's not right about all this. Do you think we should try to talk to someone else? I know PSB Chief Hao pretty well, shall I have a word with him? You gotta use your connections if you want to get anything done these days.'

'Chief Hao's your friend? Whether you talk to him is up to you, but . . . '

'Okay, okay. I got it. I'll leave everything up to you. Whatever you think is right. I wouldn't let a carpenter lay plumbing. You're the expert.'

'I'm just doing what a lawyer ought to do.' Hong Jun was glad they had achieved a conciliatory understanding. The room had windows that opened, and he opened one, letting in an icy draft of cold air, but it also let out the smoke. Zheng looked puzzled and failed to make the connection, rummaging in the mini-bar for a drink. He held up two cans of foreign beer and Hong Jun nodded. He cracked the cans and put one on the desk and sat back on the sofa with his, taking a long swill.

'Director Zheng, tell me, what brings you back to Binbei?'

'Oh, nothing special. I need to find a couple of associates for a job I'm doing, people I can trust. They're not so easy to find these days.'

'When did you get here?'

'This morning.'

'How did you know I was here? Did Miss Song tell you?' Hong Jun asked.

'Song Jia?' said Zheng. 'Your little "assistant"? I must say, Dr Hong, you're a lucky man when it comes to the girls. Those chicks we were drinking with at the leisure club the other day were amazed you weren't interested in them. But I have to say, if I had an assistant as cute as Miss Song to keep me company, I wouldn't go to the club to find girls either.' Zheng chuckled, but seeing that Hong Jun wasn't smiling, he swallowed his laughter. 'Please, excuse me. I'm just a simple man. No, it wasn't Miss Song who told me. When I got here, I figured you'd be staying at the Songjiang Hotel so I went to the reception to ask. I must be learning something about deduction hanging around you, eh? They told me you were a "special" guest, and when I showed them the letter you had me sign, they gave me your room number. What do you reckon? I'm not so dumb, am I?'

'Far from it,' said Hong Jun, thinking he'd have to have a word with the manager about handing out room numbers.

'Hah,' Zheng grinned. 'You got plans for tonight, then?'

'No, nothing.'

'Why don't we go for a bite to eat, and after we can go to a night-club I know not far from here. And don't worry. It's not one of those dodgy dancehalls . . . dead high-class. If you ask me it's as good as any nightclub in Beijing.'

Hong Jun really did like dancing. At university, he'd taken part in ballroom dancing competitions. His feet started to itch. 'So you like dancing, too?' he asked Zheng.

'Well, when you're in business, you often have to take clients out to nightclubs,' he replied. 'So I've picked up a few moves, but I'm no good really.'

'Are people into dancing up here? I would have thought—'

'Of course,' said Zheng. 'Haven't you heard the saying that a talent for ballroom dancing is a basic requirement when it comes to selecting young government officials? You have to be able to "go to meetings big and small, and never feel sleepy, drink your fill of alcohol and never feel woozy, dance the three- and four-step both equally smoothly, sleep with young girls and your own wife, and never ever worry." Hah. I'm always talking nonsense, aren't I?'

Zheng stood and looked at his watch. 'It's nearly six. Let's meet in the lobby in half an hour? Okay?'

'Sure,' said Hong Jun, trying to sound enthusiastic, but not at all confident about the direction the night would take. He didn't really like Zheng Jianzhong, but had to admit there was something intriguing about him. He was one of those people comfortable in their own skin, and if you had a problem with him, it was your problem, not his.

And, after all, Hong Jun did want to explore more of Binbei.

He arrived at the lobby, but there was no sign of Zheng Jianzhong. He took the time to chat with the manager, and mentioned that he would appreciate a call to his room before *anyone* was sent up, no matter how important they might be. The manager was embarrassed and said he would ensure it never happened again. Hong Jun looked at his watch, 6.45 p.m., and was about to walk to the entrance when Zheng Jianzhong bellowed down to him from the staircase. A young woman was at his side. She was wearing a fox fur coat and red leather boots. She was slim, a little taller than Zheng, but that was helped by the heels of her boots. Only her slightly protruding upper front teeth stopped him thinking of her as exceptionally beautiful. Her lipstick matched the colour of her boots, and she could have used a lighter touch with the eye makeup.

'Dr Hong,' said Zheng Jianzhong as they came up to him, 'this is Zhu Li, the director of our public relations department.' He turned to his companion. 'This is Dr Hong, the famous lawyer I told you about, who is helping in my brother's case.'

She offered her hand, which he shook lightly. 'Hello, Miss Zhu.'

'Lawyer Hong,' said Zhu Li with a smile. 'Director Zheng said you are very talented, but said nothing about being so stylish and handsome.'

'You are too kind, Miss Zhu.'

'We're all friends,' said Zheng, 'no need to be so formal. Tonight we're going to have some fun. So let's go. First, a place to fill our stomachs. I can't dance if I'm hungry.'

'I know just the place,' Hong Jun said.

'Lead on, my friend,' said Zheng.

When they arrived at Binbei Restaurant, there was no sign of Li Hongxing. Hong Jun assumed she'd already gone to Harbin after hearing of her father's death. He felt guilty again. If he hadn't come here to work on this case, if he hadn't gone to see Li Qingshan . . . he steeled himself. He may have set the wheels in motion, but his was not the hand that controlled the levers.

Zheng Jianzhong congratulated Hong Jun on his choice of restaurant and asked for a private room upstairs. They got comfortable. Hong Jun suggested a couple of dishes he had particularly liked, one of them the venison stew, and Zheng added his own, as well as asking for beer. 'Keep it coming,' he ordered. They began to drink and chat. Zhu Li was quick to engage Hong Jun in conversation.

'So, Dr Hong,' she said, 'I hear you lived in America for a long time. It must be an amazing place?'

'Not everything about it is so great,' he replied. Sometimes he thought the Americans far superior to China in the propaganda department.

Miss Zhu shifted herself into a more comfortable position, keeping enough space between them so they could continue their conversation. 'Everyone says it's such a rich place, and it's so easy to make money there. If you work there for a couple of years you can buy a car and live in a nice house. And Americans are *really* free, too. I mean, they can do whatever they want, absolutely anything, and no one takes the least bit of notice.'

'If you have money you're free,' he said. 'But there are a lot of poor people in America too, and if you don't have money, you're more or less a slave to the system, or you're just abandoned and left to fend for yourself on the streets.'

Zhu Li looked shocked, but Zheng Jianzhong put his arm around her shoulders. 'Dr Hong is exactly right. But if you have money, you can drive a car and live in a nice house, wherever you are. Even here in China. America is not some paradise, you know.'

'Oh, give me a break. You guys are just kidding me,' Zhu Li pouted peevishly. Then, in the tone of a TV presenter, she recited, '"We citizens of China live in paradise, while the toiling masses of the United States remain in an abyss of hellish misery." Don't give me that! If America's hell, why are so many Chinese people trying to get there? Answer me that.'

Hong Jun liked Zhu Li's feisty nature, and how she clung to her dreams.

'Don't keep pouting like that,' said Zheng. 'Did I say all America was hell?'

'I'm not pouting,' she said, 'it's just that stupid talk always makes me angry. It's just so pathetic.'

'You love to exaggerate, don't you?' said Zheng, not wanting to surrender meekly. 'What do you mean?'

Zhu Li had been hoping to give a good account of herself in front of Hong Jun, and was quite annoyed with Zheng Jianzhong for mocking her. 'Don't try to play word games with me,' she said. 'You know what I mean.'

Hong Jun found he was warming to Zhu Li. She was tough. 'We are in the presence of an honourable guest, so perhaps we can try to be a little sophisticated?'

'Wait till we get on the dance floor later, then I'll show you sophisticated,' said Zheng Jianzhong.

'Knowing the way you dance, you'll owe me a new pair of boots before the night's out,' she shot back.

Hong Jun rarely laughed out loud, but watching the pair of them go at it like husband and wife set him off. They stared at him, neither welcoming his intrusion, which caused Hong Jun to feel acutely embarrassed. 'So are you from Beijing, Miss Zhu?' he asked.

'No, I'm from Harbin.'

'Really, I would not have thought so from you accent.'

'Ah, Dr Hong, be careful. That's just what she wants to hear,' said Zheng Jianzhong. 'She wants everyone to think she's like some high-flyer from Beijing. She thinks we're just a bunch of hicks! To her, Harbin's a big village!'

'Oh, you're so irritating!' she said, glaring angrily at him.

'You lived in Beijing, no?'

'I like art. Everyone says I'm naturally artistic.' Zhu Li seemed quite enchanted at the thought.

'Yeah, even your farts sound like music,' interjected Zheng Jianzhong.

She tried to reach his foot with a slam of her boot heel, but missed.

'Ignore him, please, Dr Hong,' she told him, 'He is so vulgar. Well, you see, it's not so easy to find a job in the art world at the moment, so I went to Beijing to see my uncle.'

'And your uncle is . . . ?' Hong Jun wondered aloud.

Zheng half covered his mouth and whispered loudly, 'Deputy Managing Director Zhu, from my company, the one who came with us to the leisure centre.'

The image of Yellow Teeth came back to Hong Jun. He quickly changed the subject. 'So you're not going back to Beijing?' he asked Zhu Li.

'No, I'm going back. We were just in Harbin for three days and will only be here for a short time.'

Hong Jun wanted more details when Zheng Jianzhong said, 'It's already nearly eight! Had enough to eat, Dr Hong? It's time to get on that dance floor.' He handed Zhu Li the bill, said, 'Take care of this,' and headed downstairs. Hong Jun wanted to ask another question, but his time was up and he followed his client down the stairs.

Hong Jun followed Zhu Li and Zheng Jianzhong into the nightclub. It was small. The dance floor in the middle of the room had barely enough room for a dozen couples. Little tables, round and square, with chairs around them, spread out from the dance floor. Zheng chose a table and they sat.

Under the soft lights on the dance floor, seven or eight couples were slowly doing the four-step to the tune *Looking for the Spring Breeze*. Some of them were dancing elegantly and skilfully, some awkwardly. When the tune finished, there was a smattering of applause and several couples returned to their tables. Hong Jun noticed four couples remained at the edge of the floor, correcting wrong steps and practising turns. He recalled how hard it was to synchronise his movements with those of another so that both dancers found the same moves to match the music. Dancing looks easy, but it takes a lot of work to make it look that way and Hong Jun silently cheered them on.

A waltz began and Zheng Jianzhong told Zhu Li to dance with Hong Jun. She got to her feet obediently. Hong Jun held out his arm and led her to the dance floor. They quickly found each other's rhythm and they were moving smoothly and were soon both smiling. The other dancers gave them more space, curious about the skill of this tall, slim couple. Hong Jun caught glimpses of happy faces watching them, but couldn't shake the feeling that someone was watching him from the shadows.

The next dance was a quickstep, and the dance floor quickly filled up with couples. Zheng Jianzhong found himself a partner too, and Hong Jun noticed that despite his stocky build, he was actually quite light on his feet and was a better dancer than he had let on. With more people dancing, and the faster tempo, the dance floor soon echoed with the sound of people's voices as they bumped into each other or vied for control of the centre of the floor.

The next tune was *Give Me a Rose*, and Hong Jun thought a tango a little too exotic for this county town. Only a few couples stayed on the floor, but after a little while they seemed to tire of the music, and by the middle of the tune Hong Jun and Zhu Li were the last on the floor. Hong Jun was dancing with great concentration, his body upright, trying to keep his movements elegant. Zhu Li was also dancing carefully, but had more fluidity and showed no effort, her expression poised and natural. Their steps were lithe and graceful, swift but tidy, their bodies swaying as they whirled round, showy but still precisely focused. Sometimes their moves drew slightly envious cheers from the onlookers.

When the song finished, two hostesses ran up and gave them each a flower. An amplified voice declared them the evening's star performers. An enthusiastic round of applause rose up from around the room, with a few strange shouts of rural dialect mixed in. They took their bow and went back to the table.

'Director Zheng's a really good dancer,' he said to Zhu Li, 'and you're not too bad either.'

'He's got nothing on you, Dr Hong,' she said.

Zheng Jianzhong decided to leave them to chat while he swooped on another pretty girl and asked her to dance. Hong Jun and Zhu Li kept their eyes on Zheng and the dance floor while conversing casually.

'Do you often go dancing?' he asked.

'Only with our clients,' she replied, 'who mostly don't know their left foot from their right. It's so boring.'

'I've heard that Harbin people are very good dancers,' Hong Jun added. 'Did you go dancing much while you were there this time?'

'We only had three days. I had to stay at home with my mum and dad, and Director Zheng was always with his friends, so we hardly had time to meet.'

'So you mean you didn't stay together?'

'What are you suggesting?' Zhu Li asked, assuming a stern expression.

Hong Jun realised he'd said the wrong thing, and added hastily, 'Oh, that's not what I had in mind. All I meant was you didn't stay in the same hotel, so you don't know where Director Zheng went each day, right?'

Zhu Li giggled. 'You're very funny, Dr Hong. Even if you did mean that, I don't care. I know what you men are like, when you meet a woman you can't have a conversation for long without getting on to that subject. I'm used to it.'

Hong Jun really felt a little embarrassed. 'Actually, what I really wanted to ask you was whether Director Zheng went to see any of his old friends from Binbei State Farm while you were in Harbin.'

'He did. Several, I think.'

'Did he go to see someone called Li Qingshan?'

'Li Qingshan?' she asked. 'I think he did mention the name, but I've no idea whether he met him.'

Hong Jun scanned the tables around them and noticed a pair of eyes that seemed to stare back at him from the shadows near the entrance. They broke contact and the figure vanished into the crowd.

It was after ten when they left the nightclub. Hong Jun felt vibrant and happy until the chill of the street outside hit him. He pulled his coat closer around him. There were no cars, no pedestrians, only patches of faint orange light cast by the street lamps. They walked back towards the hotel along an icy path others had cut through the snow. It was very narrow, so they had to walk in single file, Hong Jun leading the way, with Zhu Li behind him and Zheng Jianzhong at the back.

As they reached the mouth of a side alley, four men emerged from the shadows. 'Stop!' one of them shouted. Hong Jun heard one of the others say, 'That's him, boss, the tall one, in front.'

The first man pointed at Hong Jun. 'Remember me?' he said menacingly. As he spoke, the four of them moved towards Hong Jun. He recognised two of them as the louts from the restaurant, the ones Old Bao had decided to teach some manners.

'Oh, shit,' muttered Hong Jun, who retreated a few steps and backed into Zhu Li. Zheng Jianzhong stepped in front of him. 'Hey, Old Maozi, you got little punks working for you now?'

Catching sight of Zheng Jianzhong's face under the light of the street lamp, the leader of the gang quickly dropped his raised fist and took a step back. 'Oh, Big Brother Zheng, it's you,' he said, startled. 'I didn't know you were back in town.'

'What the hell do you think you're playing at?' Zheng stood stock-still, and Hong Jun could tell by the way he held his arms out from his body that he wasn't thinking of running. Hong Jun put an arm around Zhu Li, but she looked much more courageous than he did.

'Don't worry. No one messes with Zheng Jianzhong. This will be fun to watch if they try anything. Just stay still.'

'Oh, it's nothing,' Old Maozi said quickly. 'We were having a bit of fun in the Binbei Restaurant one day, and some big bloke beat the shit out of us. And then this guy,' he pointed at Hong Jun, 'gets involved and took his side. If he wants a fight, we'll give him one. Don't know why he's still hanging around. What's he got to do with you, Big Brother? If you wouldn't mind stepping aside, we can finish our business.'

'Do you guys know who this is?' said Zheng Jianzhong. 'This is the famous lawyer Dr Hong, from Beijing. He's come here to help me with something. If any of you so much as lay a finger on him, I'll break your arm. Is that clear? He works for me.'

'Oh well, if he's your friend, then that's different. Let's forget all about it, shall we, just a little misunderstanding, okay?' Old Maozi gave a little bow to Hong Jun.

He turned back to Zheng. 'Tell me, what brings you back here?'

Zheng Jianzhong ignored the question. 'I'm kinda glad we ran into each other. I want to talk to you about something, but not here. Come see me at the Songjiang Hotel at ten tomorrow. I'm in Room 206. Come alone. I may have a job for you.' He looked at the other three and said, 'Have fun, boys,' and led Hong Jun and Zhu Li back to the hotel, waving a hand, forcing the other four to step off the path and into dirty, knee-deep snow.

Hong Jun left them in the lobby, checked at the desk for messages and went to his room. He picked up the phone and had the operator place a call to Song Jia's number in Beijing, which answered after two rings.

'Hey, boss,' she said, 'where have you been the past couple of days? I've called you lots of times, but you were never there and I didn't think you'd want me to leave a pile of messages. But I was worried something might have happened to you.'

'It nearly did . . . ' he said.

'What do you mean?' she asked, sounding anxious.

'I'll tell you all about it when I get back to Beijing. Just having an adventure, but it hasn't finished yet. I won't be back for at least a few more days,' he replied. 'But I need to ask you, how did you find out Zheng Jianzhong's blood type?'

'Hah,' she said. 'Actually it was super easy. I went to see Zheng Jianzhong, and told him the money he'd given us had run out. It was just an excuse, but not too far from the truth . . . watch the expenses, okay?

'I never imagined that he'd quite happily hand over another twenty thousand. It's in the account. I hope that wasn't wrong but it seemed the least suspicious ploy, and I like to keep the bank happy. What I really wanted from him was one of his cigarette butts. I've read several forensics articles on isolating blood type from saliva on a cigarette. I gave the butt to a girlfriend at the municipal PSB lab to test, on the quiet. She owes me lots of favours. She slipped the test in with some others she was running and came back with a result right away.'

Hong Jun smiled to himself. He chatted with her about any bills that were outstanding and asked how the accounts looked before ending the call. He picked up the phone again and was about to dial the operator to place another long-distance number, but thought better of it and replaced the receiver.

He went down to the reception counter in the lobby, gave her his room number and asked to use the direct dial phone to make a long-distance call. She pointed to a soundproof booth, number three, and turned the meter on. He closed the door and dialled Xiao Xue's home number.

'Hong Jun! Where are you?'

'In Binbei, at the Songjiang Hotel.'

'Why are you calling so late?'

'There is something I need to ask you and it can't wait until tomorrow.'

'Okay. I'm listening. I'm afraid there's not been any real progress on the case from our end. Asking lots of questions but not getting many answers . . .'

'I have some leads that might help.'

'Really? What leads?'

'Two people were in Harbin over the past week. If you can find out what they did while they were there, it might answer a lot of questions, for you and for me.'

'Let me get a pen,' and Hong Jun gave her two names.

CHAPTER NINETEEN

EVERYONE IN BINBEI had heard the Black Bear Cave story within days and Party Secretary Gu Chunshan was furious. Someone was playing him for a fool, and he didn't like it. He ordered Wu Hongfei to use the PSB surveillance network to find Old Bao's lair in Binbei. Gu wanted answers. Most of all, he wanted a scapegoat to blame for his humiliation. Having a story about being terrified by ghosts hanging around his neck would haunt him forever. It was Old Bao's cave and he had to know what really happened and who had put him up to it.

Wu Hongfei might not be the sharpest tack in the box, but he knew how to appease others, and he knew if he didn't bring in Old Bao, Gu Chunshan would not be happy with him. In the southern corner of the town lay an area of decrepit old houses, mostly inhabited by migrant workers and itinerant traders, or those from surrounding villages needing a roof for a few days in Binbei. Old Bao had rented a small house from a retired worker at the power station. It was just a matter of lying in wait to catch him.

The landlord told him Old Bao had rented the house six months earlier. He'd said that he wanted to live there full-time, but he was hardly ever there. Old Bao was a smart guy, he said. He caught a lot of wild animals, which he mostly sold to the stallholders in the market. And he was reliable too, never late with the rent, even if it meant a special trip to pay. On festivals and holidays he'd even bring the landlord a delicious selection of game for the cooking pot.

Wu Hongfei asked him if Old Bao had any visitors and with whom he spent time when he was in town. The landlord said that, with the exception of the traders who lived there, he'd never seen Old Bao with anyone else. There were a couple of young guys who'd come a few times looking for him, but they seemed to be locals, probably thugs meaning to do Old Bao some harm. The one who did all the talking had eyes like a toad, and a pretty menacing manner. He told Wu Hongfei that he'd warned Old Bao about them. He didn't want to lose such a good tenant.

With the landlord's permission, Wu searched the house. Inside there was only an earthen *kang*, with a firewood stove for cooking and for heating. On the floor was a box of household utensils and hunting gear, clean and cared for. Wu Hongfei scoured the room carefully, paying particular attention to places where something could have been hidden. In a cleverly concealed slot carved into the side of a support beam, he found a clean plastic bag wrapped up in a length of cloth. Unravelling it on the *kang,* the package revealed a small bundle of blank brown envelopes. Each contained a neatly folded strip of birch bark, similarly drawn to the one Gu Chunshan had brought back from Black Bear Cave. Wu Hongfei counted them . . . nine . . . 'I'm taking this as evidence,' he told the landlord, who was surprised at the secret compartment and could only agree. He told Wu he would call him as soon as Old Bao returned. 'Don't warn him, or you'll be in big trouble,' Wu cautioned.

Wu Hongfei saw a head peeping round the corner. He found a dishevelled looking woman sitting on the ground behind the building. 'What are you doing here?'

'I'm looking for you!' she said in a hoarse voice.

'Why are you looking for me?'

'I want to be your mother,' said the woman.

Wu Hongfei was shocked by her comment, her blank expression, her state of neglect . . . she was filthy, dressed in rags and tattered blankets. She stank. No iron rice bowl for her, he caught himself thinking, but he had no time for charity. He spat in the snow. 'Get out of here or I'll arrest you for vagrancy.' As he left, he heard her singing.

. . . My brother's a big official, hah.

Wu Hongfei was sure Old Bao would return, but he didn't trust the landlord's promise and sent some officers, none of whom wanted to sit around in the cold waiting for someone who would probably never show, and they grumbled their discontent. He had to threaten to transfer them to 'the coldest town I can find' before they moved. 'The sooner you find him, the warmer you'll be.' The next morning, the PSB had Old Bao in the interrogation room.

Wu Hongfei sat across from the mysterious huntsman. 'For the record, what is your name?'

'Old Bao!' he replied.

'Your family name?'

'Bao.'

'Your given name?'

'Oh, you mean my first name? It's Qingfu, Bao Qingfu. But everyone calls me Old Bao.'

'Your age?'

'Forty-eight.'

'And where are you from?'

'I'm from the mountains.'

'I mean what is your family's registered address?'

Old Bao laughed. 'You think people from the mountains have a registered address?'

'All right then, where do you live?' said Wu Hongfei, raising his voice a little.

'I live wherever the wild animals are. If you really want me to give you the name of a place, then the Xing'an Mountain range is my home.'

Wu Hongfei contained his anger. With these people, he thought, questions rarely yielded answers, so he'd have to try a more roundabout approach or they'd be there all day and he still wouldn't know anything.

'Tell me what you did that night in Black Bear Cave with Deputy Party Secretary Gu, Lawyer Hong and driver Liu and don't pretend you don't remember, okay?'

'In Black Bear Cave?' said Old Bao. 'All I did was go hunting with them, and then later helped when they got into difficulties. I just did what I was meant to do.'

'I want details!' Wu insisted.

Old Bao told the whole story, of how the jeep had run out of petrol, and how he'd fought his way through a snowstorm to fetch the truck.

'So you're saying you're a model communist, putting the needs of others before your own? You expect me to believe that?'

'When you're out hunting in the mountains, anyone can get into difficulties. If people need help, you just do it. And maybe the next time, they'll help you or someone else. What goes around, comes around, isn't that what they say?'

'Such lofty ideals, eh?'

'Lovely ideas?' Old Bao tapped his ear, looking puzzled. 'Not so lovely if you ask me. This time I wish I hadn't bothered. If I hadn't gone to the farm for their petrol, I might have finally been able to see the Black Bear Spirit with my own eyes. I've spent so many nights in that cave. Mr Gu and that other fellow were only there half a night and they saw it. Talk about lucky.'

'So you admit that someone else lives in the cave?'

'Not someone, *something*, the Black Bear Spirit. Everyone knows the stories, but very few people ever see it.'

'A spirit? You expect me to believe that?' Wu Hongfei signalled to an officer standing by the door. He left and came back with a black robe, a mask and a long wig, which he placed on the table. Pointing at them, Wu said unhurriedly, 'We searched around the cave and found these. They look pretty real to me. The robe we found outside the cave, half buried in snow under a bush. The mask and wig we found hidden inside the lining of your sleeping bag. Why would a spirit do that, do you think?

'Oh yes, and then there's this bull's horn . . . ' Wu Hongfei had found it forced into a crevice near the cave opening, ' . . . though of course if you blow it in this room it won't sound as good as it did in Black Bear Cave. What do you think?

'If you put all of this on, won't we all see the "Black Bear Spirit"? What do you think? And it'll have white feet, just like Secretary Gu Chunshan says he saw in the cave.' He pointed at Old Bao's white felt boots. Hong Jun had given him that piece of information, but Wu didn't want to open the way for Old Bao to digress.

They glared at each other, like a playground game of who blinks first. Wu Hongfei never lost and could hold out for minute after minute, forever if the stakes were high enough, and they were very high now.

'Chief Wu,' said Old Bao, breaking first, 'you're too smart for me. Okay. I admit it. I really thought I'd made it so realistic it would keep you guessing for months. I never thought you'd see through it right away. I'm very impressed.'

Wu was caught wrong-footed by the 'confession'. It was too early in the interrogation. Old Bao was mocking him, and he didn't like it. He liked to see the guilt in their eyes before he slammed the book closed on them. 'What do you mean by that?'

'I've always loved playing tricks on people,' Old Bao said, calmly, evenly. 'After I heard the story of Black Bear Cave, I collected all this stuff, and thought I'd wait for a chance to try it out on someone, and see how it worked. Who better than Secretary Gu? That would be sure to get attention. The others were an added bonus. I'll tell you, Chief Wu, I always love a good riddle. In case you don't believe me, here's one for you: "From the front I look like a walnut shell, from the back like a pomegranate skin, like raindrops in the sand, or a piece of melon peel pecked by a chicken." Guess what it is? . . . Too hard? It's a person with a pockmarked face, of course.' And he burst into laughter.

Wu Hongfei was annoyed, and the pockmarks on his own face began to glow bright red. Old Bao was just trying to provoke him, but he dug deep for his iciest smile. 'It was just a joke, too, to loosen the drainage cap on the fuel tank so they ran out of petrol in a snowstorm?'

'Is that what happened? I didn't know . . . those jeeps really are crap, y'know.'

'And then there are these . . .' said Wu Hongfei, tossing the brown envelopes he'd found in Old Bao's house onto the table. 'All on pieces of silver birch bark. You did a great job with them. There are nine, not counting the one left in the cave. What do they mean?'

Old Bao said nothing.

'Don't play dumb with me. In the old days, I'd have you on a truck already, on your way to some godforsaken re-education camp where you'd have spent your time hacking at the frozen ground with a blunt pickaxe. You planned all of this very carefully, Old Bao. Come clean, tell the truth. If you're lucky, you might get a nice, comfy prison cell.'

No response.

'You sure had plenty to say a minute ago, didn't you? Don't try to spin me some ghost story. I've been a cop for a long time and I've dealt with the worst. No more bullshit. Give me the truth.'

Wu Hongfei got only more silence. Perhaps a softer touch, which had worked in the past?

'Of course, I'd say this probably wasn't your own idea. I'm sure someone else told you to do it. And in any case, it didn't do any real harm in the end. Everyone's safe. If you tell us who put you up to it, you'll be fine.'

Old Bao sat on his chair, head to one side, eyes narrowed, staring at the wall. From his expression, it looked like he could have sat there until Spring Festival.

Wu Hongfei gave a chilly laugh. 'I tell you, don't dream that things will be better for you if you say nothing. Even if you don't say a single word, I'll get to the bottom of this. And the harder you make it for me, the heavier the load of shit that's gonna land on you. Think about yourself. Think carefully. Do you ever want to see the mountains again?'

Old Bao had the patience of a hunter and had barely moved throughout the interrogation, and Wu Hongfei found his refusal to respond more annoying than the fact that he hadn't given him any useful information. Chief Wu beckoned the guard at the door and whispered in his ear. He left and returned with another officer. 'Be careful, nothing too obvious,' said Wu Hongfei as he closed the door behind him.

He went to see Chief Hao, told him the interrogation was going as expected, and got permission to make wider inquiries about Bao Qingfu with other departments in the region. They quickly circulated details, including his photograph and his apparent connections with the Orochen tribe, the distinctive markings of which were found on the long black robe.

'Go ahead . . . Do what needs to be done,' Chief Hao told him. 'Just get Secretary Gu some answers, and soon.'

CHAPTER TWENTY

NEWS OF OLD Bao's arrest reached Hong Jun in a telephone call from Chu Weihua. At the gatehouse of the Binbei PSB compound, the officer checked his credentials, slowly and carefully, explaining that Chief Hao was at a meeting of the district PSB, but confirmed Chief Wu Hongfei of the Criminal Investigation Unit was there. He made a call and then waved Hong Jun through. Wu Hongfei wasn't in his office, but he saw Big Liu in the corridor who led him to another door, pushed it open and announced, 'Chief Wu, someone to see you.'

'Oh, bring them in.'

It was a meeting room. Several rectangular tables had been pushed together in the middle of the room, and chairs arranged round the sides. Wu Hongfei was sitting at one end and seemed to be in the middle of a lecture to about twenty officers. He looked up and saw Hong Jun. 'Dr Hong!' he said. 'Is it urgent? I'll be done soon.'

'Not so urgent, Chief Wu, I can wait,' he said, backing out of the room.

'Dr Hong, please stay. I'm just giving a little pep talk. Nothing secret.'

Hong Jun accepted the offer, and found a chair near the door.

'As I was saying, these days we need to combine an emphasis on science and technology while continuing to promote the revolutionary spirit of not fearing suffering and not fearing death.

'I remember soon after I became a detective, it was the last years of the Cultural Revolution, and we were in the middle of a campaign to criticise "the three scientific obsessions". You should know what those were. That's right, the obsession with cameras, fingerprints and police dogs in our work. Imagine what that was like, trying to investigate a case. In those days, the masses were highly motivated. Though there were times when they were, perhaps, a little too motivated.'

Wu Hongfei lit a cigarette, exhaled, and continued talking. 'That was the past. Now when we're on a case, we need to focus on the scientific side and make use of technology. This is a time for modernising detective work. But we can't spend all our time in labs or at computers. We still need to be out there, talking to people, finding information. It's hard work, and a lot of the time you'll be chasing down false leads, but if you want to be a detective you have to be willing and able to suffer.'

Hong Jun smiled. They might call him 'Dopey Wu', but he knew how to talk.

'Okay. Enough from me. You're all good detectives. Get back to work.'

'Nice speech, Chief Wu,' Hong Jun said as the officers filed out.

'Nothing nice about it,' replied Wu Hongfei swiftly. 'With these kids nowadays, if you don't give them a wake-up call at regular intervals, they won't get anything done.' He tossed his cigarette butt into the ashtray.

'What can I do for you this morning, Dr Hong?'

'You have Old Bao in custody.'

'We do, indeed. You have good ears.' Wu lit up another cigarette, took a long drag, sucking the smoke deep into his lungs before blowing it out through his nostrils. Hong Jun thought about Miss Song's trick with the cigarette butt, and, fumbling in his pocket for his notebook, let his handkerchief drop unobtrusively to the floor.

'And have you interrogated him? Did he tell you what happened in the cave?'

'I interrogated him, yes, and he confessed everything.'

'What did he say?'

'You also taking an interest in this case, Dr Hong?'

'I figured it was him, but want to know I was right. Why did he do it?'

'That's what we're still trying to figure out. He admits to pretend-ing to be a ghost, but he refuses to explain his motive. At first he said it was just a bit of fun, which was obviously rubbish. Then he went completely silent.'

'Can I talk to him, Chief Wu?' asked Hong Jun.

'What do you want to talk to him about? Are you an interrogator, too, Dr Hong?'

'Oh no, that's not what I meant. What I want to talk to him about has nothing to do with your case. I think he may know something about the case I'm working on.'

'The Li Hongmei case?' Wu was surprised.

'Yes.'

'Now, *that's* a good one,' he snorted. 'What possible connection could Old Bao have to the Li Hongmei case? But I'm happy to hear your insights into the matter.'

'I don't have any insight,' said Hong Jun, as calmly as he could. 'I have a feeling about him, and I think he can tell me something useful.'

'Such as . . . ?'

'It's speculation for now. But I'll certainly tell you if I get anything substantial, Chief Wu. Now, I do believe that, as a lawyer, I have the right to talk to witnesses connected with my case, and I'm sure you won't hinder my investigation.'

'It's not up to me,' said Wu. 'You'll have to ask Chief Hao. Let's go to my office and I'll phone him for you.' And he got to his feet.

Hong Jun followed him out of the room, stopped, looked back and said, 'One moment, I seem to have dropped my handkerchief.' He went back into the meeting room, picked up his handkerchief and then, using it to mask his movement, quickly picked a cigarette butt out of the ashtray. He bundled it up and stuffed it in his pocket.

By the time he got to Wu Hongfei's office, Wu was already on the phone. 'How unfortunate,' he said, cradling the receiver. 'The Chief's gone out. It's not that I don't want to support your work, Dr Hong, but I really have to get the Chief's permission for this. It's out of my hands.'

Hong Jun decided to try and get to Old Bao another way.

After leaving police headquarters, he went to the Binbei Intermediate People's Court to find Chu Weihua. The clerk at the front desk knew he was working with the court and simply let him pass. 'How are you getting on, Weihua?' he asked, as he walked into his office.

'I've just finished reporting back to my bosses on the latest developments in our case, and on what happened in Harbin,' he replied. 'Deputy Chief Judge Han was at the meeting. I proposed two possible strategies: first, that we release Zheng Jianguo on the basis of the evidence we have so far, which raises serious doubts over his conviction and to my mind exonerates him, and reopen the investigation to find the real killer. Second, that we don't rush to overturn Zheng Jianguo's verdict, but wait until we've found the real murderer, or at least until we've clarified the details of the case. My bosses prefer the second option, as I expected, and want to hang onto Zheng Jianguo until we find the real killer. Chief Han didn't say anything, but I could tell he preferred the more cautious approach. I know you want to get this solved quickly, Dr Hong, to get Zheng Jianguo released, but—'

'Oh, no!' Hong Jun cut in. 'You've done very well. Of course I want to see Zheng Jianguo freed as soon as possible, but I also want to find out the identity of the real criminal. I fully understand the position. We must find the real killer first.'

'But how are we going to do that? Just when it looked like Li Qingshan might finally give us a lead we could follow, it was cut off.'

'Have you found out what happened with the fruit knife?'

'I can't get to the bottom of it. The PSB admit it was their mistake. But these things happen, and if they won't look into it any further, there's nothing we can do.'

'Is it really just a question of an error?' said Hong Jun. 'It seems we'll first have to find out who killed Li Qingshan. I'm certain his death is linked to this case. It would be too much of a coincidence if it wasn't.'

'But that's a Harbin case,' said Weihua. 'We can't get involved in that.'

'You're right, and we can only wait for that investigation to play itself out.' Hong Jun looked at the calendar on the wall. 'Can you do me a favour?'

'Sure, what do you need?'

'Find someone to help me test the blood type of a sample.'

'That's no problem,' said Weihua. 'My wife works in the lab at the county hospital.'

'Perfect.'

'Dr Hong . . . Why do you need to test someone's blood type?'

Hong Jun took the handkerchief from his pocket, unfolded it, and said, 'I've got a cigarette butt and I understand that blood type can be extracted from the saliva on the butt. Do you think your wife would be able to test it for me?'

'She can do the test, but I can't promise she'll be able to get a result. Whose cigarette butt is this?'

'Let's just say that, as a judge, I think it would be best if you don't know anything about it.'

CHAPTER TWENTY-ONE

CHIEF HAO ZHICHENG left a message at Hong Jun's hotel that he could see Old Bao whenever he wanted. Hong Jun was led to the detention block. There was no room set aside for lawyers to talk to those in custody. He was offered use of an interrogation room, and Old Bao was brought in and pushed into a chair facing Hong Jun across a table, after which they were left alone.

Hong Jun didn't want to sit in the interrogator's spot and dragged the chair around to sit beside Old Bao. 'I'd like to ask you a few questions, if that's all right with you?'

Old Bao looked at him with an unwavering gaze, but did not speak.

'I'm a lawyer, Old Bao, not PSB. This isn't an interrogation. I just want to check some information with you.'

Old Bao looked away to the side, still saying nothing.

Hong Jun looked into Old Bao's eyes and confirmed something that had been bothering him, like a mosquito glimpsed only when he wasn't looking for it but invisible when he tried to see it properly. Now, he was sure he had it. He paced around the room behind Old Bao. He let silence fill the space between them and as it grew deeper, eased up behind him and said, quietly, 'Xiao Xiong, look at me.'

Since that night in the cave, he'd spent a lot of time pondering the question of Old Bao. He'd had the feeling all along that what happened at the cave was in some way linked to the case of Li Hongmei. And he'd studied the photograph left in the letter hidden in Hongmei's room, fascinated by the eyes, though at first he wasn't quite sure why. It had taken him some time before he realised just how much those eyes looked like Old Bao's, and pieces of the puzzle had begun to fall into place.

Hong Jun tried to imagine his face without the big bushy beard and began subtracting years. Xiao Xiong ought to have been thirty-four or thirty-five, but Old Bao looked like he was in his early fifties. He added back years of hard outdoor work and living rough, and it made sense. 'Yes, you're Xiao Xiong. The people on the farm all called you "Dumb Deer", didn't they? There's no point pretending.'

'What are you talking about? My name is Old Bao!'

'Don't get angry,' said Hong Jun. 'Since you don't want me to call you by your real name, I'll stick to Old Bao. I guess you're used to it after all these years. But I'd like to remind you that while all these years of life as a hunter may have changed your appearance a lot, there are some things about one's appearance which are very hard to change. Shave off your beard and you're a dead ringer for Xiao Xiong in the photograph of you at the Flood-Fighting Monument in Harbin that time, the one you left for Li Hongmei in that letter.'

Getting to his feet, Hong Jun continued, 'After what happened at Black Bear Cave, I was wondering how this Old Bao could have come up with the idea of getting us to spend the night in the cave by loosening the cap on our petrol tank. It was almost foolproof. Most city people wouldn't have known how to do that, let alone a hunter who'd been living in the mountains for years. But it would have been a simple trick for Xiao Xiong, who drove all sorts of tractors and trucks and jeeps on the Binbei State Farm for many years.'

Old Bao sat with his head to one side, staring at the wall through narrowed eyes.

Looking at the grizzled white hair on his temples, and the scar on his forehead, Hong Jun chose a sincere tone. 'From the first time I saw you in the Binbei Restaurant, I admired your sense of righteousness and your courage. My personal feeling is that you must have had your own reasons for arranging that whole affair in Black Bear Cave so carefully. I'm really not interested in why you did what you did. I am investigating the murder of Li Hongmei, someone you knew and loved.

'I came to investigate this case to get Zheng Jianguo out of prison, where he's been for ten years. Can you imagine what it's like for an innocent man to have to spend ten years in prison? Tragic, don't you think?'

Old Bao's body flinched a little, but still he said nothing.

'It was your eyes that had me intrigued. I have seen those eyes somewhere else, too, on someone else.' Old Bao's brow furrowed ever so slightly, confused by Hong Jun's line of questioning.

'What about your sister, Xiao Xue? She works for the Harbin PSB, you may wish to know. We were students together, but our lives took different directions and she had to go home to care for her dying father and ditch her law studies, because her brother had abandoned them. She has your eyes. As far as she's concerned you're in America. No one is looking for you now.'

Old Bao turned his head, and looked silently, steadily into Hong Jun's eyes.

'Some people can only think about the pain in their own lives, oblivious to the pain they cause other people.'

'Why are you telling me these things?' asked Old Bao, in a hoarse voice.

'Why? Your sister has suffered because of you, and I care about her. And, as a lawyer, I'm telling you all this as Zheng Jianguo didn't rape and kill Li Hongmei, as you full well know, but you let him rot in jail anyway.

'Your sister tried to find you. Your father's only wish was to see you one more time but you never came. Your sister told me this, and more. Old Bao, someone ready to stand up for justice and defend others against unfairness would have been ashamed.'

'Ha ha ha,' Old Bao burst out laughing. 'You're quite the story-teller aren't you? All the stuff you're saying, is it some kind of dream you had? I come from Jingxian County in Hebei, my dad died when I was a teenager and my sister got married years ago. I don't know this Xiao Xiong you're going on about, or this Xiao Xue. And I've never been to Binbei State Farm. If you must know, I worked in the freight yard at Alihe in the greater Xing'an Mountains, on a lifting team moving trees, and after that became a hunter. Check around there. They know me. It was a hard life. A farm job would have been cushy.'

Had Hong Jun got it all wrong? Had he convinced himself that Old Bao and Xiao Xiong were the same person because he wanted to believe they were? People, complete strangers, can look the same. How often had he stopped someone on a Beijing street convinced it was a completely different person?

Old Bao seemed to read his mind. 'I know you're desperate to sort out your case. But you can't start making stuff up. If there's something you need to find out, you should try asking *him – he* knows everything.' Old Bao was pointing at the door, behind Hong Jun.

Hong Jun looked round and saw Wu Hongfei watching them through the little window in the door. Seeing that Hong Jun had noticed him, Wu came in. 'How are you getting on with your questions, Dr Hong? Did he tell you anything?'

Hong Jun shook his head. 'No . . . nothing.'

Wu Hongfei walked across to Old Bao and said, angrily, 'Bao Qingfu, don't kid yourself. You can't bluff your way out of this one. I'm telling you, we know everything there is to know about you.'

Once again, Old Bao fell silent.

Wu Hongfei asked Hong Jun whether he had any more questions, but he shook his head. Wu walked over to the doorway and asked someone to take Old Bao out.

'So Dr Hong, wasted our energies have we?' he asked, once Old Bao had gone.

Hong Jun didn't reply to the question, but asked in his turn. 'When did you get back, Chief Wu?'

'I just got back, and heard you were over here questioning Old Bao, so I came to have a look. He's a tricky character, that one. Don't worry about it, Dr Hong. I've questioned him several times and he hasn't told me anything. It's not easy. Some things don't turn out quite how they tell you in the textbooks.'

Hong Jun nodded in agreement. As he left the detention centre, he glanced at his watch. It was after eleven, and he decided to go straight to the Binbei Restaurant. His main motivation was not to have lunch, however, but to see Li Hongxing.

*

When he walked into the restaurant, there was no sign of Li Hongxing. He found a table at the side of the room, in the section she usually worked. There weren't many customers and the atmosphere was rather gloomy. When he finished ordering, Hong Jun asked the waitress whether Li Hongxing had got back yet.

'Hongxing?' she replied. 'She hasn't gone anywhere.'

'She didn't go to Harbin?' he asked.

'No, she's round the back. Is there something you want to see her about?'

'No particular reason, I was just asking.'

'She's just round the back. Wait a minute. I'll fetch her for you.' The waitress walked towards the kitchen, calling out Li Hongxing's name. Before long, Hongxing came hurrying out, smiling broadly at the sight of Hong Jun. 'Oh, Lawyer Hong,' she said, 'what's up? We're just doing our prep work for lunch.'

Slightly baffled by her relaxed, untroubled expression, he asked, 'Hongxing, you haven't heard about your father yet?'

Li Hongxing looked taken aback, and the smile slipped from her face. 'So you've heard too?' she asked. 'I got the letter about it last night. I'm planning to go to Harbin first thing tomorrow morning since the restaurant needs me here now. It is such a shock. He had such an unlucky life.'

She pulled out a handkerchief, sat down on the chair next to Hong Jun and started sobbing. The few other diners stared at them, and Hong Jun felt embarrassed for her. He didn't really know how to comfort a crying woman, but just at that moment the first waitress returned with his food, and, seeing Hongxing weeping, put her arm around her shoulders. She stopped crying, and wiped the tears from her eyes with her handkerchief. 'It's just that Lawyer Hong mentioned what happened to my dad, and it set me off again.'

'I think you should take the day off and go home,' said the waitress. 'The way you were just now, other people will think this gentleman was being horrible to you.'

'We're short-staffed as it is. I need to keep busy.' Li Hongxing's tears vanished as rapidly as they'd come. All smiles again, she asked Hong Jun, 'Was there something you wanted to see me about, Dr Hong?'

'Well,' he said, 'a few days ago something happened in Black Bear Cave up on the mountain. Did you hear about it?'

'People are talking, but I'd say most of it is just nonsense.'

'I'm not really interested in gossip, but I've heard there's an old local story about Black Bear Cave. You come from around here and I thought maybe you'd heard it? I've always loved collecting old folk stories.'

'The story of Black Bear Cave? Of course I know it. Most of these townsfolk haven't heard it,' she whispered, 'but everyone in our village knew about it. When the old ladies in the village weren't busy they would sit at the head of the *kang* gossiping, and there was nothing they liked more than telling stories like that. I must have heard that old tale about Black Bear Cave a dozen times. I can virtually tell you it off by heart!'

'Well, if you're not too busy now, I'd love to hear it,' Hong Jun suggested.

'Oh we're never really busy at this time,' she replied. 'People don't really start coming until past eleven-thirty.' She glanced at the waitresses lolling by the counter. 'If you're interested, I'll give you the short version. It all happened back in the Qing Dynasty,' she said, 'in a village not far from Black Bear Mountain where there lived an old hunter. He and his wife had only one daughter, and by the time she was eighteen, she'd grown into a lovely young woman. Fresh as daisy she was, and all the young men in the village were fascinated by her. One day, four imperial soldiers showed up, saying they'd come to hunt animals for the emperor. The commanding officer stayed in the hunter's house and that fellow took a fancy to the young girl. He wanted to take her for his concubine. But she was a spirited girl and refused. During the night, the commander ravaged her . . . killed her too, he did. The next day, at the crack of dawn, the four soldiers fled. But crossing Black Bear Mountain, a heavy snow began to fall, and they got lost and could find no way out of the mountains. Half dead with exhaustion, the Black Bear Spirit appeared and guided them to Black Bear Cave. They thought they were safe, and, exhausted, went to sleep. But they were woken by the growling of the Black Bear . . . and a woman wearing a red bracelet appeared, and started dancing, upside down, across the roof of the cave. Their weapons were useless and they grew more and more frightened until they fainted. When they awoke, there were only three of them left – the commander was gone. They looked everywhere for him, but all they could find, in a little tunnel deep inside the cave, was his hat. They say the Black Bear Spirit dragged him away. Retribution!'

'It's a strange story,' said Hong Jun, when she'd finished.

'Oh, I don't tell it very well,' she said. 'When those old grandmas told it, it was much more fun – they could stretch it out for half an hour, the best storytellers an hour.'

'But you told it very well,' he insisted. 'Talking of hunting, it reminds me of that hunter who stepped in to defend that woman here that time. Do you remember?'

'How could I forget?' she replied. 'That guy with the great big beard, he comes here lots of times.'

'And do you still remember that guy Xiao Xiong, who lived on the Binbei Farm?'

'Dumb Deer? Of course I remember him. Why?'

'Some people say the hunter looks a lot like Xiao Xiong. What do you think?'

Li Hongxing frowned and thought for a moment. 'When you put it like that,' she said, 'they really do look a bit alike. They're both about the same build and the shape of their faces, and their eyes, are very similar. But I'd never heard of Xiao Xiong having an elder brother.' She looked at Hong Jun, thoughtfully, and lowered her voice. 'Lawyer Hong, you're not suggesting that the hunter is actually the same Xiao Xiong who vanished all those years ago?!'

Hong Jun didn't reply.

'No . . . that's impossible,' said Hongxing. 'Xiao Xiong was fresh-faced, lively, young, not at all dark and grizzled like Old Bao. Anyway, surely he's the wrong age?'

Hong Jun was asking himself the same thing, whether Old Bao and Xiao Xiong were the same person after all.

CHAPTER TWENTY-TWO

AT THE GARAGE where the County Party Committee kept its vehicles, Hong Jun found a row of high buildings with big metal doors, some open, some shut. All around was the sound of machinery, echoing, rising and falling. An old workman in overalls walked past, and Hong Jun asked him where he could find Liu Yongsheng, Big Liu, the driver. The man pointed to a garage up ahead, its door standing open.

There he found a jeep inside, up on jacks. He walked around the garage before he noticed a pair of legs sticking out from under the front of the jeep. The legs were twisting backwards and forwards rhythmically, presumably matching a set of arm movements underneath.

'Driver Liu!' Hong Jun called out a couple of times, but the legs continued their twisting. Hong Jun stepped forward and gently prodded the legs with the tip of his boot. At this, the legs instantly stopped twisting, and began wriggling towards the side of the vehicle. Finally, an oil-smeared face emerged.

Big Liu scrambled to his feet. 'Dr Hong,' he said, 'I thought you'd gone back to Beijing.'

'I've still got more work to do here,' he said. 'Something wrong with the jeep again?'

'Hah, there's always something wrong with these old model jeeps. This one's only done about thirty thousand kilometres, but there's a problem every other day. I saw someone in one of those new Jeep Cherokees the other day. Now that's a jeep.'

'What's the problem this time?' he asked. Big Liu said the lining of the oil sump was leaking and needed replacing. 'It won't take me long to fit a new one. Anyway, what can I do for you, Dr Hong?'

'Have you been hunting again since the last time?' Hong Jun asked. 'I tried to phone Secretary Gu, but I couldn't reach him. After our last trip I think I've caught the bug.'

Big Liu grinned. 'I know what you mean. You only need to go hunting once to get bitten. My old lady's always saying to me, what's the point of hunting? It's tiring, it costs a lot of money, and it takes a lot of time. You'd be better off buying a chicken on the street, or using the time to raise our own. But I told her, you've never tried it. I wanted her to, so we could go together. But she said she'd prefer to waste her time watching TV. That woman is so lazy.'

'I suppose she just has different interests,' said Hong Jun.

'After what happened at Black Bear Mountain last time, Secretary Gu hasn't mentioned hunting again. I think he got a bit of a shock that day. But I'll take you out, if you want? We can go up there for the day and have a good time.'

'Are you allowed to take the vehicles out yourself?' he asked.

'Of course!' Big Liu replied. 'If a driver didn't have that little bit of power there'd be no point doing the job.'

'Do you think you could take me somewhere else . . . not to do with hunting?

'Sure, where do you want to go?'

'It's a long-distance trip, to Harbin. I'll pay you.'

'Harbin,' said Big Liu. 'Hmm, that is a bit far. It'll take a whole day. And the road's not great either. Why don't you just take the train?'

'Well, the train times aren't very convenient, and I've got a few things I want to do along the way, too.'

Big Liu thought for a moment. 'It's not that I don't want to help you, Dr Hong, but the bloke in charge of the cars here is pretty strict. We're not allowed to go to Harbin without special permission. If it's somewhere nearby, we can just hop in and step on the gas. But long trips aren't so easy to hide in the logbooks. It's like the other day, when Secretary Gu went to Harbin, he took the train. I know because I took him to the station.'

'I see,' said Hong Jun. 'Did you pick him up when he came back, too?'

Big Liu nodded.

'Which train did he take?' he asked. 'If it was the one that arrives in the morning you must have had to get up pretty early?'

'You're telling me. The train got in at five, so I had to get up at four-thirty. When you work for other people like we do, you just have to do whatever they ask. When they tell you to get the car out, you do it. It doesn't matter whether you're in the middle of eating or asleep in bed, you can forget about having your own life.'

'That's pretty tough. In that case, I don't want to give you any more trouble.'

'Dr Hong, if you really want someone to drive you to Harbin, I've got an idea. You know PSB Chief Hao pretty well, right? Why not try him? Their cars go back and forth to Harbin all the time. Maybe they could take you?'

'Good idea,' said Hong Jun, 'I'll ask him.' But no sooner had he walked out of the garage, when Big Liu came running after him. 'Dr Hong . . . our hunting trip?'

'Let's talk about it later.' Hunting of that nature was the last thing on his mind.

*

After dinner, Zheng Jianzhong and Zhu Li were at Hong Jun's hotel room door. They were going back to Beijing the next morning, they said, so they'd come to say goodbye. Zheng Jianzhong told Hong Jun he hoped to see his brother out of prison as soon as possible.

'When I was in Harbin this time, I went to see my brother in jail. He really trusts you, he's sure you're going to get him out. But he's getting impatient. And to tell you the honest truth, as his brother, when I see him suffering like that in there, I wish I could go and take his place, just to get him out of there.'

At these words, Zhu Li, who was sitting alongside, looked rather disapproving, but she merely pouted and didn't say anything. As they were leaving, she told Hong Jun she hoped they'd have a chance to go dancing again, perhaps in Beijing.

✱

Soon after they'd gone, the doorbell rang again. It was Chu Weihua. Hong Jun ushered him in and shut the door behind him. 'Did you get the result of the test?' he asked, unable to conceal his impatience.

'My wife did it herself,' said Weihua, 'but she couldn't get a result. She said the person who smoked that cigarette might have been non-secreting. Someone who doesn't leave a measurable type. But maybe she's just not so good at it. She's never tested blood type from a cigarette butt before.'

'Non-secreting . . . ?' Hong Jun committed the term to memory.

'Dr Hong. I'm not going to ask you whose cigarette butt you wanted tested . . . I want you to know that if it comes to it, I'm prepared to go through hell or high water to help you.'

'Thank you, Weihua,' replied Hong Jun, genuinely touched.

Seeing that he looked rather weary, Weihua said goodbye and left.

Hong Jun looked at his watch and glanced at the bed, tempted. Instead, he went down to the lobby to telephone Xiao Xue.

'I've checked up on both the people you mentioned. I don't know why you're suspicious of them, but I don't think either of them is the person we're looking for.'

'Why not?'

'Because neither of them had time to do it.'

'How do you know that?'

'I went to see Section Chief Li this morning, and he confirmed Gu Chunshan and Wu Hongfei saw him on Tuesday. Secretary Gu is an old friend of his, and they came to see him about a case. They all had dinner together that evening, and dropped Gu off at Three Trees Station to catch the night train back to Binbei.'

'And Wu . . . ?'

'After seeing off Secretary Gu, Old Li took Chief Wu back to the PSB guesthouse. He was staying in a room on his own, but the night porter says he didn't see him go out again. And more importantly, the guest-house door is locked at ten-thirty. By the time he'd finished checking in, it was after ten. To get from the guesthouse to Li Qingshan's place, commit the crime and then get back to guesthouse, even if he moved fast, would have taken him until at least midnight, and he wouldn't have been able to get back in without buzzing someone to open the door. So I don't think you should waste your time thinking about those two.'

'You think your sources are reliable?'

'Hong Jun!' she exclaimed, 'You can't just go around suspecting everyone. I have no reason to doubt what they told me!'

'Sorry,' he said, 'I'm just used to questioning whatever anyone tells me.'

'And you question what I tell you too?'

'No . . .'

'Look, you're worrying me. I know you're very self-confident, and when you think you're right about something you never give up. But there are times when you get things wrong too. You've been abroad for so many years you're probably a bit out of touch with how things work in China these days. Those men are both powerful local officials.

Don't assume that just because you've got a PhD from abroad you don't have anything to fear. If you get this right, then fine. But if you get it wrong, I'd hate to think what might happen. I'm not trying to scare you. Out in the provinces it's not the same as the capital, you know. Anything can happen, including "accidents". Please be careful.'

'Thank you for the warning, but don't worry. I can take care of myself.'

'We did discover another suspicious individual who also used to live at the Binbei Farm.'

'Yes . . . ? What's the name?'

'Zheng Jianzhong.'

'And why do you suspect him?' he asked.

'Well, we spoke to the victim's daughter, and she told us that the day before Li was murdered, Zheng Jianzhong came to see her, and asked for her father's address. Do you know him?'

'Yes, he's my client, the brother of the one who's in prison.'

'Well, this case really does seem to be pretty complicated.'

'It certainly is. But I almost forgot . . . Xiao Xue, I've got some good news for you.'

'What?'

'I think I've found your brother.'

'What did you say?'

'I've found Xiao Xiong,' he said, quietly.

'You've found my brother?'

'Yes. You remember Old Bao, the man I told you about last time? I'm convinced he's Xiao Xiong!'

'The hunter?'

'I just talked to him. He won't admit to it, but this time I'm sure that my assessment is correct. Tell me, do you have relatives in a place called Jingxian County?'

'You mean Jingxian in Hebei Province?'

'Yes.'

'That's my father's old ancestral home,' she said. 'But, I've never been there, and I've never been in touch with anyone there, so I don't know if we still have living relatives there.'

'That's the piece of the puzzle that was missing.'

'Where is he?'

'Binbei PSB detention centre.'

'I've got to come to Binbei! I've got to see him. Is he all right?' She asked, her voice faltering.

'He's fine, Xiao Xue. Don't worry . . . and please don't cry. This is good news.'

CHAPTER TWENTY-THREE

A SNOWSTORM WAS coming. Hong Jun looked at the clouds building
and darkening beyond the town. He pulled the collar of his coat closer
to his chin against the intense cold of the afternoon, before giving up
on fresh air and joining Wu Hongfei in the waiting room at Binbei
Station. The train from Harbin was delayed, probably by the coming
storm headed from that direction. Neither felt like talking over the
hubbub, which would have meant breathing in the foul air. Hunched
up, they could filter it through their fur collars. Shortly before three
o'clock, people began shuffling up from the floor and leaving the hard
seats for the platform. It was even colder now outside, but they could
breathe, so Hong Jun and Chief Wu joined them looking optimisti-
cally to the south. A railway employee called through a loud hailer,
'The train from Harbin is experiencing further delays, arrival is now
expected in approximately fifty minutes,' before ducking his head
back inside the little office.

The platform resounded with curses, and many went back to the
waiting room. Those left on the platform began to briskly pace its
length. Hong Jun didn't feel like going back to the stifling waiting
room and suggested they stay outside. Wu Hongfei nodded. To the
west, the sky was filled with layers of bluish-grey cloud, through which
the afternoon sun bored a few bright holes.

'Chief Wu, a question?'

'Ask away.'

'When Li Hongmei was killed, you and Secretary Gu were at the Binbei Farm investigating Xiao Xiong, is that right?'

He saw Wu's brow crinkle in thought under his fur hat. 'Yes. We got a phone call from Harbin, asking Old Gu to investigate this Xiao Xiong's background. He was suspected of being involved in political activities and they wanted him kept under surveillance. But Old Gu took it very seriously. Probably how he made the shift to Party official. So off we went to Binbei Farm, where Xiao Xiong was supposed to be. We hung around, asked some questions, but everyone said he'd gone. I came back to town a few times. We did have other work to do. But Old Gu wanted to stay and wait. I wasn't his boss, so he could do as he liked, far as I was concerned.'

'Were you at the farm on the night of the killing?'

Wu Hongfei glanced at Hong Jun, and, after a moment's pause, said, 'I was. They were showing a movie that night, and I decided to stay over to watch it.'

'Did Old Gu go with you?'

'He doesn't like movies . . . '

'So you were both in the village that night. What happened with the Xiao Xiong case?' Hong Jun asked.

'After the Li Hongmei case, we put it aside. Old Gu insisted the cases were linked, that Xiao Xiong had conspired with Zheng Jianguo to kill her. But he'd vanished and it just got tossed on the backburner.'

They stood in silence. Wu was thinking again. 'Chief Hao was just telling me that you think Old Bao is actually Xiao Xiong. Are you sure?'

'Not a hundred per cent sure.'

'And this Deputy Section Chief Xiao who's coming today? She's Xiao Xiong's sister?'

'I believe so. I want her to identify him so we can be sure. She's on the fast track at the PSB now, so her connection to an old case like this shouldn't do any harm to her career.'

The pair kept up a sporadic conversation until the train arrived. Hong Jun spotted Xiao Xue. She worked her way to them. Hong Jun introduced Wu Hongfei, and she introduced Division Chief Ma, who had come with her. The four of them exchanged pleasantries on the way to Wu Hongfei's jeep and were driven to PSB headquarters, where they were ushered directly to Chief Hao Zhicheng's office. Court Deputy Chief Judge Han Wenqing, Bureau Chief Shen Limin and Chu Weihua were already seated.

Chief Hao explained the gathering. 'Judge Han says there are some new developments in the Li Hongmei case, which he wants to discuss with us.'

'Really, I'm just here to listen and learn,' said Judge Han. 'Dr Hong and Chu Weihua came to see me this morning and presented a theory, which I think has a lot of merit. It's certainly something we would need the Public Security Bureau's assistance with. But let's hear from Dr Hong and we can discuss what to do. Dr Hong?'

'I feel like I'm being cross-examined,' Hong Jun joked. 'I think we're all familiar with the case, and the evidence, so I'll just jump straight in.

'When I started to investigate the Li Hongmei case, my suspicions fell mainly on Xiao Xiong and Zheng Jianzhong. But after I discovered that the fruit knife, which was being held here in the police bureau, had gone missing, I began to change my mind. The envelope it had been kept in was still there, but the knife itself had vanished. This led me to believe that someone had intentionally removed it. Why? There were still traces of blood on the knife, which I had hoped to send to Beijing for DNA analysis, so taking the knife was an attempt to destroy evidence.'

Hong Jun wrote on a chalkboard in front of the group, *Fruit knife*. 'Now, based on this assumption, I drew two further conclusions. Firstly, that the person who peeled the apple, and whose blood was on the knife, was the murderer as well as the person who took the knife. Secondly, this person, or someone with close connections to this person, knew the evidence was incriminating and removed the knife. Who then? It couldn't have been Xiao Xiong, who disappeared and hasn't been seen in ten years. Zheng Jianzhong? He's spent the last few years in Beijing and was unlikely to know where the knife was stored. But a close friend of either could have done it.

'It seemed to me there were two criteria the person who took the fruit knife had to fit. One, they had to have been at Binbei Farm on the evening of April 17, 1984. Two, they had to be in a position to know where the knife was stored after the trial and have access to it, which meant they had to work either for the court or the PSB.'

He wrote *People's Intermediate Court* and *PSB* on the board.

'If we look at either of these criteria individually, there are lots of potential suspects. But if we consider them together, we discover that there are only two, because only two people who worked in the official system were also at Binbei Farm at the time of Li Hongmei's death, investigating Xiao Xiong. I'm referring to Gu Chunshan and Wu Hongfei.'

All eyes in the room were fixed on Wu Hongfei as he wrote their names on the board, but his face displayed no emotion. There was no protest at the allegations being made by Hong Jun.

'Then the Black Bear Cave incident took place,' Hong Jun continued, writing up *Black Bear Cave*. 'Once I was convinced that the "Black Bear Spirit" was just Old Bao dressed up, I asked myself who he was trying to scare, and to my mind it had to be Gu Chunshan, but why? I thought it might be aimed at me, to frighten me off this case, but Old Bao had no idea I was going to be there. From his initial arrangement to go hunting with Gu Chunshan, and the location he chose, to unscrewing the drainage cap so the jeep would run out of petrol and we'd be stuck for the night in Black Bear Cave, from using the pretext of fetching more petrol to get Big Liu out of the way, to preparing his makeup and costume, it was all planned down to the tiniest detail.

'Old Bao hadn't planned on my being there. He looked surprised to see me, but I could see in his eyes it wasn't a good surprise. We had met before and I got the distinct impression I was not a welcome addition to his hunting party. He could abandon his elaborate plan, or go ahead anyway and think of something to distract me.

'What was Old Bao's motive? Initially, I didn't see any connection between the incident in the cave and the Li Hongmei case. I thought Gu Chunshan might somehow have had a run-in with Old Bao in the past and this was some kind of payback. Or perhaps one of Gu Chunshan's political rivals was trying to stir up a scandal . . .

'I had seen an old photograph of Xiao Xiong and something that had been bothering me since I first met Old Bao became clear. The more I thought about it, the more sense it made . . . Old Bao and Xiao Xiong are the same person.

'With Chief Hao's permission, I went to talk to Old Bao. Although he never acknowledged that he was Xiao Xiong, his reaction gave him away. And I feel sure that when Chief Xiao, who has kindly joined us from Harbin, sees him and conducts her own interrogation, she will confirm my theory.

'Once I'd concluded Old Bao was Xiao Xiong, it wasn't hard to deduce his motives. He had two possible reasons for wanting to scare Gu Chunshan. The first was Gu Chunshan's role in investigating Xiao Xiong's involvement with the democracy movement back in the eighties, which was why Gu Chunshan was at the farm, and the second was the death of Li Hongmei.'

The implication of what Hong Jun was saying was enormous. But none in the room had risen to challenge him. They were all waiting to see how far Hong Jun would go. If he didn't prove his case, the Beijing lawyer was going to be in serious trouble. Hong Jun knew the ramifications of what he was saying, but he was confident.

'Now my own intuition tended towards the second possibility, but I know you can't make a deduction based on imagination. You need facts. So let's start laying them out. In Black Bear Cave, Old Bao mentioned a folk tale about the Black Bear Spirit. At that point, I had no idea what the story was about, but I sensed that he must have had some purpose in mentioning it. Later, I learned about the local legend and the message it contained. The story bears many similarities to what happened to Li Hongmei, and this convinced me that Old Bao had taken great care in luring Gu Chunshan to the cave.

'A strip of birch bark was left in Black Bear Cave. On it was a crude drawing. For a while, I was baffled as to the meaning of the pictures. But then I read up about the Orochen people, and discovered that when someone dies, it's their custom to give them a "wind burial", placing the body in a type of coffin made of strips of willow, and hanging it on a tree. I realised that the drawing we found depicted a coffin hanging on a tree, and the red circles on the coffin could have been red plums – *Hong mei*, just like her name – or a red bracelet, like the one worn by the spirit of the murdered woman in the story of the Black Bear Spirit. The person who drew the picture also drew a male reproductive organ, to imply sex, or more precisely, rape. Taken together, everything Old Bao did, from the drawing to the appearance of the Black Bear Spirit, was a warning to Gu Chunshan, a reminder of past crimes. Chief Wu found another nine strips of tree bark, with the same pictures on them, in an envelope in Old Bao's house. If his plan of action hadn't been interrupted, Old Bao would have carried on delivering these messages to Gu Chunshan. And these nine, plus the one in the cave, made ten, the number of years since Li Hongmei's death.

'Old Bao did all of these things because he believed that Gu Chunshan was the person who murdered Li Hongmei. And those pictures were designed to scare Gu Chunshan into confessing, or simply to torment him with the guilt of his actions.'

Hong Jun looked around the room. Nobody spoke.

'None of this is enough evidence to put before a court to convict Gu Chunshan as the killer. We need further proof if we're to confirm my deductions. So, let's go back to first principles, evidence. When I first identified Gu Chunshan and Wu Hongfei as suspects, it occurred to me that I ought to try to test their blood types. Of course the fruit knife had vanished, which meant we couldn't carry out DNA identification, but knowing their blood types would still be important, as it was blood type that convicted Zheng Jianguo. I'm just a lawyer, an outsider, and Gu Chunshan is the Deputy County Party Secretary, so I was unable to find an appropriate way to test his blood type. But then, quite by chance, I was able to get hold of a cigarette which Chief Wu had smoked . . . please forgive me, Chief Wu.'

'Most people's saliva or semen secretes a number of elements that can be used to identify blood type, but not everyone. Some are non-secretors, that is, the elements required for identification are not there. Our tests showed Chief Wu to be a non-secretor, so we could not determine his blood type from the saliva on his cigarette butt. This was actually helpful because, after Li Hongmei died, the pathologist was able to determine blood type by testing the semen on the victim's body. Thus, we can eliminate Chief Wu as a suspect.

'Now, if you only have two suspects who fit the criteria, and you rule one of them out, the other is obviously the criminal, so, logically, Gu Chunshan had to be the killer. But that works only if the line from the missing fruit knife leads back to the killer. However, there's another important piece of evidence, and another line we can draw.'

Hong Jun scribbled some more names and drew lines between them.

'Last Tuesday evening, Li Hongmei's father, Li Qingshan, was murdered in Harbin. Chief Xiao Xue is handling that investigation. The scene of the crime was rigged to look like suicide. It was quite skilfully done, but there were a few clues that gave the killer away. Still, from the scene of the crime it was clear that this was a murder, carefully planned down to the last detail, and the killer knew a bit about detective work. So far as we can determine, Li Qingshan had no enemies, nor did he have any valuables that would have been worth anyone going to so much trouble to rob him of. So the chances of it being a revenge killing, or murder for the sake of robbery, seem very slim. On the other hand, Li Qingshan was an important witness in the reopened case of his daughter Li Hongmei and was about to name the person he suspected of actually committing the crime. This made me think of Gu Chunshan as responsible for his death. He knew, as a former PSB officer, how to set up a suicide.

'Gu Chunshan was in Harbin at the time of the killing. But he had a very convincing alibi. He went to Harbin by train on Tuesday morning, with Chief Wu. In the afternoon they went to Harbin PSB and then had dinner with Section Chief Li, after which Section Chief Li and Chief Wu dropped him at Three Trees Station. This was at about nine o'clock. The train left Three Trees Station at 9.50 p.m., and arrived in Binbei the next morning at 5.45 a.m. We have witnesses who say that Gu Chunshan was on that train when it got to Binbei on the Wednesday morning. There were no other trains that would have got him back to Binbei on Wednesday morning, and he couldn't have taken a later, faster train that would have let him catch up with the 9.50 train further along the line.

'Li Qingshan's killing took place between ten past nine, when he was seen drinking alone in his room, and eleven on Tuesday evening, according to the autopsy. During this period, Gu Chunshan should have been either at the station, or on the train to Binbei. So this would seem to prove that Gu Chunshan could not have killed Li Qingshan.

'I was really baffled. On the one hand, Gu Chunshan had a clear motive for killing Li Qingshan, and he was also in Harbin that day. On the other hand, there was pretty solid evidence that he wasn't at the scene of the crime at the time it took place. But could Gu Chunshan have got someone else to carry out the murder for him? I thought Chief Wu might have been an accomplice, but reasoned that if Gu Chunshan wanted Li Qingshan dead, he would do it himself, to protect his reputation. It was a real puzzle.

'Now I myself had never been to Three Trees Station. I usually board the train at Harbin Station, but Chief Xiao told me that if you miss the train at Harbin, you can catch up with it at Binjiang Station. You're all much more familiar with Harbin than I am, so I'm sure you understand this. When I studied a map of the city, I discovered the railway actually runs in a kind of heart-shaped loop around the town. Three Trees Station is on the northeast side of this loop, the main Harbin Station is in the northwest, and Binjiang is in between the two of them on the north side of the loop. And there are other stations to the south, including Xiangfang.'

He drew a rough map of the city on the chalkboard and began marking out the railway route. 'As the train to Binbei heads out of Harbin, it crosses the Songhua River at the River Bridge, to the north of Three Trees Station. So if a train from Three Trees heads north when it leaves the station, it can cross the River Bridge and be out of the city within twenty minutes. But the train Gu Chunshan took that night didn't take this route. When it left Three Trees Station it first headed south, and went around in a large loop, stopping at Xiangfang Station, Harbin Station and then Binjiang Station, before finally turning north and leaving the city across the River Bridge.

'That train leaves Three Trees at 9.50 p.m., but by the time it departs from Binjiang on the way out of town, it's already about 11.10 p.m. That's a gap of one hour twenty minutes . . . And because Gu Chunshan arrived early at the station, he gains another half hour. So, after he arrived in Harbin that day, Gu Chunshan booked a taxi to meet him at Three Trees Station that evening. He made his farewells to Section Chief Li and Chief Wu, went into the station until they had left, and found his waiting taxi, which drove him to Li Qingshan's place. He probably had the taxi stop and wait in a nearby street. For an old policeman like him, half an hour should have been enough to do everything he needed to do at the scene of the crime. He goes back to the taxi and heads for Binjiang Station, with plenty of time to spare before the train to Binbei would arrive. I admire the neat precision of it.' The chalkboard looked like a tangle of intersecting lines, but the logic was solid.

Hong Jun dusted the chalk off his hands and sat back in his chair. 'Section Chief Xiao,' he said, 'there are a few details I must ask you to fill in for us.'

'There are two things I'd like to add,' she said, standing at the chalkboard and tugging her uniform jacket straight. 'After Dr Hong phoned us, we checked around the Harbin taxi companies and found a driver named Zhao, who told us that on the Tuesday night in question he had an advance booking to pick up a passenger at Three Trees Station. He took him to Binjiang Station, stopping en route near Datong Street for more than half an hour. He said the passenger was of medium build, wearing a brown leather jacket and chequered scarf, wore glasses and had on a surgical mask, not uncommon at this time of year as a precaution against catching or spreading colds and flu. The driver couldn't see his face very clearly. I checked with Section Chief Li, who confirmed Gu Chunshan was wearing a brown leather jacket and chequered scarf that day. We questioned Li Qingshan's oldest daughter, Li Honghua, who told us that Gu Chunshan had always been very concerned for her father; he came to see him at least once a year and knew her father had taken a live-in job at the school.'

Hong Jun joined Chief Xiao at the board. 'Based on everything you've just heard, I believe that Gu Chunshan killed both Li Qingshan, and, ten years ago, his daughter Li Hongmei. There are still two questions as yet unanswered. How did Xiao Xiong know Gu Chunshan killed Li Hongmei? Our information is that he wasn't at Binbei Farm at the time, and he never went back after she died. Only Xiao Xiong can answer that, but he is not talking. Why did Gu Chunshan kill Li Qingshan? Perhaps Li was about to name Gu as the person he saw leaving the house, and not young Zheng. He wanted to talk to a court official first, and I was bringing Judge Chu Weihua with me to talk to him the following morning when we found the body. Was he about to name Gu Chunshan? Did he have some evidence proving Gu Chunshan raped and murdered Li Hongmei? We cannot know.'

Han Wenqing and Chief Hao seemed lost in thought, Wu Hongfei and Shen Limin were muttering to each other about the chalkboard map and the train timetable, Xiao Xue and Division Chief Ma were whispering together. Chu Weihua was looking from Han Wenqing to Hao Zhicheng and back again, trying to read what their reaction to all this would be.

Hong Jun walked over to the window and looked out at the sky, which was growing darker as rain clouds closed over the town. He was well aware that Gu Chunshan was no ordinary person and to wrongfully accuse him of such crimes would almost certainly be the end of his career, and probably those of more than a few in the room.

'Goodness!' Chief Hao exclaimed, offering a way out of the uncomfortable impasse. 'I didn't realise it was so late. A case of "missing out on sleep and forgetting to eat for the sake of the revolution", eh? I asked the canteen to prepare a simple meal for us. So, please, let's all go eat so we can come back with full bellies.'

There was no dissent, and they all adjourned to the dining room, where a generous table was laid out for them. They sat and ate the array of delicious local dishes, chatting all the while, though no one mentioned the case. Hong Jun had said all he wanted and it had wearied him. He picked at a few dishes but otherwise sat quietly, trying not to think about his fate if he had got everything wrong.

Returning, relaxed and well fed to Hao Zhicheng's office, they resumed their seats, eager to see how the evening's revelations would play out. An officer brought in tea and, once everyone was sipping their cups, Chief Hao rose and said to Han Wenqing, 'Deputy Chief Judge Han, Dr Hong's analysis strikes me as very convincing. Would you agree?'

'As I said earlier, I am here to listen, not to express my views, which are a matter for the court since this relates to the decision about whether to overturn the guilty verdict handed down against Zheng Jianguo. But please, all of you should speak freely. This is not a formal hearing so there are no penalties for voicing an opinion, even one based on speculation, or extrapolating from what we have so far heard.'

Shen Limin spoke first. 'Dr Hong's analysis is very rigorous, however,' he paused, choosing his words with care, 'in terms of proving that Gu Chunshan murdered Li Hongmei, we don't seem to have a lot of hard evidence. It is all supposition. Chief Wu, you were working with Gu Chunshan at the time. Can you give us any more details?'

'Well,' said Wu Hongfei, 'I certainly noticed that Old Gu always seemed very keen to talk to Li Hongmei, but I really can't say any more than that. It was a long time ago. And so far there's been nothing to prove the PSB or the court got it wrong.'

Chief Hao cleared his throat. 'Deductions are all very well for cracking a case, but if you want to bring a case to court you need evidence. Dr Hong's theory seems very reasonable and sensible, but I'm afraid we're going to need more if we're to prove Zheng Jianguo was not the killer, and especially that Gu Chunshan was. It is a very serious accusation. I'm not trying to protect him, but if we're going to make the case watertight, perhaps it's worth considering how Gu Chunshan will explain it all away. Dr Hong's deductions only show that he had time to kill Li Qingshan, not that he did. Can you prove he didn't get on the train at Three Trees Station and stay on it all the way back to Binbei? Can you prove he went to see Li Qingshan, that he was the passenger the taxi driver waited to pick up?'

Xiao Xue came to Hong Jun's aid. 'We could bring Mr Zhao, the taxi driver, to Binbei, and have him identify Gu Chunshan as the passenger in question.'

'A fine idea, Chief Xiao,' Hao replied, 'but the driver himself has said that the person who took his taxi that day was wearing glasses and a mask, so I'm afraid it will be difficult for him to make a positive identification of any suspect.'

Now Hong Jun spoke. 'Although the passenger was wearing glasses and a mask, making facial identification rather difficult, we can also use identification of the way they walked, and their voice . . . This only happened a few days ago, so his memory is still clear and information on the passenger's physical appearance, gait and speech should still be quite reliable.'

'But,' Chief Hao said with a smile, 'even if we can identify the culprit in the Li Qingshan case as you suggest, we still have the Li Hongmei case, which happened ten years ago. Even if Li Qingshan was going to change his testimony and say he saw Gu Chunshan, he can't because he's dead. And we can hardly declare Gu Chunshan a rapist-murderer based entirely on the say-so of Xiao Xiong, if that's who Old Bao really is, can we? If we are guessing what Old Gu would say in refuting such a charge, it would be "I didn't kill Li Hongmei, Xiao Xiong just wants to get revenge on me because I once investigated his involvement in the democracy movement. Do you have any proof that I killed her?" And we'd still be none the wiser.'

'Chief Hao,' said Chu Weihua, 'I think there is a clear link between the Li Qingshan case and the Li Hongmei case. If we can ascertain that Gu Chunshan killed Li Qingshan, then we ought to be able to conclude that he killed Li Hongmei, too. Otherwise, why kill Li Qingshan unless it was for something he knew?'

'It's not quite as simple as that, Weihua,' replied Chief Hao. 'Gu Chunshan is the Deputy Secretary of the County Communist Party Committee and Secretary of the Political and Legal Committee as well.

We can't just pin the case on him and expect him to confess. And it won't be easy to bring charges in the Li Qingshan case based solely on identification by a taxi driver either. I think we need to think about this very carefully before we take any further steps. What do you say, Chief Han?'

Han Wenqing smiled and said nothing.

Hong Jun spoke again. 'Although it's ten years since Li Hongmei was killed, and although the fruit knife, which was such an important piece of evidence, has disappeared, there is still a way to prove Gu Chunshan's crimes. The police pathologist Yu Jinghui told me that his initial tests found two types of blood on the fruit knife, both type A and type O. He wrote this in his first test report, and he still has the original in his files. Li Hongmei was type O, but there were no wounds on her body. So where did the type O blood on the knife come from? Since no one could explain it, Doctor Yu was forced to make a decision and change his report so that it read . . . ' Hong Jun took his little notebook from his shirt pocket and flipped through its pages, ' . . . "Among the blood traces on the fruit knife, I detected type A blood" without mentioning the type O blood at all. Correct, Chief Wu?'

Wu Hongfei nodded. 'Gu Chunshan was adamant that we should adjust the report of the blood test like that. I didn't argue. At the time I thought there couldn't possibly be two people's blood on the knife and was sure there had been an error in the testing, or possibly the sample had somehow become contaminated with someone else's blood. Anyway, I didn't really think it was anything too important.'

'Why is this significant, Dr Hong?' asked Chief Hao.

'When we've tested Gu Chunshan's blood type, the significance will be self-evident,' he replied. 'I believe it will be a startling revelation.'

'What startling revelation can there be in a blood type?' said the Chief.

'Well, you see . . . ' Hong Jun began. But before he could finish speaking, the telephone on Hao Zhicheng's desk began to ring. Chief Hao walked over and picked up the receiver, which he had to hold away from his ear because the caller was shouting so loudly.

'Old Hao? This is Gu Chunshan. Come quickly . . .' They could all hear the terror in the tinny voice coming from the receiver. 'There's a ghost in my house!'

CHAPTER TWENTY-FOUR

A BIG BLACK dog woke to the noise of the police jeep as it skidded out of PSB headquarters, and dashed out to chase the vehicle, barking wildly, as the jeep raced towards the Party Committee residential quarters. From all sides, other dogs barked and howled in response, straining at their tethers or joining the chase. A lot of families kept dogs, and the chorus of barking spread to surround the speeding jeep. Soon enough, half the town was awake and alert to something happening on this snowy, stormy night.

In front of the office block, Hong Jun and Chief Hao were the first out of the jeep, and they ran up the narrow path along the wall of the courtyard towards the residential buildings at the back. Whether from age and neglect, or because residents couldn't be bothered to walk all the way to the front gate, there were several gaps in the compound wall. Hong Jun glimpsed through each as he ran and saw the shape of a person trying to flit through the shadows. Chief Hao was well ahead of him, and others were beating the path behind him, letting Hong Jun veer off to the gap and look more closely. It was that mad woman, he was sure, lurching surprisingly fast through the swirling snow towards the main road. He turned back to catch up with the others.

At the last of the four-storey buildings, they charged through the entrance and took the stairs to the third floor. Wu Hongfei was hammering on the door of the right-hand apartment. There was no sound from inside. He hammered again. Nothing. Hao Zhicheng was beside him and ordered, 'Kick it open.'

Wu Hongfei took a few steps back and ran at the door, raising his right foot in time to connect with the lock, which yielded a little, splintering the heavy timber door-jamb. He got it on the third kick, by which time the neighbouring inhabitants had all come out to watch.

The lights were on in every room. In the bedroom, on the floor next to the sofa, Gu Chunshan lay slumped, a cleaver in his right hand, and in his left hand a piece of paper, on which was written, in blood-red characters:

> *Blood debts must be repaid with blood!*
> *Li Hongmei*

Wu Hongfei rushed over to check his pulse. 'He's alive!' he shouted. 'Call the hospital for an ambulance.' Wu and Chief Hao, who had come up behind him, pulled Gu up and laid him on the sofa. Chief Hao shook Gu gently by the shoulders, calling his name, trying to rouse him, but his eyes remained tightly shut. Hao Zhicheng pressed on his *renzhong* acupoint, between the nose and the upper lip, and brought him around. Gu's eyes started to move, and finally opened. He looked round with a terrified expression at the people in the room and stared at the window in front of him. He recoiled and huddled, cowering, on the sofa. Pointing at the window, he shouted in a petrified voice, 'A ghost . . . I saw a ghost . . . Li Hongmei was . . . here . . . *her* ghost.'

Everyone was frowning. No one spoke.

Medics from the county hospital arrived and, under the direction of Chief Hao and Wu Hongfei, they carried Gu Chunshan downstairs to the ambulance.

Hong Jun crossed to the window and saw a piece of paper stuck to the glass. On it were the same characters as the note in Gu Chunshan's hand. In the glow of the light from inside the room, he also caught sight of shoe prints in the snow on the windowsill. He opened the window and leaned out. This side of the house was sheltered from the wind, but still a rush of chill air surged into the room. He looked down and around and saw a pipe running from the roof guttering to the ground; the brackets which held the pipe to the wall were clear of snow. It would have been an easy enough climb to the third floor, and onto the narrow ledge that ran around the building under the windows. He dragged his sleeve across the window ledge to clear away the shoe prints.

Wu Hongfei came back in. 'Found something, Dr Hong?'

'No, nothing,' said Hong Jun, pulling the window shut behind him, 'except this piece of paper, stuck on the outside of the window. It is really cold outside.'

Chief Hao joined them, looked at the paper on the window and said, 'Dr Hong, your powers of deduction are clearly on par with Sherlock Holmes. Would you care to analyse for us what happened here this evening?'

'It's . . . elementary,' Hong Jun said, grinning at Chief Hao's reference. 'I don't think anything happened here at all. Ghosts don't exist. It was all in Gu Chunshan's imagination. Psychiatrists call it visual and auditory hallucination.'

'But who stuck this piece of paper onto the window?' asked Wu Hongfei.

'Gu Chunshan put it there himself,' said Hong Jun. 'Didn't he have another one, with the same message, in his hand?'

'Why would he do that?' asked Chief Hao.

'Who knows? He's clearly not all there.'

That Gu Chunshan was losing his mind was simple and convenient. It helped explain a lot without really explaining anything.

✳

They returned to police headquarters, where Hao Zhicheng got someone to arrange rooms for the PSB officers from Harbin. Hong Jun walked with Xiao Xue to the door of her room. Another female visitor was sharing the room, but was already asleep. They stood in the corridor and talked quietly. 'A bit more drama than I had planned . . . Are you tired?' Hong Jun asked.

'Not in the least,' she replied.

'Do you mind the cold?'

'I'm from Harbin. I don't feel the cold as much as you,' she said. 'Why?'

'I want to take you to see someone.'

'Xiao Xiong? Chief Hao's already arranged for me to see him tomorrow morning. And it is the middle of the night.'

'No, not Xiao Xiong.'

'Then who?'

'You'll find out soon enough.'

'You really do like mysteries . . . '

'You might say that. Go get changed out of that uniform. You'll need boots, and a heavy coat.'

✳

Big snowflakes were falling almost vertically now, the wind having dropped significantly, and in the dim yellow glow of the streetlamps, the silent streets made the town look quite beautiful. They headed south along the main street, Hong Jun leading the way cautiously along the narrow icy path through the snow, under which a broad pavement lay buried.

'Where are we going?' Xiao Xue called out to him.

'To the railway station, it's warm there.'

The waiting room was full of snoring, sleeping people under and amid piles of bags and packs and blankets, unable to find or afford alternative shelter for the night. Hong Jun took Xiao Xue into a corner.

Xiao Xue looked round at the people in the room, some sitting, some lying, all with their eyes shut. 'So . . . who are we here to see?'

'See the woman sitting over there by the radiator, the one with the filthy clothes and hair like a scarecrow?'

'Some crazy woman? What's the point of looking at her, unless you're thinking of becoming a psychiatrist?'

'She's a crucial link in our case. And I don't think she's crazy.'

When it was nearly light, the mad woman got to her feet, clutching her ragged robe tightly around her, and staggered out of the waiting room. Hong Jun and Xiao Xue waited for a moment, then got up and followed her out. The snow was still falling, and the ground was virgin white.

They watched her make for the public toilet block and they followed at a discreet distance. The sky was just beginning to get light now. Occasionally someone would go into the toilet. Xiao Xue didn't look at them too closely, but after twenty minutes the woman hadn't re-emerged and she went to take a look. The toilet block was empty, but she found in the corner a rolled up bundle of the ragged clothes she was wearing.

'The mad woman's vanished,' she told Hong Jun.

'Vanished?' he said. 'That's great.'

'What do you mean *great*?'

'That means she isn't really mad,' he replied. 'But Deputy Division Chief Xiao, I have to say that your tracking skills leave a little to be desired.'

'Oh bugger off, you . . . What on earth is all this about?'

'Let's go to my hotel. It's warmer, and I'll explain everything over hot coffee.'

CHAPTER TWENTY-FIVE

XIAO XUE STOOD in the empty interrogation room. She straightened her uniform jacket. It was virtually identical to every other room used for the same purpose by the PSB. Two chairs, a table, blank scuffed walls. Time passed unnoticed, and hours could be made to feel like days. She didn't like doing interrogations, preferring to study her books on criminology and develop her psychological skills than deal with the practical side of police work.

Hong Jun had told her he thought Old Bao was her brother. She would have to reach deep inside herself not to get emotional, to focus only on the evidence that proved him right or not. She felt very uneasy. She had asked Hong Jun to join her in the interview, but he said he needed to follow up on the woman, though she still couldn't see any connection between her and everything else going on.

The heavy tread of feet in the corridor outside and the rattle of the door handle made her heart beat faster. She turned and saw a big burly man with a bushy beard. She stared at him closely, first scrutinising his face and eyes, then taking in his whole form. The escorting officers left the two of them alone.

The scar on Old Bao's forehead twitched but he was otherwise un-responsive to the woman in the PSB uniform. He sat at the table, and fixed his eyes on the ceiling.

Xiao Xue stood in front of him, staring unflinchingly at the face surrounded by grizzled, greying hair. Her lips trembled and her eyes moistened, and she felt overcome with emotion. 'Brother,' she said.

'Who's your brother? Sounds like you've got the wrong person, girl!'

'I know you recognise me.'

'Nope, never seen you before.'

There were a lot more wrinkles on his face, and a big scar on the right side of his forehead, and the greying hair around his temples made him seem much older . . . but it was Xiao Xiong.

'Did you know that in the painful days before he died, Dad talked about you all the time?' She knew her strategy was unfair, but she didn't want to play his game of denial. And besides, she was angry and needed to let it out. 'He blamed himself for making you share his suffering from such an early age, he felt he had hurt you, and he hoped you would be able to forgive him. Those last few days, he spent the whole time hoping you'd come back and be by his side, and just tell him that you didn't hate him. I tried to find you by putting ads in newspapers, but you never showed up. And just before he died, he kept calling out, "Xiao Xiong, my son. Xiao Xiong!" He was sure you would come. I sat with him, and hoped. But he died. Since then, whenever you come into my thoughts, it's always the same as what went through my mind that day, holding his cold, fragile hand. You bastard. How could you do that to him? Why do that to him?'

Xiao Xue had felt like crying at seeing him again after so much time, but instead she had tapped into a reservoir of hate and anger.

'Don't cry, please. What you just said reminded me of someone I met in the Xing'an Mountains, a wanderer named Xiao Xiong. A very righteous fellow, he was, and we looked very much alike, so we became like brothers. Unfortunately he became ill and died. But before he passed on, he told me he had a sister named Xiao Xue, who he said was the best sister in the world. And he asked me, if I should ever happen to meet her, to thank her on his behalf, and to ask for her pardon.

'After hearing what you said just now, I believe you are indeed the same Xiao Xue. So in the name of your late brother, I say, "Thank you, good sister, and please forgive him! He really did have a hard life."'

Xiao Xue slowly wiped the tears from her face, felt ashamed at letting her emotions get the better of her professionalism and looked suspiciously at the man in front of her. He sounded sincere, insisting he really wasn't Xiao Xiong. But she couldn't ignore what her eyes and intuition told her. What could Xiao Xiong have done that he daren't reveal himself, even to her? Was he protecting her?

Taking a few steps back, she leaned against the interrogation table and said, deliberately, 'You don't need to make up stories. I understand what you're saying. Whether you admit that you're Xiao Xiong or not, I just want to tell you this . . . don't imagine that you're the only good person in the world.'

'What do you mean by that?'

'Just what I said,' she replied. 'Think it over. Just don't look down on everyone else, and treat them with contempt.'

'What do you know about what I've been through,' he said. 'How can you talk to me like that?'

'I certainly do know what you've been through,' she replied. 'Maybe I didn't before, but I do now. Even if you've been wrongfully suspected of a crime, that doesn't mean you should go around trying to take revenge by yourself. I can protect myself, and I can help you use the law to resolve your problem . . .'

'The law?' Xiao Xiong cut in, and let loose a roar of incredulous laughter. 'The law, it sounds so great, doesn't it?' he shouted. 'It wears the cloak of justice, but it's always double-dealing. To the ordinary people it behaves like a stern grandfather, but when it comes to dealing with the ones who make the rules, the Party officials, it turns into a cowardly son of a bitch. And the more important the official, the more insignificant the law becomes. In this world, if you have power, then you *are* the law. If I was a big official, would you dare to lock me up like this? Even if I'd killed someone, would your law find me guilty? No way. You'd all be saying I was right to kill that person and I'd done a good thing and the wretch deserved to die, a long time ago.

'You can take your law and feed it to the dogs. But I tell you,' he added, wagging his finger, 'even the dogs wouldn't want to eat it.'

'You're wrong.' She had worked hard to earn her uniform, and its badges of rank, and still believed in what it stood for. 'The law is supposed to be fair and just. There are certainly lots of problems in how it's implemented, but that doesn't mean the law itself is unfair.'

'That law you're talking about is something they only teach in college.'

Xiao Xue remembered how her brother had always loved arguing with people when he was young. 'Grandma used to say you were "pigheaded". Remember the saying, "It's easier to move mountains and rivers than it is to change a man's nature"? I don't want to quarrel with you any more. You are Xiao Xiong. I suppose we should just use science to prove it.'

She was getting nowhere and tried a different tack. 'Why don't you tell me what you've been doing all these years?'

'What do you mean?' he asked.

'For example, where have you been living these past, say, ten years?'

'Hey, get this clear, Xiao Xiong is dead. My name is Bao Qingfu.'

'Then that should be easy. Tell me what Bao Qingfu has been doing to end up in this interrogation room. I'm not going anywhere. Neither are you. Maybe the Xiao Xiong I knew – my brother – *is* dead. So tell me . . . *who are you?*'

CHAPTER TWENTY-SIX

DEEP IN THE mountains of the Greater Xing'an range lies the town of Alihe. It was a beautiful little town, mountains on three sides and lush summer grasslands on the other, and a little river meandering past to the south. Many of its inhabitants were from the Orochen ethnic group, nomadic hunters who had settled down and made permanent homes here after the revolution. As the town grew, factories and schools were built, and a railway line too. But it wasn't until economic reforms began in the 1980s that Alihe began to flourish.

The station stood on raised ground, at the end of a broad road lined with shops, restaurants, hotels, office buildings and cinemas. Beyond them stood row upon row of neat brick houses, bristling with television aerials, under a dense mesh of power lines.

But the most impressive place in town was the freight yard to the south of the station. Here, fresh cut tree trunks roughly shorn of branches were stacked in piles by the hundreds and thousands, like so many small hills. Little diesel locomotives shunted open wagons to and fro to be filled with logs, and lined up for coupling to heavier engines that would carry them to all corners of the growing nation.

Bao Qingfu arrived in Alihe on a bright sunny day and headed straight to the freight yard, where the teams of timber haulers were loading up the tree trunks at a steady pace. The lifters always worked in teams, each member with his designated place along the tree trunk. There were no cranes for lifting the massive lengths of lumber, just the strength of their shoulders. It was tough work. But the more timber they moved, the more they got paid, and that was incentive enough. Each of the teams had its leader, who called out time, making up rhymes to ensure their movements were coordinated as they lifted. If a woman came into the freight yard, he might use her as inspiration for a chant, describing her from head to toe in such a scurrilous way that she wouldn't dare look at them as she passed, though the only thing the men really listened to was the beat. The tiniest mishap could lead to injury or death.

Bao Qingfu was allocated to join one of the lifting teams. He was a big, stocky fellow, but to the veteran lifters, his shoulders looked a little on the soft side. Nobody wanted to have a weak link in their team. Boss Du was the leader of the team, and he had agreed to take him on. 'All right? Think you can cope?' he asked.

'No problem!' Bao replied.

'I'm serious, kid, there's no point talking big. Our job's no joke and just being fit is not enough, you've got to be able to put up with a lot of pain too. I'm not tryin' to scare you or nothing, but you'll definitely lose a few layers of skin off your shoulders within the first few days.'

'If you can cope with it, then so can I,' Bao replied.

'Fine, we'll call you Big Bao,' he said, and that was it, he was part of the team.

*

At the foot of the mountain to the south of Alihe town lived a father and daughter of the Orochen minority. The father was a renowned huntsman, Uncle Mo. His daughter Yingmei was a fine-looking girl, with a round face, big eyes, high cheekbones, white teeth, long black hair and an ample figure. She'd lost her mother when she was small, and had grown up in the hills and forests with her father; this had not only given her hunting skills, but made her tough and forthright in character.

Uncle Mo was a good friend of Boss Du. One evening, Yingmei had gone to deliver some venison to the Du family. When she set off home, most of the timber yard was dark. The lights were only on in areas at work, throwing deep shadows around the rest of the yard. She was walking swiftly along the path between the stacks of wood when a man appeared from behind one, blocking her way. She saw a glint from the knife in his hand.

'What do you want?' Yingmei took a careful step back, ready to take a flying kick and knock the knife out of the man's hand. But before she could raise her leg, another man grabbed her from behind, around the throat. She barely managed to call out 'Help!' before a large hand covered her mouth. She fought, managing to break free for a few seconds, screaming 'Help! Help me!'

One of them stuffed a face flannel into her mouth and they dragged her into the shadows of a wood stack, forced her to the ground and began pulling at her trousers.

'Hey, what are you doing?' shouted a man. It was Big Bao, who had just finished a long, tiring shift lifting logs. When they first heard him coming, the two thugs had panicked, but seeing he was on his own, one of them got up and walked towards him, and pointed the tip of his knife at him. 'Mind your own fucking business! You want to die? Now get out of here.'

'This is nothing to do with me, just let me go past.' They stepped aside. Big Bao saw clearly what was about to happen, but his eyes were on the hand holding the knife and, a few paces on, he turned and with one kick sent the knife flying, raised his fists and sent one of the men sprawling with a blow to his chin. The other charged, but with a quick dodge he was sent flat on his face. They gathered their wits and charged again, and, with a fluid motion of Bao's arm they were flat on their backs. 'Get out of here, both of you,' he said, and they vanished into the darkness.

He didn't give chase. 'Are you okay?' he asked, pulling free the rag in her mouth.

Yingmei took a deep breath, then said gratefully, 'You saved me, brother. I don't know how I can thank you.'

'Just go home, quickly,' he said, and made to leave.

But Yingmei blocked his way. 'Will you at least walk me home? Those men might try again and I'm frightened.'

Uncle Mo, worried that his daughter hadn't returned, was standing outside the house looking out for her. 'Dad,' she called out, rushing over to him, and whispered to him what had happened.

Hearing this, Uncle Mo ran over to the man. 'Thank you,' he said. 'You're a hero, sir. Thank you. Please come in.'

Seeing it would be hard to refuse, Big Bao followed him inside.

The house was a single-storey building with three rooms. There was a little yard at the front, surrounded by a wooden fence. The yard was filled with stacks of firewood. The furniture inside was unvarnished wood, roughly hewn. Uncle Mo invited the visitor to sit at the head of the *kang*. Only now, in the glow of the lamplight, did they realise that he was quite young, with big eyes and bushy eyebrows.

Yingmei brought him a cup of tea and put it on the *kang* table. 'You saved my daughter's life,' said Uncle Mo. 'Please, have some tea.'

'Thank you,' he replied.

Yingmei brought chopsticks and a bowl of roasted venison, which she put down in front of the young man. 'Please,' said Uncle Mo. 'Have some meat.'

The young man attempted to decline. 'There's no need,' he said. 'I've eaten.'

'You must,' Yingmei told him, 'out of respect for us. It's an Orochen custom.'

He tried a piece of the venison, which was hot and burned his mouth, although he tried not to show it.

'And please tell me, what is your name?' said Uncle Mo.

'My name is Bao Qingfu,' he replied.

'Everyone calls my dad Uncle Mo. And I'm Yingmei.'

'*Qingfu* . . . "celebrate good fortune" . . . it's a fine name!' said Uncle Mo, outlining the characters with his finger on the table. 'You're not from Alihe?'

'My home is down south. I came here looking for work. Back home there are a lot of people and not much land, and it's hard to make money,' he said. 'Everyone says there's money to be made up here in the Xing'an Mountains, if you're strong.'

'So what are you doing now?'

'Lifting in the lumber yard.'

'Hey, are you the new guy on Boss Du's team?' asked Uncle Mo.

'Yes, I am.'

'Boss Du is a good friend of my dad,' Yingmei explained. 'I was just at his house this evening, taking him some of this meat, and he was telling me about a new member in their team. He said it was a big strong guy . . . so that's you.'

'How long do you plan to work here?' Uncle Mo asked him.

'It's hard to say,' he replied. 'If I can find steady work, I might stay a few years, if not, then maybe I'll just go back home again.'

'I tell you, Qingfu,' Uncle Mo continued, 'Boss Du is a good guy. You'll do okay with him. Where are you living?'

'In that little row of buildings next to the lumber yard . . . it's good.'

'Well, from now on,' he said, 'treat this place as your home, come whenever you like. And you're welcome to stay here too. Orochen people are used to living up in the mountains. We like it when people just come and go as they please, and it would please us if you would visit. You don't want to see an Orochen when we're displeased . . . '

Bao Qingfu nodded in agreement.

*

Winter came, and thick snow covered the mountains and the hills, as though to protect them from the fearsome ravages of the north wind. For the town of Alihe, it was the start of the busiest season of the year. Team after team of loggers set up camp in the mountains, and the valleys echoed with the sound of chainsaws and tractors dragging away the lumber. Timber trucks roared up and down the icy mountain roads, carrying the felled trees to the freight yard beside the railway station. Groups of lumberjacks, wearing green or blue fur-lined coats, were all over town, in the restaurants, at the shops, at the bars. They were big drinkers and eaters, and bought up the best cigarettes and all the canned food and alcohol off the shelves. Clever shop owners had lain in extra supplies, but they were canny too, and only replenished the shelves when others began to run out and prices rose. Local townsfolk grumbled, even though they were all making extra money too, because the loggers disturbed their peaceful lives and made everyday items expensive.

Bao Qingfu had grown accustomed to his hard life, and whenever he had a day off he would go to Uncle Mo's place, where he was taught hunting, learning more with each visit and making Uncle Mo happy to be able to pass on his skills, many of which had been passed on to him by his father. One winter morning, when the sun rose late and the team was on a rest day, Bao Qingfu got up early and set off through the hazy dawn light to Uncle Mo's house, where Yingmei met him at the door. 'Dad says he wants to test your shooting skills. If you pass, you're ready to go hunting alone.'

They headed up towards the mountain to the south, trekking through the woods until they reached a clearing. Uncle Mo handed his gun to Bao Qingfu, walked some twenty long paces away and pulled a round red radish from his knapsack. He looked at Qingfu, and, seeing that he was ready, tossed the radish high into the air. By the time it reached its apex, Bao had the gun butt against his shoulder and watched it through the sights of the gun as it fell. A single shot cracked, the radish quivered and hit the ground.

'He hit it!' shouted Yingmei excitedly.

'Quiet, girl,' hissed Uncle Mo, who threw the radish again, three times, and each time Bao scored a hit.

'Qingfu, from today, you are a huntsman. Remember, bullets are expensive and ammunition is a hunter's capital. Only shoot when you can make a profit.' He handed Bao his satchel, took Yingmei by the shoulders and led her back down the path. 'Let's wish Brother Bao good luck today.' Yingmei protested, and he shushed her. 'The first time, he must go alone. You know that is our custom.'

Bao Qingfu had gone tracking a few times before. Uncle Mo had made him practise holding the gun when they were in the house, but up in the hills he had never let him touch it before, instead explaining how to recognise the tracks of different animals, and recalling his own hunting experiences. Bao Qingfu felt frustrated that all Uncle Mo let him do was crawl around in the snow, looking at snowflakes. But now it was starting to make sense. A hunter must learn to track his prey, and how it thinks, if he was going to catch it and fill his belly.

Now it was time to put all those lessons to work. He scanned the terrain, left the mountain path and tramped up towards the forest, through snow more than a foot deep. In his imagination, he met a roe deer, and killed it with a single shot to the head. He imagined dragging the deer behind him, back to Uncle Mo's house. But the whole morning passed and he had not seen so much as a pheasant track.

Head down looking at the snow, he hadn't noticed the sky above gradually fill with dark grey clouds. His legs were tired and he looked for a place to rest, catching sight of a big tree stump up ahead. He walked towards it, but stopped when he remembered Uncle Mo's warning: 'This is the Old Mountain God's seat, you mustn't sit on it, whatever you do, or it will bring you bad luck.' He wasn't superstitious and he'd been taught from an early age not to believe in old traditions. But he needed luck to be on his side today and he stood, trying to count the circles of the stump as he ate the food Yingmei had packed for him. He kept losing count and would start again. This was a very old tree, with many rings tightly packed so it was hard to tell if one ring was really four or five.

He'd given up hope of shooting a deer and thought a brace of pheasant would satisfy Uncle Mo, or a big wild rabbit for the pot. He couldn't go back empty-handed.

Two yellow shapes moved at the foot of the hill opposite to where he was standing. He rubbed his eyes. Two deer. His heart began to beat faster, but Uncle Mo always said to remain calm and not to get excited because they could hear your heartbeat and smell your anticipation. He moved softly through the trees, taking his time circling gently into a downwind position. By the time he reached the edge of the wood, the deer had moved to the other side of the little hill but he had their tracks now and followed. He watched them edge their way across a frozen pond surrounded by piles of windblown snow. He needed to get closer, to get them within range. He thought he could find enough cover if he hugged the edge of the wood. Reaching up to use a branch to brace his next step, a twig snapped, their ears twitched in his direction and they were off, waggling their little white behinds as they bounded through the snow. He gave chase, and saw them head into some trees on the hillside and for a while followed their incautious tracks around several more hillocks, but lost them. He retraced his own steps, trying to see where their feet had taken them, but all around was virgin snow.

Weary and irritable, he leaned against a big tree. A good hunter must be a good shot, but mostly he must be patient and willing to suffer,

Uncle Mo had said over and over. Learn the habits of his prey. Where did he lose the tracks and how had they eluded him?

He went back to a patch of trees, bending often to look at the snow from different angles. There. The faintest shadow of pheasant claws, only a light dusting of snow blurring them. Gun at the ready, he followed the tracks, so close to the ground he was almost crawling. Twice they disappeared, but he found them again a little further on. He followed the tracks for nearly four hundred metres. His back ached. His eyes burned.

There: necks and little eyes intent on finding food. He raised the gun, but he was too noisy and the pheasants took flight. He raised the gun in a neat arc of his body and squeezed the trigger. Flapping wings went limp and a bird fell in a somersault into the snow.

Now he could go home, and maybe providence would reward him with something more, but at least face was saved. He felt stronger and more assured as he fastened the pheasant to his belt and began heading down the mountain. He thought he was following his own tracks, but they vanished and, looking around, couldn't find where they picked up again. He looked up and realised the sky was now grey and hazy in the near distance, with the wind coming towards him. He looked at the hillocks around him and thought that the one ahead looked familiar, but then he started to think the path beside the next little hill looked familiar too, and all the hills looked the same. He looked up again. The sky was getting darker and darker. He felt cold and pulled his coat closer around his neck.

What would Uncle Mo do? What had he told him to do? He climbed the hillock ahead, to find a higher point that might let him see the lights of Alihe.

The hillside was steep. He slung the gun across his back, shifted the pheasant to the strap of his rucksack and crawled uphill on all fours. Several times he slipped in the deep snow and had to climb again. At the top, he realised he had to get higher.

He climbed for about an hour, higher, but not high enough. All around him were hills in all directions. He looked for some hint of the sun that might let him get his bearings. He could be on the other side of the mountain, for all he knew. The clouds were impenetrable. Where was Alihe? He peered, and a row of lights seemed to be moving slowly to his left. A train? He watched, found a fixed point beyond it, and made sure the lights were moving. Yes, the railway was below, tracks not even he could lose.

✳

'Dad . . . why isn't Big Bao back yet?'

'I'm sure it's because he hasn't caught anything, so he doesn't want to come back,' said Uncle Mo, who was sitting at the head of the *kang* smoking. 'He's stubborn.'

'He couldn't have got lost, could he?' Yingmei said. 'It's the first time he's been up in the mountains on his own, and the weather's getting really bad. Even you'd have trouble out in this.'

'Qingfu's not some stupid kid, he's smart.' But Uncle Mo couldn't help glancing out of the window, and could see the snow was now falling steadily.

Yingmei got up, put on her fur-lined coat and said, 'Come on Dad, let's go and look for him.'

The gate opened and closed and Bao Qingfu was in the doorway.

'Brother Bao, how come you're so late?' Yingmei asked him. 'You had us really worried.'

'You see?' Uncle Mo said cheerfully. 'Qingfu, what took you so long?'

'I was tracking a pair of deer, and I got too caught up in the chase. Wily creatures, they taught me a thing or two. Next time, maybe.'

'So what present did the Old Mountain God give you today?' asked Uncle Mo.

'The Mountain God is, I think, still testing me. I got one pheasant, with one shot.' Qingfu laid the pheasant out.

'And a fine pheasant it is too. Not everyone gets something the first time in the mountains, so you must have done something right.'

Uncle Mo asked him to sit with him on the *kang*. 'Qingfu, there's something I want to discuss with you. If you like, why don't you give up working in the timber yard and come and live with us?'

'Oh . . . but Boss Du needs me.'

'I'll go with you tomorrow to collect your things, and you can move in here,' said Yingmei, decisively.

Uncle Mo declared that the hungry hunter needed to eat and Yingmei fetched rice and vegetables. Uncle Mo took out a bottle of grain spirit and said to Qingfu, 'Today we've got something to celebrate. Come on, you and I have a few toasts to make. You are a hunter, now . . . Drink.'

Summer is the most beautiful season in the Xing'an Mountains. The rolling hills dressed in their best green, the branches thick with leaves, the grasslands and hillsides waving with succulent grasses and flowers of every hue: bright red lilies, gorgeous purple roses, herbaceous peonies with big white flowers, golden-headed dandelions and edible amaranths dangling their little greenish-white blossoms, thoroughwort, endives, and yellow day lilies all scattered across the hills and meadows.

That particular afternoon, Bao Qingfu was at a loose end, and Yingmei asked him to go into the hills with her to pick sorghum fruit, a kind of wild strawberry. When they got up on the hillside, she immediately darted off into the trees. Qingfu looked around the meadow, but couldn't see any wild strawberries, so he lay down in the grass and watched the few white clouds bobbing in the deep blue sky. A sparrow hawk circled slowly. From the wood came the sound of a cuckoo calling out to its mate, so gentle and filled with warmth.

His eyes were starting to close when a stalk of sorghum fruit landed on Qingfu's chest. He sat up and looked round, but could see nothing other than grass and bushes. He pulled off one of the bright red fruits and tossed it into his mouth, savouring its sour-sweet taste.

More and more stalks of sorghum fruit began landing on the ground beside him, now accompanied by peals of silvery laughter. Yingmei ran out of the bushes, and sat in the grass facing him. She threw her last few stalks of sorghum fruit onto his legs, and asked, 'So Brother Bao, where are the sorghum fruit you picked?'

'I couldn't find any,' he said. 'How did you manage to find so many? Where did you find them?'

'You have to look on the edge of the woods, on a sunny slope,' she replied. Her head was leaning to one side, gazing at Qingfu. 'Do they taste good?' He nodded and picked a few more of the fruit from the stalks and popped them into his mouth.

Yingmei picked a little red flower from among the grass beside her, and fiddled with it in her hand. She turned and, with her back to Qingfu, picked two long blades of grass. Carefully, she made a little hole in the middle of each, then twisted them together, turned them over in the middle and gently spread them out flat again. She held them in her hand for a while, then turned round and handed them to Bao Qingfu.

'Brother Bao, can you separate these two blades of grass? You're not allowed to tear them!' she said.

Qingfu looked at the blades of grass, woven together in the shape of a fried dough twist. He turned them over and over, trying to figure out how to separate them, but he couldn't do it. He was baffled by the weave. He shook his head. 'Sorry, I can't do it.'

'You really can't separate them? That's great.'

Thinking that her voice sounded a little strange, Qingfu instinctively shot a glance at her. She quickly looked down at the red flowers in her hand, mumbling, 'They can't be separated.' After a little while, she looked up, her cheeks a little flushed, and said, 'Brother Bao, do you think . . . do you think I'm nice?'

'Nice? You hardly need to ask that! Both you and Uncle Mo have been so nice to me! You're like my sister!' he replied, sincerely.

'Sister . . . ?' Yingmei didn't seem at all satisfied with the word. Eyes downcast, she asked, 'Why am I like your sister, and not . . . not anything else?'

'What else could you be?' he asked in surprise. 'You really are my sister!'

'You . . . Oh, you are so stupid.' She stood sharply and began to walk off down the hillside without as much as a backwards glance.

Qingfu got to his feet and watched her silhouette disappear, with a sigh of resignation. He wasn't stupid at all, but some things were hard for him to express. He began to walk slowly after her.

*

Yingmei ran all the way home. Her father was out, probably drinking with Boss Du. She stood blankly in the doorway, as if in a trance, and walked over to the *kang* where Qingfu slept. In a daze, she gazed at the quilt she had washed for him. How could he be so . . . so infuriating? He was normally so clever and capable. He was honest, he treated people well, yet when it came to this subject he was stupid. It was almost as though he was intentionally playing dumb. But it wasn't easy for a girl to talk to him about something like this. She wished her mother were still alive.

As her imagination began to wander, Yingmei suddenly noticed a white sleeve sticking out from under Qingfu's quilt. She recognised it as one of his old shirts, and remembered that the collar was torn. She'd meant to darn it the last time she washed it, but had got busy and forgotten. Now, even though she was feeling annoyed with him, she picked it up and was about to take the shirt to her room to mend it when her finger brushed against a paper bag. She opened up the shirt and found a little white paper package protruding from a breast pocket crudely sewn onto the inside of the shirt, clearly by Qingfu himself. In the past, when she'd washed the shirt, the pocket had always been empty. She'd always thought it was strange. Once she'd asked him what he used it for, and he'd said it was for keeping money, but she wasn't convinced.

She took out the package, opened it up and found a white envelope inside. There was no writing on the outside, but when she opened it she found that it contained a sheet of folded letter paper. She knew it was wrong to look at other people's letters, so she put it back into the envelope. But as she was replacing it, she noticed another little paper packet inside the envelope, and tipped it out. She hesitated for a moment, but in the end, she had to open it and found that what Qingfu had been keeping so carefully next to his heart was a photograph of a girl – of the kind people used as a token of affection for someone they were having a relationship with. After crying for a while, she felt a little better. She wiped away the tears, and carefully scrutinised the little black and white picture. In the end, she couldn't suppress a sigh of admiration. The girl was so fine-looking, a beautifully shaped face with perfectly symmetrical features, a kind expression and a gentle smile.

She sat on the bed in silence. She felt much calmer now. She felt she understood Qingfu much better; the reason he was able to put up with so much suffering was because he had a love in his heart to inspire him. That also explained why he often sat alone, lost in thought. Yingmei now only felt even more admiration for Qingfu's character. A man who could love so devotedly was exactly what she longed for. Even if she wasn't the one he loved, she nevertheless felt he was more deserving of respect.

*

Qingfu wondered what he was going to say to Yingmei. He knew she was very kind-hearted and cheerful in her nature, if a little wilful. When she wasn't happy, she wouldn't talk to him for days. But her moods could also change very quickly. She had a natural talent for acting, and Uncle Mo had once told him that when she was at school in the town, she had played the role of Little Changbao in the propaganda team's performance of the revolutionary opera *Taking Tiger Mountain by Strategy*.

When he reached the courtyard, Yingmei opened the door of the house for him as usual. Glancing at her, he wasn't sure whether she was angry at him, or had just been play-acting on the hill.

'Brother Bao . . . ' she said. 'You've never talked about your family. Where exactly do you come from down south?'

'From Jingxian County, in Hebei Province,' he said.

'Jingxian?' Yingmei had never heard the name before. But then again, she'd only ever really heard of Beijing and Tianjin. 'Is it far from Beijing?' she asked.

'Oh, it's hundreds of kilometres from there.'

'But have you been to Beijing?'

'I have,' he said. 'It sure is a big place.'

'Really?' she replied. 'If I can go to Beijing once in my life I'll be happy.'

'That's easy,' said Qingfu. 'When I go home for the holidays next time, I'll take you with me to Beijing to have a look.'

'Really? That would be fantastic. So when are you going home next?' she asked.

'I'm not sure yet. I need to wait until I've earned enough money.'

'Tell me more about your family,' she said, as nonchalantly as she could.

'There's no one left . . . and what are you asking about that for anyway?'

'Oh, no reason,' she said. 'I was just wondering why you'd never got a letter or anything.' Then, seeing he didn't seem to want to talk about it, asked him why his accent sounded so similar to theirs. 'Not like some of those other people from down south,' she said. 'They have such weird accents.'

Qingfu laughed and said it was because he'd spent so many years drifting around the northeast. Then he began telling her the strange way that people pronounced words where he came from, and he soon had Yingmei in fits of laughter. They were like brother and sister, though each of them kept their own secrets.

CHAPTER TWENTY-SEVEN

OLD BAO SEEMED to be contemplating his own memories, and Xiao Xue sat silently, letting him tell his story at his own pace. Neither heard the door of the interrogation room open, nor were they aware that Hong Jun and Wu Hongfei had entered. Hong Jun saw them looking lost in thought.

'Brother and sister meeting again,' Hong Jun said, startling them both from their thoughts. 'This was meant to be a happy ending. How come it looks more like a tragedy?'

Xiao Xue glared at him. 'Xiao Xiong is dead. *His* name is Bao Qingfu.'

'Really?' Hong Jun replied. 'It doesn't matter.' He sat on the corner of the desk, arms folded.

'Whether your name is Xiao Xiong, or Bao Qingfu, or Dumb Deer, doesn't make any difference. Names aren't an intrinsic part of a human being, are they? They're just a symbol we use to differentiate ourselves from the next person. To borrow from the criminology textbooks, a name can't be used as evidence for the positive identification of an individual. But Xiao Xiong, or Bao Qingfu, or whatever you prefer to call yourself, there is something I want to ask you: Do you know a woman called Mo Yingmei?'

'What?' Old Bao leapt to his feet. 'You've arrested her? Listen to me. Each person alone is responsible for their own actions. This has nothing to do with her. If you dare touch a hair on her head, you'll have to answer to me.'

Hong Jun noticed that the scar on Old Bao's forehead had become red and was pulsing. 'Calm down,' he said. 'She's fine. She's staying in the Dazhong Hotel. I'm sure she's come here to wait until you get out.'

Old Bao's mouth opened, but he said nothing. He sat and looked at his hands, which had both closed into fists. Xiao Xue looked at Hong Jun, uncertain about this new approach, and left the interrogation room. Chief Wu followed her.

'Some people can only think about the pain in their own lives,' said Hong Jun as he sat in the chair in the interrogation room, 'and are unaware of the pain others have suffered, and of the pain they themselves have caused in other people's lives.' Hong Jun let the silence of the room close around them. 'You're really selfish.' He raised his voice. 'For the sake of your own safety, you're willing to let other people suffer.'

Old Bao flinched at the outburst.

'I think Deputy Division Chief Xiao Xue asked you a question. I would appreciate an answer. Do you understand? Who are you?' Hong Jun said, palms flat on the table. 'Old Bao, you've got to tell us the truth. *Now.*'

Since his earliest days, Xiao Xiong had been used to life treating him harshly. Because his father had been labelled a 'rightist' during the political campaigns of the late 1950s, the other children had given him the nickname 'little rightist'. It followed him everywhere, even after his father was rehabilitated, even when he was sent down as an 'educated youth' to Binbei Farm. Once, he and the others were playing a game based on the film *The Red Defence Unit of Hong Lake* and he wanted to play the part of the head of the loyal defence unit, but the others forced him to be the traitor, Wang Jinbiao. When he refused, the others started teasing him. 'Lit-tle righ-tist, lit-tle righ-tist,' they taunted.

He grew accustomed to the frostiness of others and he became cold and detached, silent and taciturn, a loner. He devoted the time others spent at play to reading. He was tall and strong, and trained his body so he could protect his self-respect with his sizeable fists. He rarely smiled and others grew afraid of him, though he was not known to be a bully; more one to break up bullying if he saw it.

The 'cap' of being a rightist was removed from his father's head as if it never happened, but while the official record might be easily expunged, his memories didn't fade. Xiao Xiong was intelligent and studied hard, and wasn't scared of hard labour, and so he was given a job in the farm's mechanical unit, and even got to drive a tractor. On this remote farm, driving a tractor was seen as a very important job, and the suspicion he had learned to expect from others quickly gave way to a much friendlier, more respectful attitude. Xiao Xiong was always willing to help out if anyone asked him, but he still rarely spoke. His temper retained its notoriety, and even young girls who loved to tease and flirt with boys didn't dare joke lightly with him.

To Li Hongmei, he was a special person. Whenever she ran into others, they'd always try to find an excuse to talk to her. And whenever she went to the fields to deliver food to workers, she would get a lift on the farm's Iron Bull 555 tractor. But whenever Xiao Xiong was driving her, he would help her load the food into the trailer at the back without saying a word, jump into the driver's cabin and wait for her to climb on board. When they were driving, she would be sitting right behind him, all without saying a word. Sometimes she would ask him a question, and he would give her brief replies, just 'yes' or 'no' if that sufficed.

At first, Hongmei thought he was rude, and would sometimes respond to his silence with an icy expression. But emotions can play strange games and the more the other boys tried to get close to her, the less she noticed them. Xiao Xiong did all he could to keep his distance, yet her interest in him only grew.

It wasn't that Xiao Xiong was a man without feelings. In fact, he liked Hongmei very much, and in his eyes she was the perfect woman. She was beautiful, outgoing, friendly and kind-hearted. He had even dreamt of what a joy it would be to share his life with her. The shadow cast by his childhood experiences made him defensive and a little bit frightened. He buried both love and hatred deep within his heart, showing only an emotionless face to the world. He was in love with Hongmei, but he did not know whether she felt the same way. He could cope with the pain of this love simply withering away quietly in his heart, but he definitely couldn't face the embarrassment of expressing his love, only for it to be rejected. Self-respect was what had kept him going and it was the most precious thing he had. But the way he felt when they were left alone . . .

'I'll wait for you after dinner under the big tree on the west side of the farmyard,' said the note he slipped into her hand at the canteen as they all queued for dinner. He had thought about what to say, how to say it, and thought a simple note was the best approach. If she wasn't interested in him in that way, all she had to do was not come, and he would understand. Face saved all round. Now he was standing under the big tree, trying not to look towards the little path. The sun had set now, and the clouds on the horizon had turned a deep grey. The big elm tree changed shape as the light faded away. It was an isolated spot, and there was no one in sight. He heard dogs barking and people's laughter carried across from the residential quarters on the evening breeze. Xiao Xiong walked around and around the tree. 'She'll come.'

He saw a solitary figure on the path from the courtyard. His heart began to thump. He quickly walked to meet her, slowing down as he got closer. They eventually stopped a few paces apart.

'You came, Hongmei!' he said.

'Have you been here long?'

'No, I just got here.'

'After we finished tidying up the canteen I went home to tell my dad I was going out, so I'm a bit late,' she explained.

She looked at him in silence. He'd prepared things to say to her, but just gazed at her, smiling awkwardly.

'So why did you ask me to come?' she asked.

'Hongmei, I . . . I want . . . I want us to be a couple.'

He cursed himself for sounding so unromantic. He knew what she wanted to hear, and seeing how she had carefully brushed her hair and smartened herself up before coming out, she wanted words of love that might make her blush, or for him to just throw his arms around her and kiss her. But he was frightened. It was the best he could do and he felt he had failed her.

When she didn't reply, Xiao Xiong began to panic, and quickly added, 'Hongmei, I don't have bad intentions, I just want to be with you. If you're not interested, it doesn't matter. Don't be angry.'

'Who said I'm not interested?' she rebuked him softly. She took a couple of steps towards him, and poked him gently in the chest. 'Oh you, you're so dumb,' she said. 'You really are a dumb deer.'

Xiao Xiong pulled her to his chest, bent his head and kissed her gently on the forehead. It felt really nice, he thought.

Hongmei looked up and whispered, 'Kiss me properly . . . on the lips.'

And he did, softly, with all his heart, and gently kissed her again.

*

On the eve of the mid-autumn festival one year later, Xiao Xiong and Li Hongmei drove the Iron Bull 555 out to the edge of the wood, where the tractor unit team were ploughing the fields on the nightshift. After the young men finished eating, they sat round the fire. Someone started to sing, and soon they all joined in, singing the 'Song of the Tractor Drivers'; the lyrics had been written by the Peasant Poet, and Dumb Deer had composed the tune.

> The engine's roar floats across the fields,
> the great iron bull races over the plain,
> it stirs up rolling black waves in its wake;
> an intoxicating fragrance fills the woods and hills.
> Hey – who opens up the fertile soil of the north?
> Hey! Who is it, makes the beautiful border region even more
> exquisite?
> It's us – those happy bachelors, the young tractor drivers!
> Love is like a scorching flame, burning in our youthful hearts;
> Love is like a sparkling star, brightening our little garage.
> Hey! – Who opens up the fertile soil of the north?
> Hey! Who makes the beautiful border region even more exquisite?
> It's us – those happy bachelors, the young tractor drivers!

It was their favourite tune, their pride and joy, their marching song. They'd even taken first prize in the Farm Bureau's Red May singing contest with a choral rendition.

Xiao Xiong helped Hongmei clear up the bowls and plates and put them back in the tractor, and they both climbed into the driver's cabin and drove off down the track beside the woods towards the farm headquarters. Hongmei now always sat alongside Xiao Xiong and as the tractor bumped along, she was sometimes thrown against him.

The bright white headlamps lit up the road, though its surface was so bumpy that the beams often shot off into the night sky. They had just reached the crest of a hill when a roe deer darted from the wood beside them. After a couple of paces it came to a standstill in the middle of the road, staring at the headlights. Xiao Xiong stopped the tractor and turned off its engine, leaving the lights on. He climbed down from the cabin and crept round, hoping to catch the deer unawares. Hongmei got out too, and followed him, wanting to help, her canvas work shoes slipping in the freshly churned soil, sometimes deep, sometimes shallow.

The deer still stood in the road, baring its white teeth, showing no sign of running away. Seeing that Xiao Xiong was about to creep up on the deer from behind, Hongmei's heart began to thump. Distracted, she tripped on a lump of soil and fell. The deer heard her, and leapt into the woods, and the last they saw of it was its white backside as it bounded away.

Xiao Xiong ran back to Hongmei. 'Are you okay? Did you hurt your ankle?'

She brushed the soil from her clothes and said dejectedly, 'What a shame. I'm sorry, a second more and you'd have caught it.'

'It doesn't matter!'

'Why didn't the deer run away when it saw the car?'

'It was just a dumb deer . . . it thinks if it doesn't move, you can't see it . . . don't ask me why.'

'Just like you, my own dumb deer,' she said, leaning in and snuggling against his chest. He could have stood like that forever.

The night was very peaceful, the air fresh and crisp. A full moon hung high in the sky, bathing the hills and plains in a silvery glow. The ponds to the southwest were covered in a milky white mist – under the moonlight this resembled a great fast-flowing river, meandering its way into the mountains. The woods on either side seemed like rugged cliffs, the distant hilltops like islands in the river. In the hands of nature, beauty and mystery blended perfectly together.

They held each other as they took in the beautiful scene in front of them.

'I really want . . . ' he started.

She looked into his eyes. 'What do you want?' she asked.

'I can't say it. I'm scared you'll be angry.'

'Whatever you say I won't be angry.'

'I want to do it with you,' he said.

Hongmei was silent.

'Hongmei, I love you. I really love you.'

'Could you really love me . . . for your whole life?'

Bathed in moonlight, they lost themselves in rapture. There was not the faintest shadow of anger or worry to cloud their hearts, only joy and delight. They were fully conscious of how beautiful life was, how beautiful the world could be.

Spring always came late to the valleys in the shadow of the Xing'an Mountains, but that didn't account for the vagaries of weather, because this year, a cold front cruelly swept it away. The snow and ice, which had only just melted, froze again, and the land, only just regaining its vitality, was set hard again, its early green shoots burned away.

It was after lunch, and Li Hongmei stood alone by the window of the canteen, gazing uneasily at the road outside. The previous day a Section Chief Gu Chunshan from the County PSB had come to see her, and had asked her about Xiao Xiong. He told her that Xiao Xiong was involved in illegal activities and she must break off contact with him. Hongmei knew that Dumb Deer was supposed to be coming back soon. Since he hadn't been on the morning bus, she thought he would probably be on the afternoon run. She was waiting for him in the canteen.

Over the past year or so, Xiao Xiong became a different person. He had made new friends in Harbin, all of them apparently very educated people. He was no longer satisfied simply working on the farm, and was always going off to the city. At first he'd just take some time off work and go there on a trip for ten days or a fortnight, but soon he was basically living there, and only came back once a month or two. Hongmei asked him what he was doing, and he told her he was working on something important. She didn't understand too much when he started talking about 'building democracy', nor was she interested. Life was good on the farm. Why change it? But she was sure that he would never do anything bad. She loved him, and wished that he could be at her side every day. She also hoped that the man she loved would achieve something magnificent and didn't want to stand in his way if he was passionate about what he was doing. But the things this Gu fellow from the PSB told her shattered her calm.

At last she heard the distant rumble of the bus, and soon saw its red body struggling through the snowstorm. It drove off the road and round to the north side of the canteen, where it came to a halt. Hongmei stood in the doorway of the canteen. She saw Xiao Xiong and ran towards him, dragging him inside the canteen, her head darting around to see if they were being watched.

They embraced, but Hongmei broke their kiss. 'Yesterday a PSB man came to see me, and said he was investigating you.'

'The PSB? What did he ask you?'

'He asked me about my relationship with you, whether you'd ever talked to me about a democracy movement or something, then asked when you were coming back.'

'And what did you say?'

'I said we were friends, but I didn't know when you'd be back.'

'What else did he say?' Xiao Xiong asked.

'He said you'd done some illegal things while you were away, and told me to cut off contact with you.'

'Do you believe him?'

'Of course I don't believe him,' said Hongmei. 'But I'm nervous. What have you really been up to? You must tell me.'

'Don't worry,' he said. 'I would never do anything bad.'

'But I'm afraid. I'm always scared that something might happen to you.'

Xiao Xiong pulled her close to him again. 'Don't be frightened. Nothing's going to happen to me,' he whispered.

'I don't need you to do something big, just stay with me and we can lead a peaceful life.' Pressing her face against his chest, she said softly, 'Let's get married. I'll make you happy.'

Xiao Xiong gently stroked her hair with his big hands. He wished he could stay here, enjoying the quiet life with Hongmei. But he found it hard to reconcile a life of inaction and silent acceptance with the person inside him who wanted to make things better. After what happened to his father, he had a responsibility to change the things that had led to such injustice. He was filled with admiration for his new friends. Everything they said was carefully argued and rational, the articles they wrote stirring and uplifting. 'Hongmei,' he said, 'I've got to leave again, there are some things I need to sort out right away.'

'Okay,' she said, quietly. 'You go and hide out for a while. When this is past and it's all over you can come back.'

'Hongmei,' he said, looking at her earnestly, 'my friends keep telling me I should move back to Harbin. I don't really like city life. But maybe it would be best for me, for us. If I could get a transfer back to the city, would you come with me?'

'I'll follow you wherever you go,' she said, and kissed him gently on the lips.

'Hongmei, I do want to marry you. Whatever happens, I promise I'll give you a good life,' he said. 'Do you believe me?'

'I believe you!' she answered. 'But you must go, now, before someone tells the PSB you're here.'

'You're right. I need to go to the Peasant Poet's place to pick something up, and I'll hitch a ride on the road. If anything happens after I've gone,' he added, 'write to me in Harbin – but don't send it to my house, send it to this address.' And he gave her a piece of paper. 'And I'll write to you too.'

'I'll write and tell you everything that happens here. Just look after yourself, please!' There were tears in Hongmei's eyes.

Xiao Xiong gave her a long, loving kiss, and left the canteen. Hongmei stood in the doorway, watching him.

One day in April, Xiao Xiong received a letter from Hongmei. Impatiently, he tore open the envelope.

My dear Xiong,

I miss you a lot. Even though we're not together, my heart is with you every day. I wish this time would go by faster. The only thing I hope for is to see you as soon as possible.

The police are still investigating your case. They're living at the farm now. This Mr Gu has come to see me lots of times. I can tell he doesn't have good intentions towards me. He looks so respectable, and talks in all that formal Mandarin, but I can tell that he has bad thoughts. He says it's entirely his say-so whether your problem becomes serious or not. I think it's true. So I want to give him some encouragement, so that he'll drop the case against you. For your sake, I'd do anything. But don't worry, I won't let him take advantage of me.

How are you at the moment? Any progress with organising your transfer back to the city? I'm longing for your news!

With love forever,
Hongmei
15 April, 1984

When he finished the letter, Xiao Xiong felt very uneasy. He knew he couldn't blame Hongmei, because what she was suggesting was all for his sake. But how could he let the girl he loved start flirting with another man? He wanted to rush back to Binbei Farm and give this Gu character a good hiding, then take Hongmei and run away.

After a day's agonising, he got on the train back to Binbei the same evening. The next morning, he got off the train, had some breakfast and went to the station forecourt to wait for the bus to Binbei Farm. There was still half an hour to go before the bus left, so he started to stroll around the little square in front of the station.

He heard someone hissing his name. 'Brother Xiao, brother Xiao.' He turned to look, and saw that it was Auntie Zhao, his neighbour from the farm. 'Hello Auntie,' he said, 'visiting people in town? Are you going back to the farm too?'

Auntie Zhao didn't reply, but, looking very nervous, led him over to a quieter corner of the square, and said urgently, 'Brother, what are you doing here?'

'Me? I'm going back to the farm for a visit,' he replied.

'Haven't you heard what happened at the farm?'

'No? What? Do you mean the police coming to check up on me? Don't worry about that, it's nothing serious.'

'No, it's not that! You really don't know?' She looked close to tears. 'Someone killed Hongmei!'

'What?' Xiao Xiong thought he must have misheard. 'Hongmei's dead? She's been killed?'

Xiao Xiong stood in a daze, staring into space. After a long while, he finally said, 'She just wrote to me a few days ago. Who killed Hongmei?'

'The PSB investigated and they talked to almost everyone on the farm and did blood tests and arrested the Peasant Poet and took him away. But,' she added, looking around anxiously, 'they say you were in it with him, so they're looking for you, too!'

'They want to arrest me?'

'Yes. Didn't you see the wanted poster stuck up in the station? Now look, I don't believe you had anything to do with this but you've got to get away.'

'How was Hongmei killed?'

Auntie Zhao sighed. 'Oh, the poor girl. I heard she was raped, and the attacker suffocated her with a pillow.'

'Zheng Jianguo did that?'

'That's what the police say, but I don't really believe it. The Peasant Poet couldn't do something like that. Brother Xiao, you can't go back to the farm. Get out of here quick, the further away the better. If you go back you really are like one of those dumb deer, so stunned by the light they don't know to run. That would be letting poor Hongmei down.'

Xiao Xiong stood for a long time in silence, pulled his hat down to cover his brow, and walked back into the station.

The waiting room was very crowded. Pasted on the wall, among so many other posters and messages, there it was.

WANTED

Xiao Xiong, nickname Dumb Deer; male, aged 25, worker at the Binbei Farm, local accent; 1.82 metres tall, large eyes, bushy eyebrows, accomplice in a case of rape and murder . . .

Xiao Xiong didn't read any more. He turned and walked swiftly out of the waiting room. He had no idea where he was going.

✳

Hongmei was dead! He had to accept it. He didn't believe Zheng Jianguo was the killer, just a convenient scapegoat. They were brothers. This PSB guy, Gu Chunshan, was the one, and Hongmei had said as much. She knew he meant to hurt her. But he couldn't act rashly, because Gu was already looking for him, determined to eliminate any threat to his own safety. But he swore an oath that he would make sure this Gu suffered for what he'd done.

'My darling Hongmei,' he said before the mountains. 'From this day on, you must sleep alone, but know that my heart will always be with you, Hongmei. You will always be my wife. And for as long as I live, I will never love another woman.'

He had to get back to Harbin, and waited beyond the station for the moment he could slip into the boarding crush. Securely on board, Xiao Xiong started to plan. Death by a thousand cuts appealed to him, but his cuts would be aimed not at the body, but at the mind of Gu Chunshan.

After returning to Harbin, Xiao Xiong didn't tell his father what had happened to Li Hongmei, fearing that the shock might be too much for the frail old man. He went to see his friends from the democracy movement, and told them what had happened. They all expressed sympathy, and railed against the state of China's justice system. They arranged for him to stay in a house in the countryside outside Harbin, and helped him get a temporary job driving a bicycle cart in a freight yard. He worked in the daytime, and spent his evenings helping his friends with their work to change China, but at night, in his dreams, he would see Hongmei.

Xiao Xiong wasn't sure when it happened, but his friends seemed to be giving up on working for the greater good of the nation and people, and spending more time worrying about their own future prospects. Those in university spent more time in class and less time talking about change, others began running businesses on the side that took up more and more of their time and a surprising number talked about going to study abroad. After his friends drifted away, Xiao Xiong lost his job. He couldn't go back to the farm, couldn't stay with his father. He didn't feel safe in Harbin at all because he'd heard that the PSB was still looking for him. He thought of finding his sister in Beijing, both to ask her to take care of their father and to seek some funds. After he left Beijing he began to lead an itinerant life. He was, effectively now a 'floating person', and if he tried to get a permit to work in a major city he risked arrest.

Life as a vagrant was not easy. He spent his days searching for any work that would help him fill his stomach: carrying goods, pulling loads, unloading coal wagons. At night he just slept where he could, in waiting rooms, haystacks, stables. Sometimes he wished he could go home to see his sister, but he was stubborn, had chosen his path and would have to see it to the end.

Happiness means different things to different people. For some people, dining on wild game and fresh seafood every day is nothing to be particularly happy about, for others, happiness is just eating their fill of rice sometimes. Xiao Xiong found himself staring through a restaurant window at a bowl of leftover food. He had never imagined happiness could be reduced to something so simple.

After wrestling with himself, he simply walked into the restaurant, stopped at a recently vacated table, picked up the bowl of food and poured it greedily into his mouth. He knew everyone was looking at him with disdain, and he heard voices . . . 'stinking beggar' and 'good-for-nothing'. He wiped his mouth with a paper napkin and left.

He had never felt so ashamed, but life had, little by little, shredded his self-respect and he was touching rock bottom. To survive, he had to eat. He got on a train feeling shamed, but he had no money for the ticket, and was detained at the next station, where he spent a fortnight unloading coal wagons to pay off the ticket. But he was fed.

There he met a young guy who told him about the Xing'an Mountains and the work to be had logging and hauling timber. It was hard work, but it paid well. And in the summer of 1986, he decided breaking his back lifting timber in the mountains was better than breaking his spirit scrabbling for what were really just handouts.

It was a long trek, but he made it, got to talking with some of the guys from the timber yard, and began a new life as Bao Qingfu.

CHAPTER TWENTY-EIGHT

HONG JUN DECIDED Old Bao needed a rest and asked the guard to get him something to eat and drink. Hong Jun found Xiao Xue and said, 'Come with me. Get your coat, and mine.'

'Why? Where are we going now?'

'I'm taking you to Binbei Park. It's quite a special place. I'll explain everything.'

After the snowstorm, the wind had dropped and there wasn't a wisp of cloud in the clear, deep blue sky.

'How did your chat with my . . . with Old Bao go?' she asked.

'It's a pretty harrowing story. He needed to rest and have something to eat. He told you Xiao Xiong is dead?'

'Yes. And I think I believe him in a sense. The brother I knew is gone.'

'I can understand that.'

They walked briskly up the main avenue and, once in the park, he slowed their pace as he took them through the grove and around the lake.

'You were going to tell me something?' she asked.

*

After Mo Yingmei learned Qingfu's secret, that he loved another, she never again put him under any romantic pressure. And she learned that being brother and sister was, in itself, fulfilling. What she worried about most was that he would leave. But a year passed, and then another, and he never talked of going home. Yingmei found it a little odd, but she didn't ask him about it. She still had the faintest hope, deep in her heart, that one day he would forget about everything back at his old home.

In the autumn of the same year, Uncle Mo fell ill. He had never been to hospital in his life. Normally, if he was ill, he would treat it with herbal medicine which he picked himself in the mountains, or told Yingmei to find. This time, it was worse, and nothing they tried worked. Qingfu and Yingmei looked after him day and night, but his illness only grew more severe.

One evening, Uncle Mo called them to the edge of the *kang*, and said slowly, 'Listen, you two, I don't have much time left. Don't be sad. Orochen people are not allowed to send off the dead with tears. I've lived through a lot in my time. When the Japanese were here, they didn't even treat us like humans. Once, they did some kind of experiment and killed more than a thousand Orochen in one go. The Nationalists were no good either. Only after the Communists have we been allowed to rebuild our lives. After a lifetime, all I have to say is you must ignore the nonsense people talk about politics and look to your own people.'

Then he turned to Bao Qingfu. 'Qingfu, you're not a son of the Orochen, but your heart is as bright as gold, your character as resolute as a stag. You're a good, reliable son. I can see that your heart has been wounded, but I won't ask you how. I've spent my life communicating with people and animals. I've seen every kind of wild beast, and every kind of person. There are wicked people who are fiercer than wolves and more cunning than foxes, and you must always be on your guard against them.'

Uncle Mo stopped to regain his breath. He was growing weaker.

'Two young people grew up on the banks of this little river. The boy was called Wudegema, and the girl was called Tiebukelama. They were both talented hunters, and they loved each other truly. At their wedding, Wudegema told everyone that, for the sake of the happiness of the whole tribe, they planned to go and conquer the *Luosa*, the devil that tormented their village and killed their children if tribute wasn't paid. They rode for three days and three nights until they reached the place where the *Luosa* lived, then did battle with him and finally defeated him.'

Uncle Mo's voice was growing weaker, but he took a breath and added, 'Wudegema and Tiebukelama loved and cherished each other, and lived here until they were fully eighty-one years, when they went to live in the woods up on the mountains nearby, and whenever the good Orochen people encountered any problems, they would come down to help.'

Now Uncle Mo gazed at them both in turn. 'Qingfu, Yingmei,' he said. 'I'm going to leave you now. I only have one wish, that you two should love each other devotedly for your whole lives, just like Wudegema and Tiebukelema.' He was exhausted and closed his eyes.

'Uncle,' said Qingfu quietly, 'I'm sorry, but I can't . . .'

'Dad,' said Yingmei, 'we really can't.'

'Can't . . . why?' Uncle Mo opened his eyes again to look at them. He saw them exchange looks, both realising the other knew the reason.

'But why?' Uncle Mo asked, beginning to pant for breath.

Realising that time was running out, Qingfu quickly knelt down beside the *kang*, and said, 'Uncle, I will never forget the kindness you and Yingmei have shown me. But I can't agree, because there's something I haven't told you.' He paused for a moment. 'My name is not Bao Qingfu, my real name is Xiao Xiong.'

And he began to tell a brief version of his life, and what led him to the mountain. Uncle Mo kept sighing as he gasped for breath, while Yingmei was weeping silently. The story of Xiao Xiong and Li Hongmei saddened them terribly, but it increased their respect for Xiao Xiong. After a little while, Uncle Mo said haltingly, 'You must take care . . . This devil may be even harder . . . ' Before he could finish his sentence, his voice trailed off, and Uncle Mo had passed.

Three days later, in accordance with Orochen custom, Xiao Xiong and Yingmei made a coffin out of strips of willow, put Uncle Mo's body inside and fixed it up on the branches of a big tree in the middle of the hillside, to give him a 'wind burial'. One year later, they took it down again, removed his skeleton and put it in a wooden coffin, which they buried, unmarked, near a fine birch.

Days and nights passed, freezing winters and burning summers. Living as an outdoorsman, Bao Qingfu shed the skin and thoughts of Xiao Xiong, but kept buried deep one memory. After the ninth anniversary of Li Hongmei's death he completed his preparations and, when it was all over, he might be able to cut the last thread that kept Old Bao and Xiao Xiong together. Yingmei waited, refusing all offers, though he tried to match her with solid candidates who professed, he felt truly, their love for her.

She told him bluntly she would not marry, and that was that.

'Do you really not understand how I feel?' she asked. 'Don't you know that the only person I love on this earth is you? I gave you my heart a long time ago. I don't mind, it is not meant to be. But I cannot give my heart to two people.'

It wasn't that he hadn't been aware of Yingmei's feelings for him, but he had never imagined that her love for him could be so lofty, so unwavering. After living together for so many years, he had also developed a deep affection for her. People are not made of wood, of course they have emotions. But whenever the thought of 'crossing the line' occurred to him, the image of Hongmei would always appear before him, and he would remember the vow he made: 'For as long as I live, I will never love another woman.'

'I understand your feelings, but I want you to understand mine too. I love you, but not because I want to be your wife. If I can just be with you, help you, make you happy, that's enough for me. I'm not trying to win your heart. I know you gave it to another woman a long time ago, and she deserved it. I can be your sister forever, if that's what you want . . . I'll always be with you. It doesn't matter whether you love me or not. My heart will always be yours.'

Bao Qingfu sat down beside her on the edge of the *kang* and said sincerely, 'Don't say that! You're a good, kind-hearted girl, and you deserve a wonderful, happy life. But I can't stay here forever. There's something important I have to do. And the path I'm taking is going to be a very rocky one!'

Head held high, she said directly, 'You're worried I can't take it, right? I can take it. As long as I'm with you, I'd happily put up with any kind of suffering. I decided a long time ago that, however hard the road you take, I want to go with you. Even if you go to the end of the world, I'll be with you.'

'No!' he said. 'You don't realise! Even I don't know what lies ahead.'

'But I know,' she answered. 'You want to go and find that man, Gu, and kill him to avenge Li Hongmei.'

'No,' he said. 'I don't want to kill him. That would be letting him off too lightly. If I just wanted to get rid of him, I could have done it years ago. No. I want to torment him slowly,' he insisted, 'to make him feel that Hongmei has returned to make him pay. I want him to live in terror every day, so that he can't sleep at night, so he's petrified every time he hears a knock on the door. I want to let him die slowly from terror and remorse.'

As he spoke, Bao Qingfu grew so agitated that the scar on his forehead, where a wolf had once scratched him, began to swell and turn red, and the beard he hadn't shaved for days trembled as his voice rose and fell.

*

One morning, about a month later, Yingmei found a letter on the *kang* table in Bao Qingfu's bedroom.

Dear Yingmei,

I've left! This is not about life messing us around, this is the path I've chosen myself. I'm not blaming life – life is innocent, even if it's sometimes not at all fair. I don't blame the times either, because no one can choose the times they live in. But I have to follow this path, because its destination is a duty which is more important than my life itself. If you understand me, if you are able to follow my advice this once, please don't come to look for me. In life one has to wait, particularly for happiness. As long as the sky stays blue, we will meet again one day. But please don't leave Alihe, because this place will always be my home.

Bao Qingfu
10th July 1993

As she held this letter, Yingmei's hands trembled violently, and her eyes grew hazy with tears. She realised that the day had finally come. She did what Bao Qingfu had asked and waited patiently in Alihe. But months passed, and he still hadn't come back. She carried out an 'oracle bone' divination, in keeping with Orochen tradition. She burned a piece of roe buck collarbone on the fire, praying all the while as she did so, and checked the cracks in the bone. They were long, with lines running across the bone . . . a bad omen. Too worried to wait any longer, she determined to follow him. Using her theatrical skills, she made herself up to look like a madwoman, and ate what the Orochen called 'dumb grass' to change her voice into a hoarse rasp. The disguise would ensure Bao Qingfu didn't recognise her, and allow her to help him complete his plan if needed.

*

When she arrived in Binbei town, she would often go to the restaurants and hotels, but she couldn't find Bao Qingfu. That evening in the Binbei Restaurant, she hadn't seen him come in. When he'd slammed his fist on the table and came over to put the bullies to flight, it had given her a shock. From then on, she tracked his movements, hoping she might be able to assist him in some way without him noticing. Later, when she found out he'd been arrested, she decided to carry on with the course of action which she knew he'd been planning, hoping that this might, in the end, lead to his release. And so she arranged a night of terror for Gu Chunshan.

CHAPTER TWENTY-NINE

THERE WAS JUST one story left to sort out, and it took Hong Jun a long time to get permission to speak to Gu Chunshan about what really happened. His doctors were against it, but there was little chance of getting more than a summary into evidence once he'd been certified. Chief Judge Han, keen to find out how deeply his rival had buried himself, gave permission, asking Hong Jun to give him a full report, which would be sealed under court order.

Gu Chunshan was born into an ordinary family of low-ranking officials. He was a twin, but his younger brother had died at birth. Perhaps it was because he saw himself as being the earthly representative of two lives, but from an early age he always had the sense that he was someone special. A curious belief took root deep in his mind that he would become a leader, a man of great power.

He did possess many of the attributes required to be successful. He was intelligent and studious, and a good talker, bold but not reckless, willing to struggle and work hard, modest on the surface. But he possessed a deep-seated arrogance, and was strong-willed and tenacious. He didn't care about other people, felt no shame in deceiving others and had no qualms about harming anyone else.

These singular talents meant that he made smooth, almost effortless progress in life. At primary school he was always the class president. While he was at high school, the Cultural Revolution began, and he became the leader of a faction of Red Guards. When he started work, he was quickly promoted from an ordinary worker in a power station to security officer and was later transferred to the County PSB. He rose from the rank of detective to Chief of the Public Security Bureau, before switching tracks and being made Deputy Secretary of the County Party Committee, and Secretary of the Political and Legal Committee. He felt sure that, had he not been cursed by being born in this small county town, he would undoubtedly have risen to a position of far greater prominence. Perhaps even the Central Committee of the Party. He had a very high opinion of himself. He was looking forward to the day when Binbei District was made a city, and he would become head of the Municipal Political and Legal Committee.

But Gu Chunshan was weak. He wasn't frightened of people or animals, but he was superstitious. The sudden appearance of strangely shaped dark clouds in the sky would leave him shaking with fear, and when he walked alone up a staircase at night, the sound of his own footsteps could frighten him. He was convinced that this was his twin brother trying to undermine everything he achieved.

In his eyes, life was a constant, relentless struggle. Against others and against one's self; against friends and enemies; against society and nature. In these contests, power was all important, the guarantee of victory.

Gu Chunshan's aim in life was to ensure more and more people would bow down at his feet . . . and there would be fewer and fewer people at whose feet he would have to bow. To achieve this lofty ideal, he was willing to sacrifice some of his pleasures, his desire for women among them. During the Cultural Revolution, he was held up as a model of progressive thinking, for throwing himself wholeheartedly into revolutionary work without a thought for personal matters. After the end of the Cultural Revolution, he continued to declare that 'marriage is an indication of the decline of a man's progressive will'. And he adopted the phrase 'pleasure saps the spirit' as his personal motto.

In 1984, he was appointed a division chief in the PSB with good prospects of becoming deputy chief. He was single, a solitary warrior in the struggle of life.

He never imagined that a farm girl could undermine his entire philosophy.

The first time he met the Beauty Queen, Li Hongmei, when he went to Binbei Farm to investigate the case of Xiao Xiong, every sexual nerve in his body was aroused. Her body exerted some special attraction that could drive a man to do anything it took to possess her, regardless of the consequences. Other women had aroused Gu Chunshan's lust before, but it had never been so powerful. At first, he tried to suppress his desire, but he realised it was a lost cause, because the more he repressed his feelings the stronger they got. If he didn't see her, he felt restless and uneasy, unable to sleep or eat properly.

He used Xiao Xiong's case as an excuse to stay at Binbei Farm. There was no denying it. He had fallen in love with this farm girl. But from his point of view, Li Hongmei was someone who must be conquered in a different way.

He arranged to talk to her alone many times, sometimes in the office, sometimes in her home. He was especially respectful towards her father, Li Qingshan, who had never met an important official before.

His pretext for going to see the Beauty Queen was to find out about Xiao Xiong, and to get her to cut ties with him and reveal the details of his illegal activities. But during their talks he did all he could to steer the topic of conversation towards himself. He talked about his glorious past, his grand ambitions, even his views on life and love, though of course he was careful to couch his words in high-minded constructs.

He took great care with his manners and his choice of words, trying to seem cultured and refined, but also charming and easy-going. With his position and his abilities, he felt sure he could deal a knockout blow to his rival, Dumb Deer.

As they talked more and more, Gu Chunshan formed the impression that the Beauty Queen was very well-disposed towards him, enjoyed listening to him talk and admired him greatly. But whenever they met, she continued to insist that 'Xiao Xiong is a good man, he'd never do anything against the law', and would ask him to 'use your great power to show mercy, and let Xiao Xiong alone'. Her words left a bitter taste in Gu Chunshan's mouth, but he also realised it was hardly surprising that a rural girl should speak up on behalf of her boyfriend. So long as he could have this woman, he thought, he might not necessarily need to condemn Dumb Deer to death.

On the evening of April 17, his colleague Wu Hongfei went over to the village at the back of the farm to watch a film. Gu Chunshan was at a loose end. He left his office and walked towards the living quarters. Most of the young people on the farm had gone to see the film, and the older people and children had gone to bed, so the area was quiet. Almost involuntarily, he found himself walking to the gate of Li Hongmei's house, and saw that someone was out in the courtyard taking in the washing. By the light from the window, he saw that it was her. 'Still working, Hongmei?' he asked.

Recognising his voice, she said hastily, 'Oh, Section Chief Gu. Is there something you wanted to see me about?'

'Still the same business,' he said, walking into the courtyard. 'Look, we've been here a long time, and we need to go back soon. There are a few final things I need to talk to you about. Can we talk privately, or is your father still up?'

'He had a bit to drink tonight, and he's gone to bed,' she said.

'Oh I see.' Gu Chunshan lowered his voice.

'Well, do please come inside and take a seat, Chief Gu,' she said. Carrying the washing, Hongmei led him into the west room, where she lived.

When they got inside, he saw that the quilt was already spread out on the *kang*. 'Are you about to go to bed?' he asked. 'Then I should let you be and we can talk another day.'

'It's all right, you can sit over here,' she said, putting the clothes down at the end of the *kang*, and inviting him to sit down on the right-hand side of the little table, while she herself sat on the left.

Gu Chunshan was in no hurry to discuss the case. 'Why didn't you go to the village to see the film?' he asked.

'I don't like going alone.'

'If you want to go and watch it I can go with you,' he said, looking at his watch. 'We've probably missed the first film, but I hear they are running two films tonight.'

'Oh, maybe next time,' she said with a smile. 'Would you like an apple, Chief Gu? I bought them in town, they're very sweet!' Hongmei jumped down and went to fetch an apple from the head of the *kang*, and took a fruit knife from her trunk. She put them on the table in front of him.

Gu Chunshan thanked her, picked up the knife and the apple, and began to peel it. 'I've been thinking over Xiao Xiong's case,' he said, 'and I think we can let it drop. So long as he doesn't do anything else illegal, we can suspend our investigations.'

'Really?'

'I've always been a man of my word,' Gu replied. 'But I want you to know that I'm doing this for you!' And he shot a glance at her.

'Thank you, Section Chief Gu,' she said.

'How will you thank me?' As he said this, his concentration slipped, and he cut his finger with the fruit knife. 'Ouch!' he cried, dropping the knife and the apple, and clutching his left thumb with his right hand.

Hongmei jumped down from the *kang*. 'What's the matter?' she asked, 'did you cut your finger? I'll get some cloth to bandage it for you.' She took out a sewing basket from under the table, pulled out a strip of white cloth, and, standing in front of him, began to bind his finger.

Gu Chunshan stood facing her. She was so close he could smell her body. He was seized by a powerful urge, which left him struggling for breath. Throwing his arms around her, he said, 'Hongmei, I love you!'

For a moment she was stunned, then, fixing him with a stern expression, she said, 'If you don't let go, I'll shout for help.'

By this point Gu Chunshan had completely lost reason. Caring nothing for the consequences, he scooped her up, pushed her down on the *kang* and threw himself on top of her. She managed to call out a solitary 'Help . . . !' before her mouth was blocked with the quilt he'd grabbed from behind her and pressed over her face. She struggled for a little longer, but her resistance soon ceased.

Only after he had slaked his lust did Gu Chunshan think to remove the quilt. Hongmei was no longer breathing, her heart no longer beating. At first he panicked, then managed to straighten his clothes, and slipped out of the room. Just as he pulled open the gate of the courtyard, he caught a glimpse of Li Qingshan shuffling out of his room. He rushed to hide in the shadows outside the entrance of the Zheng's courtyard. 'Who's there?' Li Qingshan called out. Then, getting no reply, he thought no more of it, relieved himself and went back to bed.

Gu Chunshan rushed back to his office. On one side of the room were three desks, and on the other side was a large *kang*. This was where he and Wu Hongfei had been staying. Wu wasn't back from watching the film yet, so Gu Chunshan hastily turned off the light, undressed, then climbed onto the *kang* and tried to sleep. However, his racing heartbeat and the return of his senses kept him wide awake.

After a while he heard the sound of footsteps outside. He lay on his side with his face towards the wall, pretending to be asleep.

Wu Hongfei opened the door and came in, calling out 'Old Gu.' But when Gu Chunshan didn't respond, he began to walk around more quietly. He bolted the door and without turning on the light climbed onto the *kang* and went straight to sleep.

Gu Chunshan lay awake for the whole night.

✳

Not long after the case was wrapped up, and Zheng had surprisingly confessed to the crime – something he didn't understand at all – Gu Chunshan was promoted to County Deputy Chief of the PSB, an advancement thanks in no small part to his running of the Li Hongmei case. There was still no trace of Xiao Xiong, and Gu Chunshan forgot about him. But he always remained very concerned about Li Qingshan, who asked in his interrogation whether Gu had called on him that night, because he thought he saw his departing shadow. It didn't take too much persuading for Li to admit he must have been mistaken. Even after Li moved to Harbin, Gu continued to visit him regularly.

After a period of contemplation, Gu Chunshan realised that he ought to get married. He chose Wang Xiuling, who worked as a clerk in the court. He had no real love or passion for her, but he felt a sense of devotion, a desire to atone. He couldn't help often imagining that Wang Xiuling was Li Hongmei, that the Beauty Queen was still alive. To make up for his crime, he devoted himself wholeheartedly to becoming a model husband.

Wang Xiuling was from a worker's family, a kind-hearted and dutiful girl. Even though she was quite attractive, she never imagined that the powerful and sophisticated deputy police chief would take a fancy to her. When she saw how caring and considerate Gu Chunshan was in his love for her, she became quite intoxicated. They had a son. In her own eyes, and those of her friends and family, her union with Gu Chunshan was one of perfect happiness. She felt very lucky to have found a husband who was both so talented and so tender.

From Gu Chunshan's point of view, his marriage and his behaviour towards Wang Xiuling helped restore his mental balance. He could never forget the crime he had committed, but he felt he had already served his punishment, and had sincerely dedicated himself to undergoing 'reform and re-education'.

But after the incident at Black Bear Cave, all the concerns which had more or less faded from his consciousness suddenly resurfaced with a vengeance. It was as though he had suddenly been plunged back into that period ten years earlier when he had lived in constant fear. He had the feeling that some terrifying, intangible fate was awaiting him.

He had no doubt that the incident in the cave was connected to Li Hongmei's death. The moment Old Bao mentioned the story of the Black Bear Spirit, he had felt a nagging sense of fear. When it turned out they had no choice but to stay the night in the cave, he again felt a vague premonition of danger. But he had told himself that it was all just coincidence, and that his reaction was a sign of his own cowardice. After the incident that night, and after he saw the drawing on the strip of birch bark, he realised someone was taking revenge for Li Hongmei's death.

But who could it be? How could anyone know the truth about her death? He thought of Xiao Xiong, but a guy like that would have forgotten about Li Hongmei a long time ago, and would be far away.

The more he thought about it, the more he felt sure that the only person who could know, or might have guessed the truth was Li Qingshan, and that incident must have had something to do with him. Perhaps he had arranged for someone to stage it to help him take his revenge.

He decided he would have to eradicate this potentially fatal threat before it was too late. He had no desire to involve himself in killing, but he had taken the first step on this road ten years before, and now there was nothing for it but to carry on down the same path. There could be no turning back, that way lay only disgrace and disaster.

✳

Gu Chunshan's final undoing was his own mind, and a piece of paper slipped under his door . . .

> *Blood debts must be repaid with blood!*
> *Li Hongmei*

He was convinced that people had souls that survived after they died, and that ghosts and spirits really did exist. No longer caring about the consequences, he ran into the sitting room, picked up the phone and dialled Hao Zhicheng's home number. There was no answer, so he dialled his office. When he finally heard Chief Hao's voice on the other end of the line, he felt like a drowning man who finally had a straw to clutch at. 'Come quickly!' he shouted. 'There's a ghost in my house! Quickly!'

He hung up, but still he felt scared. It really seemed like there was some kind of spirit in the apartment. When he stood in the living room, he heard sounds from the bedroom. When he stood in the bedroom, he heard movements in his son's little room, which he knew was empty because he and his mother had gone to her parents'. He ran from one room to the other, grabbing a meat cleaver from the kitchen as he went. Gasping for breath, he sat on the sofa in the bedroom, lowered his head and shut his eyes. 'There's no ghost,' he told himself loudly. 'Ghosts don't exist.'

Strange sounds came from the direction of the window. Instinctively, he opened his eyes and looked up. On the window ledge stood a woman with long, flowing hair, staring in at him.

Gu Chunshan screamed in terror, and collapsed on the floor beside the sofa.

CHAPTER THIRTY

AT NIGHTFALL, THE Binbei Restaurant was as busy as ever, and almost every table was taken. At a couple of tables, people were playing drinking games and shouting excitedly as they tried to guess how many fingers the other person was going to hold up. But sitting by the window, Hong Jun, Xiao Xue and Chu Weihua seemed hardly to notice the hubbub.

Hong Jun remembered it was the same table he'd sat at the first time he'd eaten here. Over these past few weeks, he'd been rushing around on the case, even analysing it in his dreams, but he hadn't felt the slightest bit weary. Now, with everything resolved, he felt utterly exhausted.

Xiao Xue glanced at him, and then at Chu Weihua. 'What's the matter with you two?' she asked. 'You look like you've just been to a funeral.'

Swiftly raising his glass, Chu Weihua said, 'I don't know what it is. I just feel totally drained. Let's drink a toast! Firstly to congratulate Dr Hong on his great success, and secondly to wish you both a safe journey home, and that all your dreams may come true.'

They clinked glasses, and drained them. Hong Jun said Chu Weihua could insist on one *baijiu* toast, but after that, it was beer all the way.

'Deputy Chief Judge Han came to my office today to ask me to give you both a send-off on his behalf. So I may have to demand another round of *baijiu*. Over the past couple of days, he's asked us all to reflect on the lessons of this case, and write a report summarising them for the Regional Party Committee. He told us not just to write about Gu Chunshan's failings, but also to look for mistakes in the system, and in our thinking, that let this happen. He's not happy about sloppiness in the way we collect evidence, giving too much priority to the prosecutors, only going through the motions of checking evidence during the trial, and putting too much emphasis on arresting suspects and not enough on ensuring the quality of our work. Still, I can tell that Chief Han is very happy with the outcome. And word is that he's pretty much got the promotion to Secretary of the new Municipal Political and Legal Commission.'

Hong Jun tapped his glass with his fingers. 'Hmm . . . even though the original verdict he passed has been overturned, clouds really do have silver linings.'

Chu Weihua said, 'You have to say, we really did a fine job of solving this case.'

Xiao Xue nodded and said, 'Some things in life are really hard to predict. Sometimes you feel sure that they're moving in one direction, but then some tiny thing happens, and everything changes completely. People are the same too.'

'You can say that again!' said Chu Weihua. 'Take Gu Chunshan. Everyone saw him as a very honest and upright official. They said he wasn't interested in sexual favours and he wasn't greedy for money. If I hadn't worked on this case myself, I'd have found it very hard to believe he could have done something like this.'

'Well,' said Hong Jun, 'it's not necessarily as simple as that. Normally, people suppress their own needs, to varying degrees, to satisfy what they perceive as the needs of society or other people. But it's not their natural instinct to do this. So you need a moral code of right and wrong, and where that fails, law must channel and restrain behaviour.'

'If you make one bad choice, it can haunt you for life,' said Xiao Xue.

'Indeed, "a wrong decision can never be undone",' Hong Jun replied.

Chu Weihua finished gulping down a large swig of beer. 'Sometimes I can't help thinking that people are quite scary and unpredictable. Today they might be like this, but who knows what they'll be like tomorrow. I mean, I'd never imagined that even their blood could be two different types!' he added, eyebrows raised. 'To be honest, when I saw the results of the blood tests from the hospital, I really thought my wife was joking with me. How could one person have two types of blood – both type A and type O at the same time? She said it was the first time they'd ever come across anyone like this. But one of the doctors looked it up.'

'In genetics it's called the phenomenon of blood type reciprocity,' said Hong Jun. 'I've been reading a lot about it because of this case, and about forensic science. Zheng Jianzhong mentioned something young lawyers are doing in the US, The Innocence Project, and modern forensics is proving many people were wrongfully convicted, even executed, for crimes they didn't commit.'

'But how did you know Gu Chunshan had a double blood type?' Weihua asked.

'Well I can't say I actually knew until today,' he said. 'I was mostly speculating. When I first heard there were two types of blood on the fruit knife, I thought it might have been a set-up arranged by the killer. But as my suspicions began to focus on Gu Chunshan, and I got a clearer understanding of the details of the case, I started to look at it again. It seemed to me that the criminal had either killed Li Hongmei unintentionally while raping her, or had decided to do it on the spur of the moment after she tried to fight back. It definitely wasn't a premeditated murder. Now, in those circumstances, the criminal would probably have fled the scene in panic after committing the crime, and was unlikely to have had the presence of mind to think of this kind of trick. If he'd thought at the time that the blood on the knife could be used as evidence against him, wouldn't it have been simpler just to wipe it off the blade? And, if he had put the blood on the knife intentionally to confuse the investigators, he wouldn't have needed to remove the knife from the police store afterwards. So the fact he took it away seemed to confirm that the killer realised it was his own blood on the knife.'

Hong Jun paused for a moment and looked at Weihua. 'And then I remembered that while I was in America I'd read that a couple of scientists had discovered an unusual phenomenon in human blood type heredity. In such people's blood, hereditary elements of two different types of blood are present. These two elements co-exist peacefully in the human body, and one of them is always dominant, but when the blood is tested, it will display characteristics of both types. It's only found in a tiny proportion of people, probably one in a few million, usually in twins,' he went on. 'We didn't know Gu was a twin until later, but I guessed that he had a double blood type.'

By now, almost everyone knew who Gu was, and a few better informed individuals began filling in the story for those around them as to the events of the previous night. The whole restaurant was talking about Gu Chunshan's arrest for the rape and murder of Li Hongmei all those years ago, and then the killing of her father in Harbin just the week before. And that Secretary Gu had been scared out of his mind by a 'ghost woman'.

Hong Jun and Xiao Xue looked at each other without speaking for a long time. Finally, Xiao Xue sighed and said, 'Poor Wang Xiuling.'

Hong Jun nodded. 'She's innocent in all of this,' he said. 'And she's a good person too. If she was one of those greedy, arrogant official's wives, I'd find it easier to accept.'

'And there's the child too.'

'The person who's guilty goes crazy and has no idea what's going on, so whatever punishment he gets won't really affect him. Legally speaking, because he was in a normal mental state and in control of his actions when he raped and murdered Li Hongmei and killed Li Qingshan, he ought to bear criminal responsibility. But even if the court gives him a suspended death sentence, what will that mean for him now? And in the circumstances he might not even be sent to prison, more likely to an asylum, or he'll just be locked up in hospital. But poor Wang Xiuling. She'll have to be responsible for him, and endure the punishment and shame meant for him.'

'Ah, well, there's nothing we can do about it,' said Xiao Xue. 'There are so many unjust things in this world. Let's focus on the things we need to do now.'

'Yes,' he replied, 'shouldn't you go and see Old Bao before you leave? I suppose he won't want to admit his identity while he's locked up, but I reckon once he's out he'll acknowledge that you really are his sister.'

She shook her head. 'I'm not going to see him. I've said everything I had to say. If he wants to acknowledge me then he can come and look for me himself.'

'But, how did you find out about Mo Yingmei?' Chu Weihua interrupted.

'Actually it was very simple,' said Hong Jun. 'Do you remember I told you that the first time I saw the crazy woman, in this restaurant, I thought she didn't look really mad, so I felt then that there was something puzzling about her? I never thought there was any link between her and the Li Hongmei case. But the other night at Gu Chunshan's flat, I saw a pair of footprints in the snow on the windowsill. There was no doubt that someone had really been there. When Gu Chunshan made that call to Chief Hao, he hadn't gone crazy yet. He might well already have found some signs of her presence, and judging by the piece of paper in his hand and the cleaver he was carrying, he may have heard something outside the door, and found that piece of paper. After he hung up the phone, he saw the woman outside the window. And from the moment Chief Hao put the phone down to the time we arrived at Gu Chunshan's house, only about twenty minutes had passed. So by the time we got there, the woman couldn't have got very far away. As I was arriving, I saw her through a hole in the compound wall not far from Gu's building. And on such a stormy, windy night, I felt pretty sure this wasn't just a coincidence.'

Hong Jun paused for a moment and sipped some tea, making sure he had the next part of the story clear in his own mind. 'Later I started thinking about the link between the woman and this case. Judging from what was written in that note, she was there because of Li Hongmei. And the methods she used were very similar to the ones Xiao Xiong used. Now of course, I didn't believe that Li Hongmei had come back to life, and so it seemed very likely that she was someone else with some connection to Xiao Xiong. And when she abandoned her disguise at the station, where she waited every night for the train, it proved my theory was correct. I felt sure that she wouldn't leave Binbei. She'd wait for Xiao Xiong, and might even try to find a way to rescue him. Now, the waitress in the restaurant had told me the crazy woman wasn't from Binbei, so if she wasn't a local, I figured she would have to stay in a hotel like anyone else. I went round some of the hotels and enquired who had checked in that morning and found there was a guest named Mo Yingmei at the Dazhong Hotel, who came from Alihe town. I knew Old Bao had come from Alihe, so there was our answer.'

'Aha,' said Xiao Xue. 'The simplest solution is usually the correct one. It's just that before we have it, we don't usually know where to start looking for it.'

'To be honest, I actually wish I hadn't discovered this answer,' Hong Jun said.

'Why not?'

'Well,' he said, 'as someone who works in the legal profession, I know that what Yingmei did was not legally permissible. She intentionally scared someone so badly he went out of his mind. Even though that person was a criminal, she also ought to bear some criminal responsibility, or at least the responsibility to pay compensation in a civil case. And, my own behaviour also contravened the professional ethics of a legal professional. I swept away her footprints on the ledge and I'm covering up for someone who's broken the law. Xiao Xue, do you think I've done something wrong?'

'Hey, come on,' she said. 'Forget about all that! It's not as though you told her what to do.'

'But I destroyed evidence.'

'I think you did the right thing,' she replied. 'And anyway, even if the footprints were there, what would they prove? How could anyone prove that Gu Chunshan went crazy because Mo Yingmei scared him so much? Don't torment yourself, Hong Jun. You've done a brilliant job solving this case. But Deputy Division Chief Xiao Xue will issue you with a caution if you like. I'll be watching you. Happy now?'

Dinner was over by the time they got back. Chu Weihua had paid the bill, courtesy of Deputy Chief Judge Han Wenqing of the Binbei Intermediate People's Court, and they headed for the door. Hong Jun, on a sudden impulse, turned and looked back at the corner where the crazy woman had sat the first night he saw her and he wondered about invisible lines that connected people in the strangest ways.

CHAPTER THIRTY-ONE

SONG JIA PUT on a pot of coffee to brew and placed that day's post on Hong Jun's desk, noticing a new picture frame. She picked up the frame. It was a photograph of a woman who looked very like her. Song Jia was staring at the picture, trying to work out what it meant, when she heard the outside door opening. She replaced the frame on the desk, adjusting it just so, and walked nonchalantly out of the room.

It was Hong Jun, accompanied by a young woman. She didn't look quite as young as the girl in the picture, but Song Jia could see it was her.

'Song Jia, let me introduce you to Deputy Division Chief Xiao Xue of the Harbin PSB. Xiao Xue, this is my invaluable assistant Song Jia.'

They shook hands, and looked each other up and down. Hong Jun watched them and said with a smile, 'I imagine you both feel a bit like you're looking in the mirror.'

'There really is quite a similarity,' Xiao Xue murmured.

Song Jia suddenly remembered her professional responsibilities, and said politely, 'Chief Xiao, please take a seat. May I get you some coffee or tea?'

'Oh, no need,' said Xiao Xue quickly, 'I can't stay long.'

Song Jia shot Hong Jun a questioning glance. 'Xiao Xue came yesterday to do some work at the Ministry of Public Security, and today she's going back to Harbin,' he said. 'I'm just taking her to the airport, so I thought I'd give her the grand tour of HONG JUN LAW OFFICE, such as it is.'

Xiao Xue was looking at Song Jia as though there was something on her mind. 'Are you from Beijing, Miss Song?' she asked, when Hong Jun finished speaking.

'Yes,' she replied. 'Beijing born and bred. My family's really straight-forward. There's my dad, my mum and me, and currently there are not yet any plans for further population expansion.'

'You're very humorous, Miss Song.' Xiao Xue hesitated for a moment, and seemed on the point of asking another question when the door buzzer sounded.

'Excuse me, please.' Song Jia went to open the door. It was Zheng Jianzhong and Zheng Jianguo.

As they walked in, Zheng Jianzhong said to Hong Jun, 'Dr Hong, my brother arrived in Beijing yesterday. So I brought him here first thing this morning to thank you for your kind assistance, and to wish you a happy new year too.'

Zheng Jianguo stepped forward and bowed deeply to Hong Jun, apparently quite overwhelmed with emotion. He seemed to want to say something, but no words came.

'Please, there's no need to say anything,' said Hong Jun. To Zheng Jianzhong, he asked, 'Have they dealt with all the people involved in the case?'

'Well, the political and legal commission issued some document, asking all the public prosecutors and legal departments at all levels throughout the region to study and learn from what happened, all that kind of stuff,' said Zheng Jianzhong. 'But as for the officials, they didn't really do anything to them. All the blame conveniently landed on Gu Chunshan's head, and of course he's not in a position to defend himself. Deputy Chief Judge Han made a voluntary self-criticism, which keeps him in the clear and scored points with the regional leaders, who felt he'd handled this miscarriage of justice in a professional manner in keeping with correcting past wrongs and it looks like he's up for promotion.' Zheng shook his head. 'I don't care. My brother is out of jail. His record has been wiped clean. And we'll just have to see how fast we can make up for ten wasted years.'

Hong Jun looked at Zheng Jianguo, who was looking a lot younger in his suit and tie. 'How's your novel coming on?' he asked.

'I'm still revising. I really like parts of it, but I need to work on some of the other sections. It'll be a while.'

'I've rented a flat for him,' Zheng Jianzhong said, 'and I don't want him to do anything except sit at home and write his book. I told him, it doesn't matter whether you finish the book or not, just give it a try anyway.'

'Please, send me a copy of the manuscript,' Hong said. 'I mean it.'

As he was talking, Song Jia led Xiao Xue into the other room where they continued their conversation. After watching them walk out, from behind, Zheng Jianzhong gave Hong Jun a rather curious look and said, 'You should be a bit careful, you know, Dr Hong.'

'How so?' asked Hong Jun, who had no idea what he was talking about.

'Well, you don't want to exhaust yourself now, do you? Looks like your big assistant and your little secretary are out of the same packet. Did you get them from the same shop?'

'You'd better watch your tongue,' said Hong Jun. 'That one is Deputy Division Chief Xiao of the Harbin Municipal PSB.'

'Oh goodness, I'm sorry,' said Zheng Jianzhong. 'I must make sure I settle my bill before I leave today.'

They chatted for a little longer, until Hong Jun looked at his watch and called out to Xiao Xue that it was time to leave for the airport. Zheng Jianzhong sat with Song Jia while she went over the accounts and he began producing stacks of banknotes from his pocket. Zheng

Jianguo looked at the painting of The Heavenly Lake and moved to the window, admiring the old maple in its shaded garden.

*

Hong Jun slid a cassette of blues music into the player and they listened as he whisked the car to the airport. As he neared the freeway turnoff, he glanced at Xiao Xue. 'Have you had any news of Xiao Xiong?'

The question seemed to bring Xiao Xue back to reality. 'Oh yes,' she said, 'he asked the Binbei County PSB to deliver a letter to me. He thanked us both, a lot, and said he wants to go back to Alihe with Mo Yingmei, to start a new life. But even though he called me sister in the letter, he still signed it Bao Qingfu. He said he met Xiao Xiong on the mountain, spent some time with him, and that he was dead. I should stop looking for him. I understand what he means.'

*

Hong Jun waited while Xiao Xue checked in, which her PSB badge made a lot easier, and they passed untroubled through security. They reached the passengers only point beyond which Hong Jun could not go. He stood, unsure of what to do, and followed her lead. They shook hands in farewell.

'Do you remember the lines of that Song poem you once gave to me? "If our love is everlasting, what does it matter if we cannot be together day by day",' Hong Jun asked.

Xiao Xue lowered her head, thinking about the meaning of the lines. She looked at him and he let her slender hand slip from his palm . . .

CHINA  LIBRARY

WANG XIAOFANG

THE CIVIL SERVANT'S NOTEBOOK

Dongzhou City needs a new mayor. Devious plots, seduction, blackmail and bribery are all on the table in a no-holds-barred scramble for prestige and personal gain as the city's two vice-mayors compete for the top honour. At the centre of it all is a humble witness to events, a notebook whose pages contain information they should not …

Penned by a former insider, *The Civil Servant's Notebook* is a political page-turner that offers a glimpse into the complex psyches of those who roam the guarded halls of Chinese officialdom.

www.penguin.com.cn

CHINA  LIBRARY

SHENG KEYI

NORTHERN GIRLS
Life Goes On

Qian Xiaohong is born into a sleepy village far
from China's headlong rush towards development.
A scandalous love affair launches the buxom but
unwordly sixteen-year-old on a journey to the southern
boomtown of Shenzhen. There, released from the
stifling conservatism of her rural upbringing, Xiaohong
must navigate a strange new world with unfamiliar
rules and values, and learn to go on in the face of great
adversity. Along the way, Xiaohong finds support and
solace from her fellow 'northern girls', with whom
life's challenges and pleasures can be shared.

Northern Girls explores the inner lives of a generation
of young, rural Chinese women who embark on life-
changing journeys in the search of something better.

www.penguin.com.cn

DIVERSE STORIES
UNIQUE PERSPECTIVES

Comprising literature and narrative non-fiction,
twentieth-century classics and contemporary bestsellers,
the China Library brings together the best of writing on
and from China, all in one dedicated series.

www.penguin.com.cn